GORDON R. DICKSON

OTHER

Tor books by Gordon R. Dickson

Alien Art
Arcturus Landing
Beyond the Dar Al-Harb
Delusion World
The Dragon Knight
The Far Call
The Final Encyclopedia
Gremlins Go Home (with Ben Bova)
Guided Tour
Hoka! (with Poul Anderson)
Home from the Shore
The Last Master
Love Not Human
The Man From Earth
The Man the Worlds Rejected
Mission to Universe
On the Run
Other
The Outposter
The Pritcher Mass
Pro
Secrets of the Deep
Sleepwalkers' World
Soldier, Ask Not
The Space Swimmers
Space Winners
Spacepaw
Spacial Delivery
Steel Brother
The Stranger
Wolf and Iron
Young Bleys

GORDON R. DICKSON

OTHER

A TOM DOHERTY ASSOCIATES BOOK
NEW YORK

OTHER

Copyright © 1994 by Gordon R. Dickson

This book is printed on acid-free paper.

A Tor Book
Published by Tom Doherty Associates, Inc.
175 Fifth Avenue
New York, N.Y. 10010

Tor® is a registered trademark of Tom Doherty Associates, Inc.

Library of Congress Cataloging-in-Publication Data

Dickson, Gordon R.
    Other / Gordon R. Dickson.
        p.   cm.
    "A Tom Doherty Associates book."
    ISBN 0-312-85198-7 (hardcover)
    I. Title.
    PS3554.I328O84   1994
    813'.54—dc20   94-12916
                                                      CIP

First edition: September 1994

Printed in the United States of America

0 9 8 7 6 5 4 3 2 1

This book is dedicated to Marguerite Brodie Dickson

I'm indebted to the following people, for their remarkable helpfulness with this book:
Harry Frank
Joe Haldeman
Yoji Kondo
Dennis Lien
Michael Longcor
John Miesel
Sandra Miesel
Dr. Robert Passovoy
Dave Wixon

—GRD

GORDON R. DICKSON
OTHER

Chapter 1

It was not until the small hours of the morning that Henry MacLean had finished the cleaning and reassembly of his power pistol, that had lain buried deep these twenty years.

It was only then, when he put the energizer coil into the thick handle, that he found his right hand suddenly white-knuckled on the pistol, the heel of his left hand resting where he had slapped it in—as he would have done with a fresh reserve coil, in combat as a Soldier of God.

For a moment, it all came back; the sound of weapons, the smell of burning buildings—and the dying Militia soldier, that one time, who had taken a burst of needles in his throat. Who begged him, with gestures, to hold his bloodless hands together and be his voice, in a final prayer before death.

For a moment he paused, bowed his head and put the edges of his joined hands for a moment against the edge of the table.

"God," he prayed, "he is like a son. Like Joshua—and like Will, who is in Thy arms now. I love him equally. Thou knowest why I must do this."

He sat for a moment more, then parted his hands again and raised his head. He had mastered the image and the long-dead reflex, risen from the grave of memory. They were gone. He put the pistol with its shoulder rig into his suitcase, with what few other possessions he was taking.

Only a little later, before he left, Henry stopped in the pre-dawn darkness of the kitchen to leave on the kitchen table a letter to Joshua and Joshua's family. A single sheet of paper on which he told them where he was going, that all that had been his was now theirs, and that he loved them.

Then, soundlessly in his stocking feet, and carrying his boots and suitcase, he went to the front door, opened it and let himself out, softly closing it again behind him.

He stood on the top one of the three wooden steps for a moment before putting his boots on. It was the end of the brief few days of spring here, on the planet of Association, under the star of Epsilon Eridani, after the long, long rainy winter and before the mounting heat of the equally long summer.

There had been only a brief shower during the night. Now the air was still; and in that moment on the top step, he felt the cool pleasant dampness that would so soon pass away.

Dawn was just below the horizon. But a whiteness from the east had already washed the stars from the cloudless sky overhead. About him lay the gray earth with its fields already tilled and sown. Epsilon Eridani's light, even from just below the horizon, made everything seem to stand out, strangely clear and three-dimensional. Even a puddle in the trodden earth about the steps made a clear and perfect mirror. Beyond the puddle, the yard was wetly dark; so that, here and there, the clean-washed tops of white-veined, blue stones, like those that plagued their fields, projected from the earth, sharply visible.

The puddle threw back at him the whiteness off the cloudless dawn sky; and, against it, his own lean, square-shouldered, tight-knit figure, hardly showing the beginnings of middle age.

Now, with his everyday boots, his dark, heavy pants below his equally dark and heavy jacket, he was in the winter wear of an Association farmer, such as he had been for so many years now. Only the white shirt and dark beret, which were normally reserved for church-going, and the tie that made a black cross at his throat, made a difference.

The suitcase he now carried, heavy with the pistol, its holster and his scant burden of other belongings, was of scuffed brown plastic. He set it down again for a moment; and bent over to tuck his trousers into the tops of his ankle-high boots, with one neat fold apiece. Then he picked up the suitcase and walked out of the yard, over the railless bridge that crossed the ditch by the road; and turned to his right, in the direction he had determined to go.

An unusual stillness held the air about him. No breeze stirred. Even the variform and native insects were silent; the night insects had ceased their voices and the day insects not yet taken up the chorus. There were no native birds—and no variform birds; it had been decided that it would be an unnecessary luxury to import them from Old Earth. Parasites among the variform insects kept their part of the ecology in balance.

But the vegetation about him was almost all of Earth variforms. All the trees and the hedges that divided the fields owed their original genes to the home planet. Only, alongside the road down which he walked, was a species of the original native vegetation of this world.

These were the so-called Praying Trees. They were like nothing so much as a temperate zone version of Earth's saguaro cactus, but with thick white bark. They had the same candle-like branches as the saguaros; although these limbs grew out horizontally at regular intervals up two sides of the tree-high plant, each one opposite from the one below and the one above; and then crooked themselves after four or five feet to grow straight upward.

They were like sentinels lining his path. In the early light of the pre-dawn sky, they, like everything else, threw faint ghost-like shadows, stretching long back the way he had come, and away from the way he was going.

A little more than a kilometer down the road, he passed the small church to which he and his family had belonged all these years. Gregg, the minister, always held a morning service for those who could get here at that hour, in this rural community. But in all his years here, Henry had never been able to get free from the work of the farm to attend. Now he paused for a moment to listen, as the small congregation within burst out strongly into the morning hymn—"Greet We the Day!"

> *"Greet we the day!*
> *The day of work and striving*
> *The day of God's contriving*
> *Greet we the day!*
>
> *"Greet we the sun!*
> *The sun that rises o'er us*
> *The sun the Lord made for us*
> *Greet we the sun!*
>
> *"Greet we the earth!*
> *The earth that keeps and feeds us . . . "*

The song ran on to its end and ceased. Gregg's resonant voice, so large for such a small, crippled man, announced the text for the sermon.

"Joshua 8:26." The words reached clearly to Henry's ear. *"Joshua drew not his hand back wherewith he stretched out the spear."*

A cold memory touched Henry at the sound of the text—but the beginning of the sermon itself went unheard. Behind him now was the sound of an approaching hovercar. He turned to see the vehicle coming toward him.

He put the suitcase down and stood, waiting. The white hovercar, already splashed from the road ruts, though it had been fresh-washed at the time Henry had left home, pulled up beside him, and sank to the roadway as the air-jets on which it traveled ceased blowing.

In the back were his son's wife and his two grandsons, aged three and four. At the control stick in the front sat Joshua, his oldest—and now his only—son; since Will, the younger, had been killed on Ceta, as one of a levy sold off to fight there by Association's government.

Joshua touched the control that threw open the door of the front seat on Henry's side, and spoke across the short space now open between them. His square face under its brown hair was angry with unhappiness.

"Why?" he demanded.

"I told you why," said Henry, calmly. His light baritone was, as always, level and self-contained, "I told you in the letter I left for you."

"But you're leaving us for Bleys!"

Henry took a step closer and lowered his head to speak into the car itself. He looked at the strong face of Joshua under his brown hair and above his stocky frame.

"Bleys needs me," said Henry, in a quieter tone. "You no longer need me, my son. You've got your wife and children. You can handle the farm as well or better than I can. It was always yours, anyway. You don't need me now. But Bleys does."

"Bleys has Dahno!" said Joshua. "He has money and power. How can he need you more than we do?"

"Your life is safe," said Henry. "As a married man with children and the farm, you're not draftable, as Will was. Your souls are secure in God's keeping; and I do not fear for them or you. But, I fear greatly for Bleys. He has fallen into Satan's hands and only I can protect him—perhaps— so that he lives to the time when he can break loose."

"Father—" Joshua ran out of words. His father's decisions had always been as immovable as a mountain, in all things human, worldly and spiritual. He stared at the spare man before him, so lightly untouched by time despite the gray showing in his brown hair. Still strong. Still certain.

"We'd hoped you'd always be with us—all of us," he said, his voice breaking on the word "us." "With me, Ruth, and your grandsons."

"Man proposes, God disposes," said Henry. "In spirit and love, you know I'll be with you always."

There was a long moment more in which they simply looked at each other. Then Joshua made an abrupt gesture, beckoning his father into the car.

"Where did you think you were going, on foot?" he demanded harshly. "Were you going to walk all the way to Ecumeny?"

"Only to the store, to catch the Thursday bus," said Henry. "The car is yours now."

"I'll drive you in it, to Ecumeny and Bleys!" Joshua repeated his gesture. "Get in!"

Henry got in beside him; and Joshua closed the door, putting the hovercar once more in motion.

They drove in silence for a few moments. The main highway, with its built-in control cable, was only minutes away by magnetic-levitation vehicle or hovercar. The single-story store with its living quarters in the background flickered past them, seen through the right windows of the hovercar. Henry suddenly heard and felt a small, warm and breathy voice almost inside his left ear.

"Granddad . . ."

It was the voice of William, the three-year-old, named after Henry's dead son buried on Ceta. He swiveled his car seat around and opened his arms to those in the backseat.

"My children," he said.

They all came into his arms together. Four-year-old Luke clung as tightly as young Willie; and Ruth, their mother, also hugged him, the faces of all three pressed against his chest and shoulders.

He held them tightly, and kissed the top of the three heads; the two light-blond ones of the boys, that would darken with age to the color of their father's hair, and the wavy reddish-brown of Ruth's. They simply held together without speaking as the long moments slipped slowly by; and then suddenly they were enveloped in gloom, as the window glass of the vehicle automatically darkened around them. Their sun, so like that of Earth's, had broken clear of the horizon and was shining directly upon them.

"I'll come and see you whenever I can," he murmured to the three, gave them all an extra squeeze, then let go and turned back his seat toward the front. The windshield had darkened automatically almost to black, except for one spot of brightness where Epsilon Eridani, directly ahead, burned through in a glow that carried the same signature the star wrote on the sky above.

"It's all right," said Joshua. "We're on the cable road now. On automatic."

Following the impulses from the cable buried in the concrete surface beneath it, under its cushion of air, the hovercar rushed onward, guiding itself toward Ecumeny.

Henry did not answer.

He had opened the package compartment in the dashboard panel before him, and was rummaging within it. After a moment he found and drew out one of the several spindles of recordings that were kept there. He closed the compartment and slid the forefinger-length, pencil-thin spindle into the player.

Immediately the space around the compartment disappeared, to give place to a three-dimensional image of a room with a desk. Behind the desk, a tall, young, remarkably handsome man, in a shirt as white as Henry's but with a black cloak lined in red hanging from his shoulders, sat and spoke. It was clearly a broadcast speech, recorded.

"Call me Bleys," said the figure in a soft but resonant baritone that had the ability to send a thrill—of what, they did not know—through those now listening, even though they knew the man who used it. His eyes were dark brown, dark almost to blackness, under level brows and equally dark brown, slightly wavy hair, cut short about his head.

"I speak for no church," he said in that oddly memorable, compelling voice, "for no political party or policy. If I am anything, I am only a philosopher. A philosopher in love with humanity, and concerned about its future . . ."

The voice went on, filling the car, holding the five people in it captive with its sound and its words, in spite of their familiarity with the message and the one who spoke it. Only Joshua, glancing for a moment sideways at his father's face, saw that Henry's eyes had gone as hard as the blue-white stones of yard and field.

Chapter 2

Bleys Ahrens paced.

It was an hour since he had come back from an early-morning recording session. The brilliant daylight that had dawned on Henry's farm struck through the window wall that was one full side of his private lounge, with daylight at an angle of nearly noon.

The scarlet-lined black cloak that was his trademark had been thrown aside on one of the lounge's chairfloats. One edge of it half-hid the pages of an ancient printed book on Old Earth avian fauna, left open on the float, leaving revealed the image of a hunting gyrfalcon of Old Earth, head up-right and turned sideways, beak closed and fierce, eye cruel.

Bleys was no longer aware of it. Without thinking, since he had started to pace the strides of his long legs had unconsciously lengthened until they crossed the spacious lounge in only six steps. His unusually tall, slim but powerful figure in its black jacket, narrow gray trousers and ankle-high boots seemed to tower under the ample ceiling of the room. Even without the cape, he appeared too large for the available space, as a falcon might, locked in a cage spacious enough for several canaries but not for a single, swift-winged hunter like himself. —An impatient falcon, who did not intend to remain long in any cage and soon would be found gone from it.

He had never intended to remain, in any case. It was more than seven years since he had faced the decision of which way he should go in life. As he saw it then, and as he still did see it, he had only two choices. He could live out his years with humanity as it now was and let it confine him in its own limited society.

—Or he could try to change everything else.

Those years and thousands of hours of relentless training had made his body and mind into the tools and weapons he would need. Sixteen years now since he had first come to his Uncle Henry MacLean's farm here on Association, banished there after forcing his mother to send him from her; by making himself a living reminder of a truth about herself. He had spent his first seven years becoming aware of his terrible loneliness, and two more, coming to realize that among the billions of people on the sixteen worlds, there could be no one to understand him. And at last two years deciding to push his mother to the point of putting him out of her life.

Still, because religion was a way of life for Henry and his two sons, and because hope of belonging somewhere, somehow, was not entirely dead within him, Bleys had tried to find his own future in the faith they held. But he could not believe, and he could not pretend to believe. In the end when the religious community of farmers around the little church where Henry's family also worshiped had driven him out, he had gone gladly; and for the past years with his older half-brother Dahno (possibly full brother—someday Bleys must find out) he had faced his decision.

For the lonely way he would have to go, and for what he needed to do, he required strengths. He had realized that, those seven years past, and had set out to build them in himself. And now he was satisfied with the weapons he had gained—all but one of them.

He had learned to face the fact that he stood apart from all other people; and that meant that he had to have a power to reach across the gap to them—he had to have a glittering eye that would hold them . . . that was a line from some Old Earth poem. Yes . . .

> . . . *He holds him with his glittering eye—*
> *The Wedding-Guest stood still,*
> *And listens like a three years' child:*
> *The Mariner hath his will.*

For seven years that had been the final inner power he had worked to build. Thousands of hours of training his mind and body, able to judge only by his inner feelings that each skill mastered pushed him always closer to possession of it. But he could sense he did not have it yet. That was why, with a very few minor exceptions, he had limited himself to recording what he wanted to say.

Training could do no more; this ability would need to be honed in accomplishment—like the ultimate end of a sword, found finally only in actual combat. He must leave Association to acquire it, in actual action on the other New Worlds.

Now he could not wait to go. But something barely felt in him, yet surely known, was warning him, holding him back. He was not yet fully equipped to go.

The certain knowledge of this came as such things always did to him, in an unmeasureable but unarguable signal from what he had thought of as "the back of his mind."

Those words for this part of him had been with him as long as he could remember, back into early childhood. It was as if his mind was something like a large room divided into two sections. One, a short but wide space before a high counter with no doorway in it; but all clear, visible and provable.

Behind that counter was a space equally wide but shallow, a short step to a great semi-transparent wall or screen—something like a barrier of leather scraped thin enough to barely see through, as if there were light behind it. In that light, through that barrier, it had seemed to him that he could see, or feel—or somehow sense—the moving of great, portentous shapes that occasionally sent messages of meaning to the clear front room.

He had known somehow, even as a child, that if he allowed himself to be forced to live only in this small front part, with the light extinguished behind the screen—cut off from all that could be learned from there—that what was essentially *him* must eventually be destroyed.

So he had chosen instead to try to understand the vaguely seen shapes, to somehow reach through that semi-transparent, curtain wall. He would find a way to make use of the massive hidden machinery there; and put it to work in an attempt to change all grown-up things. So that he and everyone else in the future could live as they should.

An Exotic medician, a specialist on emotions and one of the many medicians of various specialities imperiously summoned by his mother to keep this highly intelligent toy that was her son in top working order, had once gently remonstrated with Bleys when he tried to tell the man he could feel the workings of the back of his head.

"No one can *feel* his unconscious working," the medician had explained gravely, going on to give Bleys an explanation adapted to someone of tender years as to why this should be so.

Bleys, at five of those years, was too wise to try to argue with the man. He merely listened and went on believing as he had always believed. For already his listening and reading had told him better.

He had overheard an author—friend and guest, temporarily, as all his mother's male acquaintances turned out to be—mentioning that after years of writing, he even worked in his dreams on scenes from a book he was writing; literally re-playing and re-directing the action of his characters in the dream.

Also, in his reading—for Bleys had begun to read shortly after two years of age—he had already come across the account of Kekule von Stradonitz, the great nineteenth-century German chemist on Old Earth; and his struggle to determine the atomic structure of benzene. The scientist, after months of frustration, had reported finally dreaming of a snake with its tail in its mouth and wakened, saying essentially (and correctly), *"Of course! It's a circle!"*

It did not matter to Bleys, as it had not to Kekule von Stradonitz, or to the author who had been a storyteller in various media, that what they had experienced was something ordinarily not believed. The point was, it worked. That was all that mattered.

Now it was that back of his mind which had given him the unmistakable message—*not yet*. Something was still lacking to him. Something he had overlooked, he had missed—something, perhaps, that had been forgotten, or not achieved yet.

He saw history in his own mind as a strip of fabric made up of the threads of countless individual lives, continually weaving its pattern forward. Perhaps, he told himself, it was pressure from that pattern he now felt. But—message or pressure—it was there.

For a moment, the thought slipped through his mind that what was missing was Hal Mayne—that elusive youth whose three tutors had been killed on Old Earth five years ago, by gunmen with Bleys, before Bleys could stop them. But the chance of Hal's suddenly being caught now was too small. He put that answer from him.

Deeply, he wished Antonia Lu were here at this moment, so that he could talk to her about this. He had never been able to open himself completely to anyone. Always he had been alone. But she was the closest to confide.

It was over five years now, since he had met her, a wrestling coach at one of the college preparatory schools in the area; and she had agreed to work with him. He had come to need to talk some such concerns out to her—not so much to demand opinion or help from her, but to put order in what was in his own mind by forcing himself to explain it to a sympathetic ear. But at this of all moments, she was gone.

She had left to get her father's approval to go with him off-planet— off Association, if and when he went.

An adult seeking parental approval for anything, was a strangely archaic thing to do in this twenty-fourth century; even with a family as conscious of its Nipponese heritage as Toni's. But this was Association, one of the two ultra-religious Friendly worlds; and the people on this early-terraformed planet, who after three centuries had little else, possessed firm beliefs and minds that did not change on a whim. They followed their own ways.

But she should be back by now. And she was not.

Impatiently, Bleys tried to think of anyone else to whom he could talk safely about his need to be at work. He did not want advice or suggestions. He wanted a sounding board. Somebody understanding, to listen and be safe to tell.

He thought of Dahno. His half-brother was unpredictable. Dahno was much more likely to want to inject his own ideas into this—so interfering with the free working of Bleys' mind. On the other hand, he was the best other mind available. After a moment's hesitation, Bleys lifted his control wristpad to his lips and touched the stud that gave him a private phone connection to Dahno.

"Dahno?" His resonant voice echoed in the empty and now-quiet lounge. "Where are you at the moment?"

"Under your feet, brother. In my office. No, Toni hasn't come in yet. I'll tell you the minute she does, and I'll pass on the message you'd like to see her as soon as possible."

"Are you reading my mind now?"

"Sometimes," said Dahno, "and I'll let you know the minute anything new comes in on Hal Mayne's whereabouts."

"Good," said Bleys.

"You know, you could catch Toni when she comes in, yourself, if you were down here on the office floor, with me."

"You like offices," said Bleys. "This, up here, is my office."

"—With fireplace, Mayne-map and usually Toni. Looks remarkably like a lounge to me. Anything else?"

"Nothing," said Bleys.

"Then I've got some things to talk to you about, myself," Dahno said. "There's some interesting spaceship mail in from New Earth. I was going to bring it up myself, anyway; because there's something else as well I've been wanting to talk to you about for a while now and I'd like to talk privately. How about my coming up now?"

"Fine."

"Right. I've just got a small matter here to finish off. Be there in five minutes." Dahno broke the connection.

So did Bleys. Dahno, with any kind of news or problem, would give Bleys' mind a relief from its galloping pursuit of the thoughts that had been occupying it for the past half hour. That might be even better.

Bleys went over and took one of the padded chairfloats that was high enough off the floor to give his long legs room, half-facing a chair equally high and perhaps a little more spacious.

But his mind would not stop simply because his body had. His longing for the signal he waited for was still like an ache within him, but his conscious mind had already leaped to consideration of whatever information Dahno would be bringing up and its possible effect on his outgoing. All events were potentially important.

That concept he had always privately called "the Historic Pattern," and which he counted on for reshaping the future of the whole human race, had always been like a bright multicolored ribbon in his imagination.

It was not his insight alone, this idea that all human history built forward in a continuous pattern that was the sum of individual human efforts by all those alive at any single moment. So that by working together and against each other, they created the social forces with which those of following generations would have to wrestle.

The Annalist school of historical writing on Old Earth, in the early twentieth century, had also seen that same forward-building movement of history, created, not only by all human actions but also by their environments, beliefs, social conditions and just about everything else.

A few years later, but much earlier in history, Bleys found, in St. Paul's Epistle to the Corinthians—I Corinthians, chapter 12, verses 12 to 31—a passage in which Paul had used the symbol of Christ's body to much the same purpose: as a metaphor for all the members of the early Christian church. And even earlier than that, in the first century B.C., there had been the Roman writer Livy, in his *Parable Of The Belly* . . .

* * *

"—There you are," Bleys said, gratefully discarding thoughts about the Historic Pattern, as Dahno entered the lounge through the particular one of its sliding doors which opened on the private elevator to Bleys' suite.

Dahno stepped off the float plate on which he had come up and walked in, his size for a moment half-hiding the wall-wide Mayne-map he had mentioned, with its red line showing what they knew so far of Hal Mayne's movements between the New Worlds.

Bleys' brother was as tall as Bleys, but heavy with muscle as well. A literal giant. The red Hal Mayne line he had partly obscured had started on Old Earth and stretched through New Earth to Coby, the metals-rich mining world. There they had lost track of Hal among the miners; whose only valuable concession from the mine owners, on that small, airless but rich world, was the fact that they could take jobs under false names, and no record would be kept of when or how they got the job. So that a man or woman who took successive jobs at different mines broke his or her trail several times and was almost impossible to trace.

For some time now they had searched Coby for Hal, with no success. Bleys felt a necessity to find the boy. It should not have been so difficult even when the quarry had such a strange history as young Mayne.

Dahno was coming forward, looming beneath the ceiling. He took a chair-float opposite Bleys.

"The spaceship mail," he said, as he sat down, "was a Private-and-Secret from Ana Wasserlied, herself, on New Earth. One of our secret Others members there, who's openly a member in the CEOs' Club, has told her the CEOs—it'll have to have been with the agreement of the Guildmasters—have just signed a full-planet contract with Cassida and Newton for the manufacture of a more compact power unit for vehicles using magnetic levitation."

"Ah," said Bleys.

He put no emphasis on the sound; but this was one of the developments he had been waiting for. A full-planet contract, pledging the cooperation, by law, of all manufacturers, would make for a single body of opinion on New Earth, with which he could begin his work. Good news.

But now Dahno stretched his massive arms out lazily and settled comfortably into his chairfloat—and Bleys tensed, suddenly on guard. The jolly giant that was the external Dahno was indeed the actual man. But within him, deep-hidden, waited another Dahno that was a legacy of their mutual mother.

What Dahno valued above all else was personal freedom. Not wealth, not power—he had these—not anything that Bleys had been able to discover or imagine; only complete freedom of action. It had led him finally to literally run from their mother, and so Dahno had been the first of them to be shipped off to Henry MacLean, here on Association.

But before that there had been years in which the young giant had struggled against the invisible bars of her control over him. What had resulted inside the grown-up Dahno was a very cautious, brilliant mind that concentrated first and foremost on making sure it stepped into no traps that might endanger that valuable freedom; and stayed at arm's length from any close contact with another person who might entangle or hold him against his will.

Dahno had been thirteen when he was sent here to Association. Ten years later, Bleys had been only eleven when he, more clearheadedly and coldly, arranged his own exile. But the wound inside Bleys had been deeper; and whether Dahno had ever really understood the difference between them was something Bleys doubted. He knew that he—himself—could reach no one. No one could reach him.

Bleys still seemed to remember a short time after his birth, when his mother—or someone—had loved him. Otherwise, Bleys reasoned, he could not have felt his loss as he had, when later he began to realize she did not; that to her he was no more than one more toy, or expensive piece of jewelry.

He did not like to think of his mother, now; or anything to do with the subject of whether love existed or not. It was as if the very thought of it stirred unseen monsters beyond the semi-transparent curtain. He was aware that there were those like Henry MacLean, Dahno, and possibly Antonia Lu, who had some feeling for him—he pushed that thought away. It must not matter how anyone else felt about him.

That movement of Dahno's just now, seeming to stretch and relax, was not encouraging; an unconscious reflex that warned of unpleasant news to come.

"I've copied the letter into our private files," Dahno said. "Was this something you were expecting? A New Earth full-world contract?"

"More or less," Bleys said. "I'll want the best possible social climate on any New World I include in any speaking tour I make. New Earth's the one I was hoping to start with. This kind of news makes it that much more attractive."

He gazed at Dahno, but Dahno did not look encouraging. Rather the opposite.

"I know you've been busting a gut to get going, brother," Dahno said bluntly. "I suppose it's been bound to happen, any moment. But I suggest you take a close look at this letter from Ana Wasserlied I just filed and make sure it's a good sign; not just an excuse for what you want to do anyway. But, on another topic—I've been thinking for some time about what I told you on the phone just now I wanted to talk to you on. For your own good—"

He broke off. One of the sliding doors of the lounge had just been unlocked and opened. Toni had stepped in, just in time to hear the last words. She halted, barely inside the room. Instantly, even though it was Toni, Bleys felt the soundless *click*—the shift of adjustment inside him, when the unexpected appearance of an extra person altered the social equation abruptly.

"Am I breaking in on a private talk?" she said. "Sorry. I'll be down the hall in the floral lounge, Bleys."

"No. No, come on in," said Dahno. "I'd like you to hear this. You may want to back up something I say."

She looked at Bleys questioningly.

"Yes," said Bleys. He would have liked to ask her immediately about her family's reaction—but privately. "Come join us, Toni."

She smiled, and both Bleys and Dahno smiled back. It was almost impossible not to, when Toni smiled. She came forward with the smooth walk of a trained athlete—and indeed one of her assets, which Bleys had already appreciated when he first asked her if she wanted to work for him, had been the fact she could keep training him in the martial arts at which he had worked for these past ten years.

She was slim and tall, in an aquamarine knit dress that picked up some of the color of her blue eyes, under surprisingly black hair. Her face was fine-boned and oval, giving her a delicate appearance in spite of her size. As with many people on the New Worlds who traced their ancestry back to Japan, she did not look particularly oriental. She took a chairfloat and sat down.

"Feel free to speak out, if you've got something to say for or against what I'm going to say," Dahno told her. "What I wanted to tell Bleys is something I've been thinking about for some time."

He turned his attention back to Bleys.

"It's over four years now," he said, "since you put me to work searching out, training and re-training the best and most capable members of our Others' organizations on all the worlds we've got organizations on. Obviously, you're looking to the future use of these people; and I don't mind you not telling me the specifics on that, because it's the way I'd do something myself. I'd just as soon never find something I said in the past tripping me up in the present."

Bleys smiled. "I know. It seems as if we're both up against that."

"It comes to anyone in the public eye at all," said Dahno. "But the point is, you've got the best minds of our Others on half a dozen worlds working away at this without knowing what it's to lead to. What all of them think now is that it'll make them into someone like you—and they've all got you up on a pedestal in their minds. They're all expecting that what's going to happen is you'll turn out to be a new King Arthur over all the worlds—and they'll be your Knights of the Round Table."

"Actually," said Bleys, "that isn't too far from what I hope to do. But it'll depend on whether I can get control of some of the Worlds first—at least enough people on enough worlds changing their attitudes and beginning to believe in a planned future. If I can, I'll need these Others of ours to be leaders on the rest of the New Worlds. So when that time comes,

I'll want them able to go to work as trained. I'll still be in control. I mean we—the three of us here—will still run things, but from back out of sight. These trained people are going to have to be the leaders in the spotlight. You follow me?"

"Maybe," said Dahno. "Spell it out."

"I'm saying," Bleys went on, "that I want the peoples of the New Worlds to know about me, and they will; but only that. They'll have seen me on broadcasts and on tape, and to a certain extent in person when I've given talks. But that's the most direct contact I want. They'll be free to believe or not in what I say; but the day-to-day, item-by-item leading should be done by these Others you've trained."

"Hmm," said Dahno.

"Once it's like that, our Others can move into place," Bleys said. "They'll be working for us with whatever planetary government each World already has, disturbing as little as possible the existing machinery there. They'll be the ones seen as controllers. It's the only way to control that many worlds at once. But it's no more than what you've been doing yourself for years here on Association, Dahno, as a lobbyist and advice-giver to the delegates of our Chamber, governing Association. You, I, Toni—we'll be working at one rank removed—that's all."

He waited, but Dahno's expression still did not change. Nor did he answer immediately.

"You understand?" Bleys said. "I want to change people's minds, not the way they live—immediately, anyway. For that I have to be more an Idea than a Human, someone seen always and only at a distance—a sort of mythic personage, a symbol of what I tell them they can be."

"And you're sure that all this is going to go off all right?" Dahno asked slowly.

"Yes," said Bleys.

He stared directly at Dahno.

"You've seen how my recorded tapes have caught on on other worlds. The overwhelming majority of people on most of the New Worlds are hungry for leadership. It's been three hundred years now since terraforming allowed the first immigrants to go to the New Worlds. For a long time those who left Old Earth were too busy struggling to survive, to consider where they were headed in the long run. But they've had time now. The Fanatics, the True Faith-Holders, the Dorsai and the Exotics believe they've already found their future and they're satisfied with it. But everyone else on our New Worlds is reaching out for something they can't describe or put their finger on but know they want—just like our ancestors back on Old Earth for several thousands of years knew that there was an eventual future in which everything they needed and wanted could be had and they themselves would be happy. I promise them that in my dream of the future, and in a little while it'll seem as if there are people on their own worlds who are steering them in exactly the direction I talked about. It's that simple."

He paused. Dahno looked less doubtful, but still not completely convinced. After a moment, Dahno did speak, soberly.

"That business of being a symbol—that's always been a strange and dangerous notion you've been playing with," he said. "It'll end up with the three of us trying to drive something like a dozen different juggernauts in single harness. Dangerous—not only for our Others, Toni and myself; but mostly for you. People can turn against symbols—and when they do, they destroy them. Anyway—since I know better than to try to talk you out of it—how would this lecture tour of yours lead into it?"

"It's the first step"—Bleys began, but at that moment Toni's wrist control pad chimed and she lifted it to her lips.

"Yes?" she said. She listened a moment, her control pad obviously on *mute*, so that only her end of the conversation was audible to Bleys and Dahno. "Hold a moment."

She looked back at Bleys while touching the control that would block off their conversation from the open phone circuit. "Someone's here to see you," she said. "Apparently, he's being insistent about seeing you. Do you know an Association Militia officer who just got back here from Harmony, named Amyth Barbage?"

"I do," said Dahno. "Oh, that was the other matter I wanted to talk to you about, Bleys. This Barbage called me from orbit on his way in. I've been maintaining contacts within the Militia of both our Friendly worlds for some time, and I know this man. He's a Fanatic; I don't care for him, but he's useful. And he's ambitious—he's been wanting to talk with you, and now he's come up with news he says you have to hear—from him. Didn't want to tell me; but I got it out of him. He thinks he's located Hal Mayne finally—with an outlaw Command on Harmony."

"Harmony!" said Toni, for Hal Mayne could hardly not know that Harmony was the other so-called "Friendly" world, a place where the Others were strong.

"Yes," said Dahno, "Barbage seems to think Mayne's been there some months; all these last few months we were still having the Coby mines searched for him. In fact, Barbage thinks you saw him yourself—or should have seen him—when you were on that speaking tour on Harmony just four months ago. Damned if I know why you attach so much importance to finding this Mayne, anyway!"

"In that case, I probably better have this officer up," said Bleys. "But you sound as if you don't really trust his information."

"I don't know whether or not to trust it," said Dahno. "And I didn't want to raise your hopes until I'd checked it out. But, make your own judgment as to whether you want to use him further, or not. Anyway, since the cat's out of the bag on his current news, maybe you're right. Maybe you'd better talk to him now and judge for yourself."

Bleys nodded, and Toni lifted the control pad again to her lips.

"Send him up," she said.

Chapter 3

Bleys looked directly at Dahno.

"According to Barbage, Hal Mayne's been there how long?" he asked.

"Some months, apparently," said Dahno. "I'm checking the information, of course."

With his gaze focused on Dahno, Bleys was still able to see the Mayne-map, but only with the outer corners of his eyes. He did not like to betray his intense interest in this news by looking to see if the map had just been updated. As it was, he could not be sure upon which black world-dot the end of the red line now rested; but the line itself seemed longer than it had been the last time he looked. Dahno was probably playing safe—more sure than he sounded, that Barbage's information was correct.

"Anyway," Dahno was going on, "I ought to have my answer in six days. I sent a letter on *Favored of God*—you remember? One of the space-ships we've got a majority interest in. *Favored*'s got to go on from Harmony to Ceta. But there're other ships coming straight back to here, any one of which can bring back the answer."

Bleys nodded, thoughtfully. He had not only remembered *Favored*, he had wanted to do his entire speaking tour using that spaceship. But the answers on the Hal Mayne question were important—important enough to him so any delay of the trip would be worthwhile, whenever he might decide to go.

"When will *Favored* be back here and free?" he asked.

"Eight days," said Dahno.

Bleys nodded again. With all the near-magic of which phase-shift physics seemed to be capable, the fastest way to get letters across an interstellar distance was still by sending them aboard spaceships. It was even more practical between two worlds under the same star, like Association and Harmony. He should probably be glad he had an available technology like that to make his multi-worlds speaking tour possible. But the Exotics had once been supposed to have a secret and faster way of sending messages between the stars that gave them a commercial advantage in inter-world trade. Bleys lost himself in possibilities.

Phase-shifting could be made to translate properly equipped ships from point to point—the word "move" did not really apply—completely disregarding the limiting speed of light. It did not so much move the ship, as simply restate its position with regard to the theoretical centerpoint of the galaxy.

But the best calculated phase-shift was only an approximate approach to any destination. Traveling this way was like zeroing in on a target point. The smaller the shift, the more accurate it was. But there was always some error, requiring re-calculation, until the destination was close enough to be approached with an ordinary mass-drive unit.

That took time, but if there was some way to compensate for the error factor—

"—In fact," Dahno was saying, as Bleys came back to the present, "Barbage, as I say, claims you were right in the same room with Mayne four months ago. In any case, as I say, Barbage is here, hotfoot from Militia Headquarters with the news. I don't like the little man."

"I gathered," said Bleys. "Why? You've dealt with enough Fanatics in your lobbying work—Bishops of wild-eyed churches who've managed to get themselves elected to the Chamber, and are there, helping rule Association."

"I have," said Dahno. "But Barbage out-fanatics them all. He's like a knife blade, a very sharp, very cold knife blade. And he always wants something."

"What is it this time, then?" said Bleys.

"He expects you'll be going with him to Harmony to run Mayne down," Dahno went on. "He wants us to pull strings for him. He'd like to pick out troops for his own search force, from here on Association; rather than simply getting authority to use the district militias on Harmony, as he passes through their districts."

Dahno leaned back in the float, spreading his wide shoulders. His brown eyes watched Bleys intently.

"I told him I didn't know how it could be done," he added, "but I said I'd talk it over with you first."

"No, I don't want him taking Association Militia to Harmony," said Bleys. It was an obvious decision. As a Fanatic, Barbage would be one of those people on the two Friendly Worlds who made his religion an excuse for his own desires, not a standard by which to measure them. Even if it occurred to him, he would ignore the fact that the appearance of numbers of Association Militia on Harmony would arouse feelings of rivalry, resentment and non-cooperation from the Harmony Militia.

"There're good reasons for not using Association Militia there," Bleys went on, "particularly with a rare two-worlds election for an Eldest coming soon. I'll talk to him—"

"Come over here, Captain," Toni interrupted with unusual sharpness. "Bleys Ahrens will speak to you now."

Bleys looked up quickly from Dahno, and saw a man who must be Amyth Barbage already standing just inside the door from the office elevator to this lounge. He had plainly been there long enough to hear Bleys' last words. Possibly even long enough to hear Dahno's opinion of him. He came forward now with no expression; a slim, wiry young man, slightly above average height and wearing a perfectly fitted black-and-silver uniform of the Militia—as the planetary paramilitary police forces were called on both Friendly Worlds.

Bleys saw Toni examining Barbage as he advanced. He was young to have reached the rank he had in the Militia and unusual enough in appearance to invite interest.

He stood rod-straight; and the first impression he gave was that of someone thin and young trying hard to look impressive—but achieving impressiveness no more so than a rabbit. A second glance told Bleys more. The impressiveness was real. This was a saber-toothed rabbit.

Barbage's face was lean with almost the leanness of near-starvation. His hair and eyebrows were almost as dark as the impeccable black uniform he wore. In contrast, that face was beardless and so white-skinned that he looked pale, as if with emotion.

Under his eyebrows, Barbage's eyes burned with little brightnesses, like fire opals of that same color. His mouth was a straight line, as if his lips were locked tightly between the thin nose above and the narrow-but-square jaw beneath. He walked directly toward Bleys, but with his gaze equally on all of them. There was no expression on his face, unless what there was could be called an expression of aggressive politeness. It was not far removed from an expression of contempt.

And indeed, thought Bleys, it could be contempt. As a Fanatic, Barbage would think of himself as one of God's chosen—possibly the Chosen among those chosen. This would mean that everyone else anywhere was necessarily less than he was, no matter what their worldly office, power or authority.

He came to a halt before Bleys.

"Thou honorest me by seeing me, Great Teacher," he said.

"I believe I saw you briefly the last time I was on Harmony," said Bleys. "Are you a member of the Harmony Militia or a member of Association Militia who was temporarily on Harmony?"

"I was on Harmony, Great Teacher, on a training transfer from the Association Militia, to which I belong. I had volunteered for a spell of training on Harmony, to broaden my experience and usefulness to the Militia and to God. Clearly, thy memory is as great as thy other parts, Great Teacher. You would have seen me only briefly, when I brought in the detainees there under orders to display them to you. You spoke to them, and they went away no longer abandoned of God and committed to outlaw ways, but seemingly back in the path of righteousness once more. Though, certainly, some of them must have strayed again from that path; otherwise I would not have seen the man you call Hal Mayne sometime later with an outlaw band in the mountains there, where I was temporarily leading a small arm of the Militia in search of such."

"Yes," said Bleys. "I'm not surprised you found Hal Mayne with the outlaws, Amyth. He's not an ordinary man."

"Satan upholds him, clearly," said Barbage.

"Doubtless," said Bleys. "But, to come back to present matters. I called you in because I just wanted to be sure you understand the reasons for what I've decided."

Suddenly his voice became quiet and warm, and a little flicker in Barbage's gaze betrayed his taking note of the change.

Bleys went on, "You were expecting to be going back to Harmony to search for Hal Mayne, of course, and I want you to do just that. How sure are you you'll know him when you see him?"

"Very sure, Great Teacher. I do not forget faces. I knew him from an image of him, an artist's rendering of his boyhood face as adjusted by a computer, which your people have circulated. And now I have seen him twice." He paused only briefly.

"And now," he went on, "there is evidence he is with some of those Abandoned by God, one of the self-styled Resistance Groups, outlaw commands that have sprung up in opposition to the Chamber of Government on Harmony—as other such groups have here."

His use of the antique-sounding "cant" speech of some of the ultra-religious on Association and Harmony could have sounded artificial and ridiculous. It did nothing of the sort. Instead, it seemed only to put him farther from having ordinary human feelings and responses. His voice itself was a light baritone, held taut by some inner tension, so that the sound of it had an edge which cut like a tight-stretched wire.

"—But surely, Great Teacher," he wound up, "thou wilt be with me there, on Harmony?"

"*There is a tide in the affairs of men,*" said Bleys, "*Which, taken at its flood, leads on to fortune . . .* "

"Great Teacher?" Barbage's eyes suddenly burned on him. "Thou quotest a scripture not known to me. Nor one spoken in the common tongue."

"It's not scripture, Amyth," said Bleys. "It's from the secular pen of a remarkable writer. He wrote those words some eight hundred years ago. A man named William Shakespeare. Those words are his, in Old Modern English, not our present-day Basic. They mean I'll not be going to Harmony with you. I've got other things to do. But you can carry a letter from me to the Harmony Militia saying you speak with my voice. Now, do you know which Resistance Group—or outlaw command—this is, that Hal Mayne's supposed to have joined?"

"Not yet, Great Teacher," said Amyth. His face had returned to its normal expression. "But I will find someone who hath that knowledge—and that I will do much quicker with a force of my own men."

"Perhaps," said Bleys, "and I think we could possibly get you permission for such a force. Particularly, if it's Association's Over-Bishop McKae who wins the upcoming run-off election with Harmony; and becomes the first Eldest in eighteen years to rule over both our worlds. But if I arrange such a command for you now, or even then, I'm afraid the local Harmony Militia commanders are going to be only too likely to leave all the searching to you; and do only a halfhearted job of looking on their own. I want them doing their best, as well as you. In the end, Amyth, I think it'll save time if you let them work for you. I can understand how you'd rather have a force of your own. But I think in this case—no."

Barbage's face registered no emotion. "If such is thy decision, Great Teacher. God hath made known to me that thou art one who decides. I will do as thou sayest and take what force is needed from the local militias. But it will be necessary to arrange authority for that. Also—"

Barbage was interrupted by a single chiming note on the air of the room.

"What is it?" asked Dahno.

"Great Teacher Bleys Ahrens, do you and Dahno Ahrens have an uncle named Henry Mack Klane?" It was the voice of the receptionist some forty floors below them, in this building that was both offices and living quarters for all present now in the room, except Barbage. "He's asking to see you."

"Uncle Henry!" Bleys was on his feet suddenly. He realized only then that the surprise of this announcement had sounded in his voice. He made himself go on with nothing more than his usual enthusiasm. After all, the visit might be just that, a casual drop-in because Henry was in town.

"Send him up," Bleys said. "The lift shaft to my private lounge."

"He's coming, Bleys Ahrens," said the receptionist's voice, after a moment's pause. "Thank you for your orders."

Bleys turned to Dahno.

"Uncle Henry!" he said. "Did you know he was coming to town?"

"No." Dahno shook his head. "It'll be good to see him. I wonder if he's got the family with him?"

"The receptionist didn't mention it—"

Before Bleys could finish, the door of the elevator from the lobby slid open, and one of the lift circles stopped level with the room. Henry stepped off it, into the room, carrying his suitcase. The door closed again.

"Uncle!" said Bleys. "Are you alone? Where's the family?"

"They drove me in at dawn," said Henry. "They will have been back at the farm for some hours now. But I've come to stay with you."

"Dawn, Uncle?" said Dahno. "Into town, here? And you're just getting to us now?"

"I had some old friends to look up first," said Henry.

His voice was no different, in its warm but unyielding statement, from the way it had been any time Bleys could remember. Henry put down his suitcase.

"—But you're busy at the moment?" he added.

"No, no," said Bleys. In a couple of long strides, he and Dahno had passed by Barbage to stand within arm's reach of Henry. Barbage was only now turning to look at the three of them. Henry MacLean was not someone whom people other than young grandchildren would normally hug, and neither Bleys nor Dahno made any attempt to. But the way they stood close to him radiated their affection for him. As for Henry, he stood—in his own way—apart and alone, but perfectly still and composed. In spite of his relative lack of height, he did not seem to need to look up at Bleys or Dahno.

"No," said Bleys, "and if it was business, it could still wait. But what do you mean, Uncle—you're going to stay?"

"Just that," said Henry. He looked first at Toni, and then at Amyth Barbage. "Are you sure you don't have business with these two?"

"Any business has just been finished," said Bleys. "You've never met Toni before, Uncle. This is Antonia Lu, my right hand—or left, if you want to call Dahno my right. This Militia officer is Captain Amyth Barbage. Come over here, now, and sit down."

He led the way, and Dahno with him, to the chairs. He and Dahno dropped into theirs. Henry followed, but stopped, still on his feet. Barbage turned back again, standing silent, now not much more than arm's length from Henry; and Toni was still over by the wall map.

"I've been sitting for most of the morning," said Henry, "after Joshua and the others drove me in—"

"They should've stayed, too," said Bleys.

"Joshua has work at the farm," said Henry, "and so has Ruth. Even the children have their duties. They should not really have taken the time to drive me, but Joshua chose to."

"Of course, Uncle," said Bleys. He and Dahno both sat tall in their large chairs, looking at Henry. "Tell us why you're here."

"I've come because of my love for you, Bleys," said Henry. "I would not for anyone I did not love as a son. You have fallen into Satan's hands, and perhaps only I can keep you alive until you save yourself."

A touch of bitterness made itself felt in Bleys.

I went seeking God and found him not, thought Bleys, with bitter irony; but he did not utter the thought aloud. Henry would have taken it as a personal reproach at his failure to help Bleys to believe in a deity.

"We're all in Satan's hands, Uncle," said Bleys aloud, instead.

"No," said Henry, "I am not—"

He glanced briefly at Barbage, as if a second's glance was all that was needed.

"—Even this man, in spite of his twisted wrongness toward God, is not. But you are. And I—"

"How darest thou!" snapped Barbage, stepping forward. "To say *I* am wrong in God's eyes—and that the Great Teacher is in Satan's hands, but you are not! It is blasphemy! I will take thee—"

"Barbage," said Bleys.

He had not needed to raise his voice. The training he had put himself through in the years since he had come to Dahno had honed sharp his natural talent for putting his full strength into words without raising the volume of their sound. The room rang suddenly with that strength; and Barbage took a step back, as if he had been on the receiving end of a blow. He stood silent.

"You are in Satan's hands," repeated Henry, inexorably, in the same calm voice in which he had first spoken the words. After that one glance, he had ignored Barbage. His gaze had returned to Bleys. "But it may be I can guard you from him, until you are strong enough to break free."

Bleys considered him thoughtfully and calmly; but his mind was racing, all his plans undergoing alteration. Luckily, Dahno spoke first.

"What do you mean, *'Guard'* him, Uncle?" Dahno asked.

"I think maybe what Uncle Henry means," said Bleys, "is that he'll form a guard—possibly of some of those friends he saw this morning—and with these keep me alive long enough to see the error of my ways. Am I right, Uncle?"

"But Great Teacher!" Barbage burst out, the words breaking from him in spite of an obvious desire to keep them penned, "thou dost not need this—this old prophet—to guard thee. Thou canst have as many of the Militia as thee needs. Militia may be set about thee at all times. *Militia*, I said! Not—not whatever this, thine uncle, can sweep up."

Now Henry did turn to look at Barbage, still without any excitement in his voice or posture.

"I say nothing against any man in his will to do the best he can to protect whoever he feels he should protect," he said. "But I have fought Militiamen and found them wanting."

A physical slap could hardly have changed Barbage's face more than Henry's last words. His pale skin went paper-white as the little blood that was in it drained out.

"If thou hast fought the Militia, thou art a felon!" he said, his eyes burning once more. "Accordingly, I put thee under arrest. Thou—"

He had taken a step forward and lifted his hand to grasp Henry by the shoulder. But his fingers never touched their goal.

Instead, Henry's hand caught his forearm in midair and held it there.

Barbage stared at him in utter disbelief; then, although his body hardly moved, it was obvious he made an effort with all his strength to break loose. Not only did he fail, but his arm stirred only slightly. Then Henry held it again, completely still.

Barbage still stared at the older man. He was a little taller than Henry; and while Henry might have weighed a few kilograms more than he did, that was the only other visible difference. But it was almost as if the hand holding his arm were Dahno's hand. From his chair, Bleys chuckled softly.

"You haven't run a farm for twenty years, Captain," he said. "My uncle Henry has. You grow strong doing that kind of work. Let him go, Uncle, please. And Captain, I do not want to hear talk of arresting my uncle again; and if he ever is arrested, I'll hold you accountable."

Henry let go, and Barbage's arm dropped as if the strength had been drained from it.

"Yes, Great Teacher," he said expressionlessly. But his eyes burned now on Henry alone.

"And I think you'd better go now, Captain," said Bleys. "I believe I answered the question you came to ask?"

"Yes, Great Teacher."

Barbage turned back to a door in the wall behind him. The door slid aside for him. He passed through it and was gone as it closed behind him.

"You must not condemn him," Henry said to Bleys. "He is Fanatic and probably will never be a True Faith-Holder. It is clear in him; and sad as true. But even as a Fanatic, he's closer to God—much closer—than either you or Dahno have ever been. In his twisted faith—within its limits—he may well be an honest man."

"How can you know so much about him?" said Toni unexpectedly from across the room. Henry looked at her.

"I have met his kind, many times," he said. "I have fought them, talked with them—and prayed with them. I know that in certain things, in his own way, like other Militiamen I've fought, he's not unworthy of respect. But I do not love him or his kind; and I, myself, fight only for those I love."

Toni plainly checked herself just in time from saying any more. She continued to gaze at Henry with an expression Bleys felt fell between deep interest and mild shock; and, as well, something that was possibly admiration. Bleys could not be sure.

He stood up.

"Uncle," he said, "I think I know whom you'd recruit. Once, a few years back, I needed to infiltrate the Defenders of Bishop McKae. Those bodyguards of his were former Soldiers of God, all of them experienced in the fighting between churches, and against the Militia. I know, even if Amyth Barbage doesn't, that they're more capable than Militia; and I'm glad to have you with me, with or without help. But it's true, the time may come when I'll need the personal equivalent of a small strike force. Why doesn't Dahno find you a suite of rooms? Then we'll all get together at dinner."

He turned to Dahno, who had also stood up from his chair—and, without warning, it was as if some inner part of him over which he had no control spoke in him.

"Wait a minute," he heard himself say, turning back to Henry. "Can you put together as many Soldiers of God as you think you'll need in the next two weeks?"

His mind was suddenly exploding with new possibilities, new plans. He heard his voice, going on calmly, with hardly a pause.

"I'll be making a speaking tour on some of the other New Worlds in a couple of weeks. Could you get your group together in time if we left that soon?"

He was aware of Toni's and Dahno's eyes suddenly hard on him; but the focus of his own attention was all on Henry.

"New Earth?" asked Dahno.

"New Earth," said Bleys, still looking at Henry. "I'm going there first. Can you do it, Uncle?"

"Two weeks?" Henry said, quietly, as if Dahno had never interrupted. "Yes."

He turned to Dahno. "You were going to find me a room."

"A suite of rooms, Uncle," said Dahno. "A suite. Come along."

They went out.

"That's excellent. It's just what I needed," said Bleys, looking after them.

He turned toward Toni and found her also still looking out the doorway by which the two men had left. Her eyes were bright. A change had come over her since Henry had arrived.

"I'm sorry to spring this New Earth trip on you and Dahno without warning this way," Bleys said, as she finally turned back to him. "You went to talk to your family . . . "

He found himself oddly hesitant and very nearly superstitious about ending his question.

"Oh, yes," she said. "It's all right. I'll go with you."

"You heard. I'll be going beyond New Earth," Bleys said bluntly.

"That's all right," she said. She smiled at him suddenly. "Anywhere."

Chapter 4

Bleys woke as a wild animal might if an unknown, possibly threatening, sound had reached its ears. Suddenly he was sitting up—all senses alerted.

But the seconds passed, and no reason for the sudden wakening appeared. His first impression was that he had been asleep barely a few minutes. But a glance at the clock glowing among the light-points of the starscape on his ceiling told him it had been four hours. Whatever had brought him awake was not apparent now.

However, as he sat in bed, he began to recognize a feeling of excitement, like that which had driven him earlier in the day now just passed—but now uncomfortably mixed with a nameless uneasiness.

But there was no reason for the uneasiness.

Dinner with Henry last night had been happy. There were no more questions, he had thought then, to delay his outgoing. Henry had said fifty former Soldiers of God would be needed for the protective duty on which he and Bleys decided. But there should be no problem assembling that force.

He had not talked to anything like so many before coming to see Bleys and Dahno, that morning. In fact, only to twelve. But these would know how to contact others, through the network that connected veteran Soldiers. In three or four days he should have the full complement.

The night breeze came through the open doors of the balcony of his bedroom and cooled the upright part of Bleys' body, lifted above the force-field that was both mattress and bedding on his expensive bed. He rolled off it and stood upright in the dark bedroom, all in one motion.

The breeze was fluttering the thin, white curtains before the balcony doors. The moving air was cool on the dampness of his skin—for he had sweated as he slept—and he could feel the light chill over the whole surface of his body.

As usual, he had been sleeping in only a pair of brief athletic shorts. Before he had left his mother, like all Exotic children he had slept entirely without bedtime clothing. But when he had been sent to live with Henry MacLean, he had found Friendlies shocked by this, and he was expected to wear a nightshirt.

Because he had been only eleven then, because he had wanted so badly to become part of Henry's family, he had begun wearing the night-shirt Henry gave him. Like most of the other clothes he was put into at Henry's farm, it was a hand-me-down from Joshua, Henry's oldest son; and he had hated the tangle of its cumbersome folds about his legs.

Grown at last, when he was driven out by the local church community and Henry sent him to join Dahno here in Ecumeny, Bleys had thrown away his nightshirt, only to find that habit had made him come to feel unprotected, sleeping naked. The shorts were an answer. They did not tangle around him as he turned in bed, and he slept comfortably in them.

Now the feel of the nightgown came back to him; and it seemed that even the spacious luxury bedroom was stifling, like a closed box with all the dimensions of a cage. He walked through the gauzy, white curtains, dancing in the faint breeze, through the half-open door beyond, and out onto the balcony.

The open air was a relief. But the glowing spectrum of ghost-lights of an advertising sign, projected into the air above one of the hotels nearby, lit this side of his building.

Thirty-seven stories below him, at the street level, the trafficway be-fore his building ran to intersect with others like it to make a gridwork of ruled lines, like bars on a prison window.

He lifted his eyes to the stars above all of this.

It had been in stars like these he had found comfort, when he first began to understand the love he sought from his mother was not there. What he gazed at now, out here on the balcony, was different from what was duplicated on the ceiling viewscreen of the bedroom behind him. These were the stellar bodies, themselves, not just their captured image. He looked through atmosphere and light-years of space to their actual selves; and a desire to reach to them for help in understanding the uneasiness he felt, moved in him.

Driven by the excitement and this uneasiness, one of his rare wild impulses took him. He looked about. Along the front of the building, underneath every row of balconies, ran a continuous decorative ledge twenty centimeters wide. He gazed at the one just beneath him.

He was tall enough so that by standing on the ledge running below his balcony and reaching up, he could close his hands on the ledge under the balconies of the floor overhead; and so move out along those narrow roads to where he would stand with only air and space between him and the stars.

Bleys stepped to the corner at his left, where his balcony met the wall of the building. He would need to move along the ledge with his back to the wall. He turned his back to the building's surface; and, reaching up with his left hand, felt for and easily found the overhead ledge. Closing his fingers on it, he put his left leg over the railing, his bare foot feeling for the surface of the lower ledge and finding it.

He pushed both left arm and leg out along their separate ledges, while still holding the railing with his right hand. Then he took hold of the ledge overhead with his other hand, took all the weight of his body on them, lifted his right leg over the railing in turn and, when it was firmly on the lower ledge, distributed his weight equally and stood, free of the balcony and supported only by the two ledges. Vertigo threatened him for a moment—but he overrode it.

Spread-eagled, with his back against the wall of the building, he stood looking out, over the city, unimpeded at last, at space and the stars.

He looked out at them, ignoring the faint light and noise drifting up from below. Gradually, he narrowed the focus of his attention. With the experience of thousands of hours of mental self-discipline, he began to shut out his awareness of anything but space, stars and the surface against which he pressed. The excitement mounted in him.

I am Antaeus, he thought—wrestler and son of ancient Greek gods, Poseidon, of the sea and Gaea, goddess of Earth. The wrestler Antaeus, whose strength was renewed each time he touched his mother, the Earth. But, unlike Antaeus, I draw my strength fresh and fresh again, not like him from the earth under me, but from each time I see the stars. The stars, and the whole human race renew my strength—over and over again, without limit.

He recalled his years of study with the martial arts and the concept of *ki*—the centering of his consciousness at a theoretical balance point, two inches below his navel and an inch within his body.

He remembered, once concentration was achieved, how thinking of his *ki* as extending downward into the surface below his feet, could make him seem so heavy that two, or even three, other people, who should have been able to lift him easily, could not. The term for this in Old Earth Japanese came back to him: *"Kioshizumeru."*

Yes, said the wildness in him.

He had centered his *ki* unthinkingly, from long training, before stepping over the railing. Now he closed his eyes and thought of it as extending itself—not down, but backward, like a pin through a mounted butterfly in a display case, from his body deep into the upright wall of the building, so that he could not fall. So that, instead of standing on the ledge, he would feel as if he were lying—as he had lain, a boy upon a hillside, at Henry's farm—so that all that was visible of his universe was space and stars.

He was motionless; but gradually the feeling of lying on a flat surface, rather than standing against a vertical one, grew in him. It became more and more real, until it was the only reality.

Now he no longer thought—but knew—that he lay flat, looking only up and out.

Slowly, he loosened the strong grip of his hands, letting the force alone hold him, as if by the weight of his body only, on this level surface. Slowly a relaxation crept over him, moving downward like a warm wave through his body until it reached his feet and possessed him literally. He no longer stood. He lay relaxed, with the stars, alone.

But not quite alone. Misty, winding among their lights, but growing clearer and brighter as he watched, he saw a rainbow-colored ribbon that was his own mental image of the thousand-year fabric of historic forces that connected the beginning of the fourteenth century to the present moment in which he lay on the side of a building, on a world called Association.

It was a ribbon made up of the many colors of the innumerable threads, each one representing the force which one individual during his or her lifetime had exerted on the whole pattern of the race's development.

Many of the threads lived only briefly and disappeared without effect on the pattern. But a few—a very few—gathered other threads to the direction of their own life's force, so that during their existence—in some cases even after their death—the pattern was changed permanently. These rare few—great religious, military, or philosophic leaders, for the most part—disappeared from the later memory of the ribbon—but the effect of their existence did not.

But all the billions of lives from the fourteenth century until now were there; and it was the combined mass of their lives that eventually determined the present pattern and direction of movement of the whole race, so that the life of every individual person had its effect and lent its color to the threads around it—determining the direction of other threads in its lifetime and beyond.

Something new would be proposed and seem to die with its proposer; only to resurface and grow strongly, later on. There, in the sixteenth century, Bleys' imagination could now envision the life-thread of Delminio, who had proposed what he called the Theater of Memory, which had seemed to die with the unsuccessful efforts of his life, but had emerged again in the late twenty-first century to eventually become the unique satellite that circled Old Earth now, and was known as the Final Encyclopedia.

Further on, in the twentieth century, were the two developments that had made massive, sudden differences in the colors and direction of the pattern. One, the first humans actually lifting above Old Earth's atmosphere for the first time in the world's history, out into space. Two, large social groups of humankind beginning to gingerly entertain, at least in theory, the idea of each individual's having a universal responsibility—not only toward his fellow humans, but toward his planet and everything on it.

—And a little further, in the twenty-first century, was the thread of those in the Chantry Guild; that had given rise to a specialized society on two New Worlds—Mara and Kultis—of the Exotics. He looked further forward and identified his own thread, Dahno's, Toni's—and Henry's. Henry's had joined his own again just hours since. With Toni's and Dahno's threads, tightly clumped, they were already thickening and beginning to spread their color and direction all about them.

Bleys concentrated on the thread of Henry.

His breath increased, with sudden slow depth and strength. What he looked at was entirely subjective, colored by his own beliefs and desires. But the part of his mind that had been concerned, demanding a reason for the sudden, apparently reasonless uneasiness mixed with the excitement in him, suddenly saw a possibility of answer in the ribbon threaded among the stars.

On rare occasions before this, Bleys had been able to squint at that section of the ribbon that represented the present moment; and looking at the lines—all blurred then, but still recognizable in relation to each other— he had sometimes been able to believe he saw how they would project into the immediate future.

These insights—they could hardly be called much more than guesses—were, at best, some calculation by the back of his mind of how the threads affected each other to weave the ribbon forward. But they had helped by inspiring his plans for the immediate future, as data reduced to a graph might help. Though, at best, the kind of aid they offered was good only for the very close future; for a few days, a week, or two—rarely as much as a month.

The wildness that had brought him out to this strange position on the side of the building certainly arose from deeply buried inner promptings. If he could go a step further in his mind, and see what he could visualize of the possible, immediate future—perhaps the back of his mind would now be able to let him know the reason for the uneasiness which he was now sure had been the reason for his awakening.

Accordingly, Bleys imagined himself trying to see forward along the ribbon; and his effort seemed to show him that Henry's thread remained bonded closely to him, to Toni and Dahno—in every way supportive and useful as far forward as he could see it. The thought came to him suddenly and clearly, that he had been looking a gift horse in the mouth; suspicious because it was more than he had been expecting.

With Henry's arrival, he had felt his opportunity open before him; and, in a flurry of decisions, he had begun to act. And the back of his mind had reacted with unease, cautiously skeptical of apparent good fortune. Years of careful planning and making sure he looked before he leaped, had made him wary of anything that came too easily. He had worried automatically.

This train of thought brought him at last to relaxation and calmness. The uneasiness was gone. With it had gone a great deal of the excitement that had driven him out; and he realized now that the excitement had been a gearing up of his defensive nature in reaction to the uneasiness behind the curtain at the back of his mind. He lay, comfortable and happy, looking at the stars.

Sounds from the street, drifting up from beyond his feet, brought Bleys back to awareness of his body and its location.

For a moment longer, he stayed as he was, on the face of the building, reluctant to leave what he had found, looking up and out into the universe. Then, slowly he began to reverse his mind-set.

He seemed to swing, but without moving, from the horizontal to the vertical. So that finally he stood, once again, his weight on his legs, his bare feet pressing the ledge; and only his grip on the ledge overhead helping to keep him there. As he did so, he became conscious that the noise far below him had increased.

Slowly, almost indifferently, he looked down between his toes and saw that he had attracted a crowd on the trafficway below. They would not be able to make out who he was at this height; or even be able to tell that he was taller than most men. But they would be thinking that he was a possible suicide, a jumper.

Bleys' identification was threatened. If he returned to his room now, those below would know too much; and there would be at least a rumor that someone—even if that someone was not him—had attempted suicide from a floor which belonged exclusively to him.

He could not go back to his own balcony. But the corner of the building was only a few meters off, and there was no other balcony projecting between him and it. And at that corner the trafficway below ended in a spiral down to another one-way vehicle route, leading away from his building. If he could get around the corner on his ledges, he would be lost to the sight of those below; and none would be sure where he had gotten back inside. With sudden decision, he began to move along his ledge again, away from his balcony.

He inched carefully along toward the corner of the building—luckily it was not far—and reached it.

For a moment, he paused; then, holding with only his left hand above, standing on only his left foot, he flung his body weight around the corner in one swift spin, pivoting on his left toes and fingers to swing his body in a complete turn by momentum around the corner, snatching a grip on the new upper ledge with his right hand, finding the ledge below it with his right foot—and, as soon as these two could hold all his weight for a necessary moment, bringing his left hand and foot around the corner to share the load. He now stood facing the building; but above a side of it that looked down the spiraling ramp, at the moment empty of traffic.

Here he was not only away from the watchers, but from the light of the advertising sign. No faces gazed up at him. This side was in deeper darkness, and the ledge still ran past balconies that belonged to the outside rooms of his own personal suite. He inched along to the first such balcony, reached for the top of its railing, and pulled himself up and over.

He stood for several moments while his breathing slowed.

The doors had not been left open here, but they were not locked. He pushed through them into the gloom of what turned out to be his dining lounge. In the dim light from the nighttime city outside, the top surface of the long table-float gleamed. The room smelled faintly of cleaning fluids. It had been readied for whatever tomorrow would have in store.

He turned to a side door, passed back through the unlit rooms, through the interior, lighted corridors, and once more into the darkness of his own bedroom.

He stood for a moment, glancing at his bed, then sat down at the desk to one side of the fluttering curtains. He touched a control, and a little light came on, a small pool of illumination that lit only him and the float-table with its keyboard and screen.

He touched another control stud on the table itself. The keyboard rotated out of sight, leaving him a blank desk surface, to which clung a pad of paper, a writing stylus, and a disposal slot.

He pulled the paper to him, releasing its magnet-like hold, and picked up the stylus. In the small area of illumination, he began to write by hand on a sheet of the paper. At the top he set the word *NOTES*, followed by the date, hour and place.

Each handwritten page began to fade back to blankness as soon as he had finished writing on it. But, to make doubly sure, what he wrote was encoded. No code was unbreakable nowdays; but he changed to another one every half-line.

The room about him—like all of his rooms—was checked routinely once a minute by automatic sensors, and by human engineer daily, for any spy-eyes that might have been sneaked in, or listening devices. Moreover, no one watching would be able to break the quick succession of codes quickly enough to follow what he wrote. His final completed note would be stored in his memory where it could not be lost; but where he would be able to find it in the future if he wanted to remember exactly what had been in his mind at this time and place.

"Today," he wrote, *"Henry appeared unexpectedly to begin to 'save me from Satan,' as he says, which means that he is trying to save me from myself and what I'm trying to do. I wish I could make him understand. But the only words I could use would have a different meaning for him. Nonetheless, he and the security group he will form for me is something I needed but did not know I needed. Now, that much is settled.*

"Toni came back from her father to tell me that she was free to go with me anywhere. This, like Henry's appearance and help, is something that I now see as an absolute necessity. These things all appearing at this one time when I'm just about ready to go out among the stars with my message, is something that ordinary thinking would simply label 'coincidence.'

"But, as any thread in the historic pattern multiplies and grows, it comes closer to other threads, also multiplying and growing to influence the pattern—as like people in everyday life come in contact with each other, simply because they follow similar paths and these paths feed at last into a thoroughfare that they have in common.

"So what I expected from the pattern is already beginning to show itself. This indicates that it is more vital than ever to find and recruit Hal Mayne. I have no direct evidence of his unusual worth; but even though his beginning is shrouded in mystery, as a two-year-old child found floating in an empty spacecraft in space, but with directions for his upbringing by three very remarkable old men.

"I have only these strange bits of evidence, plus the scanty record of his activities in eluding me, getting to the Final Encyclopedia, and from there by way of New Earth to the Coby mines, and now—according to Barbage—to Harmony. But just this, and the fact that on Harmony he has become associated with one of the outlaw Commands (which automatically puts him legally on the other side of the fence from me), indicates so strongly to the back of my mind that he is far and above the ordinary run of people, that I would give almost anything to have him with me.

"Toni, Henry and Dahno will stand about me now like three mountain ranges, protecting and influencing what comes to me in the way of future sun and rain. But there is still part of my personal territory that needs to be shielded. Particularly, from what I realized today, I am desperately in need of an outside point of view that can give me a full picture of myself at any time. Dahno tries hard to do this, as he did today with his questions about why I was training the best of our Others for—as he put it so aptly—management duties.

"But we are at the same time too similar and too different. He thinks too much like me to notice what he should notice as I change, and at the same time he had his growing-up years with our mother when she was younger than when she had me. While there are similarities, there are other areas in which we do not understand each other; though I must feel that I understand him better than he understands me. No, Hal Mayne would be the ideal answer, if he is the kind of mind that I think he is. He would be able to see me, dispassionately but loyally,

from the outside, and tell me the truth about myself so that I could make adjustments accordingly.

"That is all for this note."

Bleys noted the time he finished writing below his last line, together again with the date, and put the stylus aside. Shuffling the papers together, he held them in his hand for a second and then slipped them through the slot in a raised panel at the back of the desk, where phase-shift physics had been applied to make the ultimate form of a destructor of documents.

As he fed the sheets in, their far ends disappeared, resolved into their least-component parts, which were then scattered through the universe—just as a spaceship was scattered for an instant of no-time all through the universe, while being relocated from one position in the galaxy to another—except that here it was desired never to bring them together again in their original form.

He sat for a moment gazing at the empty slot where the pages had disappeared. They were gone now, beyond recovery. They existed only with earlier, similar records, in the already-thick file of his memory, labeled *NOTES*.

After a moment, Bleys added another line to the blank paper on top of the stack remaining, a line which faded out like a wistful voice, dying, even as he fed it into the destructor slot.

"I wonder if Hal Mayne has ever seen in the stars anything like what I seem to see there, every time I look at them."

Chapter 5

"Did you expect trouble here?" Dahno murmured.

"Possibly," said Bleys, in an equally low voice, "from either the CEOs or Guildmasters or both. As well as from other possible unnamed groups."

The two of them were standing together facing the exit port of *Favored of God*, which would open in a few moments to let them out on the landing pad at New Earth City, New Earth. A space was being held clear for them to talk privately by a three-deep arc of Henry's Soldiers of God, who passively resisted any attempts from the passengers not of Bleys' group—for *Favored of God* was technically classed as a general passenger space liner; and there were about as many aboard who were not of their party as there were of it.

The Soldiers of God were experts at such apparently passive resistance. They smilingly ignored the accidental-on-purpose shove or elbow jab from curious passengers trying to push through; and then—only if such activities became too bothersome—with an equal smile trod on the inquisitive person's toes or returned hidden blows or pressures, apparently as accidentally as these had been inflicted on them.

"Well, you'll have it," said Dahno. "The minute you seem to get friendly with either one, the other outfit will be down on you like a gang of outlaws. Unless you go along with the wishes of both—and no human being could do that—both organizations'll be after you to associate yourself exclusively with one of them. There's also an important third group here, though I couldn't get anyone to even name it to me."

"I'm not surprised," murmured Bleys.

Dahno had come up by shuttle to join *Favored* before it landed on New Earth.

He had gone to New Earth ahead of the rest of them to begin to test the climate. And indeed, thought Bleys, looking at him now, it was one of the ways in which he was invaluable.

Dahno could learn more in two hours in a strange place where he had no personal contacts at all than a dozen others could learn through people they already knew there. He had a knack for threading through the maze of personal connections to the one person who could give him the most information on any point.

"Well," he said now, "I'm sure I can find out, given a little more time. In any case—"

A ship's-address system interrupted him, waking to life overhead.

"WE WILL BE TOUCHING DOWN IN TWELVE SECONDS," boomed the speaker over the noises of the lounge. "PLEASE DO NOT MOVE UNTIL WE ACTUALLY TOUCH. REPEAT, STAY WHERE YOU ARE UNTIL WE ARE ACTUALLY ON SURFACE."

A hush fell generally on the conversations of those waiting.

"Tell you later," said Dahno hastily. "You'll learn most of what I know from Ana Wasserlied, anyway, as soon as we reach the hotel."

He, too, fell silent. Bleys glanced away from him back into the body of the lounge, grateful once more for his height that allowed him to see over people's heads and locate Toni next to one of the windows. She was standing with Henry.

They had a strange likeness, these two. Bleys studied them from a distance. It was not a matter of any of the usual marks of similarity. Henry was spare and taller than average on the New Worlds, but not outstandingly so. While Toni, slim and tall even for a New Worlds woman, was almost exactly his height.

Their faces could hardly have been less alike. Toni's was not particularly Oriental, as could have been expected from her last name—shortened and misspelled as it had become since her Nipponese ancestors left Old Earth. Henry was a Scot, and looked it; with the brown hair, lean features and steady gaze of his ancestors from the islands of the Hebrides, west of the main Scottish land in the north of the Old Earth island of Britain.

Perhaps, thought Bleys, it was because they were both islanders by heritage. Perhaps it was something in the way they both stood and moved. Neither was someone an oncoming stranger might elbow aside casually as he or she approached them in a passageway.

Indeed, Bleys' thoughts ran on, that was probably it. Both radiated the same signal to the instincts of those who faced them. They each had an utter faith in themselves and in what they believed; and each was utterly fearless in acting in accord with her or his conscience.

In any case, they had become very close in the past few weeks. Bleys smiled to himself, whimsically and a little sadly, feeling his warmth for the two of them. He wished he knew what Toni was thinking now; and perhaps later on he would find the right time to ask her. Meanwhile he made a mental note that when the chance came he would like to listen in on one of their conversations. Bleys winced internally. Playing the Peeping Tom was not something he found comfortable.

But things had moved swiftly in these last days, and he would need as much information as he could get. In the time since his arrival, Henry had recruited nearly sixty former Soldiers of God and made a working unit out of them while the trip was being arranged and Dahno sent ahead.

Bleys looked through a small window just beside the port, and at the ground below. Their descent had slowed until they were settling surfaceward more gently than a bubble—down to the spaceport pad. Even with the softness of that parking surface, however, the slow descent was necessary, for the mass of the ship could crush its underside like an eggshell if it came down too fast.

Its outer shell was strong, but only strong enough to face the winds of atmosphere. Otherwise, the mass of the ship was far out of prudent proportion for surface landings in planetary gravity—New Earth's was a little less than that of Association, a little more than that of Old Earth. If the "Other" organization Bleys and Dahno controlled had not been a majority owner in the vessel and demanded a surface landing, *Favored of God* would have discharged its passengers to shuttle-craft beyond the atmosphere.

Outside, now, Bleys saw a row of black limousines lined up, waiting. They had been driven out here in the landing area itself in special exception to all ordinary Customs and transportation procedures. The rest of the passengers who were not members of his party would have to take a surface-bus to the nearest underground departure point. But that would be after his group had left first; and he, first of all.

At that moment, the spaceship grounded itself with hardly a jar. The port swung open heavily before him, and at the crewwoman's gesture, Henry's advance party trotted down the landing stair, to spread out watchfully on the field. Bleys walked down onto the yielding surface of the landing area, a whiff of cool air—different, but invigorating—filling his lungs. The spring sunlight of Sirius, so yellowishly different from the white light of Epsilon Eridani over Association and Harmony, dazzled him briefly out of a beautiful sapphire-blue sky as he set foot outside into what was obviously a hot summer day.

He stood aside so that the rest of his people, who had been waiting just behind him, could come off. Henry and Toni were among the first few the Soldiers allowed to follow. Henry led Toni directly back to the fourth limousine in the row. Some of the Soldiers were already getting into the first three black magnetic-lift limousines with their dark one-way windows.

Bleys stood waiting at the foot of the ramp in the remarkable sky and the different sunlight, feeling unusually satisfied and elated. He could think of no particular reason for this. Then it struck him—of course, he was finally in action, committed to what he had planned to do-all time for doubt was over—

Henry's voice beside him interrupted his thoughts.

"I've put Toni in the fourth vehicle," Henry was saying. "You go in the second one with the local Others' Headperson—Ana Wasserlied?"

"She came to meet us, then?" said Bleys, absently. "Dahno thought she'd be at the hotel."

"She's here and wants to ride with you. I'll have Dahno ride fifth, in that limousine," said Henry. "I'll be up front in your limousine."

"No, why don't you ride with Toni?" Bleys murmured back. Henry looked at him for a moment.

"All right," he said.

He led Bleys to a limousine. Bleys stooped and got in.

Ana Wasserlied, in one of the two individual chairs of the back seat, was a capable-looking, tall, blond, rather angular woman. She was in her late twenties, wearing a three-quarter-length semi-formal dress of some silky blue-green material. Already seated in the car on the far side, she smiled a somewhat weary-looking greeting as he joined her and the door was closed upon them.

"It's good to meet you at last," she said. "I've always wanted to thank you in person for appointing me last year to be Head of the Others' branch, here."

"Thank Dahno," said Bleys. "He runs the organization, you know. I'm just a sort of roving philosopher, although he lets me advise from time to time."

"Oh, I will thank him," said Ana. The tone of her voice clearly refused to give lip service to the idea that Bleys was nothing more than a roving philosopher. A foolishly unreasonable small point to impress on Bleys himself in particular, Bleys noted absently. "But I wanted to thank you as well."

"That's very good of you," said Bleys. "Did you bring that recording spindle I messaged for? The one with the latest information on our membership here, with a breakdown into those in training, and those we think able to hold a high administrative position?"

"I have it right here," said Ana, producing it. Her voice was a rather pleasant soprano; which, however, developed a slightly metallic edge when she became brisk. She handed it to him.

He reached for one of the personal readers that was hanging against the back of the front seat, below the window there that shut him off from the driver and the Soldier who had stepped in to sit beside the driver a moment since. Bleys put the reader on. It was like a dark rectangular mask, with insert plugs for his ears and an elastic band behind to hold it on his head. Out of long practice, he put on the mask with one hand and slid the spindle into its slot below the viewing area of the mask with his other.

"Before you start," said Ana's voice, hastily if distantly, now that the plugs were in his ears, "I wanted to tell you: you've got an invitation by the local CEO Club for dinner tonight with some of their most important members. You remember that the CEO and the Guildmasters are the two important organizations on this world? CEO stands for Chief Executive Officers, of course—although these men you'll be meeting are much more than that. They're the heads of multiple corporations."

"I see," said Bleys. "We'll talk about that more when we get to the hotel."

Ana fell silent. Unobtrusively, Bleys touched the controls on his wrist-pad. The page of names that had filled his mask a second before disappeared; and the screen filled instead with a one-way connection to the intercom between his car and the one that held Henry and Toni.

While Bleys and Ana had been speaking, the limousines had all been filled and had already started to leave. The one Bleys and Ana were in plunged downward into a tunnel; and, as the picture of Toni and Henry in theirs came up, their voices began to sound in his ears. Bleys' limousine came out of the tunnel on to a magnetic roadway, almost certainly the direct route into New Earth City.

" . . . Does your Soldier need to keep watching the driver like that?" he heard Toni saying.

In the screen, she seemed to be looking directly at Bleys, from which he assumed that she was looking instead into the front of the limousine through the window that sealed off that part of the vehicle from the seats in back; and made the conversation of the passengers back there private unless an intercom connection like this was opened up.

" . . . The driver's an Other, isn't he?" she was going on.

Henry nodded.

"We hope he's trustworthy, but we play safe," he said.

"Your people seem to like doing that," she said. Bleys knew that she had had little to do with the Soldiers until the trip.

There was a momentary look of pain on Henry's face. Then he was himself again.

"All of them have learned to be aware, all the time, whether on Harmony, Association or any other world," he said. "You're a woman of Association, yourself. You should know what being a Soldier of God means."

She nodded. "I do."

Her own temple—the temple she had gone to in her childhood—had, she remembered, once been embroiled in a battle with another religious body; and Soldiers of God, volunteer fighters from other churches, had come to help on both sides.

"I saw some once when I was twelve," she said. "But most of them weren't like this."

There was a pause before Henry answered. "These are all afflicted. Not with a physical affliction. The affliction of a sin. I have that sin, too."

She stared at him, obviously hesitating. But surely, thought Bleys, watching, she and Henry were close enough now so that she would venture on the personal question that had plainly and instantly come to her mind.

"What sin is that, Henry?" she asked, gently.

Henry turned his head slowly to look at her. Without warning his face had become implacable. Suddenly, he looked deadly—as deadly as he had the one time Bleys had seen him so before. It was the time when Henry had rescued Bleys from the anger of a mob of their fellow church members; the time when Bleys had been forced to leave Henry's farm for Dahno and Ecumeny.

"What it is," he said slowly, "is something I myself have told only my family; and I believe these men would want an equal privacy. You'll have to do without an answer, I'm afraid."

He looked at her steadily until she nodded. Then he looked away from her again and directly forward at the front seat; so that, in the reader screen, he now seemed to look directly at Bleys.

Toni stared at his profile for a moment. To Bleys—and he thought also to her—it must have seemed that Henry's attention had gone a long way away from her, from everyone. But then the expression on his face faded. He turned back and offered her his brief quirk of a smile. She smiled forgivingly in return; and they both sat back in silence.

Bleys touched his wrist control pad and went back to the names, figures and other data in the recording spindle.

Memorizing these and turning over various plans in his head kept his mind occupied for the twenty minutes or so at the six hundred kilometers an hour with which the motorcade approached their hotel. Once arrived, they were shown to quarters that were, if anything, more luxurious than those they had occupied back on Association.

"As soon as everyone's unpacked and ready," Bleys said to Toni, Dahno, Henry and Ana in the entry lounge of the Master Suite, "we'll gather in my private lounge here for a talk. Say, in twenty minutes, standard time. You can wait here for us if you want, Ana."

A little later, the private lounge saw them seated around a conference table not only long enough to accommodate all of them comfortably, but also two individuals who had since joined Ana. Both of these were wearing a padded single-garment type of business suit which disguised whether they were men or women, and there were two blue blurs of light where their heads ordinarily would have been seen.

Bleys sat at one end of the table, Ana at the other, facing him with one of the two disguised persons on each side of her. There seemed to be emotional brittleness to the atmosphere in the room, like a miniature rotary storm system with its locus in the air above Ana's end of the table. But it was not greatly disturbing. Bleys decided to ignore it for the moment.

"All right," he said, once they were settled, "Ana, want to bring us up to date on the situation here?"

"The whole world knew you were coming," said Ana. Here at the conference table, her strong soprano voice was surprisingly pleasant, in a way that went far to cancel out her somewhat rawboned, overdressed appearance.

"That couldn't be helped," said Bleys, pleasantly. "I can't control any but a few of the ships that leave Association and later call at New Earth. Also, now I'm part of the Government on Association, as one of the Speakers in the Chamber there—even if I do have a deputy holding down my seat regularly—the Chamber has to be notified if I go off-planet. That means it was no secret on Association about my going to New Earth; so it could hardly be kept a secret here."

"Well, in any case," said Ana, "the general population of this world knew almost as soon as we did; and that includes the CEO Clubs and the Guildmasters. By the way, let me introduce these two on either side of me."

She pointed to the faceless figure seated on her right.

"We'll call this person Jack," she said. "Jack is an Other who's graduated from our ordinary training. He's also a member of the CEO Clubs."

Her finger moved to indicate the figure on her left.

"And this will be Jill," she added. "Jill is another graduate Other, and in her case she's a Guild member. Both are fairly high in the hierarchy of their"—she paused a brief moment—"secondary organizations."

"Honored to meet you," said Jill.

"Honored to be here," said Jack.

There was practically no difference between their voices, each of which could be the voice of a man or a woman behind the filter being used to distort it.

"I commend their caution," said Bleys, smiling at each of them in turn.

"I trust you all, myself," said Ana—though she looked hard for a moment at Toni as she said it—"but these two are literally risking their lives. Both the CEOs and the Guilds have a death penalty for any one of their people who belongs to any other organization. That rule was originally made to keep the spies of one out of the councils of the other."

"But in spite of that, I'd guess there are still CEO spies in the Guild ranks and Guild spies among the CEOs, aren't there?" said Dahno.

"Of course," answered Ana, "and spies from other groups beside ours as well, in both organizations. None from either in ours, in case you were thinking of asking. We have ways to check that neither the CEOs nor the Guilds could risk using. However, the point is, Jack and Jill are here now to answer any questions you might like to put directly about those two organizations, themselves."

"All right," said Bleys, "both of you, then, what's the general attitude of the CEO Clubs and the Guild Leadership to my speaking tour here? I assume they're familiar with recordings of the speeches I've made for Harmony and Association, before?"

"Your tapes are very popular with the ordinary people—the job-holders—the rank and file, I suppose you'd call them," said Jack. "We call them job-holders as opposed to the job-givers, the executives of the CEOs. Both want to see you for their own reasons." He paused. "Wouldn't you say so?"

There was an uncomfortable pause in the conversation.

"I'm sorry!" Jack's voice burst out again suddenly. "I keep forgetting you can't see my face. I was looking at you, Jill, to answer for the Guild."

"The Guild—" The filter made Jill's voice so anonymously similar to Jack's that it was almost as if Jack answered again. She hesitated. "I could say exactly the same things. You see—I'm sorry, I'm looking at *you* now, Great Teacher—until now, the CEOs and the Guildmasters have completely controlled the job-holders; and the Guild worries about you getting a separate influence over them. It's a matter of survival, you see—"

"Perhaps I'd better explain that part of it," Ana broke in. "Bleys, the fact is—"

"No need," said Bleys. "I think I already know that, and it's part of a much larger picture. See if I'm right—New Earth is essentially a manufacturing world, buying new technical information from Cassida and selling its products and manufactory knowledge to all the other New Worlds. But what Cassida sells are developments of technologies derived by them from the basic free research going on upon Newton. This chain of connections will only go on working as long as your job-holders are willing to produce what's considered most profitable by their CEO or Guild leaders, the Cassidan leadership and the Newtonian researchers. Correct?"

"Of course it is," Ana said. "All right. You ask the questions."

"I want specifics," said Bleys. "Tell me—any and all of the three of you—what actions, if any, have the Guild and the CEOs in mind to take about me? What are they planning to do, or try to do?"

"I don't think they've made definite plans yet—Jack?" said Ana. "Jill?"

"No," said the two similar voices. Jack went on. "They know they can pick you up anywhere, anytime, anyplace on our world. So they're both waiting to size you up."

"One thing's certain," said Ana. "The CEOs control the management of everything but the smallest business establishments in this world; the Guilds control the people who work in those establishments. Together, if they want to crack down on you, you won't be able to move, let alone speak. For one thing, you could be out of here and in the street with one call by the CEOs to the hotel manager; and theoretically at least, no commercial vehicle, not even an autotaxi, would stop to pick any of you up."

"Would they do that now, in the face of public interest in me, if what I was just told about the job-holders was correct?" Bleys asked.

"Not right away, at least," said Ana, almost grudgingly. "Maybe Jack or Jill can tell you more."

"I think—" Jill began, then hesitated. "Jack, do you want to answer that, first?"

"If you like," said Jack. "The CEOs, anyway, are going to begin by smiling at you. In fact, as Jill knows, Great Teacher, because we were talking a bit about it before the rest of you joined us, you're invited to dinner with the top CEO people of the New Earth City Club, tonight—"

"I told him that on the way here from the spaceport, since the invitation was passed through me," Ana said, sharply.

"Sorry," said Jack, "I didn't know—"

"Well, the point is, the Great Teacher did know. Go ahead," said Ana.

"Well, then, with my apologies to you, Ana Wasserlied, and to you, Great Teacher," said Jack, his anonymous voice masking any embarrassment. "The people you'll meet tonight if you go—and it would probably be wisest to go, if you want my opinion—are going to be the most powerful in the world. They're sort of an unofficial governing body for the actions of the Clubs in general; or, to put it another way, where they lead, the other Clubs and their members always follow."

"What do they hope for, by seeing me at a dinner?" asked Bleys.

"To impress you with their power," Jack answered, "and to size you up, to see if you'll do what they want."

"They'll hope they can get you to use your influence for them against the Guilds," said Jill.

"Yes," said Ana, "the balance of power between CEOs and Guilds has been essentially equal for years now—but they'd both like to turn that balance in their own favor as much as possible."

"Would they go so far, either one, as to try to kill me, if I won't work with them?" Bleys asked.

"No, no!" Jill managed to convey shock, in spite of her voice filter.

"I don't think so, either," said Jack. "Not as things stand now, anyway."

"Copies of your earlier speeches have been sold on all the worlds—even Old Earth—haven't they?" Jill said. "They wouldn't dare—unless there was a job-holders' revolt threatening because of what you say. Also, you've got your own bodyguards, haven't you?"

"Fifty-seven people," said Henry, breaking, for the first time, the silence in which he had sat since they all sat down together. "Enough to stop any ordinary assassin or mob; but nothing like what would be needed to handle any serious military attack."

"Oh, they'd never go that far!" said Ana, finally sounding shocked in her turn. "Anyway, besides your security people, I'm going to have you surrounded by Others I trust. We could even arm them if you want—"

"No," said Bleys.

"Anyway," Ana went on, "even though the CEOs, in particular, control whatever police, military, or paramilitary forces we have—"

"They don't control those in the ranks," Jill said. "Only those in command."

"There's that," said Ana, "still, what I was about to say was that for over a hundred years everything's been settled on this world with nothing but talk, bribes, and some use of Tough Squads."

"I've got some information on these so-called Tough Squads, already," said Henry. "But perhaps, Jack and Jill, you could talk to me later and fill me in on some details?"

Jack and Jill murmured agreement.

"That seems to cover the main points," said Bleys, "and I'll leave the rest of you to fill in the lesser ones—like the information Henry would like from our two incognito advisors. Ana, you've got the official invitation for me to this CEOs' dinner this evening?"

"Yes," said Ana.

"Then, when we break up here, I'd like to talk to you about the individuals I'm likely to meet there—or would Jack know more about them than you?"

"No," said Ana, sharply, "Jack doesn't move in those social circles. Because of the Others—as you know, we've got over half a million registered members on this world, now; since it was known you were coming, they've been crowding in faster than we can handle them, literally—I'm the one who meets and knows the important people."

"So much for the moment, then," said Bleys. "If the rest of you don't mind, then, I've got some things to talk over with Dahno."

The rest got up and left the room. Jack and Jill stood back to let the rest out first, and Bleys watched with interest as they turned their backs and walked through the door.

"What's wrong with Ana?" Bleys asked Dahno privately, after the door had closed and he was alone with his brother.

"Can't you guess?" said Dahno. "She was head of a large, wealthy, perfectly legal operation here, personally welcomed and accepted among the other movers and shakers of New Earth society. Now, if what you say or do here rubs the CEOs or Guilds the wrong way, what's going to happen to her Others—and her?"

Chapter 6

"Why did you want them dressed like starving outlaws?" Toni asked.

They were being driven to the CEO Club for dinner in two of the limousines; Bleys and Toni in the first with one of Henry's crew riding next to the driver, and the other five security people they had brought along, with Henry himself, in the second limousine. It was just twilight now, with Sirius setting, so that the blazing-white Dog Star, two-fifths the apparent size of Sol from old Earth, was already safely hidden from direct sight behind the tall buildings—but its light filled the air of the city above the passageways with a faintly greenish-golden glow from the reflection of its rays off a thin but widespread cloud cover that had spread across the sky in the afternoon.

Toni was referring to Henry and the six men he had handpicked. Bleys had told Henry to have them dressed—and, so they were—in the worn, rough clothes and heavy boots of farmers and workmen, common away from the cities on Association and Harmony.

"It's a test," said Bleys. "A small but interesting one. To see how badly these CEOs want me. One of the prices of having me there is going to be their admitting Henry and the others along with us."

He smiled at her, suddenly almost mischievous.

"It's also a small reminder that most of my faithful following on this world, as well as others, are working people," he said.

Toni nodded. She looked out the window of the limousine at the tall buildings about them, bathed in the golden twilight.

"Such an orderly, well-off world to be so troubled and torn apart," she said. Bleys watched her sympathetically. She would be thinking, he knew, of the poverty on the two Friendly Worlds and the struggle for survival of most of the people on them these last three hundred years.

"It's what you've heard me say so often now—a world with promise still," he said. "The trouble is, like the rest of the other New Worlds, its sights've always been fixed too much on its own present moment. It's ignored the past; what it could learn there, and from the past on Old Earth. If it hadn't, it'd have seen how history is sweeping New and Old together toward a point of crisis—"

Toni smiled.

"What is it?" asked Bleys.

"You're getting to sound a little pompous, aren't you?"

Bleys frowned. Pomposity was certainly not one of the impressions he wanted to give anyone listening to him; and Toni was only doing one of the duties of her job to point it out to him.

"I suppose," he said. "It's just that some things are hard to say without being pompous."

He waited for a second, but she only smiled.

"However, thanks for telling me. I'll work on it."

"No payment necessary," said Toni. "Now, you were about to say?"

"Just," said Bleys, "that for New Worlds and Old Earth, it's a matter of establishing the different personalities of the New Worlds from Old Earth's—their social patterns, for example, as they had to be dictated by different conditions."

"Still you'd think—" Toni broke off. "What are you expecting to happen at dinner this evening?"

"It'll be a war of nerves," said Bleys, "or perhaps you could call it a war of character. They'll try to intimidate me—and I'll try to intimidate them—at least enough to keep them guessing while I get at least some lectures accomplished without interference."

"How many do you need?" asked Toni.

"I've no idea," said Bleys. "But even one will let this world know I'm here; with that done, things should start happening both with the CEOs and the Guildmasters, and I'll adapt as things develop. My great advantage over organizations like them is they've got to take time to talk things over before they take action. I can walk around behind them while they're still debating."

"I see," said Toni. She was silent for a moment, then smiled again. "At least I didn't have to dress up as an outlaw or a working person."

"No," said Bleys, looking at her. "Also, you and I are the contrast to Henry and the others. For that matter, your acceptance here may be another small test; but my main reason for wanting you with me is so we can go over what's said, afterward, from two different viewpoints."

He continued to look at Toni with approval. There was that tall, trim body of hers, that had been shaped by a lifetime of exercise in the martial arts and wrestling; beautifully clothed at the moment in a long ivory evening gown, under a short jacket of imitation black fur. Fur which matched the color of her hair and focused all attention on the brilliance of her steady and intensely penetrating eyes, which were a blue almost as dark as hair and fur.

He, himself, was dressed as usual for public occasions, in his black cloak with red lining, over a tight-fitting, light blue jacket and narrow black trousers which tapered to scallop-topped ankle boots, also black. All these, except for the cloak, were in current evening fashion, as far as men's clothes went on New Earth. Together, he and Toni made an expensively tailored-looking couple—particularly in contrast to Henry and the Soldiers.

The limousines had reached their destination. They pulled up in front of the CEO Club, which turned out to be a tall building at the corner of a block in the business section of New Earth City, its front faced with stone that looked like a dark granite.

That front, unbroken by windows, faced out on the passageway by which their limousines had arrived; and the side of it that was next to the equally high side of a neighboring building was separated from it only by a bare narrow cul-de-sac of an alleyway. So narrow, in fact, that it would have been too dark to see into, if it had not been for a single glaring light above a double door, grimly closed and of service-entrance appearance, some twenty meters back from the alley opening. The day's-end gloom would have left it a place unknown.

By contrast, pleasantly open to the evening air in the still-bright twilight, the front entrance had a number of wide steps before it, leading up to the open doorway, tall and wide enough for at least four people to walk abreast through it.

Only the hinged edges could be seen of the pair of heavy doors, swung back inside, leaving the doorway itself unblocked except for the customary invisible weather-shield that would be guarding the indoor climate against that outside. Two pink-faced, healthy-looking young men of identical size, in sky-blue uniforms with oversized lapels edged in gold, stood one on either side of the doorway and just inside it, looking out. A third young man, in the same livery, turned and disappeared back into the club's dark interior, at the sight of Bleys emerging from the limousine.

Bleys waited for Henry to organize his people from the second limousine and bring them up behind Toni and himself, so that they went in as a single group. It was a small pause, but long enough for the young man to return, along with a man in his late thirties or early forties, who wore a dark gray business suit with similar oversized lapels. He stopped and stood, stage-center in the middle of the doorway looking down at Bleys and the rest of them as they began to mount the steps.

He towered over the doormen. In fact, he was plainly no more than a dozen centimeters shorter than Bleys himself and wider in the body. He had a broad, strongly-boned face and a mane of graying black hair mounted from his forehead in a sweeping curve backward, matched by a heavy black handlebar mustache that would have looked ridiculous on anyone not his size and bulk.

Everything about him—the suit with the wide lapels on a body that was already wide-shouldered and very strong looking, the mustache, the mane of hair—was clearly orchestrated to give the impression of an over-powering, almost domineering figure of authority. But in this case, the half-frown with which he had first stepped into the doorway faded into an uncertain look, as with Bleys' steady mounting of the steps it became obvious that Bleys would loom over him—he who was clearly used to looming over others.

Bleys kept the smile inside himself hidden. He was used to a reaction from men more than normally tall who suddenly noticed he overtopped them. He merely nodded gravely at the man as he reached the top of the steps.

The mustache and gray suit pulled itself back into some semblance of authority. Plainly, he recognized who this guest must be.

"Bleys Ahrens! Honored to meet you, very honored!" he said. But then the smile thinned as his eyes shifted to Toni and the men with Henry. He looked back at Bleys. "I'm Walner Mathias, Club Manager. I've got you down for dinner in the upper private dining room. But—I'm sorry, my book's marked only for you, not for anyone else with you."

"This lady with me," said Bleys, letting some of the long-trained power of his voice roll out in the tone of someone who states an inarguable truth, "will be with me at dinner. I'm sure you'll find my hosts agree. These others—perhaps you can find some side room for them. They're students of mine, a few I allow to come with me from time to time, to observe and learn. These six were lucky enough to be the ones I chose this evening. We'll all come in."

The Manager hesitated.

"I'm sure you can find a place for my pupils," said Bleys. This time there was the slightest edge of impatience to his voice—an edge that could hardly be said to verge on annoyance over the other man's hesitation, but hinted at it; the way a distant roll of thunder below a horizon might threaten storm from a sky presently cloudless.

Mathias hesitated only a second more. He was clearly uncomfortable, his only choices other than accepting them being to directly refuse admission to Toni, Henry and the rest—or admit publicly that he had to consult Bleys' hosts, and damage his obviously-valued appearance of ultimate authority in this place.

He chose to surrender, and led them all along a wide hall past a succession of rooms half-filled with people sitting, reading, talking or drinking. The furnishings seemed odd, as if a deliberate attempt had been made to make the club look like something out of the historic past, the nineteenth or possibly twentieth century on Old Earth.

The furniture was all float-furniture, but this was about the only concession to modernity. Underfoot were rich individual carpets—in all sizes. These, the paneling and the upholstery of the furniture were dark, as if with age. Antique floor lamps pretended to light the rooms with a yellowish glow, while actual modern lighting supported this from the illuminated ceilings. Even with that, it was dimmer here than Bleys would ever have expected to find in a present-day New World building.

The hall led them at last to another pair of floor-to-ceiling doors, green metal this time, that barred further passage. These, however, opened automatically before the Manager; and when they passed through, they were suddenly in a totally different section of the building, completely modern in furnishing; and with full-spectrum Sirian daylight beaming upon them— safely now—from three-dimensional outdoor scenes, shown in viewing screens built like windows into the walls on either side of the hallway.

In another moment there were only three of them—Bleys, Toni and

Mathias. Henry and the others had been conducted away by another blue-
uniformed young man.

Mathias led Bleys and Toni a small distance farther down this new
section of hall, then turned to face one of the wider screen-windows. It,
and the wall around it, slid aside to reveal an elevator with a fixed compartment waiting. Clearly a private elevator, judging by the padded floats
and tiny drinks-bar the compartment contained. He led them into it. The
wall closed behind them and they went up.

The building was a tall one, and there was silence for several moments
as they rose. Mathias was sternly wordless; Toni, as was usual on occasions
like this, was simply being silent and giving out no signals whatsoever.
Bleys was immersed in his own thoughts. He had made a habit of keeping
his plans to himself unless it was necessary to tell even Toni or Dahno
about them, and at the moment there was nothing more to tell. He was
thinking that one of the things the CEOs at the dinner would try would
be to buy him.

He had no intention of being bought. But he would get a much clearer
picture of what his position was on this planet, and therefore what his own
bargaining powers were, if he seemed to listen to their offers. They would
probably follow the timeworn method of donkey control, by first offering
him the carrot, to make him move in the direction they wanted, then
threatening him with a stick if the carrot failed to produce results.

Only a dozen seconds had actually passed before the lift stopped and
its entrance opened again. They stepped into the small anteroom of a
much larger oval chamber, which was either dining room or boardroom—
it was impossible to say which—and which had more of the viewscreen
windows in its walls. The ones visible from the anteroom showed wide
expanses, in all directions about the building, down on the now-twilit
streets of New Earth City, seen from a considerable height.

The Manager led them into the larger chamber. A dozen or more
men—but no women—were seated on floats with individual side tables,
at the room's far end. They looked at Bleys and Toni with open curiosity.

"Wait here," Mathias said to Bleys under his breath.

He made his way to the man seated farthest from them; an individual
well into his fifties, with some remnants of an athletic body, now over-
padded with fat. His face had been open and generous once, with clear
blue eyes, which still remained.

But there were lines of habitual ill-humor between his eyebrows and
around his mouth, which deepened in his reddening face, as Mathias
whispered in his ear. When he opened his mouth, the voice that came
out was loud and angry, ignoring the fact that Bleys and Toni were there
to hear.

"Well, there's no point in your telling me now! You've already let
them in!" he half-shouted at Mathias. "What good does it do to tell me
about it now?"

Mathias started to whisper in his ear again and was interrupted. The expression of his face, the angle of his body all silently cried out at the discomfort of suddenly having to live the role of flunky, rather than that of Manager.

"Oh, let them stay! Let them all stay!" the red-faced man waved the manager off; and turned his still-angry attention on Bleys and Toni.

"I see you misunderstood, Bleys Ahrens!" he shouted—unnecessarily in a room plainly so acoustically perfect that an ordinary tone of voice could be heard clearly from one end to the other. "You were the only one invited to dinner. We didn't send invitations to half the Friendly Worlds!"

Bleys smiled, letting the tone and words bounce off him.

"Allow me," he said, "to introduce Antonia Lu. She comes with me everywhere—particularly to dinners like this."

"It doesn't matter to me what her name is—" the man was beginning, his face darkening as blood flowed into it; but he was interrupted by another of the CEOs, two chairs from him, who looked to be by far the youngest there.

This man, who hardly seemed more than in his late teens, had the same sort of round face and blue eyes that the older man had. His face, however, was surmounted by a shock of blond hair above a slim body that sat erect in its float, instead of slumping as most of the others were doing in theirs, to one degree or another. His voice did not have Bleys' smooth, penetrating resonance, but it was like Bleys' in being low-pitched and unruffled.

"Oh, I don't think we ought to make an issue of it, Harley," he said.

Harley opened his mouth to speak again, but the younger man was going on. "I'm sure the lady will be as welcome here as Bleys Ahrens himself. In fact—"

For a moment, his eyes were almost mischievous.

"If you'll come sit by me, Antonia Lu, and Bleys Ahrens will sit on the other side of you, you'll be only one chair from my uncle, Harley Nickolaus, who's just been talking to you. Then perhaps we can make introductions all around and get on with the occasion."

There was—it could not be called a murmur, but something between a murmur and a mumble of agreement—from the others in the room.

For a moment Harley Nickolaus glared about him. Then slowly the color began to fade from his face, the lines lost some of their deepness; and he looked, if not friendly, at least not unreasonable.

"Have it your way!" he said. He turned to the Manager. "That's all, Mathias."

Mathias went out. Two chair-floats had moved themselves from the wall into the positions the younger man had spoken of, by the time Toni and Bleys reached them. Not only that, but the table-arm on each one now held a tall glass of orange liquid.

"We understood this was what you wanted to drink," said Harley in a voice that still seemed to struggle with the remaining rags and tatters of his anger, "but if you'd like something else . . . "

"This is exactly what I like," said Bleys, picking up his glass and drinking lightly from it before putting it back down.

Toni also sipped from hers.

"Why, it's Association orange juice!" she said.

"Oh, we get our shipments in," said Harley.

It was, Bleys thought, a massive bit of ostentation. For anything of as little intrinsic value as variform orange juice to be shipped by spaceship from one world to another spoke of a use of interstellar credits that could only have been planned to impress.

"I see," he said. "I take it, then, you knew our taste before we got here."

"Harley," said the younger man, "seems to know everything. None of us have any privacy from him—"

It occurred to Bleys that "everything" Harley knew was something that would have to be measured. There was no secret, of course, about what Bleys himself usually drank. He was well known for preferring fruit juice to other drinks. But the younger man was still talking.

"Let me introduce you all around," he was saying. "Next to you, Bleys Ahrens, is Harley Nickolaus, my uncle. Just beyond Harley is Nord Pulaski. Then Ky Bennen . . . "

He continued around the room, giving names Bleys recognized from the information he already had about New Earth, as the heads of consortiums of multiple corporations.

"—And finally," the young man wound up, smiling engagingly at Bleys, "I'm Jay Aman, CEO of only one company, as opposed to Harley's thousands."

"Yes. The single largest company on New Earth," said Harley bluntly. "General Services."

"Ah, but lonely—the man at the top of a single company." Jay Aman smiled, eyes and all, at Toni.

Bleys watched him, interested. Harley Nickolaus had shown all the signs of being the leader here. But he had allowed himself to be stopped in mid-tirade by this nephew of his.

This did not fit at all with Harley's first reaction. And, if Jay Aman was capable of controlling what must be one of the most important assets on the globe, and was important enough to be here, he could hardly be as irresponsible as his open approach to Toni seemed to indicate.

That he was more than usually intelligent was plain.

But now someone else was speaking.

"It can't be too lonely," said a thin, dry-skinned man, in middle age, with a long, narrow, rather sour-looking face and a voice to match, speaking from farther down in the room. "Jay seems to find someone to sleep with most nights. They even say he sleeps with the Guilds."

"While Orville Learner," responded Jay, without taking his gaze off Toni, "sleeps with no one at all these days."

His answer came with a wide smile and in a light, inoffensive tone; but the words were waspish and plainly calculated to sting.

"Dinner," said Harley, interrupting.

As if this was a signal, table-floats, each bearing one or more serving dishes, plates and silverware upon them, began wafting in amongst them, until they were all surrounded by a variety of foods.

The attention of the CEOs was suddenly all on food. They took plates, helped themselves and commenced eating.

This put an end to all conversation. Evidently, thought Bleys, as he, too, went through the motions of taking a plate and helping himself lightly from some of the serving dishes, eating took precedence here over everything else. The dialogue between Jay and Orville Learner had been completely disrupted, and everyone's attention was on the food and the filled wineglasses, or whatever else they had taken to drink, on their chairfloat side-tables.

Outside of the occasional brief exchange of a word or two among the CEOs, nothing was said until the dinner came to an end. Then, in response to a control signal from someone, possibly Harley Nickolaus, the floats carrying the food dishes began to leave them. The diners put their plates back on the traveling tables as they passed by them through the air on their way out of the room; and finally it was once more a meeting place rather than a dining hall.

The CEOs sat back in their floats, replete. But the atmosphere of the room had changed. Bleys read it both in small differences of the facial expressions and the way they sat. But most of all, he felt it instinctively—a sudden gathering together by the CEOs, as a pack of half-wild dogs gather before making an attack on some prey.

He glanced at Toni and saw his feelings confirmed. Her face had changed subtly.

Now it held no expression at all.

Bleys recognized the change from his years of study of the martial arts. It was what was called a "white-mind" face—not achievable until one had moved fairly high into the ranks of one of the martial arts. But it was recognizable by anyone having to do with the person who displayed it. To those who did not understand its significance, the almost-inhuman lack of expression in an opponent could be terrifying in its implication. To those who did recognize it, it was the greatest of warnings. It told of a mind floating in its own center, a body free to achieve lethal harmony with any attack from any direction.

In sum, it signaled a situation in which the person was at his or her most dangerous. There was no specific intent. All was possible. Nothing was planned. Now, instead of being focused on any one thing, the mind was prepared to focus on anything, in any direction, and the body was a perfectly balanced sword in the hand of the mind.

Growing up as she had, Toni was capable of it. Bleys still was not.

But it underlined, as nothing else could, the sudden predatory threat that he now sensed all around him.

With the removal of the food, the attitude of those around had changed completely. Gone was any sense of individual conflicts or enmities, such as that between Aman and Learner, that had made them all seem separate individuals with separate points of view and points of desire. Suddenly they were unified—a team of hunters long used to working together, poised and ready to attack. Just as, in spite of the fact that they both sat relaxed in their chairfloats, Bleys and Toni were, each in their own way, ready to meet that attack.

"So, you come here, a stranger among us, Bleys Ahrens," said Harley, sitting comfortably back in his float-chair like a sated lion, "to teach us all how to be better people."

Chapter 7

Bleys looked agreeably back at him. Clearly, it was to be the stick first, then the carrot—instead of the order of procedure he had expected.

"How well you put things, Harley Nickolaus," he said.

Harley's face flushed.

"Here on New Earth," he snapped, "we usually address CEOs as 'Sir.'"

"Do you indeed?" said Bleys.

His slight emphasis on the *you* was not mild enough to be missed. Harley looked almost appealingly at his nephew.

"Well, now," Jay Aman said softly to Bleys. "We understand you call yourself a philosopher."

"Yes," he said, "I do call myself that."

"Say something in philosophy!" Harley said, jovially; and, scything a glance around at the other CEO Club members, he reaped a small grumble of laughter in acknowledgment.

"I think what my uncle means," said Jay, "is that he'd like to hear a sample of what you call your philosophy. What, in other words, you'll be telling your audiences here on New Earth. In short—could we hear you philosophize, sir philosopher?"

Jay's voice had stayed pleasant enough, but there was the hint of a less-than-pleasant smile at the corners of his mouth.

Bleys ignored it. "Well," he said thoughtfully, "one of the things I tell an audience—any audience—is that one of the problems with all of the people on our New Worlds is that they don't pay enough attention to what can be learned from their past; not only from the past on the world they colonized, but before that, on Old Earth. Because those pasts made the present they live in right now; and unless an effort is made to avoid the past's bad solutions to problems, the present may end up unpleasantly determining their future; making what a few clear-sighted people long since saw as possible become inevitable."

Harley gave a snort of laughter.

"I don't think we should laugh at this situation," said Bleys. "Remember, it's over two hundred years since an Exotic thinker made his case for the fact that the Splinter Cultures necessarily had to decay on their own and eventually disappear. We're still divided into those same Splinter Cultures, and there's been no real attempt made to weld all the people of all the New Worlds into one community."

"A two-hundred-year-old prophecy?" said Jay Aman. "Is that the best you're going to have to offer our New Earth audiences?"

"The prophecy's entirely valid," Bleys said, mildly. "But you have to do what only a few people have done, and that's to look ahead more than just a couple of generations. Most people don't, simply because beyond their grandchildren, possibly beyond their great-great-grandchildren—what seems to be the future is so far outside the expectations of their own personal lives that they can't rouse themselves to any real interest in it. Their views vary from one extreme, which is 'there's no hope anyway, but at least I won't be here to see it,' to 'future generations will take care of things.' "

He looked directly at Harley.

"Future generations won't, you know," he said directly to the older man. "For future generations to do anything about it, the process needs to be started now. That's my message, essentially. We have to start now to make a change."

"Juvenile nonsense!" said Harley.

"I don't think so," said Bleys. "Would you be interested in hearing a little story I tell my audiences at this point, in a great many of my talks, that illustrates what I just said?"

"Please," said Jay. His voice was suddenly serious, and it brought about a startling change in his uncle.

"Oh, certainly," said Harley, waving a dismissive hand. "Tell us."

"I tell a story, a true story from my own experience," said Bleys. "When I was a boy, I was moved around many of the worlds, and met a number of men and women; some of them recently out from Old Earth. One woman gave me a recording of her visit to one of the natural preserves they have there. This one was in a mountainous area of North America; and included a talk by one of the Preserve Rangers that care for the place—its flora and fauna. It happened that this particular preserve was one on which the North American grizzly bear still thrives. You all know what a grizzly is like?"

Heads nodded. Old Earth history and geography were taught in the primary and secondary schools of all the Younger Worlds. Later, Younger Worlds' adults might have only the haziest remembrance of the shape or number of the continents of Old Earth, or of its languages or history.

But—and Bleys himself was no exception to this, only better read and informed than most—they all had lively memories of hearing about the great whale, the giraffe with his impossibly long neck, the massive elephant, with his curious nose extended into a supple trunk—and all the other marvelous and strange creatures they had seen pictured in three dimensions simulated to act as if they were alive. But which, unless they became so very rich that they could make a visit to the Mother World, they would never see in actual life.

"Four meters tall and three to four thousand kilograms," said Orville Learner, the sour-faced CEO, suddenly no longer sour.

"I think your figures might be a little oversize," said Bleys. "The biggest have been more like two and a half to three meters and weigh no more than two thousand kilograms—nine feet and a thousand pounds, roughly, in the Old Modern English measures. At any rate, the Ranger warned against getting too close to any of them; and he also said if anyone in his audience was charged by one, to climb a tree. If no tree was available, that person's best chance of escaping alive was to fall to the ground and play dead. With luck, the grizzly would just come up, shove their limp body around with a paw and then lose interest—but there was no guarantee of that. It depended on the grizzly."

Bleys had the people in the room as captive as those in the Ranger's live audience undoubtedly had been. Even Harley's attention was fixed.

"The point was, the Ranger went on to say," continued Bleys, "that most of those listening to him would remember this for a little while— some might even write it down. But the chances were that unless they really appreciated the danger, they'd forget all about it if they came across a grizzly bear and it charged them. They'd panic and run for their lives, even though they had just been told that the animal could run faster for short distances than a human could, and would catch them. But, the Ranger said on the recording—and as a child I remember being very impressed by the grin on his face when he said it—if there was anyone in the group he was speaking to who'd ever been chased by a bear before, and there was no tree close enough to climb, there would be no hesitation. That person would drop, almost without taking time to think, as if he or she had been shot."

Bleys stopped speaking. The CEOs were silent, clearly envisioning a grizzly coming at them.

"You see my point," said Bleys into the silence. There was a pause.

"So you're telling us," said Harley, with an obvious effort, returning to his normal acerbic manner again, "that nothing you say is going to be advising the people on New Earth on what would change our society?"

"Not as specific advice, no. I only lay the facts before them and tell my audiences I'd like to see each one there concerned with developing his or her share of the human race's full potential."

"Hmph!" said Harley.

"But," Bleys went on, undisturbed, "I merely offer general information. Specific advice is something I give only if asked. Like teaching, advice is wasted until the listener already has a vital reason for wanting to know it. When that's true, then suddenly that knowledge makes immediate sense to them. But until that moment of recognition, all they've gotten from me is nothing more than a bagful of words. They may listen to those words. They may even write them down; but until it connects with something important to them, what they hear is just that—words."

He paused.

"Forgive me," he said, "I see I've slipped into speech making, after all."

"You damn well have," said Harley, "and what it sounds like to me is you're going to try to give our people some rabble-rousing—"

"Uncle!" Jay's higher-pitched voice cut sharply this time across Harley's words, and stopped the older man, in mid-sentence.

"You'll have to forgive him," Jay said, smiling in turn at Bleys. "Harley has a tendency sometimes to go a little too bluntly to the point. What he'd really like to know—what we'd all like to know—is what these speeches of yours, here on *our* world, have as their ultimate aim. If, for example, you're planning to go on from these parables to suggest that changes should be made right now in our New Earth society . . ."

He left the end of his sentence hanging delicately poised in the air.

"Actually," said Bleys soberly, "I don't believe I'll be mentioning New Earth specifically, at all. The message I have is universal—for all humans on all worlds, Old or New. I'll be talking somewhat specifically only about Old Earth—and in particular, the Final Encyclopedia, there."

"Now, why should New Earth's women and men have any kind of concern with Old Earth and the Final Encyclopedia?" asked Jay.

"Why, all of you here are educated people," said Bleys. "I'm certain you've heard before this of that early prediction of an Exotic I just mentioned, in which he also said that several hundred million years of Mother World evolution aren't safe to tamper with in a few hundred years of social and individual specialization."

None of their faces reflected confirmation of Bleys' certainty in this. Every expression there but Jay Aman's showed no connection of these words with the prediction about Splinter Cultures Bleys had mentioned earlier.

"Ah, yes. Of course," said Jay. "But it's always been understood that idea was at best a theoretical opinion."

"It is that," said Bleys, "but consider it in connection with the need of the Younger Worlds to survive *independently* of Old Earth's continual attempt to control us; which nowadays is hidden in their tool for doing just that, which is the Final Encyclopedia."

"This is all nonsense!" Harley burst out.

The majority of those there clearly agreed. There were scowls here and there around the room directed at Bleys, now.

"What the hell," said Harley, "does it matter to us what some Exotics, or Old Earth and their Final Encyclopedia people think or do? The point is, we've got a good society here on our own world; and what we want to know, in plain, unvarnished Basic, is if you're going to try to disturb it!"

"Forgive me," said Bleys. "But my interests are much larger than the situation on any single New World."

"So you say," said Harley. "It doesn't sound like it to me."

He drew a deep breath, looked down, and took the stem of his wineglass between his fingers. He began to twirl the glass, watching it rather than Bleys.

"You know, Bleys Ahrens," he said, more quietly, still toying with his wineglass, "New Earth is ours. It's the world of those of us you're looking at right now. We're the top people of this CEO Club. And this CEO Club is the top Club of all those in all our cities. In short, the planet's more our responsibility than it is anyone else's; and, of course, with that responsibility goes control."

"Of course," said Bleys gently. "I understand."

"We hoped you would," said Harley, in an even more reasonable voice. Now comes the carrot, thought Bleys. "Particularly, considering what you've done so far, you're the kind of man who realizes the facts of life when you run into them. Now, you're going to start on this tour of yours soon, aren't you? Leaving New Earth City for other points around our globe?"

"The day after tomorrow, for Blue Harbor," said Bleys. "As my schedule stands now. It could be several days from now, but not many."

"Yes," said Harley. "Well, you understand, then, that once you start your tour, and even now here in New Earth City, you'll be keeping in mind the fact that we own the hotels you'll be staying in. Whatever transportation you'll take, the availability of your meals—wherever you find them—and essentially everything you'll touch while you're here, is owned or controlled by us."

"Yes," Bleys said.

"Fine," said Harley. "We'll be counting on you, then, not to try anything that will do the CEO Clubs any harm." He raised his gaze from the wineglass, let go of its stem, and smiled a smile that in spite of his obvious efforts, was rusty and unconvincing.

"I've already told you," Bleys said. "My concern is with something greater. Philosophies make history; machinations by CEO Clubs hardly would."

Harley did not look particularly pleased with the association of the word "machinations" with CEO Clubs. But he made an effort to hang onto his smile.

"Good," he said. "Then, that subject's taken care of. There's one other matter to talk about."

"Is there?" said Bleys; and this time, so delicate was the irony in his voice that it was questionable how many of those there besides Toni and perhaps Jay Aman even heard it.

"Yes," said Harley. "You know of course that we're not the only power on this world—though we're the main one. The other is the job-holders' Guilds"—his face reddened—"unions are what the damn outfits are! Never mind that fancy medieval name they call themselves—"

Harley swallowed the wine that was left in his glass; and the sudden surge of blood that had come with his last words faded again. Bleys thought of the obvious effort that had been given to produce an impression of great age in the outer portion of the Club building.

But Harley was going on.

"Don't ever think the Guilds won't be approaching you," he said. "They'll want you to use your talks to advertise them, to give them credit. We can't have that. If they ever got control here, everything'd fall apart—everyone his own job-giver. Anarchy! So we don't want you encouraging them. We've got trouble enough keeping them in line now. All right, then, you've told us how you're not concerned with doing anything about changing our world, here. Have you got it clear that we're in a position to outbid the Guilds in anything—including interstellar credit, which is the only thing that really matters?"

"Is it the only thing that really matters?" said Bleys, a little wistfully.

"What else could?" demanded Harley. "Credit's everything. All right, so the Guilds have strength in numbers. Also, they've got financial resources; but, talking about amounts that count, only in local currency. They can't begin to touch us in interstellar credit. We're the ones who buy from Cassida and Newton, who sell to all the other Younger Worlds. If you plan to visit here, you also plan to visit other worlds—am I right?"

"You're right," said Bleys.

"Of course I am," said Harley. "So, since these other-world trips of yours have to be expensive, a large chunk of interstellar credit banked with us is always going to be useful to you. Particularly if all that you had to do to get it was to make sure that you helped people to look always to us for guidance, not the Guilds."

"A bribe?" asked Bleys.

"Call it anything you want," said Harley.

"I'm afraid," answered Bleys, rising to his feet, "you're one of the people for whom my little anecdote of what to do if chased by a grizzly bear doesn't yet have a personal application. I think Antonia Lu and I will leave you all, now—"

"I don't think you will," said Harley. "Not until we've got the kind of assurances from you we invited you up here to get."

As he spoke, he was very visibly pressing a stud on his wrist control pad.

Bleys nodded, but he also stayed on his feet. Toni had risen to stand beside him. He did not move toward the lift; neither did she.

"Looks like you didn't think of all that could happen," said Harley. "Anyway, just for your further education, we'll let the answer to that signal

I just sent out carry on through—for *your* education. Stand, or sit if you want—but it'll only be a couple of minutes."

"Then of course we'll wait," said Bleys.

There was utter silence in the room, a silence which continued while the seconds ticked off. Both Bleys and Toni knew how to stand still, but relaxed. Less than two minutes after Harley had spoken, the lift arrived. He and Toni turned to face it, with the others in the room who could not see the lift doors without turning their chairfloats around.

The doors opened. Through them stepped Henry MacLean.

He stood aside to leave the entrance clear, and Bleys and Toni walked to and into the lift. Henry stepped back in beside them; and they all turned back to face the startled expressions of those in the room they had just left.

It was only then that Harley came out of whatever shock had held silent not only him, but all those with him. He shouted at Bleys as if the words within him had a life of their own and were now finally exploding into speech from the emotional pressure.

"Where's Mathias?" he shouted. "What have you done with him? You"—he stared at Henry—"how did you get in here?"

Henry did not answer. He had already touched the row of studs in the elevator wall beside him. The doors closed and the lift began to descend.

"It was almost too easy," said Henry to Bleys as they started down. "They made a common mistake. Once we were inside, we were past their main security elements. We'd been scanned, just as you were, for weapons and were found unarmed. Anyway, we didn't look like enough force to make trouble for them. We waited until we were alone with only a few of them, disarmed and tied them up, then took care of just those that could give us access to this lift, including the Manager in his office. Nobody else saw anything happen. Then we waited for a call to him from upstairs. When it came, I came."

"Anyone hurt?" asked Bleys.

"None of us," said Henry. "A few of the club employees may have sore heads, but I doubt if any of them were really hurt. I took a void pistol from the Manager. We didn't have to touch him, at all. When he saw how easily we'd taken control, he simply handed the pistol over."

"That's interesting," said Bleys. "I'd guess they thought something like this might happen; and the Manager had been given orders not to risk any of the people with us getting hurt, unless he was sure he could win. But I don't think they ever expected you to turn on them like that."

"No," said Henry. "I don't think so. In any case, we left the Manager with his thumbs tied behind him in his office. I think he'll stay there—at least until we're out of here."

The lift stopped abruptly and unexpectedly.

"They may have planned a little more sensibly than we thought, Uncle," murmured Bleys.

"It's possible," said Henry.

The elevator started again. Moments later it stopped a second time, and the door opened. Mathias stood just outside, his hands unbound and Henry's men with their own hands tied behind their backs looking embarrassed.

Henry glanced at Bleys.

"I don't think there'll be a problem," Bleys said to him. He looked at Mathias. "Will there?"

"No, Bleys Ahrens," said Mathias. "We have certain standard emergency measures," he went on, once Bleys, Toni and Henry were out of the lift. "The one we'd designed for your visit didn't work too well. But we've managed, anyway. However, since you're so well known and a governing Member on your own world, it's been decided you need some time to think things over."

"Of course," said Bleys. "But you might tell Harley Nickolaus for me that their bluff didn't work. You see, I knew they weren't ready yet to get rough."

Mathias did not seem to have heard Bleys at all.

"So," he went on, "I've just been told the Club considers any questions between you and it deferred for the moment. I'll show you out."

He turned and led off. Bleys, Toni, Henry and the rest followed. The men who had their hands tied behind their backs had their bindings cut by Henry as they left.

They retraced the route they had followed coming in, according to Bleys' memory. But as they passed through the door that let them into the outer section of the Club, they found themselves in halls swarming with people.

They halted.

"Forgive this, please," said Mathias, turning back to Bleys, "I forgot there's a special meeting going on. Let me show you another way out."

They turned aside, into a room that held a long, empty dining table set with silverware and glasses; and through a farther door into a large kitchen area, through which they threaded their way amidst various pieces of equipment and people working with food, to a double door of gray metal, with a lift bar locking it.

Mathias picked up the lift bar and pushed on the right hand section of the door. It opened on the side alley Bleys had noticed on entering. Nighttime had made the darkness without into an opaque wall surrounding a small circle of alley pavement lit by the glaringly bright light above the door.

The air outside felt cool now, and slightly damp. It was all black to their left. To their right, it was a tunnel of gloom, giving way gradually to the light from the alley's farther opening to the trafficway on which they had driven to the club.

"Take Intertrafficway Forty-one," said Mathias, pointing to their right. "Your chances of picking up autocabs for your hotel are best there."

Henry led his men out first into the alley. Bleys and Toni followed. Mathias stood for a moment in the doorway behind them, watching as they started toward the lit passageway to their right.

Suddenly the outside light went out; and the total length of the alley was plunged in darkness, except for the light coming past Mathias through the service door. At the same moment, figures with thick rods like policemen's nightsticks, erupted from the dark at their left in an attack at Bleys' group from behind. Mathias stared for a second; then hastily stepped back inside, closed, and locked the door behind him, leaving them blinded in the sudden lightnessness.

Chapter 8

But the darkness did not completely blind them. There was still the light from the alley mouth; and that, as their eyes adjusted, began to let them see almost as well as their attackers.

Henry and the Soldiers, who had gone out first, had immediately dropped to the floor of the alley, spinning around as they lay on their backs, so that their feet were toward their attackers. Taking one long stride over the three steps to the alley floor, Bleys had shut his eyes to let his sight adjust as quickly as possible to the dimness of the alley, and was going completely with the momentary glimpse of the attackers rushing toward them, which was like a picture imprinted on his mind—a picture which acquired movement as his ears picked up the sounds of the people rushing at them, and turned it from a still image to a moving, developing one.

Within seconds Bleys had his eyes open again and could see enough better to make out that the attackers had run into the Soldiers, and unexpectedly found themselves being flipped off their feet as the Soldiers' heavy work boots caught them with one toe behind one of their ankles and another kicking out at the front of the lower leg above it. The floor of the alley was concrete, and some of those who went down that way stayed down.

Bleys' first concern was for Toni. But she had been behind him going down the stairs, and as long as she stayed in that position relative to him, the two of them could handle just about anything that was likely to come at them, clubs or no clubs. Four of the attackers had peeled off from the general rush to concentrate on him, but those four now had the light from the alley mouth in their eyes while he had it at his back, and his own vision was about as good as it could be in this dimness. That advantage, at least, was clearly with him.

At the same moment, the first of his club-wielding attackers reached him, and he lashed out with his right foot, feeling it connect solidly. The leader of the four had made the same mistake so many people made, which was to underestimate the unusual reach of Bleys' long arms and legs.

Bleys' sight was good enough now that he could see that the man he had kicked was sliding limply down the opposite wall of the alley. But his attention was on his other three opponents.

His action had brought a sudden check to the other three fronting him. Out of the corner of his eye he could also see that Toni had slipped past the blow aimed at her with the nightstick of one attacker, at the same time as she accelerated the momentum of the man's rush to propel him on past her—so that he slammed face foremost against the wall of the building—and dropped. Now she was turning to help Bleys.

Meanwhile, the other three had decided to spread out and move in on Bleys, but by this time, between vision and hearing, he knew their movements well; and, from the corner of his right eye, he saw Henry's group rising from the alley pavement and taking down their remaining attackers, one-on-one or two-on-one.

Toni had already moved past Bleys, and in behind the next closest of Bleys' opponents. She twisted his stick from his grasp, over his shoulder. At the same time, she drove the point of her toe into the hollow of his left knee from behind and pulled him to the pavement backward, where he lay still. Now warned, one of the two coming toward Bleys, turned to face her.

He lifted his stick in good baton fashion—a foolish move against someone like Toni, who had grown up with the art of kendo. She spun in underneath the blow and hardly more than tapped him on the side of the head with the stick she now carried. At the same time, Bleys, dropping to a crouch on his left knee, used his long right leg to sweep his one remaining opponent's legs from under him with such force that his head also hit the pavement and he lay still.

Around them the battle was ending.

"Henry?" Bleys peered through the gloom for his uncle, who emerged from the mass of dark bodies.

"They're all taken care of," Henry said to Bleys. He seemed only slightly breathless.

"Are you hurt?" Bleys asked. Henry shook his head. "Anyone else hurt?"

"A couple of our men might be concussed," Henry's matter-of-fact voice came out of the obscurity. "They're still out, and we'll have to carry them. Nothing to speak of, otherwise."

"Good," said Bleys.

"But I think we'd better be moving," Henry added.

"Yes," said Bleys, "I can carry one of the men who's hurt, if you'd like."

"No need," said Henry. "The Soldiers are used to this. They're already on the way. It's only a short distance to the road—passageway, I mean—that the Manager pointed out."

They did not have to hunt autocabs, as Mathias had suggested. When they reached the street, the limousines which had brought them to the dinner were still waiting for them, a small distance down the curb from the doorway of the club. They backed down to the alley-mouth as soon as Bleys and the rest emerged.

Bleys took Toni and Henry with him in the leading car; he turned to Toni the minute they were out in traffic.

"Toni," he said, "this is your department, since Dahno's not with us to deal with the political aspect. Call the local police and report an attack on us as we were leaving the CEO Club. Tell them Dahno's the one they should go through for any further questions. He can arrange to have our Soldiers available for them. Then get Dahno on voice only. He's having a private dinner with the New Earth City Governor, I understand. Brief him and say we're headed back to the hotel. But contact the police first."

"Is there any real point in that?" asked Toni. "The CEO Club must have the local police in their pocket."

"Probably. But I want it on the police record," said Bleys.

Toni started to lift her wrist pad to her lips, then hesitated.

"You're looking unusually pleased," she said. "Did you like our being attacked in that alley?"

"Not that specifically," said Bleys. "But I'm pleased with the whole evening as more than fulfilling my expectations."

"I'd have called it a standoff," she said. "We walked out of that dining room when we wanted to, but on the other hand, Henry's men were captured and helpless; and we ended up being attacked by their—what do they call it on this world? Tough Squad. We ended up getting attacked by that Tough Squad in the alley. We did take care of them, but if we'd had a few less of Henry's Soldiers with us, we might not have been able to."

"The point is, we had enough people with us," said Bleys. "Remember, Jack and Jill briefed Henry on the Tough Squads, so looking ahead, perhaps he had an idea of how many men they might send to give us a lesson. And, of course, it was planned to be just that: a lesson. They wanted to knock us around a bit, not do any real damage—nothing that could cause interplanetary complications."

"Well, then, why isn't it a draw?"

"They gave themselves away," said Bleys. "They tried to impress me, then made their offer—and neither one worked. I posed them a rather hard question. I'm obviously a potential danger to them; and obviously I'm not going to be easy to take care of quietly, without violating my diplomatic status, or even making the kind of fuss that would arouse their job-holders when they don't want them roused. If they let me go, I may rouse the job-holders, myself. If they don't let me go, and stop me—but the word gets out—the job-holders may be kindled to action by that. It's a no-win situation for them both ways. That makes it a win situation for me."

"Possibly," said Toni. But she lifted her wrist control pad to her lips and spoke into it.

Back at the hotel, Bleys paced up and down their private lounge while they waited for Henry, who had left them to get a medical check on those of his men who had taken any possibly serious damage in the alley.

Bleys had not taken off his cloak, which swirled and flapped about his legs at each turn, as he paced the room. He was aware of Toni's watching him from a sofa-float, and of Henry's arrival, shortly after; but only with the edge of his mind. At the center of it, it was as if the energy being generated inside him by his thinking would burn him up if he did not burn it off.

His eyes were focused nowhere in particular. He was concentrating on nothing and everything at the same time; including the possibilities suggested by what they had experienced at the dinner. These possibilities engaged the full cognitive machinery of his mind. The room, Toni and Henry—even the world around them—for the moment had only a shadowy existence. Only his thoughts existed.

"It's all right," he came back to his surroundings to hear. Toni was saying in a low voice, "He's well into it."

Bleys looked and saw Henry and Toni sitting with their heads close together; and, since he was still pacing, he saw they did not realize he had come out of his whirlwind of thought.

"How are your men?" Toni was asking.

"Fine," Henry answered. "No one got seriously hurt."

"I'm glad to hear it," answered Toni. She nodded at Bleys. "Was he like this as a boy?"

Henry shook his head.

"No," he said.

"When did it start?" asked Toni.

"I saw it first a few months before he left my farm—my son's farm—to go to Ecumeny and be with Dahno. That was shortly before he tried fasting to find God—and did not. It was at least half a year after that before I saw him again; and somewhere in that time he'd made the decision that brought me to him now."

"The choice for Satan?" said Toni.

"Not a choice for," said Henry, shaking his head again. "No, he wouldn't do that. He's too big in soul—too big in every way—for that. But it was a decision that put him in Satan's hands, whether he admits it to himself or not."

"If he really doesn't know," said Toni, "can you still hold him responsible for being the way he is and doing what he's doing?"

"Yes," said Henry flatly.

"Why?"

"No one who walks with Satan can avoid the guilt of it," said Henry. "A man may try to hide it from himself, but the hiding is known by him, even if what's hidden is not admitted."

"You're very hard in some ways, Henry," Toni said.

"I'm very sinful in many ways, myself," said Henry. "But in the end—for me as for Bleys and everyone—the answer's the same. Alone, you take the responsibility for any decision. And alone, you bear the consequences."

"It's cruel to think that way."

"To live in God's way is not easy," said Henry.

Bleys stopped his pacing abruptly and stood facing them. Their heads lifted and their faces turned to him.

"Henry," he said, "are there any of your men who won't be able to move on to Blue Harbor tomorrow?"

"None," said Henry. "But I thought we were going to stay here another day or two."

"That was my first plan, yes," Bleys answered. He looked at his wrist control pad. "Just a little after nine in the evening, now. There's plenty of time yet. Toni, will you take the phone and make arrangements for all of us to fly tomorrow, late afternoon, for Blue Harbor? Make it about dinnertime."

Toni frowned.

"I don't know if I can arrange scheduled transportation for as many people as we've got at that short notice," she said. "At the very least, the local space-and-atmosphere lines are going to want to split us up into groups on different ships."

"Charter a space-and-atmosphere ship if you have to," said Bleys.

"There's that, of course," said Toni. "Maybe I'd better ignore the regular flights and go directly to that."

"I'll leave it to you," said Bleys. He came over and took a chairfloat by them. She keyed in the phone by her sofa, spoke briefly to a travel agency and broke the connection.

"You look pleased," said Henry, watching him steadily.

"Things are moving," answered Bleys, stretching his long legs out before him toward the fire in the fireplace, which the hotel staff had replenished. It crackled as merrily as if there were not a problem in the universe. It was ridiculous that something originally designed to heat a room should be retained for merely decorative purposes. But Bleys enjoyed watching it, as—for very different reasons—he appreciated the starscape in the ceilings of his bedrooms.

"They could be moving much faster than I expected," he went on thoughtfully. "There are some possibilities—"

He was interrupted by the chiming that signaled a phone call. Toni answered. It was a return of her travel agency call, and she was immediately immersed in the details of the move.

"Interesting that none of those who jumped us in the alley used anything but sticks or clubs," Bleys went on to Henry.

"They planned to hurt us—but not seriously," said Henry.

"So I just said to Toni," Bleys answered. "That's why it's interesting.

Whoever sent them did it with orders to hurt and scare us, but not to do real damage—to the important ones among us, anyway."

"Also," said Henry, "to give the appearance of being a simple gang off the street. Not part of any organization."

"That, too," Bleys said. They looked at each other and nodded. Bleys turned to Toni, who had now finished the call. "Everything set?"

"Everything. I set takeoff for six P.M. tomorrow," said Toni. "All right?"

"Fine," said Bleys, gazing at the fire again. "Now, we wait. I think we're going to have a late visitor."

"A visitor?" Toni asked. "Who?"

"That I can't guess," answered Bleys. "We'll wait and see. Whoever it is should be here by midnight."

However, it was less than an hour and a half later that their phone chimed. Toni picked it up and spoke into it.

"Bleys Ahrens' suite. Yes?"

She listened a moment, then thumbed her control pad to mute and turned to Bleys.

"For you," she said. "A Guildmaster Edgar Hytry. News travels fast in this town."

"And decisions are just as fast," said Bleys, a second before he thumbed the phone stud on his own pad to *talk*. "Guildmaster Hytry?"

He listened a moment.

"Not at all," he said. "I'm usually up later than this. If you'll go to the north tower of this hotel, and press the stud of private elevator A2, its door will open, and you can come directly to me, up here."

A pause.

"Not at all." Bleys said. He touched the stud again and cut off contact.

"What does this mean for me and my men?" Henry asked.

"Nothing," said Bleys. "The Guildmaster's coming to suggest a lunch with him and some of his associates tomorrow, he says. I'll agree to it, but here in my suite. They'll agree—after tonight, it'll only be natural caution on my part. Your men—most of them, anyway—can rest until we go to Blue Harbor. I suppose we'll have to leave the hotel a couple of hours ahead of time to be sure of getting clear of the city and out to the chartered ship—not that it wouldn't wait for us."

"I'll go tell them, then," said Henry. "Both about the change in plans and the fact that they can relax. A few of them who were in that CEO alley might like to celebrate a little tonight."

"Your Soldiers of God aren't going to fit the popular New Earth idea of a Friendly in many ways, besides the ability they showed as alley fighters," Bleys said, smiling.

Henry looked at him grimly. He did not return the smile.

"They are what they are," he said.

Bleys nodded, becoming serious. "I'd like them to stay in the hotel, however, if you and they don't mind," he said. "Outside of that, as long as they get enough sleep, their off-duty time is their own. But they should stay in touch at all times. We just might have things for them to do, once we get to Blue Harbor."

Henry got up and moved toward the door.

"But don't go yet," Bleys said. "I'd like you here when this Guildmaster comes."

Henry came back and sat down.

Guildmaster Edgar Hytry, when he appeared, was a round-faced, round-bellied man with thinning black hair and a pleasant, smiling round face. Like New Earth men in general, he was closely clean-shaven. The dark purple business jacket and narrow purple pants of his business suit seemed at odds with his overweight body, as if he had put on some extra kilos of weight since he had acquired it. Nonetheless, he beamed at them all, halting just inside the door through which he had entered.

"Bleys Ahrens!" he said in a thick tenor voice. "It's good—very good of you—to see me at this time of night."

Bleys looked at him across the distance that separated them. "As I told you on the phone, it's no intrusion at all. Sit down."

"Thank you," said Hytry.

He came around the chairs between them and took one opposite Bleys, cautiously perching himself toward the forward edge of his float, as if he might need to jump up from it at any minute.

"You're wondering what brings me, of course," he said to Bleys. "I'm a member of the Select Council of the Guildmasters here." His voice had added a ring of importance. "In a way, I suppose, you could say we speak not only for the Guildmembers of this city, but of all cities on New Earth. We welcome you here to New Earth, Bleys Ahrens. In fact, we were hoping to give you some more solid indication of our welcome than just a few words from one of us. But we understood you were going to be here several days longer, and, well, word has it—" he waved vaguely at the city beyond the windowed walls of the lounge— "that you're leaving tomorrow evening. That doesn't give us much time to make you properly welcome. I was hoping I might be able to persuade you to go back to your original plans and stay an extra day or two, here in the city."

"I'm afraid not." The tone of Bleys' mild answer passed over any question of how Hytry had learned about their leaving so swiftly. "We've been going over our schedule and come to the conclusion that I've less time before needing to be back on Association than I thought originally. A shame, but what can you do?"

"A shame, indeed," said Hytry, managing to smile and frown at the same time. "The whole of New Earth City, of course, knows you had dinner at the CEO Club here tonight, and we'd be ashamed if you left with . . . what should I say? Say—without a balancing opinion, from our Steering Committee. Our Committee, Bleys Ahrens, would like to have a meal with you. That is to say, we'd like to have you as our guest at a dinner worthy of a visitor like you. But with the time so short . . . you're sure you can't at least put off leaving until perhaps midnight, tomorrow night?"

"No," Bleys said slowly. "We've just been talking about the immediate schedule, and I leave at six P.M. These tours take it out of us, you know."

"Oh, I do—wait a second!" said Hytry. "I've got it! There's still time for lunch tomorrow. It's not going to let us really give you the kind of welcome we'd like to show you, but it would give all our Steering Committee Members a chance to meet you—which they very much want to do; and if I do say so, Bleys Ahrens, it'd be to your advantage to meet them, seeing we're the First Guildhouse, the leading one on our world."

Bleys shook his head slowly.

"I'm afraid not," he said. "I'd planned to spend all day working here tomorrow before I left, getting my talks ready, as well as other pieces of business. To take time out for even a lunch would mean going to meet you, eating lunch, and then getting back here again and back to work. No, no. It'd kill off the best of my available afternoon and, in any case, I don't want to leave this hotel tomorrow until I go to the spaceport."

"I quite understand. I quite understand," said Hytry. "How about this? We'll have lunch right here at your hotel. It won't take more than a couple of hours of your time. I promise you."

Bleys shook his head again, regretfully.

"An hour and a half, then?" said Hytry. "I guarantee we won't keep you longer than an hour and a half. No? How about an hour?"

Bleys smiled ruefully. "I don't see how you can have a lunch for me even here in the hotel, that'll give us time to eat at all. Wait . . . perhaps. Yes, possibly. We could use part of my quarters here, and set the lunch up in that. You people would pick up the cost, of course."

"A splendid idea!" said Hytry. "Of course. Absolutely. We planned to be the hosts. What time would you like it?"

"Twelve noon," said Bleys. "Twelve noon sharp, and you'll have to leave at one o'clock sharp—I warn you."

"That's quite all right. We understand," said Hytry. "Just leave it to me. I'll talk to the hotel and take care of everything. All you'll have to do is to get up from whatever room you're in and move to another that's large enough to hold us all and the lunch table."

"Very well, then." Bleys rose. "Now, if you'll excuse me, I still have some time before I'll be going to bed, and there's work still, tonight."

Hytry was on his feet in an instant.

"Yes. Of course." He was already moving toward the entrance to the lift. "I'll say good night, then. Good night to you all. Good night to you all!"

Bleys had already touched the stud on the control pad of his chair. The door to the room slid open, Hytry stepped through, and the door closed again, swallowing him up. Bleys sat back in his chairfloat, almost grinning at Toni and Henry.

"Well," he said to them. "There we have it. The bidders of the opposition. On second thought, Henry, in spite of all his agreeableness, you can expect him to show up with an armed guard of his own people. I suppose we ought to display a guard of our own."

"I guessed as much," said Henry. "I'll have Soldiers out of sight but ready."

"As a matter of fact, you can put them right in sight," said Bleys. "They'll expect that, I think, knowing about the attack on us tonight. They'll also expect me to be jumpy about another attack—but I don't think there'll be one—this time."

Chapter 9

"Bleys Ahrens." Edgar Hytry said, sweating lightly at the head of the table that had been set up in one of the lounges of Bleys' suite. "We've looked forward to your coming. Unlike the attitude you probably encountered at the CEO Club, ours is that a Great Teacher like yourself will always be welcome on New Earth. Let's all drink to that!"

There were twelve men and women around the table, counting Bleys, Toni and Henry. The other nine were Guildmasters, Council-people all. Now, these lifted glasses holding a curious, sweet white wine with an acid aftertaste, and drank.

Bleys lifted his glass barely to his lips with them and set it down again. He noticed that Toni also avoided having to actually drink the orange juice in hers. There was nothing wrong with it—for anyone born and brought up on New Earth. But of course the hotel could supply only New Earth orange juice, and it tasted little like the Association orange juice that the CEO Club had been able to produce. Henry, sensible man, was drinking coffee; made, of course, with New Earth water, but the different taste of which was less apparent, since the taste of coffee could be standardized, though it was expensive to do so. Dahno was not with them. Some errand of his own had taken him away.

"Thank you," said Bleys. "It's always cheering to hear that your coming is welcome."

Since he had specified no more than an hour for lunch, it had necessarily ended up being more of a snack than a meal, though the Guild-masters had arranged for it to be served with as much ceremony as the hotel could manage; and this was the first time anyone at the table had shown any intention of approaching the subject that must have caused them to want to meet with him. Half the hour had already gone by.

"You see," Hytry was leaning forward confidentially, although the full length of the table was between him and Bleys, "we know—we have ways of finding out these things—how the dinner you had with the CEOs went. Naturally, they'd be suspicious of anyone like you coming in. They feel they own this planet—though they don't. I'm proud to say they don't, because we of the Guilds hold them back from becoming absolute tyrants. We of the Guilds speak for the common job-holders. We know you speak to the jobholders. Therefore you're with us, and we with you."

"Who speaks for the non-job-holders?" asked Bleys.

"There are no non-job-holders," said Hytry, and the other Guildmasters, of whom only three were women, nodded. "On New Earth everyone works; and everyone who works—at any job—has to belong to a Guild."

"Including farmers, ranchers and such people?"

"Yes, indeed," said Hytry. "Everyone. So that in the next few weeks when you talk to the people of this world, you'll be talking to Guild members—all except the stray CEO who might come to listen."

"That's interesting," said Bleys. "Then you aren't worried about some of the job-holders having to switch jobs or be thrown out of work, as a result of this new contract with Newton? Though I suppose a number of them will have to move to different places and face that sort of disruption."

The Guildmasters looked at each other.

"Oh," said Hytry, "it'll all go smoothly. We know how to handle such things."

"Well, that's good," said Bleys. "I hadn't been able to see how something so massive could be done without a good deal of disruption and people changing jobs, a general hardship on at least a certain percentage of your job-holders."

"Well, of course," said Hytry, "there has to be a certain amount of re-adjustment, naturally. But we keep it to a minimum. The job-holders understand. It's all done for their own good, for the planetary good. As a matter of fact, Great Teacher, you should realize that the job-holders don't represent the total population of the planet. There are others of our society, also outside CEO ranks, who stand to benefit by such a contract. It's for the good of all. I do assure you of that. But to get back to what we were talking about, your audience is going to be almost wholly made up of Guild members. You might keep that in mind."

"I will," said Bleys.

"That was why we wanted to have this lunch with you," said Hytry. "Bleys Ahrens, you need never fear the CEOs, for the Guilds are with you."

"As they were last night."

"Yes"—Hytry broke off, frowning—"of course we were . . . but you couldn't have realized it then—just what are you referring to, Bleys Ahrens?"

Bleys laughed.

"You aren't going to pretend that those men who attacked us last night were CEO men?" he said. "You know as well as I do that they were yours."

They were just now finishing the dessert course, a frozen pudding of some kind. Hytry's fork went down with a clatter on his plate.

"You don't really think those men were ours?" he said.

"I know they were," said Bleys. He smiled at all of them. "I believe you when you say you have ways of knowing what went on when I met with the CEO men for dinner. You would have found out very quickly, but not quickly enough—am I right?"

"Great Teacher"—said Hytry, staring at him with a shocked expression—"I don't know what you're talking about."

"I'm talking about the fact that the news of what the CEOs said to me and what I said to them reached you a little bit too late, didn't it? You'd decided even before I got here that the CEOs would be able to invite me to a meeting before you could. So that I'd see them first before I saw you. You decided to let it happen that way, but turn the fact to your own advantage. You were sure, weren't you, that no matter what you had to offer me, the CEOs could outbid you; and that one way or another, either by bribe or threat, they would enlist me to speak for them, in the process of my seeming to speak to everyone on the planet?"

"Certainly not!" said Hytry. He rubbed his napkin between the palms of his hands.

"Certainly yes," said Bleys. "You were quite sure that I wouldn't be able to resist the threat, if not the bribe. You were sure that, even if I was sorry later I had agreed to their terms, I'd either do what they wanted or immediately flee New Earth, to get out of their reach. Accordingly, you sent a Tough Squad to speed me to take my speaking tour to some other world."

"But this is ridiculous!" Hytry exploded. "How could we know you were going to come out into that alley? There was no reason for you to do that!"

"Not unless you arranged for me to come out that way," said Bleys. "But it wouldn't be too hard for you to do that. You've got your own people, undoubtedly, in the CEO Club itself—for all I know one of them may even be Mathias, the Manager. Anyway, you arranged for the halls to be jammed with people and for us to be let out through the alley. It seemed to me at the time there was something of a guilty conscience in the way Mathias cooperated by pulling the door closed, locking it behind us and turning out the light; leaving us in the dark to be attacked by men with clubs whose vision had already adjusted to the dark there."

"I absolutely assure you, Great Teacher," said Hytry with ringing sincerity, "we had no pre-judgment of you whatsoever; and we were in no way responsible for the attack on you in the alley!"

Unfortunately for that sincerity, however, the faces of at least half of the rest of them around the table did not echo it. They showed varying mixes of guilt and resentment.

"Do you?" said Bleys. "Then it will do you no harm if I give you the same answer I gave them. I am a philosopher. I speak to people out of my own convictions and my view of the historic situation we're all in at its present critical moment. Both I and what I might be able to do for them would be utterly destroyed if I allowed my message to be influenced in any way by anything at all outside my own thinking. In other words, with the best will in the world, I could not associate myself either with the CEO Club, or you, or anyone else."

Hytry, although with some obvious effort, had made a remarkable transition to calmness.

"If you insist on feeling that way"—he made an effort to lower his voice—"but at least you might let us tell you what we came here to tell you, what we—the Guilds—have to offer you."

"Go ahead, then," said Bleys, "but please keep it within the twenty minutes or so we have left."

"I'll be brief," said Hytry. "First and foremost, we can offer you protection against the CEO Clubs. Believe me, without that protection you and your handful of security people could be chewed up and swallowed at a gulp."

"It would be very bad publicity on all the Younger Worlds for the CEOs, if they did anything like that," said Bleys; "as bad, say, as if your Guilds were to do the same thing. Remember I'm a member of the Chamber on Association; and I have a diplomatic passport. Besides, either the CEOs or you would be foolish to make the first move against me, for fear of pushing me directly into the other camp."

Hytry stared at him down the length of the table.

"You're implying that we and the CEOs block each other off from taking any real action against you?" Hytry asked.

"I'm stating a fact," said Bleys. "You and the CEOs created a balance of power on this world. Now it seems to me you're more or less stuck with it. In the end, you both depend upon the general population, and the opinions of the general population, for your own status and popularity. If you've paid any attention to the popular opinion on your world—which has already been influenced by recordings of speeches I've made on Association—I believe you'll find your job-holders, as you call them, look at me as something not only harmless, but also extremely interesting. I can promise them a hope of something that will let them control their lives. Everybody, I think you'll find, wants to be more in control of his or her future. Perhaps even yourselves."

Hytry waved aside Bleys' last words.

"What we were prepared to offer you, Bleys Ahrens, in addition to protection against the CEO Clubs, was some aid in building your audience. If the Guild, in effect, sponsors your speaking, you can be sure that our people will pay more attention to it—and that means nearly all the people on this world."

"Does it?" said Bleys.

"Yes, it does," Hytry replied. "We know what the CEOs planned to offer you—interstellar credit, a high payment in interstellar credits for using your speeches to shore up the job-holders' opinion of them. You turned them down, you say—as was quite right. We, of course, can't match them in offering *interstellar* credit. But if you want the job-holders to listen to your words, believe me, our goodwill—the goodwill of everyone on New Earth we represent—is worth a great deal more than any interstellar credit could be to you."

Bleys glanced at his wrist control pad again.

"I see our time is almost over," he said. "If what you say is true, Guildmaster, it's a shame that I can't take advantage of it—"

"But—" began Hytry.

"But"—Bleys cut him off—"I'm afraid I'm going to have to give you the same answer I gave the CEO Club. Few people seem to hear what I say. I've no ax of my own to grind, and I refuse to try to grind anyone else's ax. I repeat only what I've said so many times before this—I tell people what I've learned and what I've experienced, and leave it to them to apply it or not to anything they may have experienced themselves."

He stood up. Looking down on Hytry suddenly from his full height, even from the far end of the table, he towered over them all.

"It's been good to meet," he said. "I tell people no experience is wasted. No interaction with another human being is without value. I've gained by sitting here with you and listening to you, Guildmaster, and I thank you. But now I'm afraid I've got to get back to work."

Henry and Toni had risen at the same time. Bleys led the way out of the dining room, leaving silence behind him.

Once back in the private lounge, Bleys dropped into one of the float chairs that was adapted to his height.

"What made you so sure?" asked Toni, as she and Henry sat down with him. "How could you know certainly it was the Guild people, and not the CEOs, who arranged to have Mathias let us out into the alley, and that the thugs out there were Guild thugs?"

Bleys smiled.

"I didn't," he said. "But how could it be any other way? The CEOs had nothing to gain by it. Also, for them, it would have been like committing a crime on your own doorstep when you could just as well do it on someone else's. As for the Guild's knowing we'd come out that way— I don't doubt that Mathias is a Guild member."

"How can you be sure of that?" Toni asked. "Working in the CEO Club the way he does?"

"He'd have to be a Guild member legally or illegally," said Bleys. "Remember what Hytry just told us at lunch? Anyone who works belongs to a Guild. I think he told me more than he meant to—if you work on this world, you're a Guild member whether you want to be or not. And Mathias would be ideally positioned to be a double agent; for the CEOs on the Guild and for the Guild on the CEOs. In fact, I'll bet both organizations know of his double allegiance and make use of it. All he would have been asked to do, after all, was to let us out by the side door. He may not even have known the Tough Squad was there."

"All right," said Toni. "But still you had to be guessing somewhat. Admit it."

"I wasn't," said Bleys. "Add all that I just said to the fact that the attack didn't fit the CEOs' pattern of trying to influence me, at all. Harley, as I expected, gave me the donkey's choice: between the threat of a stick or the offer of a carrot. They were clearly reserving force as a later weapon. On the other hand, the Guilds, as I said to Hytry, had a happy chance to test my security force dropped in their lap, with the further chance of teaching me a lesson for the decision they were sure I would have made— whether I planned to stick with it or not—if I wanted to give my talks on New Earth at all."

He grinned at them once more.

"Also," he went on, "it gave me that chance to drop a bomb into their laps at lunch, to see their reaction—which was just what I expected it'd be."

"You told them what's not true, yourself, however," said Henry. "You've now told both the CEOs and Hytry you've no ax to grind. You know that's false, Bleys."

"Why, Uncle"—Bleys glanced at him—"what ax have I to grind?"

"I don't know—" said Henry. "And it doesn't matter. It's enough that I know it's not God's ax. But I know as well as you do you've always got a reason for everything you do. Now, tell me *I* lie."

Bleys shook his head.

"I'd never call you a liar in anything, Henry," he said, very seriously. "Of course, I've a path of my own. If I didn't, I can't think of any cause I'd have for living. I don't talk about my goal or goals, though, only because it's too early to talk about them. I want to keep my mind open to the chances that may come up later, as they so often do."

"You may even believe that," said Henry, "but I think, in your soul, you know better."

For a moment, Bleys said nothing.

"Henry," he said, then, "some day, I'll tell you everything."

He looked up.

"You, too, Toni," he said.

"I've never asked to be told," said Toni.

"No. You never have," Bleys answered soberly. His attitude suddenly changed. He ceased his lounging in the float and sat up straight. "Toni, have you checked on the weather for tomorrow? We had a clear day picked out for my outdoor talk at Blue Harbor. What's the weather to be there, tomorrow?"

"Light, occasional showers, but mostly sunshine," answered Toni.

"Well, that's all right, then," said Bleys. "Those who come will simply wear weather-shields, if they need them. They're invisible, won't take up any room, and any rain will bounce off them. Henry, you said your men would be ready for the trip tonight and for tomorrow?"

"Yes," said Henry, "I did. They will."

"Good," said Bleys, "because I want to make the last of my approach on foot to the broadcast building through the crowd; and for that, I'll want to be completely surrounded by Soldiers. I don't really believe there's any danger; but there'll be a number of spectators who'll want to press close to me, and I want them all held off well beyond touching range."

"We can do that," said Henry.

"Well, then," said Bleys, getting to his feet, "we'd all better get busy with the last of whatever we have to do to get ready to leave—"

He broke off as the sliding door from the adjoining room of his suite slid open and Dahno came in, seeming to fill the doorway not only from top to bottom but from side to side as he did so. The door slid closed automatically behind him as he took several long steps to one of the larger chairfloats and dropped into it.

Chairfloats were supposed to be engineered not to give, no matter what weight was dropped on them. But this one descended at least three or four centimeters before coming back up again. Dahno let out a heavy breath of air, stretching out in the chairfloat and extending his massive arms along its arms.

"I had a follow-up lunch today after my dinner last night with the Governor-Mayor of this city," he said. "I talked to her again today, but she's a woman of straw. You're going to have to make all your arrangements either with the CEO Club or the Guilds, Bleys. Speaking of the Guilds— I came in through the dining lounge on the way here, and it was empty. Did they leave happy, or not?"

"Not," answered Bleys.

Dahno sighed again. "In that case, I guess I've got bad news for you. I know it isn't credit you want, but free access to talk to the people. But if you're alone, either the CEOs or the Guilds can tie you up completely; and if you're talking to one of them, then the other isn't going to agree to give you anything it doesn't have to give—and that means nothing at all. They've been about a hundred years getting the present fine balance of power between them, and they're both scared out of their skins of anything that might give their opponents the edge—and both of them see you as a potential troublemaker. Did you just touch up the Guildmasters a bit, or did you do something more on the order of burning your bridges to them?"

"I think I burned my bridges pretty thoroughly," said Bleys.

"Well," said Dahno after a minute, "there's no bridge, once burned, that can't be rebuilt. If you'll give me the details, I'll see how to go about putting you back into bargaining position with them. You have to understand the situation, Bleys. I know it's ridiculous, but while New Earth's still got all the apparatus of local and planetary government, nowadays, to all intents and purposes, it's nothing but show. Apparently, in the last hundred years, its powers have gradually been taken away from it; and now the only people who really make decisions on anything are the CEO and the Guild. You've definitely got to have those two bidding against each other, because only while the bidding's going on are you going to have any freedom of action here."

"But I don't want to rebuild my bridge to them," said Bleys.

He was conscious of not only Dahno, but Henry and Toni watching him with a particular intensity. For a moment he felt a touch of that sense of isolation, the loneliness he could remember feeling all his life. He found himself wondering whether all of them would be with him at the end, if he succeeded. And if he was not to have all, which would he lose? He did not want to lose even one of them—in this room were all the people in the universe who meant anything to him.

"I told them the truth," he said to Dahno. "I said that my credit to people in general as a philosopher would be lost if I committed myself to any particular group or cause other than my own ends; and I told them those were simply giving my views of the present historic moment."

"But if you won't talk to the Guild, and you can't talk to the CEO Club—or won't, now that you've said the same thing to them you said to the Guild," said Dahno, "who in hell will you talk to?"

"I'll talk to everybody," said Bleys.

Chapter 10

The following day at Blue Harbor—a large city on a great inland lake— was as the weather people had arranged and Toni had repeated to Bleys. Sirius shone hotly down through occasional, small rain-filled clouds. Generally, he shone on the wide expanse of open field, rising gently on all sides around a circular, depressed area, bright green with fresh variform spring grass, that Bleys had chosen for his outdoor speech. There was room on those gentle slopes for up to one hundred thousand people, although less than half that number was expected.

In the center of this area stood a temporary dark brown building of pre-formed materials that Dahno had arranged to have set up. It would be large enough to hold Bleys, his broadcast equipment and his immediate party; and it had a flat roof above which his image could be projected during his speech. The situation could hardly have been better chosen.

"I'm worried," said Toni, looking out through the one-way window

of the limousine in which she, with Bleys and Henry, were riding out to
the broadcast point, with Henry's security people in other vehicles before
and behind them. Bleys looked at her.

"What do you suppose the CEOs or the Guilds are likely to try here?"
she said.

"Nothing," said Bleys. "We might run into the occasional stray crazy,
but the Soldiers should handle anything like that; and Dahno's waiting for
us in the broadcast building. I don't think we'll hear anything from the
two organizations for a bit. They'll want some time to negotiate with each
other."

Toni turned her head sharply to look at him.

"Negotiate?" she echoed. "The CEO's and the Guilds? What will
they be negotiating?"

"How to join forces and get rid of me."

"Those two join forces?" said Toni. "Do you think they'd do that?"

"They don't have much choice. I said I wouldn't work with either of
them, but of course they'll both go on trying to twist my arm to get me
on their own side. However, if that won't work, they'll both want to have
a plan for working together to get rid of me—off New Earth altogether."

"But could they work together?" Toni said. "I'd have thought they'd
never trust each other that much."

"They don't and never will," said Bleys, "but a common foe makes
unlikely friends. It wouldn't be the first time in history that two deadly
enemies worked together to destroy someone they both wanted out of the
way—"

"You don't think either one of them might try to use you to break
the power of the other then use your doing that as an excuse to get you
killed or run off their planet?" Toni broke in.

"Either outfit would have to be controlled by fools to try it. That
would really bring interstellar repercussions down on their heads; and
there's no way they could keep their responsibility for it hidden—" Bleys
broke off suddenly, gazing at her.

Toni looked back calmly. For several seconds, their eyes held, and
then Bleys breathed out softly.

"Toni," he said, "thank you. I'm a fool myself for not thinking of it."

He remembered suddenly how when he was still very young he had
gone through a period—thankfully brief—in which he had first realized
that the people around him, though they might all be adults, had never
been as perceptive and intelligent as he was. He had assumed that all
grown-ups were just like him—only wiser and more experienced—and he
had been shocked when he began to find this was not true. Here and now,
he had been overlooking one of the most obvious of dangers, simply because it was so obvious. Toni had thought of it at once.

"You're absolutely right," he said to her. "Of course, the fact they
might be doing something stupid has never stopped some people; partic-

ularly, if they're not used to looking closely at consequences. I should have realized that."

He looked gratefully at her and fingered his wrist control pad to talk to the building just ahead of them.

"There's another example of how valuable you are to me," he said to her. "—Dahno? Are you in the broadcast building there? If you are, what's the count of the spectators?"

"Better than we expected," Dahno's voice came back. "The rooftop scan gives an approximate figure in the seventy thousands."

"Good," said Bleys, "we'll be there in five minutes or less. I'm going to start my walk in shortly."

He shut off the phone connection and turned to Henry.

"I'll want to walk only the last twenty meters or so," he said. "Everyone here is going to claim that they saw me in person, anyway, so there's no point in my making more than a brief appearance. We'll drive into the fringes of the crowd and stop when the crowd gets thick."

It was barely a minute before they were among a loose scatter of people standing on the grass; a moment later, the crowd had thickened to the point where the limos were almost crawling. Bleys spoke again.

"I think here," he said.

Henry picked up the car phone and began giving orders to his Soldiers in the other limousines. A moment more, and they were all out of the vehicles, pushing through an ever-tighter press of people, with the Soldiers in a close group encasing Toni, Henry and Bleys. Bleys smiled over the heads of their protectors and waved to the people on both sides as they went, but without answering the voices that called to him.

Though Bleys found it easy enough to keep a smile on his face for those they passed, he was aware of a tension in him, an armed feeling, as if an attack might come without warning from the crowd. *I work better behind the scenes*, he thought. The tension stayed with him until at last—and it seemed a much longer time than twenty meters should take to cover— they reached the building on foot, went through the door and shut it, leaving the Soldiers outside to guard against those still thickly following.

Within, the sound of the crowd was muted. There was little space, however, and much to fill it. Chairfloats, and the equipment for broadcasting, recording and projecting his image above the roof of the building as he talked, took up nearly all the space.

Only, in a small area left clear, was a chair set up for him, on whom the equipment was focused.

"Take it away," Bleys said. "I want to talk standing." He discussed a few points with the equipment technicians—all members of the New Earth Others' organization—then took his position, cape over his shoulders, head erect, feet spread apart slightly.

"Now," he told the equipment-people.

There was a moment's cessation of sound from outside the building, followed abruptly by a rising sound of voices from the crowd. The projected image of Bleys, twenty meters tall, appeared in three dimensions in the monitors, showing it as if standing on the roof of the building. By a function of the projection, Bleys knew, he would seem to face in all directions about him at once. So that to each of those watching, his eyes would appear to look directly at him or her, alone.

He waited for a moment until almost total silence came back. Then spoke.

"You are all Pioneers and the children of Pioneers!"

At that first phrase, flung at them like the challenge of a trumpet, the last murmurs died away, slowly but completely; so that his words that followed seemed suddenly to echo into the complete and listening silence.

"While there were those on Old Earth who preferred not to leave their safe and comfortable quarters on the home world to adventure among the stars, you or your ancestors went forth and populated these New Worlds. As always, it was the best who went out. The bravest. The most hopeful. The strongest.

"For nearly three hundred years, your Younger World forebears wrestled with insufficiently terraformed earth, to build it into livable territory. They transformed wild planets into tame ones. They created a new society, with a common language—Basic—of their own. A language to which Old Earth still pays only lip service; so that while most back there understand it, few can speak it with comfort, even now. But for you, it has become your native tongue.

"You are the inheritors of what your ancestors did. And, like them, you still struggle with an alien environment; to dominate it, to make it useful, to make it profitable, to make it a place you can call home. Recognize this, all of you!"

For the first time since the silence began, it was broken. Penetrating the walls of the brown building came a murmur from the listeners outside. It rose to a low roar and then died away again. Bleys waited until they had quieted once more.

"Now you stand on the earth you inherited and had a share in making," his voice went on.

"Tell me, are you satisfied with what the effort of three hundred years has gained you? Are you satisfied with what you have?"

Once again the murmur rose to a roar, this time a little louder than before, and once more it died away while Bleys waited.

"If you are not satisfied, let us ask ourselves who is to blame . . ."

He had them with him now, and he spoke on.

Old Earth it was, Bleys told them, that had deliberately been guilty of keeping them from full development. That guilt had been shown clearly by the Mother World's attempts, first to dominate the Younger Worlds directly, then—when it failed in this—to direct and control them by indirect means.

It had been abetted in this, both consciously and unconsciously; by the Dorsai, the Exotics and even by certain elements in the societies of all the Younger Worlds. Now, for the last hundred years, Old Earth's effort had been directed and focused by the Final Encyclopedia. In stunting their growth as worlds, it had stunted them as individuals. If they would grow as individuals, they would see clearly the shackles with which Old Earth had bound them and the means to throw them off for good. They must strive as individuals to learn and think clearly about the interstellar situation. And the way to do that was to think clearly about themselves.

There were ways to do this, and he would be talking about them in his later speeches here on New Earth.

As he walked through them afterward, they cheered and struggled to get close enough to touch him.

"Hytry," said Toni, when they were at last being driven back to their hotel. She was crammed this time between the large bodies of Bleys and Dahno. Henry sat beside the driver, in the front two seats. Bleys and Dahno looked sideways and down at her.

"What about Hytry?" asked Bleys.

"He did all the talking for the Guildmasters we had lunch with," said Toni. "He acted as if he was their leader. But did he seem like a leader of leaders to you? I can believe Harley Nickolaus as the dominant one among the top CEOs in New Earth City. He's not someone I'd like to know better; but he gives the feeling of being strong enough. Hytry, though—nothing about him seems to show the strength you'd expect in the top Guildmaster."

Bleys and Dahno exchanged glances over her head.

"What do you think, Dahno?" Bleys asked.

Dahno shrugged, almost lifting Toni off the limousine's backseat, so pressed together they were.

"I didn't see him," Dahno said.

"Yes," said Bleys thoughtfully. "You weren't back from your dinner with the Governor-Mayor."

"I know something about Hytry through our Other contacts," Dahno said. "But it's not enough for me to give you any kind of sure opinion, one way or another. He's called First Guildmaster of New Earth City. But what that means in terms of his leading the other Guildmasters of that Steering Committee of theirs, I'm not sure. If this was Association, or even Harmony, I could tell you."

"Hytry did seem weak," Bleys said thoughtfully, "but there could be other reasons for his doing all the talking. He could be a puppet for the real leader. Or it could be that they decide everything by committee vote or agreement and he just announces that decision. Finally, he could be a lot brighter or a lot stronger than he pretends."

"I thought you said anyone could tell how intelligent other people are by measuring them against herself—or himself." Toni said to Bleys.

He looked down at her. "Did I tell you that? I haven't had enough to do with Hytry to be sure what he's actually like. Within limits, what I

said is true enough. But I must have told you, too, there's an exception—
for me, for everybody. At best, none of us can see any higher than the
level of own eyes. We can be sure of an equal, but we've no way to
measure a superior."

"But have you ever met anyone you thought was even an equal?" she
asked. "You've never mentioned it to me if you have."

He thought a little ruefully of his error (Henry would have called it
a sin) of arrogance. Apparently he had fallen into it in spite of his long-
standing determination not to let it trap him.

"Isn't that right?" she said.

"That's right, but"—he hesitated—"there's you and Dahno here."

"Thanks," she said. "But I'll steer clear of being compared."

"Second the motion," Dahno said.

"All right, then," Bleys said, "there's Hal Mayne. I don't know his
limits, so that means they could be anything. My guess is—just at a wild
guess—there's a chance he could be my equal or better. Or I could be
jumping at shadows; it's just that there's so much mystery about his beginnings."

"Hm," said Dahno, whom Bleys knew did not believe in the possible
importance—not to say dangerousness—of the boy they had chased off
Earth.

They were pulling up now, in front of the door to the lobby of their
hotel. They left the limousine. Walking into the lobby, they found themselves confronted by their baggage in a pile on an open spot of the lobby
floor.

It appeared to be the baggage of all of them, including that of the
Soldiers, which should still be up in their rooms. Henry, and those Soldiers
who had entered the hotel just before them, were standing around it as if
on guard. Henry glanced at Bleys, now, without a word.

"Dahno," Bleys said. "I think this is something you should be the
first to look into."

"You're right," Dahno said harshly, the normal good humor of his
expression completely gone. He stalked off toward the registration desk
and began speaking to one of the clerks behind it.

He was not raising his voice, and he was at a distance where they
could not hear either him or the man he spoke to. Bleys settled himself
in a chairfloat and beckoned Toni and Henry to join him. They took seats
and waited.

Normal expectations would have been for Dahno to return almost
immediately. But his talk with the clerk continued for several minutes and
ended with his following the clerk around the counter and through a door
in the wall behind it, into the regions behind the registration area.

He was gone a good half hour, during which time Bleys chatted cheerfully with Toni and Henry, about further plans for his tour, as if their
baggage had never been brought down to the lobby at all. The other two

were caught up in what he was saying, despite the situation. Bleys had worked at developing the skill of making even small talk interesting. He was successful with it now. Toni and Henry relaxed visibly. At the same time, however, Bleys himself was controlling and hiding a strong feeling of excitement within him. It was too soon to be sure, but he felt that things were beginning to happen.

At the end of the half hour, Dahno emerged, accompanied by a small, tubby man, wearing a dark business suit and an unhappy, determined look on his face. They came across the floor silently and Dahno was the first to speak when they reached the chair in which Bleys lounged.

"This is the general manager," Dahno said abruptly, as he reached them, with nothing pleasant at all in his voice. "He insists we were due to check out today; and that he had another reservation for the rooms, which have since been taken over by the people who had the reservation."

"I'm very sorry, Bleys Ahrens," said the tubby man, perspiring, "but our records are definite on the subject. Your reservation called for you to check out today; and the people who had an ironclad reservation for your suites and rooms have already moved in. Since they're actually in their rooms, I couldn't evict them, even if they were there by our error. As you know that's the law—in fact, a universal law on all the Younger Worlds, and, I believe, even on Old Earth itself."

"I believe it is," Bleys murmured.

"So now, I'm afraid, Bleys Ahrens"—faced with the mildness of Bleys' answer, the general manager drew himself up and his voice became more authoritative—"I'm going to have to ask you to vacate the lobby. You and your people are in the way of our guests. You've no more reason to be here now."

He turned toward the concierge's desk and snapped his fingers. There were three men in their green uniforms standing there, and they all came over. The leading one was a small man in his thirties with a deeply tanned face. His eyes met Bleys'.

"Two of you start to carry this luggage out to Bleys Ahrens' vehicles," commanded the general manager. "You, there—I don't know your name— go get a few more bellpeople. At least three more."

"Yes, general manager," said the tanned man. He turned about and went off.

"And hurry!" the general manager called after him. His round face was sweating.

"Well," said Bleys, standing up, "Toni, Henry, Dahno, I guess no one's going to turn up to help us. We might as well get going. We ought to be able to find some quarters—temporarily, at least—until we can find another hotel with rooms to hold us all under one roof. The doorman outside should know the city and the hotels."

He led the way toward the door by which they had come in, while

Henry gave orders that sent the Soldiers ahead in a kind of skirmish for-
mation.

The other three followed him. They stepped outside and into the
golden glow of another sunset, and the air filled their lungs with a freshness
that the conditioned atmosphere within doors had not seemed to have.
The passageway in front of the hotel was damp from what must have been
a brief shower while they were inside. Some of their luggage had already
been carried out by the bellpeople, but it was not waiting for them on the
sidewalk before the passageway. It was simply nowhere in sight.

A bellperson came out just then—it was one of the men, with four
carrycases, one under each arm and an extra one in each hand. Turning
right, he went off around the corner of the hotel to their right.

"Interesting," said Bleys, feeling a small inner excitement. He was
humming a tune to himself cheerfully. Suddenly aware of Toni, Henry
and Dahno gazing at him, he stopped and made his face expressionless.

But he strolled in the direction in which the bellperson had gone.
Toni, Dahno and Henry went with him. They turned the corner, but the
bellperson they had just seen was nowhere in sight. They continued along
one short, blank side of the hotel, turned again and found themselves
looking into something like a cave in the side of the hotel building.

A vehicle entrance cut through the curb of the walkway they were on
to the relatively open space that terminated in a loading dock. A flight of
concrete steps led up to it; and their bags were being piled on the loading
dock there.

The bellperson, who had just put down the four bags he was carrying,
turned and went back past them again without looking at them.

"What's got into them?" Toni demanded. "What're they bringing it
all here for?"

Bleys' inner excitement sharpened.

"I think someone's come to our rescue, after all," he said. She
looked at him. At that moment, still another bellperson loaded with luggage came around the corner, carried his load up the steps to the loading
dock, and set it down. He was the short man with the heavy tan on his
face. He stopped and turned to them, and Bleys noted that his name-tag
read *Anjo*.

"It's all right," he said. "You'll be back in your own rooms in a few
minutes. Nobody actually moved in there. I'll be back in a moment."

He went from the loading dock through a pair of swinging doors in
the wall behind it. He was gone only a few moments before he came back
with a room waiter, in white shirt and black jacket, and with a name badge
pinned to the jacket. The room-service man picked up as many of the
bags as he could handle and carried them away through the swinging doors.
The bellperson picked up the rest and followed him.

He was gone for some minutes—not many—and came back empty-
handed, followed by two more of the room-service waiters. He watched as

they picked up some more carrycases, since delivered by bellpeople. He turned to Bleys.

"Most of us watched the broadcast part of your speech, Great Teacher," he said. "Don't concern yourself. We'll take care of you."

With that he turned and went away down the steps and back toward the front of the building.

Very shortly, the last of the luggage was delivered by two of the other bellpeople, one of them a woman, this time, with dark, curly hair.

"Shall we stay and help?" the woman asked the brown-faced bellperson, who had just brought an armful of bags himself.

"No, you'd better go back," Brown-face said. "Bring those guards of the Great Teacher with you."

"Wait," said Henry, "I'll need to go back with you."

"Right," said the woman. She and Henry went off. Brown-face turned back to the pile of luggage, but it was almost gone by this time, carried off by the waiters. He picked up the last few cases himself.

"Come with me," he said.

He led them back through the swinging double doors, into a kitchen area and to a wall in which there was a lift entrance.

He punched an ordinary button set in the wall, rather than a wrist control pad, that was normally all that was necessary to give access to a hotel's customer lifts. The elevator tube they stepped into was half again as large as the one leading to Bleys' rooms; and its walls were hung with thick padding.

"Service lift," he explained briefly, punching a combination on the wall control pad.

The lift rose swiftly, then slowed. Its doors opened, and they stepped out into the kitchen area of Bleys' quarters.

"As I said downstairs, there's no one here," their guide said.

He was speaking as he moved, heading deeper into the living area of Bleys' suite and into the bedroom in which the bags belonged. Clearly, he knew whose carrycases they were. The room he led them to first, like the cases he carried, had been Toni's, and she began to unpack immediately. He led Dahno and Bleys back out into the hall and returned to the kitchen of the suite, pausing outside the doors of the service lift.

He pushed the button to open the lift and turned to Bleys. Bleys saw that the man was younger than he had assumed before. The tan was misleading. Bleys had "filed an image"—as he called it privately—of this man in his memory when Anjo had first spoken to them. The tan, and later the shadowy dimness of the loading dock, had seemed to deepen the color of his face and emphasized the lines at the outer corners of his brown eyes under the black eyebrows and hair. But the lines were squint lines from long hours out in the sunlight. He had noticed such lines on Henry when, as a boy of eleven, he had first seen the man he called "Uncle."

Anjo was no more than in his thirties—possibly under thirty.

"As I said, Great Teacher," he said, turning to Bleys, "we'll take care of you. Most of the service people at work here now will help, and by tomorrow I think there won't be anyone around the place below managerial level who won't.—Oh, I almost forgot."

He reached into his upper jacket pocket and pulled out a piece of paper with some numbers listed on them. Next to each number was a word. He passed the piece of paper to Bleys.

"Your inside lines are cut off from the switchboard, you'll find. But they can't cut off the outside lines. If you want to reach room service for food, or anything like that, make an outside call back in to the number I've printed here. You'll be put through the switchboard automatically, directly to the department you want. By tomorrow, everybody on the switchboard will be safe. Meanwhile, use the safe way and seem to call in from outside."

He pointed to the top number, opposite which Bleys now saw was written the word "bellperson" and one other word he could not quite make out.

"That's my name, Anjo." He indicated the second word with his thumbnail. "If you call for a bellperson, don't trust whoever answers just yet. Ask for Anjo. Then, when I get on, you can tell me what you want."

"Thank you." Bleys took the paper between his long fingers. "Indeed, we all thank you, very much."

"It's nothing, Great Teacher," said Anjo. "A lot of us have seen and heard your recordings before this. The manager may try to give you some trouble, but it won't amount to anything—that is, once he finds out you're up here, and he may not find that out until tomorrow. Don't be surprised though, if some people show up wanting to move in. If they do, just send them back down to the desk—"

"We'll do that," said Dahno, with a merry smile.

"Yes," Anjo went on. "When you do that, the manager will probably come up; but he really can't make you get out of here, now that you're back inside. That's the law. Just say there was someone here all the time, so that the quarters weren't unoccupied; and the bellpeople will swear that when they helped pick up baggage from here and pack your things, they saw a couple of people still here."

He started to turn away toward the lift.

"Just a moment," said Bleys. Anjo turned back.

"We're going to need to know who else around the city will help us," Bleys said. "Would you find out what you can? Particularly, see if you can find out whether our drivers will still show up with their vehicles if we call for them. In fact, if you can round up people who can speak for a large number of others, why don't you bring some of those leaders here to us, so we can plan what we'll do?"

"Be glad to, Great Teacher," said Anjo. "Make yourself comfortable now. Call for room service for anything you want—"

He broke off and smiled suddenly, his brown face looking less formal and almost as merry as Dahno's.

"—And, by the way, you won't be charged for anything you order from room service. In fact, you won't be charged for anything at all from now on unless the manager somehow forges a bill for you and enters it in the records, himself."

He turned away and stepped into the waiting lift, and the doors closed behind him. Almost at the same moment, the door to the adjoining room opened, and Henry joined them.

"I called in the Soldiers and sent them around by the loading dock with that bell-lady as guide," Henry said. "They'll be mostly back, by now."

"You told them to stay there until further notice?" Bleys asked. "You might explain to them that if they leave their rooms, they could be locked behind them. Better phone now and tell them that—but call outside the hotel and then in again to their room numbers so you don't go through a live operator. Here's a list Anjo gave me of department phone numbers in the hotel. Would you make copies of it for Toni and Dahno?"

"Yes." Henry took the paper.

"Obviously," said Bleys, "we'll have to get out of this city, unless Anjo and his friends have some place in it where we can stay. Clearly, the CEOs are showing me what they can do in the way of cutting off services and everything else to me. Something has to have happened to trigger that reaction so quickly. I'd like to know what it is, but I imagine we'll have to wait a bit to find out—again, unless Anjo and his friends can tell us."

"No more of this New Earth orange juice!" said Toni, looking at a room-service menu.

"They've a fairly good local ale," said Dahno. "It's different, but not bad. I know you don't care for alcohol, either one of you. But Toni, you could drink several bottles of this without even knowing you'd had any alcohol; and Bleys, you could probably drink three or four times as much."

"All right," said Toni, "I'll try it."

"So will I," said Bleys.

"Water." Henry shook his head.

"All right," said Bleys. "Look at the room-service menu. As soon as you've all decided what you want to order, tell me, and I'll try getting hold of them through the outside line, the way Anjo said, and see what happens."

What happened was that a very excellent dinner, including everything they had ordered, was shortly delivered to the lounge.

"You're acting pleased again," said Toni, as they sat down to dinner.

"I think I mentioned it to you," said Bleys. "Reaction is faster than action, particularly in this case. I wanted the CEOs or the Guild to act, so I could take advantage of it. You know, when we first got here, Dahno mentioned to me an unnamed third element in the social situation here—"

One of the doors of the room they were in burst open, and the same manager they had encountered downstairs stepped in. His face was ugly with congested blood and anger.

"You're here illegally!" he shouted at them. "I've called the police. Did you hear me? I've called the police! They'll be here in a few minutes to put you out!"

Chapter 11

Casually, Bleys got to his feet from behind the table and started around it toward the manager. The manager's eyes widened in his furious face, and he ducked back through the door, which closed behind him. Bleys came back to the table and picked up the fork he had just put down.

"The police," said Toni. "What about them? What'll we do about them when they come?"

"I don't think they will," said Bleys. "Arresting me would be news. We'd be on the front page of every news-sheet on this world. Even if he actually called them, they won't move without checking with their superiors, and I can't see their superiors letting them go ahead without first checking with the CEOs. The CEOs don't want me to have that kind of publicity. For one thing, it would mean we could bring a damage suit against the hotel for everything from slander to false arrest. The CEOs wouldn't like that. Don't you think so, Dahno?"

"Absolutely," said Dahno.

"Are you sure the laws here would let you do that?" asked Toni. "They may be different here."

"Not that different," said Dahno. He stopped eating and wiped his lips with a napkin. "But, come to think of it, there's no reason why we shouldn't make some publicity for ourselves out of it, anyway."

He lifted his wrist control pad and spoke into it.

"Give me a screen," he said.

The image of a screen about three feet on a side appeared in the air before him.

"Directory listing, local," he said. "Lawyers. Estate Planning." A number of names began scrolling down the screen. Names with addresses and phone numbers beside them.

He punched studs on his control pad. The scrolling stopped, the screen disappeared, and he spoke again into the air.

"Yes," he said. There was a pause while he waited and the others watched—Toni with considerable interest and curiosity. "Hello. This is Dahno Ahrens. I'm a lawyer from Association. I was directed to counselor Lief Williams, on a rather important matter, with ramifications both on Association and here on New Earth. If I could just speak to him?"

Dahno had either forgotten or not elected to make audible the answering voice. The others heard only his side of the conversation.

"—Yes, of course I'll hold."

He touched his phone to *mute* and looked at the rest of them with a small mischievous smile.

"The notion of a possible interstellar case should bring the credit signs into Lief Williams' eyes," he said.

"Do you know this Lief Williams?" Toni asked.

"No," Dahno said. "I'm just hooking into the network."

"Are you a lawyer?" Toni demanded.

"Among other things," said Dahno. "That is to say, I read all the books and passed the Board—there may have been a few shortcuts I made along the way as far as the ordinary route for becoming qualified as a lawyer goes, back on Association. But legally, I am one there. I thought it could be useful—"

He broke off.

"—Yes, counselor!" he went on in suddenly warm tones. "Good of you to drop what you're doing and speak to me. This is Dahno Ahrens . . . Yes. Yes, the brother of Bleys Ahrens. The Others' organizations we have on the various worlds come directly under my control. Oh, yes, I did say that to your receptionist, or secretary—whoever it was I talked to. As I mentioned to him, I'm a lawyer myself on Association, though I'm not in general practice. My job is advising my brother—yes, the 'Great Teacher'; you're quite right. Someone on Association mentioned your name—"

He paused, listening.

"Oh, I don't remember just how it came up, but I remember you were mentioned as someone I should remember . . . in estate planning, obviously, you get to know other specialists—"

Once more he interrupted himself to listen.

"No, no," he said. "You're to bill me—directly, of course—for this call. No. No, I absolutely wouldn't think of accepting it as a courtesy. I just need some local advice from you. Can you tell me who would be best to handle a large damage case against a hotel, here on New Earth?"

"Oh? You think so?" Dahno touched his wrist control pad again. "Could I have that name and number once more? Thank you. Yes, yes, indeed, I'll mention your name when I speak to her. No, certainly not. Now, remember, we definitely want to see your bill for this time of yours I've taken. Thank you. Yes, we must. The moment I have a little free time, you and I. Lunch. Yes. Good-bye, then."

He set his pad to *off* and looked at them.

"I'll mull a bit," he said to Bleys, "if you don't mind, about how I'm going to present our situation to the lady he recommends. I want to make an actual court action so possible that she can practically taste it. But we don't actually want one to tie us up in court on this world, do we?"

"No," said Bleys. "Or on any other world, for that matter. I want to stay personally remote, even if it carries a high price."

They finished their dinner and the police did not show up. After a little while, the phone chimed with a call for Bleys. It was Anjo.

"Great Teacher," he said. "I've some news. The Guilds and the CEO reached some sort of agreement on you this morning, after some overnight talks. Also, some of our people have already had time to do some organizing. I've got those you wanted to talk to here with me now. Shall I bring them up?"

"Fine," Bleys said. "That's what I've been hoping you'd do. By all means bring them up."

He punched the phone connection to *off* and told the others.

Still no police appeared. Anjo and five other people did—three men and two women. They were invited to take chairs and offered food and drink, which they all turned down.

Once seated, however, Anjo began with introductions.

"This is Zara Ben," he said, commencing with a small black-haired, olive-skinned woman in a tailored trouser-suit of muted orange, in her early thirties with a sharp-featured, combative-looking face. "She's a traffic engineer for the city, here; and this is Vilma Choyse."

Vilma Choyse, the only other woman with Anjo, was possibly in her late forties. She was in a light blue dress, erect, and tall and brown-haired, with a round face.

"Just call me a free-lance ombudswoman," she said. Dahno nodded at her, and she smiled professionally back at him.

The others—all men—were Bill Delancy, blue business-suited, owner and operator of a stamping company that made small metal parts. He also was in his forties, but looked, if anything, older than Vilma. He was square-bodied, square-faced and had dark brown hair, with no touch of gray, but with something of a wave to it. Like Zara Ben, he appeared combative, but much more cheerfully so. Next was a younger, tall, slim, black-haired man named Trey Nolare, who had come wearing the black trousers and white shirt of a service waiter. Last was another business-suited thirty-year-old with a lean black face, dressed in gray, who turned out to be a local newsman for one of the information stations in Blue Harbor. His name was Alann Manders.

Once they were seated, they all looked directly at Bleys, effectively ignoring Toni, Henry and Dahno.

"In twenty-four hours, your nondiplomatic people will be arrested on sight," said Zara Ben, almost with relish, the moment Anjo nodded at her. "No hired vehicle will carry you now; and you've already lost your limousines. The drivers would bring them, but the companies won't let the vehicles out of their garages. There's been a general clamp-down on you by both Guild and CEOs."

"I see," Bleys said, gravely.

"Yes," she went on, "almost all the job-holders would be on your side if they dared, but the CEOs ordered every job-holder not to give you any service. The Guildmasters said almost the same thing. There are too many eyes watching for most of the people to go against orders. We were thinking about moving you out of the city, one or a few at a time in private vehicles."

"There's no immediate rush," said Anjo, not so much breaking in as taking control of the conversation away from Zara. "As I may've said before, you've a perfect right to be here, and neither CEOs nor Guilds want to be seen publicly as deliberately forcing you to leave this world."

He stopped, with a look at Zara, who appeared ready to speak again— she had leaned forward on her float. She sat back once more, and he went on, "we can keep and feed you here. But you'll still be pretty much a prisoner as long as you're in the hotel."

"Your hired atmosphere ship—and drivers for it—are still available at the airport," said Alann Manders, the newsman. "But if you take it to the next stop on your itinerary, you'll find the situation there as bad, if not worse."

"The general opinion among us who more or less head up an organization to take care of you, Great Teacher," Anjo told him, "is that sooner or later you'd better disappear, so that neither the Guilds nor the CEOs can find you, and do the rest of your speeches on recordings."

He paused. Bleys nodded.

"I've been thinking of that. The job-holders are going to need to know, though, that I'm still with them. I may have to leave New Earth unexpectedly, but even then they should know I went of my own wish, and I'll be back."

"Both letting the job-holders know and your leaving can be managed," said Anjo. "Now," he went on, "we could hide you around the city, two or at most three to a single place."

"No," said Bleys, "we'll stay together."

"I thought so," said Anjo. "Then we take you out of the city entirely. A long ways out."

"You're a sort of explosive material, you see," said Bill Delancy, in a deep, friendly voice. "Neither the Guild nor the CEO ever imagined anything like you could come in here and upset their applecart."

"That's right," Manders put in. "Both groups have been tightening down on the general population here. Getting them more and more under their control for a hundred years. But CEOs and Guilds have both got complacent. Now, your coming and talking, and so many people showing up at your first talk and responding to it, has panicked them, confronted them with a situation where they don't know what to do."

Dahno chuckled.

"So they feel something's got to be done right away," Manders went on, earnestly. "They don't dare frame you on some made-up charge and haul you into court because that would be too obvious. They're not up to killing you or attacking you openly—yet, anyway—because that'd be very bad for their reputations, not only worldwide here but off-world as well. Also, and more important, it could damage the CEOs' strong commercial connections with the other Younger Worlds. In special, this world's necessary relations as a part of the Newton-Cassida-New Earth tech-production channel. You know that they just signed us in a worldwide production contract with those two planets?"

"Yes, I heard of it," said Bleys.

"They treat us all like serfs—or slaves!" Manders' dark face was suddenly dangerous.

"That's right," said Bill Delancy. He took out a small tube and inhaled from it into each of his somewhat hairy nostrils, alternately. "And also, neither the Guild nor the CEO wants to look to Newton and Cassida as if they don't have their working people under tight control."

"A cold?" Bleys asked him sympathetically.

Bill Delancy shook his head and put the tube away hastily.

"A sort of arthritis," he said. "The tube's something new out of Cassida from a medical research group my outfit makes equipment parts for. The nose is just a quick way of getting the medication into me several times a day."

His voice became a little wistful. "I understand that," he said, "on Old Earth, for years now, they've had a way of permanently taking care of any of the autoimmune diseases."

"We aren't really here to talk about that, are we?" Zara said. "I agree with what Anjo says. The Great Teacher and his people can stay here and be taken care of for some time. But I still think we ought to start moving them out as fast as we can, little by little—trickle them out two or three at a time in private cars from the loading dock."

"I agree," Bleys said thoughtfully. "As Bill Delancy just said, we seem to be like an explosive material—or perhaps, more aptly, like the trigger to some already-primed explosive. The deeper you hide us, the better. I seem to have happened along at a critical time on this world of yours."

He smiled at the visitors, for Toni had frowned at his last words; and Henry's face was suddenly stern.

"Yes," Bleys went on musingly, "but I've always been deeply interested in New Earth. Perhaps I could have come at a better time."

His voice had ended on a humorous note, but he glanced for a second at Toni and Henry with no particular expression. Toni erased her frown. But Henry, stubbornly, did not change expression.

"Would you lead us, Great Teacher?" said Delancy. "If it came to an actual revolution?"

"No," Bleys said, firmly. "I've said it many times, and I apparently have to keep on saying it. I'm a philosopher, not a revolutionary. But occasionally, it seems, the philosopher has to run and hide like a revolutionary. And where do revolutionaries traditionally hide when those in power start hunting for them?"

He looked around at their faces. But when none of them spoke immediately, he answered his own question.

"Why, in the mountains, of course," he said. "This world doesn't lack mountain ranges, and among them there ought to be places where we can hide, even from searching atmosphere craft, while staying all together—which is important."

Anjo gave a small sigh. "Great Teacher, that's where I wanted to take you all. You read minds."

"No," said Bleys, a little sadly. "I just use logic. But we should leave as soon as we can. Tonight, if possible."

Chapter 12

It was past midnight before Anjo could make the necessary arrangements. They went in small parties down through the now-quiet, white-walled service-ways and kitchen of the hotel and out onto the loading dock. Here they were taken, several at a time, into a variety of different vehicles.

Bleys felt an inner excitement. The same sort of strangely disturbing excitement that had sent him out on the side of the Others' building back on Association, the night following Henry's unexpected appearance to offer what help he could. But, he told himself now, it was not the same.

He had expected Anjo's appearance—or at least the appearance of someone like Anjo—representing the unnamed third element in New Earth society that was at odds with the CEOs and the Guild, as those two were at odds with each other. Anjo had not been the surprise—even the shock—that Henry had been, appearing so unexpectedly and so fortunately.

All that the present moment had in common with the way things had been then was this excitement that verged on uneasiness—as if with the inarguable good fortune of what had happened there was mixed in a potential danger of some kind. Clearly, there had turned out to be no such danger with Henry; but, as Bleys had decided there, too much luck, too suddenly, always tended to make most people uneasy. There was probably no reason for uneasiness. Still, in this case, he would probably do well to stay alert with Anjo.

But, certainly to begin with, there seemed little reason for him to be concerned. Their escape from the city began, at least, by being almost humdrum—more dull, ordinary and uncomfortable than anything else. Bleys pushed the excitement and the uneasiness from him.

Bleys, Toni, Dahno and Henry went first in the relative luxury of a delivery van—unfortunately merely wheeled, as most of the other nondescript vehicles also were—but the windowless interior of which had been furnished with carpeting, a couple of sofas and two oversized, cushioned armchairs, all non-float furniture, for Bleys and Dahno. The Soldiers went by fours and fives into the vehicles that followed them.

It was morning before they reached—and stopped briefly for breakfast at—a small town named Guernica, hardly more than a wide spot in the road. It consisted of three houses with unpainted, weathered, shake-shingles covering sides and roof of their gaunt two stories; two squatty stores and a restaurant-bar, facing the houses across a short stretch of the road.

"Don't let the looks of this bother you," Anjo said, as they stepped out of the van on travel-cramped legs. "You'll be staying with people farther out in the country."

They ate breakfast in the restaurant-bar, with more tiredness than appetite, and went on.

The upland that now surrounded them was of the altiplano desert variety, with hard, reddish earth and little vegetation. It was attractive in a stern, hard, almost forbidding, way. A land of truth, Bleys found himself thinking—but could not remember where he had read or heard the phrase, or why it should come to his mind now.

A number of cactus-like plants were the most prominent native flora. The rest of the plants—obviously imported—were small patches of variform desert grasses and bush, sown about here as part of the original terraforming operation. They had obviously been introduced both to hold down the earth which had been top-tilled, to make a soil of sorts; and to provide eatable vegetation for whatever variform herbivores were raised in the area.

"The people in this district," said Anjo, "are nearly all ranchers."

"What kind of ranchers?" asked Toni.

"Rabbit and goat." Anjo half-turned from beside the van's driver, in one of the front two seats, to speak to Toni in the back. "Beef cattle struggle up here; and even if they could do well here, the ranchers here could not compete with the laboratory-raised beef—any more than the small ranchers down on the green plains were able to compete. When the CEOs imported that lab technology from Cassida, they kept it as a monopoly for themselves."

"And the ranches died?" Bleys asked.

"Well, they're still there," Anjo said. "But they're not owned by the same people anymore."

"It seems a waste," said Toni. "I mean, on one of the few among the New Worlds on which Earth beef cattle can successfully be bred—they don't bother."

They had turned off the main highway only a few hours after leaving Blue Harbor; and from then on the roads had become more and more primitive. The road they traveled after leaving Guernica was more a barely-visible marked trail in the hard, red-tinted earth, than anything else. Their van bumped and shuddered over the uneven surface.

They were headed directly for mountains now. These could be seen ahead through the windshield of the van, looming, as the day wore on, over them in colors ranging from slate blue to deep purple and black, and back to blue again, then off to a bluish-green and finally to red. In a certain light, they might have looked forbidding. To Bleys, who liked mountains, at this moment they were like old, massive friends.

"It must be something to see this range at sunrise or sunset," Toni said.

"It is," answered Anjo from the front seat. He did not turn to say it.

They came finally to a low building at the very foot of the mountains' first steep slope, a building with stone walls and a shake roof. The walls were gray; and the shakes were grayish with a red tinge like the reddish earth—clearly made from the outer bark of some plant or tree; and each one arched upward in the middle, longitudinally, like ceramic roof tiles.

The van stopped; and, stiffly, they got out of it. A middle-aged couple—a tall man with a face as sharp as a hatchet and as brown as Anjo's, with a wife of middling size and weight, dressed in an ankle-length blue-and-white checked dress—came rushing out, followed by three girls and one small boy, in ages ranging from six to sixteen.

"This is Mordard Cruzon and Yala Cruzon," Anjo made the introductions. "And their family."

"Great Teacher," said Mordard, "we're happy and honored to have you here. You four we have room for in our home. There are tents behind the house for those with you."

"I'll be going on, to stay with some relatives," said Anjo. "I'll see you all later."

He and the driver got back into the van, turned it about in a cloud of dust, and went back along the road they had just traveled and which ran along the feet of the first slopes of the mountains.

"Come inside. Come inside!" cried Yala. "Let's get away from this dust before we all choke!"

They went in. The interior was unexpectedly spacious, with wooden furniture, and brilliantly colored rugs hanging on the plank walls of all the rooms. The rugs and furniture, like the house itself, were obviously hand-made and all spotlessly clean.

In the end, they were there for three days before Anjo showed up again, this time with a short, broad man in his fifties and with a full head of thick iron-gray hair, who showed a clear resemblance to Anjo himself.

"A campsite for you is ready," said the older man, whom Anjo had introduced as his uncle, Polon Gean. He spoke formally, with a trace of accent, as if from some Old Earth language; either acquired by him on Old Earth, or inherited. "We should start for it now. We've got—"

He glanced in the general direction of the eye-searing dot that was Sirius; placing it, without making the mistake of looking directly at it.

"We've got only eight hours of daylight to get there. It's not so far, but the last part's a hard climb."

He turned toward the couple who had played host to Bleys, Dahno, Toni and Henry.

"Mord, you got a goat-cart for me with runners and wheels both— and a team that can make the trip?"

The tall man nodded.

The luggage of Bleys, Toni, Dahno and Henry went into the goat-cart behind a team of twelve goats, harnessed two by two. Variform goats were larger and much more trainable than natural Old Earth goats, and consequently the variforms were commonly used for hauling on the Younger Worlds. For a moment, Bleys felt a touch of something almost like nostalgia for his early years at Henry's farm on Association, where he had traveled in Henry's cart, pulled by goats. Then they started off.

It took them until mid-afternoon to reach their destination. The last fifth of it justified Polon's statement that it would be steep going. Here, the skids came into play. Up on the sides of the mountain, oddly enough, there was a great deal of long, matted dry grass; and the skids operated well on this after being jacked down below the wheels. The goats seemed at home on the slopes; but as the climb threatened to become nearly vertical, all of them—including Bleys, Dahno and Toni—took to pushing the cart to help the animals.

They reached a more level place at last, an island of tall variform pines, which grew close enough together so that they almost shut out the daylight.

Bleys saw Toni, once she had seated herself on the stump of a re-cently cut-down tree and caught her breath, looking around with some obvious skepticism at the unfinished state of the camp. There were the beginnings of permanent structures built here. But it was far too completed to have been started only four days before. Anjo led them to a row of conical lean-to structures constructed of very long branches from the tall pines surrounding them, with their tips laid together.

"They're not bad," said Anjo. "Look inside."

He led them to the first of the lean-tos and in through an upside-down, V-shaped slot in the stacked branches. There was a board floor within, raised above the ground, and all the interior walls had been hung with blankets. Altogether, there was an unexpectedly cozy feel to the space inside; and a full-spectrum, hundred-year light bulb was burning under a shade which softened its light to something not too different from what they had been used to in the way of daylight on Association.

The wooden floor was partly covered with a section of red-and-black carpeting. For furniture there was a folding campbed, covered with some colorful heavy blankets, like those the Cruzons had hung on the walls of their home; a desk, and four armchairs cushioned with blankets—all hand-made. For some ridiculous reason, possibly the long, wearing trip, the sight of the carpeting seemed to move Toni deeply. Indeed, thought Bleys, the idea of these people struggling with a roll of such heavy material up that last steep section of mountainside, just to help create an illusion of comfort inside a makeshift shelter like this, was thoughtfulness carried to the extreme.

"You're right," Toni said to Anjo, blowing her nose, "it's positively beautiful. Do we each get one of these shelters? Or how did you plan to distribute us?"

"One apiece for you four—except for the Great Teacher, who'll have an extra one for his office," said Anjo. "The others with you, as they arrive by various routes, will be six to a residence—theirs just have beds. The conveniences are outside. They're camp-style, I'm afraid. If you have to go out in the middle of the night, better put on something warm. It gets cold up here."

He looked deliberately at Toni.

"This one's for you," he said. "For the Great Teacher and Dahno Ahrens, we've made them with larger beds and chairs. Will they do, until the permanent buildings are up?"

"This is going to be just fine for me," said Toni. "But when will the permanent buildings be ready?"

"Maybe only a few days. Maybe a week," Anjo answered. "We've had to scavenge most of the materials from homes around here. We didn't dare order in anything, for fear of signaling unusual activity in this district."

He looked at Bleys, Dahno and Henry.

"Will they do for you, too?"

"Certainly," Bleys said. "Your people have worked a miracle here in what must have been no time at all."

"Actually," said Anjo, "we started some time ago. This was to be a sort of headquarters for our own use."

"I see," said Bleys. "Well, I don't need to look at my residence now. But I'd like something to eat, and then a chance to sleep."

They all had something to eat—roast rabbit, of course—in the communal combined kitchen and dining room; the largest structure so far erected—and turned in to the cots prepared for them.

Waking, about twilight, Bleys went to inspect the nearly-finished building in which he would record his speeches, and which also acted as a communication center for the security setup of the camp.

He found eye-and-ear spy units had already been set up in a wide band encircling the camp. The units were placed unobtrusively in rocks and trees so that any attempt to creep up on the camp unobserved could be detected. He put on the monitor, using the controls for a while to acquaint himself with the terrain immediately surrounding them; and in moving from one camera viewpoint to another, found himself suddenly an invisible companion of Toni and Henry, walking together under the soft day's-end light that was now filtering through the high branches of the pines. Curious, he stayed with them.

" . . . You know," Toni was saying to Henry, "what was Bleys like when he was young? When he first came to you?"

"Different," said Henry. "Different—and lonely."

"Yes," Toni said, looking at the ground as they walked along, "in some ways he's the loneliest man I've ever met. I can feel it so strongly sometimes when I'm around him that it's like a deep hurt in me."

She looked at Henry. "But he has you."

"That's so," said Henry. "I love him like one of my own. But he's still alone—I believe he's been alone always—since the day he was born."

There was silence for a few moments. They continued walking along—Henry looking ahead of them, Toni looking thoughtfully downward at the pine needles. Alone in the security center, Bleys switched to another eye-and-ear unit, to stay with them.

"—Something else," Toni said then, as they moved now through the greater sunshine between the sparser tall pines near the border of their island, "if Bleys hadn't told me your name before I saw it written, I wouldn't have known it was pronounced 'MacLain.' How does it happen you say it that way?"

"Ah, well," said Henry, "the name's Scottish, you know. You know where Scotland is on Old Earth?"

"Let me see," said Toni. There was a slight pause as they paced along together. "It's part of the British Isles, isn't it?"

"In a manner of speaking. Put it that the English part is to the south of Scotland in the main island. But the Scots also lived in the Hebrides, the so-called Western Isles, off the west coast of Scotland; and it was from the Hebrides my ancestors came."

"I remember now," Toni said. "The Scots spoke Gaelic to begin with—do they still do so in parts of Scotland?"

"That I don't know," said Henry. "I don't myself, but the way we say 'MacLean' comes because the MacLeans are descended from a man called Gilleathain na Tuaidh. I don't say that as a Gael-speaker would—" he gave her one of his quick, quirky smiles—"but it means 'Gillian of the Battleaxe,' and he lived in the Isles, back in the thirteenth century of the Christian calendar. Two brothers of his—Lachlan and Lubanach—were ancestors of two separate clans of MacLeans: the MacLeans of Duart, and the MacLeans of Lochbuie."

He paused.

"—Those are other parts of Scotland, you see," he said. Toni nodded.

"In the Hebrides—or on the main island?" she asked.

"Both," said Henry. "The MacLeans lived mainly in the Western Isles at the time of Gillian of the Battleaxe; but they gained more lands on the mainland of Scotland and ended as four separate clans. When I was young, I was told that my father's line went back to the MacLean chief, Red Hector of the Battles, who was killed at the battle of Harlow, fourteen hundred and eleven, if I remember right."

"Such names!" Toni shook her head and smiled a little. "Both Red

Hector and that other you mentioned, whose name is hard to say—Battleaxe—Battles. They both sound as if they ate people for breakfast."

"The MacLeans were always a fighting race," said Henry. He looked somber, his gaze going away from Toni into the distance.

Toni's smile disappeared and she glanced at him with a touch of concern.

"I'll tell you why it stuck in my mind to ask you about your name," she said. "You see, my name isn't the way it's said—or written—either."

"Is it not?" Henry's eyes came back to focus on her face.

"Yes," she said. "My family is Nipponese—you'd probably call us 'Japanese'—but Lu isn't a Nipponese name. You'll find it in people of Chinese ancestry, but not from Nippon—Japan."

"Your name isn't Lu?" Henry studied her.

"It is—and it isn't," said Toni.

They stopped. They had come to the very edge of the island of variform pine and they stood now on top of a small cliff of bare, gray rock, that overhung the long metallic brown-green slope of the grass downward until it lost itself against the flatland below, stretching off purple in the shadow, grayish-red in the sunlight, far and far to the perfect horizon in every direction without a rise along it anywhere.

"No," she said, after a moment's pause. "Correctly, my family name is Ryuzoji, not Lu. My immediate ancestors were some of the first Nipponese to emigrate from Old Earth to Association. They didn't really plan to stay. You remember how it was—how we're all taught in the history classes in school? The coalition of many religions that bought the settlement rights to both Friendly Worlds from the large terraforming companies that were formed to make the Younger Worlds livable, had put out nearly all their credit in the hope of getting only religious emigrants to them. To begin with, there seemed to be a great many people who wanted to emigrate."

"I know," said Henry. "We've letters from my family of those early times on Association."

Toni looked at him sympathetically.

"Yes," she said, "but a lot of the people from the religious groups didn't go after all—wouldn't, or couldn't afford it—and with so few settlers on the two worlds, the coalition feared the colonies wouldn't be viable. So they began to offer bonuses to attract more immigrants."

She looked at Henry, who nodded knowingly.

"Well, my family were bonus immigrants," Toni went on. "And, as you know, along with the bonus, there was a promise by the terraforming companies to ship them back to Old Earth after five years if they didn't like the bargain they'd made. The companies didn't want to spend the money to do that, of course, but it was the only way to get enough people to go. My family planned to take the bonus and go out, build up a property that could be sold to other people who intended to stay there—and then come back before their five years were up."

She looked at Henry. "I don't suppose your family did that."

"No." Henry looked out at the land below. "My family came for religious reasons."

"Oh," said Toni. "Well, at any rate, we were one of the few Nipponese families coming out to Association, and we were widely separated from other such families. But we found ourselves in an area that had a number of Chinese families, and these grew into quite a community over the generations. Meanwhile, my family hadn't gone back, because like just about everyone else who'd come out, they had underestimated the problems of building anything worthwhile in as short a time as five years on a newly terraformed world. They'd have gone home poorer than when they came out. So they ended up staying."

Henry nodded again, his mouth now a straight line. "Even today, it's not very easy to work the land for a living, on most worlds."

"Yes," said Toni, "we know that now. But—as I said, where my family settled, they were surrounded by Chinese; and the proper pronunciation of Ryuzoji is one that sounds to the Chinese ear as if the Nipponese speaker is saying 'Lyuzoji.' So the result was that we eventually became known as 'Lyuzoji'—and finally this became shortened to just 'Lu,' and it's been that way for probably the last hundred years or close to it."

"I see," said Henry.

"But as for notable ancestors," said Toni. "Our family traces itself back, too. As I say, Ryuzoji's the family name. *Ryu* stands for 'dragon,' *zo* for 'to create' or 'to construct' and *ji* for 'temple.' The *u* and *o* in Ryuzoji are long vowels. My illustrious ancestor was a sixteenth-century *daimyo* in a warring period that lasted over a century. His domain was roughly a third of the island of Kyushu, and he probably commanded an army of samurai warriors of a few tens of thousands. In those years, a *daimyo* had the absolute power of life and death over his subjects. When he died in 1584 of your Christian calendar, Takanobu was fifty-six years old. After his death, his domain was dismembered by other warlords. Unless you read Japanese history, you probably never ran across mention of him."

"I did not," said Henry. "So, Takanobu was your direct ancestor?"

"Specifically," Toni said, "the direct ancestor of my family was Ryuzoji Masanobu, a great grandson of Takanobu. His grandfather, Takanobu's son, had sought solace in religion—Christianity in his case—after witnessing the ephemeral nature of earthly glory after the death of Takanobu and the subsequent fall of their clan. Then there was a Christian uprising in the Amakusa-Shimbara region on the island of Kyushu in 1637, twenty-four years after the prohibition of Christianity in Japan and two years after the Tokugawa Shogunate's total ban on overseas travel by Japanese nationals. Perhaps you read of that?"

"I did not," said Henry again, but this time watching her with sharper interest.

"Masanobu was, of course, a Christian; and one of those whose persecution was carried out relentlessly by the local daimyo, whose fief had the largest concentration of Christians. The local peasants were overtaxed inhumanely, and they rose in rebellion and joined the Christians. Together, Christians and peasants entrenched themselves in the Hara Castle on the Shimbara Peninsula, under the leadership of Amakusa Shiro Tokisada, who was barely sixteen years old at the time. He led the rebels with great courage, and they held off the assaults by much superior forces of trained samurai warriors for four months."

"They were strong in the Faith," said Henry.

"Yes," said Toni, "but eventually the castle was overrun, and only a few escaped with their lives—because the attackers tried deliberately to slaughter them all. One of the few who did escape was Masanobu, and so my family descends directly from him."

She stopped and smiled again at Henry. "So, you see, we Ryuzoji are a fighting race, too."

Henry nodded soberly and thoughtfully. Their eyes met and held for a moment. Watching and listening at the security console, Bleys felt a sudden twinge of something like shame for witnessing this moment secretly. It was clear that with Toni's words something like a bond had been sealed between her and Henry.

"I wonder," Toni said, after a second's silence, "what it would be like for either one of us, with what we think of our forebears—to be back on Old Earth right now, and how would those of that time look at us?"

"Whatever they felt and whatever we felt," said Henry, "it would make no difference in us nor any difference in them. We are as God made us—whether we believe in Him or not."

"He can hardly blame us, then, if we're like our ancestors," Toni said.

Henry looked at her abruptly.

"God looks at not only what's done, but at the reason for doing it," he said. "It may be my ancestors knew no better than to do what they did. I do."

Toni merely continued to look at him, as she had been since she last finished speaking.

"You have been told of my sin," Henry said. "The one I would not tell you of in the limousine."

"No." Toni shook her head. "Who could tell me? Bleys or Dahno? Neither of them have."

"Dahno does not know," Henry said. "Bleys does—my sons told him, which was wrong of them; but at that time they knew no better. If Bleys did not tell you, how do you know?"

"I know only that that pistol of yours is always there under your shoulder," said Toni. "The only times I've seen you without it were when we went through customs here on New Earth and when we went to the CEOs Club. But I've watched you with it. Do you know you walk differently when you're wearing it? And I can feel that you carry some sort of unhappiness with it. I couldn't help thinking it might be connected with the sin you mentioned."

Henry looked at her for a long moment. She met his gaze candidly.

"I'll tell you, then," said Henry. "When I was young and first went as a Soldier of God, it was for God I went—or I thought it was for God I went. But I went again and again—and I found that it was not just God I went for, but for something in me that liked the warfare and the fighting. Only . . . there is never any justification for fighting and killing. Justification may be found here, in this life, among other sinful human beings; but in the life to come—"

He broke off suddenly. Then started again.

"So I realized that my soul was at stake. I buried my pistol, nearly twenty years ago. And it remained buried until the day when I came to Bleys."

"Burying the pistol saved you?"

"It was not all, but it was necessary," Henry said. "I had thought I was doing good with it, but with each time I fought, I fell deeper into Satan's hands."

"But you dug it up again and brought it to Bleys," she said. "You've gone back to risking your soul again, haven't you?"

"Yes," he said. He did not say anything more for a short moment. "But I can save Bleys."

"With a pistol, a single pistol?"

"Yes," said Henry. He gazed out over the level ground far below them.

Toni's face paled slowly. "You don't mean you'd use it on him, if you thought he was going the same way?" she demanded.

Henry turned his head and looked into her eyes. "Yes."

"But you love him," she said. "You love him like a son, you said. How could you bring yourself to kill him, just because you believed he was taking the wrong path?"

Henry had looked away from her as she spoke. Now he looked back, and she saw his eyes—tortured, but as unyielding as stones in the earth.

"The soul is more than the body," he said. "If it comes to the choice, I must save his soul—if God gives me the courage."

They stood looking at each other for a long moment.

"You can tell him this," Henry said—and the words came out painfully. "But I don't think you're one to do that."

"No," she said. "But I have my own duty. And from this moment, Henry, I'll always be watching you."

"I know."

Neither said anything for a breath or two. Then, gently, Toni put out her hand to him; and, after a moment, he took it, as he might have taken the hand of another Soldier of God who, an old friend, was now fighting on the opposite side.

Bleys wrenched off his glasses and earphones, suddenly flooded with disgust at himself for watching and listening to them at a moment like this.

He turned and started out of the building. There was no one else in it, and he encountered no one as he crossed the small distance to his private shelter. He pushed his way through the triangular entrance and threw himself down on the long bed made for him there.

For a little while he lay, looking up at the converging tips of the needle-heavy branches forming a tight, dark point at last above him. Then he got up and sat down in a solid wooden chair before the simple four-legged table provided as a desk for him.

There was a neat stack of paper, a stylus and a folder containing maps of the camp and the area.

Bleys picked up the stylus, took a piece of untouched paper from the stack and began to write upon it.

"*NOTE*—" he wrote automatically and, after that, the date and the current hour and minute. He moved the point of the stylus a little farther down the paper, hesitated, then began to write.

"*I watched today over the spy system set up in the trees that surround our camp here on New Earth, and found myself with Toni and Henry. They were talking.*

"*I should have thought—I should have known—the full reason behind Henry's sudden appearance that day on Association. Of course, to Henry, the soul must always be more important than the body.*

"*But how could I have been so blind as not to realize he was taking the need for such a heartbreaking decision on himself, knowing how he thinks and how he feels about me—*"

He dropped the stylus and crumpled the paper into a ball hidden by the clenched grasp of his long fingers.

After a moment, automatically, Bleys smoothed out the crumpled piece of paper and looked about for the slot of a phase-shift document destructor.

There was none, of course. Getting to his feet, he stepped to the floor-mounted heating unit that stabilized the temperature inside the building. He turned up its thermostat, and it came on, projecting a small, hot wind abruptly through its vent, an aperture not unlike the wider, deeper slot in a document destructor.

Bleys waited a moment, until the air from the slot in the heating unit burned the skin of his hand. Then he fed the paper into the vent. The white sheet disappeared as it went, as if an invisible tongue licked it up. At the last, a corner of curled ash clung to the lip of the slot as if in defiance of the outrushing air. Then it, too, was gone.

Chapter 13

The sound of feet on the two steps up to the entrance of Bleys' office structure the next day, and the sound of a knock on the slab of wood provided for that purpose, made Bleys look up from the sheet on which he was drawing what looked like the skeleton of a spiderweb; but which actually was a coded version of his latest thinking on his future plans, described in terms of their combined effectiveness in working to his eventual goals. It was only a thinking aid, and unreadable by anyone else; but the habit of caution made him fold it and conceal it in a pocket of his jacket before responding.

"Come in," he said. Anjo appeared.

"Great Teacher!" he said. "I just took a chance and thought I might find you here. They said you'd just left the recording building, and I didn't find you in your own private place."

"I thought we'd seen the last of you for a few days," said Bleys, smiling.

"You would have," answered Anjo, "but something's come up. I was hoping to take care of it without bothering you, but it seems it's bothering Ana Wasserlied, this woman who leads your Others here on our world. She wanted to talk to you, and I took the authority on myself to have her brought here—though she didn't at all like traveling in a closed van; but we don't want her to be able to find her way back here, later."

"Perfectly understandable," said Bleys.

"At any rate, she just got here," Anjo went on. "She's at the eating hall, and I'll go get her for you if that's what you'd like. She wanted to talk to you alone, but this is something that concerns me and my people as much as it concerns her and hers. Shall I get her?"

"By all means," said Bleys.

"I rather expected—" said Ana Wasserlied, once she was seated with Bleys and Anjo in the office lean-to. She darted a glance with no friendliness in it at Anjo. "—I rather expected you'd keep me informed of where you were going to be."

Bleys looked at her with mild concern. "You did?" he said.

Ana's mouth opened, closed and opened again.

"I certainly did!" she answered. "After all, I'm Head of the Others, here on New Earth, aren't I? It was we Others you were going to work with while you were here, I thought."

"Ana," Bleys said mildly, "I work with everyone in the whole human race."

Ana stared at him for a moment. "Well, I don't understand! I naturally assumed we were to be kept informed of your arrangements while you're here—all of your arrangements! And then suddenly you disappear, and I have to find out where you are from the organization *he* belongs to!"

She darted a momentary pointing finger at Anjo.

"I'm always happy to take advantage of the help of any of the local Others' organizations," said Bleys. "But I'm here to talk to all the people on this world, not just those that belong to the Others. So, sometimes, I have to make my own plans; and, in emergencies, change them quickly without necessarily letting the Others know. Anyway, you're here now."

"Yes, I am," said Ana, "after days of desperately trying to get in touch with you."

She looked at Anjo once more.

"—And hours more in a sealed van with a little glowworm of illumination I could hardly read by," she wound up.

"That wouldn't have been pleasant, of course," said Bleys. "But did you have something—some particular reason for wanting to get in touch with me? Or were you just worried because I wasn't at the hotel in Blue Harbor any more?"

"Something, indeed!" said Ana. Once more she looked angrily at Anjo, then back at Bleys. "His organization has started blowing things up, and we're getting the blame for it—we Others!"

"Are you?" said Bleys. "That's interesting. Why? Is it because I'm connected with the Others?"

"No!" Ana almost shouted. "Because some of their people have gone and joined our organization, so they belong to both."

"And how many would that be?" asked Bleys, glancing in his turn at Anjo, whose face was still immovable. He looked back at Ana.

"I don't know, of course!" said Ana. "These people don't tell us when they join that they belong to this thing of his!"

This time it was Bleys who held his gaze on Anjo.

Anjo looked back.

"You've got over four hundred thousand members in your New Earth Others' organization," he said. "A good twenty percent of them are our members."

"Twenty percent"—Ana stared at Anjo—"I don't believe you."

Anjo shrugged.

"I do, Ana," said Bleys. "It's possible the people you have checking on new members haven't been doing quite the job they should. I take it you two have known each other some time, then?"

"We know about each other," Ana said. "I never met him until today. I don't even know if he's just one of their members, or their leader, or what."

"Well?" Bleys asked Anjo. "What are you, Anjo?"

"Technically I lead the Shoe—as it's called," said Anjo. "But I don't really control everyone in it. No single man or woman does. If I had, what she's excited about wouldn't have happened."

"What, specifically, happened?" Bleys asked.

"Two explosive devices," said Ana. "One went off in that side alley of the New Earth City CEO Building. The other in the doorway of the CEO Club building in Bjornstown. The second one hurt some people and may have killed some—so far the CEOs aren't letting us know exactly. But they say it was our people doing it, and of course they're right. But it was people of ours who were also members of this 'Shoe.' "

She took a deep breath.

"—And I emphatically don't believe that twenty percent of our people belong to that group! There may be a few who slipped in through our normal checks; but not that many!"

Bleys had been watching her as she spoke. But now he moved his gaze back to Anjo.

"We're twenty percent, all right," said Anjo.

"And why so many?" Bleys asked the other man gently.

"Simple enough," said Anjo. "The Shoe's an illegal organization. Both the CEOs and the Guilds supported that measure through our rubber-stamp government, forty years ago—the Shoe's been growing for nearly a century. But your Others is a perfectly legal organization, and we needed a place where local leaders could meet openly and frequently without attracting attention to their positions in the Shoe."

"That seems reasonable enough—" Bleys was beginning, when Ana cut him off.

"I tell you he's lying!" she said. "Our Others can't be—can't—simply can't—be made up of twenty percent Shoe people. It's inconceivable."

"No," Bleys answered her. "I don't think it is. Our Others organization was started on Association by my brother less than fifteen years, Absolute, ago. After I became active with it, a little over four years ago, the general pattern of it was loosened considerably. We didn't exactly invite other organizations to make use of our group on the various worlds, but we left openings, so to speak."

Now Anjo as well as Ana stared at him.

"You knew of the existence of the People of the Shoe four years ago?" Anjo asked.

"Not more than about two and a half years, Absolute," said Bleys. "I did a little private checking on all the Worlds where we have branch organizations, starting about that time."

Anjo continued looking at him in the ensuing second silence.

"If you knew about us, Great Teacher," he said, then, his voice hardening, "why didn't you get in touch with us, either before you came or right after you got here?"

Bleys answered, "My way has always been to let people like you come to the Others in your own time, rather than having the Others try to push a connection with you."

Anjo's eyes narrowed.

"Why?" he asked.

"On this world, where everybody knows everything about everybody else," Bleys said mildly, "you probably know that when I talked to the CEOs at dinner in New Earth City, I told them an anecdote as an illustration. An anecdote about what to do if you're on Old Earth and are attacked by a grizzly bear. If you know about that—"

"I know," said Anjo.

"Then you realize the point," said Bleys. "People tend to act on advice only when they can see a clear reason for doing so. I didn't want anyone joining the Others unless they came with a real willingness and a reason for joining."

"But"—Ana began, then broke off, stared at Anjo for a second—and they both looked back at Bleys.

"You're wondering," said Bleys, "how the parent organization of the Others, and particularly myself and Dahno, could think to reconcile different-thinking people on a number of different worlds, when on each world they had their own aims. Am I right?"

They both nodded.

"To answer that," said Bleys, "think of your own People of the Shoe, Anjo. Aren't they made up of many different occupations, many different ways of looking at matters on New Earth—and with very many different ideas about what should be done about it? And yet they all belong to one organization that has a general purpose—which is taking the feet of the Guild and the CEOs off the necks of the job-holders. Am I right?"

"You're right in that, anyway," said Anjo.

"But that wasn't why you formed us, certainly?" Ana said angrily. "The Others organization I joined was one that was looking to a greater future for all of us; that greater future for the race that you mention so often when you speak."

"But there are almost half a million people," Bleys said, "in your branch of the Others, here, Ana. You've got to be as aware as I am, and as anybody would be, that each one of them probably has his or her own idea of what that future ought to be like. Isn't that true?"

"Well, of course," Ana agreed. "But meanwhile they ought to all work together."

"Exactly," said Bleys, "including those who also belong to the Shoe, wouldn't you think?"

He looked at Anjo, who met his gaze with no expression at all. Ana said nothing, and Bleys took advantage of her momentary silence to go on.

"But this is all somewhat beside the point, isn't it?" he said. "You're actually here because you're both concerned about these bombings some Shoe/Others members have committed. And that isn't what I meant by the Others working together. I'm right, aren't I, Anjo—you aren't too happy yourself about that?"

He broke off. In the silence they all listened to what he had just heard, a distant droning on the air, growing swiftly in volume. He rose and led the way out of the lean-to. They followed him.

Outside, everything that was going on in the camp at the moment had come to a standstill. Those Shoe members who were still at work erecting camp buildings, aided by those of Henry's Soldiers who had reached the camp, were hastily putting any bright objects, such as carpenter's tools, out of sight. This done, they all waited and watched, although the droning could have only one meaning.

Approaching them from the southwest, at a low altitude—perhaps less than a thousand meters—was a fan-powered atmosphere ship. Not a space-and-atmosphere ship, but the type of airship built to operate only in atmosphere, at low altitudes, and capable of traveling only at slow speeds—down to the point of hovering overhead.

Bleys looked at Anjo as the most likely to have an answer for him.

"Can you estimate how fast that ship is coming toward us?" he asked.

"At a guess," said Anjo, "no more than two hundred and fifty to three hundred kilometers an hour."

"And will they come directly over us?" Bleys asked.

"If they don't, they'll come pretty close," Anjo said. "For the record, he'll want to investigate any clump of pines like this."

"By 'he,'" Bleys said, "you mean whoever's driving the ship?"

"Yes," said Anjo. "It won't hurt if we all stand perfectly still until the ship passes over. Don't look up when it's passing. It should be over us in a minute and gone again in another two or three."

They stood. The whole camp was still and silent. The ship went by overhead, its drone suddenly rising in the last moment, when it was directly above them, to a muted roll of thunder, which as quickly faded away again in the distance.

"I don't see how we can hide from that," Bleys said, thoughtfully. "It'll have camera facilities, and the pictures can be studied later by machines and experts to make out what's down here."

"They aren't using cameras," said Anjo. "New Earth doesn't have the experts—for that matter, it doesn't even have the atmosphere craft—to do a complete close-coverage of all the land surface of this world in anything less than a couple of years. The wealth this planet has built up has been put into other types of assets. So these Militia observation ships have drivers who've just been told to look for possible signs of a camp like this. Besides, since most of them are our people, they have nearly all promised us they'll report they found nothing. I'd bet you that ship was on automatic, and that its driver was doing anything from taking a nap to listening to a recording of one of your speeches."

Bleys did not answer immediately. He was looking among the people who had watched the ship pass above the thick net of pine branches that shielded then from direct view overhead, searching out Toni and Dahno. He found them both standing just outside the entrance to the eating hall. He beckoned then and, as they started to move toward him, he turned back to Anjo and Ana.

"We'll go back inside now," he said. "Toni and Dahno will be here in a minute, and then we can go on."

Ana, Bleys noted, had been silent since the craft had passed overhead. It seemed to have convinced her of Anjo's better knowledge of the planet.

"There you are," he said, as the other two entered. "Sit down here and join us. Ana and Anjo have come in because of something that's happened as a result of my New Earth visit. Anjo, you haven't been doing much talking yet. Why don't you tell Toni and Dahno what the situation is."

Anjo did so.

"Well, there you have it," Bleys said to the now-seated Toni and Dahno. "In addition to what Anjo's just told you, he was telling me just before you came over that we didn't need to worry about this airship that passed above us because most of the people belong to his organization of the Shoe and had committed themselves to give no report, even if they did catch sight of us here."

He turned to Anjo.

"I didn't say anything to that outside, Anjo, but I'll say it now. I don't operate simply because the odds are in my favor. I operate only on certainties; and there's no certainty that the driver of that craft wasn't someone *not* a Shoe, or else an agent for the CEOs or the Guild."

"You don't mean you want us to abandon this place, where they've only gotten started?" Toni said.

"I do," said Bleys. "But not right away. I think we can risk staying here another week, and in that time I'll try to record as many speeches as I can. I ought to be able to do at least a couple a day. Then, Ana, you work with Anjo here and make sure these speeches are broadcast to crowds at outdoor meetings like our one in Blue Harbor, at the rate of one speech every four or five days—always in a different location. You needn't emphasize the fact that I'm not available in person. On the other hand, if anyone asks, you don't need to hide it."

"I don't usually offer opinions. You know that," Toni said.

"Go ahead," said Bleys. "That's the reason I asked you and Dahno to join us—to hear any opinions either one of you had."

"Then I think you ought to take into account the fact that Anjo ought to know his own world," she said. There was a steady look in her eyes, more than a little determined. "If he thought this would be a safe place for you for the rest of the time on this planet, you ought to give some weight to his opinion. It doesn't seem to me, just because one airship happened to fly over, that we're necessarily in danger of immediate discovery. And it seems rather hard on Anjo's people, after they've gone to so much trouble to build this place, for us to leave it before it's even half-done."

"It is that," said Anjo. "The fact is, even if your worst fears about whoever was flying that aircraft are right, still—with nothing reflective down here and no one moving—he wouldn't see anything through the pines over us, anyway. Also, there's a great difference, Great Teacher, between your being here with us on New Earth, even if you are in hiding, when your tapes are played to large outdoor audiences. A big difference between that and your being off-planet completely when they're played for the first time."

Bleys nodded thoughtfully.

"You could both be right," he said. He looked across at his brother. "Dahno?"

"I'm still thinking about it," said Dahno. "But, in any case, I always did believe you were crowding too many things in, trying to get here and make this speaking tour and still get back to Harmony or Association for the Eldest and Chamber elections. As it is, you'd have to leave in just a few weeks, anyhow."

"That's right, Anjo," Bleys said. "I was due to be back on the Friendlies before the elections, in six weeks, in any case. If nothing else, there'll be an election for the seat I presently hold in the Association Chamber."

"Still," said Anjo, "if you stayed even that one week you talked about, we'd still have you on hand for at least the start of your recorded tapes— at the rate you said you could make them. We People of the Shoe have fought for over a hundred years to free ourselves. All we ask of you is a little time. Do you know where our name comes from?"

"I think so," said Bleys. "As I understand it, you picked it up from a revolt on Old Earth in the year 1525, Christian calendar. The revolt of some German peasants who called their group the *Bundschuh*—'the Union of the Shoe.' "

"That's right," said Anjo. "And when their revolt was put down, a hundred thousand of them were killed. Many more than a hundred thousand here are fighting for their survival as human beings under the situation we live with on our world. Over the last century, we've lost our own thousands, taken, tortured and killed by our so-called forces of the law, which are under the thumbs of the CEOs and the Guilds. Still, the Shoe survives. But it has to do more than survive—and your talks can help it manage that. Your speeches can make a unified force out of people in all sorts of occupations, people with all sorts of different attitudes, as you were pointing out a little earlier. All you have to do is take a small chance—by staying here, with the odds you won't be discovered and nothing will happen to you. I promise you our people will give their lives for you, if necessary, to keep anything from happening to you!"

"I believe you," Bleys said gently, "but a willingness to die doesn't solve all problems. Things happen that no one can change. Remember why you and Ana are sitting here together in the first place. Why don't you tell me now from your point of view what caused these bombings? I take for granted the fact that they weren't by your direction, or even with your agreement; or even, come to think of it, that you knew about them before they happened."

"You're right about that," said Anjo. "They kept it secret from me. Just as you're right about our organization having to be made up of people with different ideas about how to reach the end they all dream of—we've got our dreamers and our fools. We've also had our trigger-happy few who want to throw us into open revolt against the CEOs and the Guild, without stopping to think what the results will be, or the cost. Some of them, using your speeches as an excuse, simply went ahead and planted the bombs."

He paused and looked around at all of them.

"There was no real useful end they could gain by it; just to make a noise, to do some damage—make an empty threat, in effect. But they did it; on their own and without telling any of the rest of us first. We've caught up with them now, and they won't do it again. But there are always others—not *your* Others, but other Shoe members—who may not be quite as quick to blow things up, but who may be close to thinking they can get what they want simply and quickly, with threats. Your speeches, backed up by your presence on this planet, even if you're in hiding, can make enough of our people think about finding some better way to solution than threats or force. A way that shows the CEOs and the Guild they have no choice but to recognize the overwhelming strength of our enormous majority; under a few strong leaders, or even—if we're lucky—one strong leader."

"Yourself," said Bleys.

Anjo looked him squarely in the face.

"If I knew anyone better than myself, I'd be standing behind whoever it was, right now. I'd tell you who he or she is," he said.

"How many of the People of the Shoe would accept you in a referendum vote, as their paramount leader, right now?" asked Bleys. "I'm right, aren't I—you're leading right now by a majority approval of their sectional leaders?"

"Yes. And I do think the rank and file would give me a majority," said Anjo. "No! More than just a majority. Most of them. Those who aren't too anxious for open warfare, but aren't too fearful of it. However, I'm not sure how many of those who'd accept me would still follow me if I sounded the call to action today. But I do know how many would follow you, if you were their one leader. With a handful of exceptions, everyone would listen to you—they'd all follow."

"You know what I told the Guild and the CEOs," said Bleys. "I'm a philosopher, not a revolutionary. Particularly, I'm not a revolutionary on a world that's not my home."

"They'll still follow you," said Anjo. "And they'd follow whoever walks in your footsteps, whoever speaks in your name, as long as he or she's already proved his or her loyalty to the Shoe."

Bleys looked at him for a long moment, quietly.

"So," he said, "you want me to endorse you as the one to lead them all, in the speeches I'm now planning to record?"

"No," said Anjo, "I only want you to talk. I'm already walking in your footsteps. I'm already identified with what you say because most of it's what I've been saying for some years now. If, in some of your speeches, you say some things that I haven't said—even things that I wouldn't have said—I'll still follow what you say because I believe in you and for the sake of the People of the Shoe."

Bleys looked at him thoughtfully. He had left pushed to one side the two branches that normally barred the opening to this lean-to and acted as a bar to outside weather, so that the entrance had been clear for Toni and Dahno to walk in.

Dahno, the last to come through, had not replaced the branches; and his big body, shouldering through, might even have widened the opening. In any case, since the four of them had started to talk, the entrance had been open and a cool breeze was now circulating through it. The temperature was not so much lower outside that the breeze was uncomfortable, but there was enough of a difference for Bleys now to be suddenly aware of it.

It seemed to him that it eddied around the other three to come to him, and that the coolness came partly from both Dahno and Toni. They were looking at him with expressionless faces, but Bleys felt strongly that they were with Anjo in what he had just said, though they would not say so here and now.

"What you say, is interesting," Bleys said to Anjo, "but it doesn't change the facts, the situation or my mind—at least, in itself. Toni? Dahno? If either of you have something to say about this, now's the time."

Toni still said nothing, but Dahno spoke.

"You know what my job was on this trip," he said. "I was the one to look into political situations; and I've already told you that the regular governmental apparatus here has no real power of its own, but just lets itself be pushed one way or another by the Guild or the CEOs—whichever one is strongest at the moment. So I haven't wasted too much time with the government, but I have made some independent assessments of the CEOs and the Guild. So I'll say this. You've got at least one thing going for you, if you want to chance staying around longer. They're both massive organizations. That means they're both slow to decide, slow to act; and, in this case, both the Guild and the CEOs have got to agree on any joint action first. Until they've done that, all they'll dare do is to try to locate you and immobilize you while they make up their minds on how to deal with you."

"How much time would you guess would be safe, then?" Bleys asked.

Dahno shrugged. "Two weeks, maybe three," he said. "I really don't see how they can take any solid decision and move with it in under two weeks."

"All right, then." Bleys looked back at Anjo. "Then I'll stay here while we keep watch on the situation, and record speeches. Meanwhile, Anjo, you can tell your People of the Shoe I prefer to have any contacts with them through you."

"Thank you—" Anjo began, but Bleys' voice cut in on him.

"Understand, I won't say so in so many words in my speeches, but what I do say will leave my high opinion of you to be inferred. At the same time, I'll come down hard against the idea of any kind of physical action, like these bombings. The watchword I'll give them will be that they should wait. Wait until they're in an unbeatable position to act; and when that moment comes, to do so—but not yet."

"Thank you!" said Anjo. "Great Teacher, thank you—not so much for choosing me, as for promising to stay, at least as long as you think you can. Believe me, it means everything to us!"

"I do believe you," said Bleys. "But now, if I'm staying, things need to be set up so that when I do go, I can go quickly, and without anyone knowing it. For that, I'll need the help of both of you—you, Ana, and you, Anjo, working together."

"You know you've got my support," said Ana.

"And I don't need to tell you you've got mine," said Anjo.

"I never doubted it," said Bleys. "But we're going to have to be ready to leave at a moment's notice; and get off-planet both secretly and quietly. Ana, if you'll check your records you'll find the ship we came in, *Favored of God*, is still in the New Earth City spaceport—technically undergoing some equipment overhauls, but actually standing by to carry me and the rest out. Get in touch with her First Officer and let him—him only—know that anytime after the next four days, he should be ready on a moment's notice to lift with us for our next planetfall. He's prepared to hear this."

"You might leave that soon?" she asked.

Bleys shrugged.

"Who knows?" he said. "Also, by the way, tell the First Officer about Anjo; and give Anjo a letter from you authorizing him to speak for you. Can you get that done right away?"

"Of course," said Ana.

Bleys turned to Anjo.

"Anjo, once you've got your identification, make personal contact with the First Officer and explain how we might be coming in at any time. Also, at the same time, make your own arrangements on the same basis, so you can get us all aboard secretly through whatever spaceport security is in the way. If and when I leave, I promise you I'll be back as soon as I can, and you can keep in touch with me through Ana."

"I understand, Great Teacher," said Anjo.

"Fine," said Bleys. "And meanwhile, I'll get as many speeches recorded here as I can; and in them I'll support your authority among your People of the Shoe as strongly as I can."

Bleys stopped speaking. There was a moment of silence, and then Dahno stood up.

"Then I guess we'd all better get about it," he said.

Toni also stood up and she smiled at Bleys. The lean-to seemed warmer now. Anjo was already on his feet, and they went toward the door, as Bleys himself rose.

"I'll leave right away," Anjo said. "I'll call you at your headquarters in New Earth City."

"Very well," said Ana.

Anjo and Ana left, followed by Toni. Dahno held back for a moment. He looked at Bleys and nodded at him.

"I think you made a good decision," he said.

"I hope so," said Bleys.

"Come on, now," said Dahno. "You know you didn't want to leave so early. You're waiting for at least one more development from either the Guild or the CEOs or both, aren't you?"

"If we get one before I have to leave," said Bleys, "it'll be most welcome."

He and Dahno smiled at each other. It occurred to Bleys that their kinship caused them to understand each other, perhaps sometimes a little too well.

Dahno nodded his head again and went out.

With his going, the lean-to felt empty, and once more Bleys was conscious of the cool air coming in through the opening that was its entrance. He walked over and put the two protective pine boughs, each a good meter or more taller than he was, back into place, blocking out the draft.

Chapter 14

Anjo did indeed leave as the afternoon was ending. He was the last of the local people up at the camp to go for the next five days.

He went back down the mountainside with Ana, the goats being harnessed curiously, but with practical common sense, *behind* the cart, rather than in front. The goats were obviously used to it, and began to brace themselves and slow the descent of the cart on the slope at the edge of the pine island, like veterans. Standing with Polon Gean, Anjo's uncle, who had been in charge of building the camp from the beginning and was a permanent resident of it, Bleys and Toni watched the cart with its passengers and its goats until the shadows on the lower slopes hid them from sight.

The next morning, however, Polon came to Bleys and Toni as they were having breakfast in the mess hall and sat down with them, carrying a cup of coffee.

"There's something you might want to look at," he said to them. "If you're finished here, I'll take you out to the edge of the island and you can see it. It's pretty impressive for someone who's never seen it before."

"What is it?" asked Toni.

Polon smiled, his weathered, round, middle-aged face creasing in a slow, teasing expression of cheerfulness.

"Don't you want to see for yourself?" he asked. He took them out to the same point where Bleys had seen Toni talking with Henry over the spy system around the camp.

From this height on the side of the mountain they could ordinarily see a good hundred kilometers out to the perfectly level horizon of the altiplano. But now that horizon was no longer regular. It seemed much closer, no longer the hard semicircle of sharp demarcation that it had been before. Now there was a blurred, uncertain line where earth and sky came together.

Also, the desert below them seemed smaller; and, as they watched the horizon, it seemed to continue to grow gradually, not only in area but toward the sky; although there was no perceptible thickening of its line. It was only after Bleys had been watching for several minutes that he realized the reddish-gray, flat country before him appeared to be literally shrinking at a snail's pace, becoming smaller and smaller.

"Something's coming!" said Toni, staring out at the land below them. "What is it, Polon?"

"Sandstorm," answered Anjo's uncle, his brown face unsmiling as he watched, just staring at the horizon. "It'll reach us in another hour. Then, until it's over, no one here will risk going down, or anyone down there risk coming up. You can hardly see your hand in front of your face even indoors. When the sand's blowing all around you—it's more like fine dust than sand, really—it can get into even tightly sealed rooms. Try to touch your nose outdoors, and the only way you'll know your hand's there is by feeling it. You don't see anything, outside, when it's like that. Even the lower slopes down there are too risky to try traveling blind—up or down."

"I can believe it," said Toni.

"The only good thing," Polon went on, "is that while we can't get out, nobody can come up and find us here, either. Also, that wind with the sand in it can suffocate you in minutes, if you're not in shelter. That means you're safe here for another several days, anyhow."

"You knew this was coming?" Bleys watched the growing line of the storm.

"Everyone here knows that," said Polon. "There's a special weather pattern that says it's coming. Good thing, too, so our people down there can fort-up for it."

"No one mentioned it to us."

"Probably took it for granted you'd know," said Polon. "Just hit me this morning you might not."

"Will the sand get to us here, too, finally?" asked Toni.

Polon shook his head. "The top of the sand won't reach higher than two hundred meters above the level ground. Even the strongest blow can't lift the fine grains higher than that."

"How long will it last?" asked Bleys.

Polon shrugged. "Two, three hours? Five, six days? Who knows?"

"A five- or six-day sandstorm," said Bleys, "particularly one widespread as this—"

He shook his head.

"But it's real enough, all right," said Polon, looking darkly at the encroaching semicircle of brownness. "Though you won't find it anyplace else. Weather, land, the season of year—everything's got to be just right; and they aren't like that, all together, on any other World people've seen yet. Some of that sand starts coming a couple hundred kilometers away; in desert out beyond the horizon—a desert along the shores of the big lake we call Inner Sea, beyond where the high land here drops off gradually to lower level. These mountains stop the storm from going farther, so its circular motion will end up making it slide away to the north. Until then, if you really want to see something, wait a while more, until it's covered all the ground between the mountains and the horizon."

What he said proved true. As Bleys and Toni stood watching, the brown area changed constantly. It was now beginning to show a steady, ominous growth in size, both up into the air and across a farther stretch of flat land in front of them. But more than this, they could now see from above that the sand mass was constantly in motion within itself like a cauldron of boiling water. There was nothing about it that remained the same, for even a moment.

Polon left them after a little while, but Toni and Bleys stayed, anchored by the sight.

As it grew even closer, the height of the storm's front began to show itself, at first as a thin but perceptible line, then as a thicker and thicker bar against the horizon, until at last it was visible as an actual front moving toward them, seeming not so much to cover the ground over which it passed as to devour the very earth beneath it.

As the storm neared, it could be seen to be coming much more swiftly than they had thought before. It also gave the impression of closing in on the point from which they viewed it, although its line of advance was still apparently straight across the open landscape.

By the time the storm was a kilometer from the bottom of the mountain slope at their feet, the height of its front was plain to see. It seemed to loom over everything before it, threatening even them, though they stood high above it on the mountainside.

Now the storm was very close indeed, probably less than half a kilometer from the base of the abruptly rising slopes where the mountains began. Now it was clear that the whole mass was in continual motion—not merely moving toward them, but in motion within itself. Looking across the wide top of the storm, to a horizon that was smudged and uncertain instead of the sharp line they had seen on their first view of it from this height on the mountain, it was possible to see that the storm's whole wide body was rotating like stirred batter as it moved forward.

But the large general rotation was simply the mainspring of the storm, the largest of its movements. As the storm reached the foot of the mountain, they could see innumerable smaller whirlpools of action within the one great circling that moved the whole; and lesser eddies within these, becoming progressively smaller, down to the point where every least part of the flying sand seemed to be in an independent dance of its own. But the smaller these motions were, the more they were erratic; until it was clear that the mass was twisting and writhing in all its parts, even as it drove forward like a snowslide down an ice slope.

At last the storm reached the bottom of the mountain; but instead of stopping there, as they had expected after what Polon had said, it started to creep up the slopes; and Bleys found himself holding his breath unconsciously from moment to moment, until the creeping ceased finally; breaking down at the point where the whirling brown surge turned into something like a series of waves crashing on the shores of an ocean, except for the fact that they were finally shattered into spumes and spoutings, that tried to climb higher but could not.

They watched it for a while even after it had clearly reached the limit of its ability to climb. It was so malignantly alive, it seemed that now it should acknowledge its failure to go any farther. But, mindlessly, it continued its attempt to climb the slope, on and on and on.

"It's like an animal," said Toni, staring down at it. "How can Anjo, his relatives and these other people face living under it, maybe for days? You get the feeling that when it finally goes away the houses will be ruins, and the people inside them will be nothing but bones scoured clean."

"It's only a cyclonic movement of the atmosphere," said Bleys, "made visible by the sand it carries."

Toni flashed a glance at him that was very close to being angry. "You think I don't know that?" she said. "How you can"—she broke off suddenly, her eyes steadily watching him—"you like it, don't you?"

"No." Bleys shook his head.

"*—And I was not lying when I said it,*" he wrote to himself later in the privacy of his office lean-to, setting down one of his Notes to Memory. "*I was not lying because Toni would have known it if I had been. But perhaps she saw through my answer to the lie beneath it? I could honestly say I did not like it because I did not. I felt a repulsion, an anger against it, just as she did. But somehow, at the same time, I was feeling a kinship with it—an identity—the right word for what I felt does not exist. In any case, whatever I felt was something that linked me to it on a very deep level. I think this is a matter I should give to the mechanism of the back of my mind, with a special tag to note that the answer is important.*

"*The longer I know her, Dahno and Henry, the better I understand them; and, apparently, the better they understand me. Toni, I'm sure, to those looking at her with me, seems to do nothing for me except be a companion to me. In reality she is uniquely valuable—a counterweight to the decisions of my own purpose, the stone against which I can sharpen the edges of my understanding and decisions.*

"*When, just that short while ago, she flashed out at me with 'You like it, don't you?' I answered without thinking with what I thought was the truth. The storm repelled me—just as it did her. But she was right. Also, something about it fascinated me. It was almost as if I was glad it was there; so that I could go out and meet it, fight it, and single-handedly finally drive it back over the horizon from which it came.*

"What signal had there been in me or my words to understand that?

"I do not think she realizes how much I would like to tell her about how I feel, but how hard it is for me to imagine anyone else being able to live with my vision of what I am trying to achieve; and how much, with this necessarily locked inside me, I depend on her, Dahno and Henry—Henry, whom I had not even thought of including until he brought himself, and his own reasons for joining me— to me, just weeks past in Ecumeny.

"But the bigger problem in all this is not with how well they see through me— or into me. It is the matter of my utter dependence upon them. How I would go on if I was to lose any one of them, let alone all three? Yet, when the back of my head—against my will—goes looking forward at the future with them it seems to see only dark possibilities; in which at least one, but often all three, are eventually lost, or turn against me. That must not happen.

"I don't know; I simply do not know. I'll have to wait for the moment that comes and face it then."

Bleys put down his stylus, looked for a moment at the sheets he had filled, and then, carefully, he reduced them to ashes in the heating unit of the lean-to, as he had done with the note he had made before.

Three days later, he was still keeping up his pace of recording two speeches a day. It was the second this day, and he was beginning to blunder from weariness . . .

" . . . I have explained that growth is inevitable in all of us—" he was saying into the recording equipment.

He broke off.

"No, scratch that. I'll rephrase it." One of the women technicians brought him a glass of water. He drank thirstily.

It seemed far longer to him than three days since the coming of the sandstorm. The madly whirling sands were still filling the level land of the horizon and attacking the mountain slopes. The atmosphere among the locals was still tight-lipped and silent. But they worked with him as long as he was willing to keep going.

"All right. Starting again from just before." He cleared his throat. *"I have explained that growth is inevitable in every one of us. It is one of our instincts as a race and part of our natural urge toward survival from the time we are born. Instinctively, we learn and adapt.*

"Just as flagstones laid down to cover the earth at first prevent plants from coming up, when the shoots from the germinating seeds reach the impenetrable stone; but, in time, the shoots learn to grow sideways and come up between the stones— or to exploit cracks already in them, eventually splitting the stones apart with their determination to grow so that in the end we have stones broken and hidden by the victorious plants—"

He broke off.

"Stop," he said. "This isn't coming out the way I want it. Mark a 'hold' at that point and note that what follows will be a brief tie-up of points and conclusion—and I'll stop recording here for today."

Wordlessly but patiently, the technicians operating the equipment obeyed.

Their silence was not aimed at him. It was part of the common attitude among the local people throughout the camp. Before the sandstorm came, Bleys would have assumed that all of them up here in the pine island, safely above the whirling sands, would have felt, if anything, protected and snug beyond the reach of what was below.

He had come to realize now how many of these people must have experienced living under sandstorms before this one; and nearly all would have relatives down under the storm right now—wife, husband, children, other family, friends. If anything, it was harder on those up here because they could not physically share the imprisonment and deprivations of those who were enduring the storm down below, right now.

"Print what I've said on this one out for me, will you, please—as far as I've gone?" Bleys went on, now, to the chief technician. "I'll go over the copy and make what changes I want in the printed form. It's not that I'll be changing how I say things, so much, as I'll be changing the order I say them in. The part about the plants pushing aside and breaking through the stones is something I might use earlier as a preparation, before I get off on the inevitability of growth. Maybe the example should come first."

The small gray-haired man who led the technicians nodded.

"What time is it now?" asked Bleys.

"Sixteen hundred," said the tech-leader.

"Time for us to stop anyway, then," said Bleys. "I'll see you here at seven hundred hours, tomorrow morning."

He left the recording building. His first feeling was that he wanted only to lie down and collect the myriad of thoughts that had been galloping through his mind for the last couple of hours. But, smelling the aroma of food from the dining hall, he realized he was hungry and went in that direction instead.

He had not reached the hall, in fact he was only a little more than halfway there, when Polon came out of it and walked quickly to him, holding up his hand to stop him.

"What is it?" Bleys asked.

"Anjo came back. He was just here," Polon said unhappily, "and left again almost immediately. Dahno Ahrens went with him. Neither of them told me why. You were busy recording, and Dahno said not to disturb you. Anjo backed him up on that, and they went away down the mountain."

"I thought you told me—" Bleys was starting, when he saw Toni emerge from the hall and come hastily to join them. He waited until she was with them, then looked at Polon again. "I thought you told me no one could get up or down the mountain while the sandstorm was on."

"I meant it, Great Teacher!" said Polon. "They're taking their lives in their hands. They'll be like blind men going back down the slope. Even if the goats can dig their feet in solidly the minute they feel the cart tip any way it shouldn't, the chances are they'll already be in a situation where all of them—the cart, the goats and everything—are just going to fall, either to their deaths or so they're so badly hurt they just lie there until they die. That is, if they don't suffocate on the way down!"

He stopped and stared at Bleys. Bleys did not say anything immediately but looked at Toni, and waited. Toni, on the other hand, was already looking at Polon.

"Polon," she said, "would you go back to the dining hall and have them send some lunch over to my personal lean-to? I have to talk to Bleys Ahrens, privately."

Polon looked at Bleys, who nodded. Polon turned about and went back toward the dining hall. Toni caught Bleys' eyes and nodded toward her shelter.

"Do you know why Dahno left, or Anjo came?" Bleys asked as soon as they were inside.

"No," answered Toni. "That's what I was going to ask you. Sit down there. Take the sofa—it's the only piece of furniture that'll fit you—and I'll pull up an armchair."

They sat, and Toni leaned forward in her seat.

"I don't know why Anjo came either," she said. "According to Polon, the odds of his getting safely up the mountain were ten to one against him, and the odds against the two of them getting down again as little or less. Polon did say they could follow the land-line the technicians laid for Dahno our first day here, so he could phone-connect with Mordard Cruzon's house; and, through the phone there, connect undiscovered through a communication satellite to anyone on New Earth. I do know Dahno's been busy using that phone and land-line ever since the storm came."

She paused and looked at him questioningly.

He nodded.

"I knew that, too," he said. "But Dahno works best left alone. He didn't tell me what his calls were about."

"Well," she went on, "Polon did say, too, when I asked him, that there were sealed vehicles capable of operating in the sandstorm—atmosphere vehicles—that could fly in and pick Dahno and Anjo up from the Cruzons and take them out, over the storm. Dahno could've set up something like that by phone. Of course, that kind of atmosphere transport is too expensive for any of the ranchers around here to own. But it's available on a hire basis in large cities, if Dahno or Anjo could convince someone at the other end that his credit was good enough so that they could simply send such a vehicle, like a taxi, to pick him up."

She looked intently at Bleys. "I didn't say it to Polon, but I think Dahno could convince anyone over the phone that his credit was good enough to send anything out to him."

Bleys nodded again, slowly.

At that moment, lunch came, and their talk was interrupted until the man who had carried it in had gone out again, pulling the door branches closed behind himself.

"Go ahead and eat," said Toni, gathering the dishes that had been brought in on a coffee table, which she pulled between Bleys and herself. "I've already had lunch. Then, if you know something and want to tell me about it, it would ease my mind a lot to hear it. I don't like to think of Dahno—or Anjo, for that matter—lying broken or dead at the foot of a cliff under that sandstorm."

"Yes." Bleys said nothing more, but began on the food that had been brought in. Eating gave him a few minutes' excuse not to talk, so that he could gather his wits.

It was not really so unusual for Dahno to do something like this—to take off on some project without leaving word for him about it. But Dahno was cautious; for him to take off under such conditions suggested that something serious was in the works, somehow.

Bleys had begun their history together on Association as Dahno's inferior and, later, pupil. One who took orders and did not question them, rather than one that gave them and could question anything Dahno might do. But that situation had reversed itself, with Bleys becoming the leader, Dahno the follower. Still, Bleys had always believed that most of the people he worked with—but particularly Dahno—did best with a free hand. It boiled down to how much he trusted Dahno—not merely to be loyal, but to do nothing that was not wise or safe for all of them.

Bleys pushed away the dishes in front of him. Much of what Toni had brought was still uneaten. He sat back on the sofa and looked into the eyes of Toni's perfectly calm face, which was still waiting.

"No," he said, "I was never told Anjo was coming or Dahno was leaving with him when he went. Neither one said anything to me about it."

Toni continued to watch him steadily.

"That doesn't mean you can't come up with a very good idea of what it was all about," she said, "if I know you. So tell me what you think he was up to."

Bleys smiled and shrugged.

"I'm not omniscient, you know," he said mildly. "Also—"

He felt an inward twinge, remembering his listening-in on Toni and Henry over the spy-system on the first day they had all been here.

"There are private areas I try not to stick my nose into," he went on. "Dahno, of all people, hates anyone looking over his shoulder as he works. To even guess at his reasons for going—and if I guessed wrong, that wrong guess might confuse my own thinking later on. I'd rather leave the whole matter with a question mark for now. I'm sure his reason was good, and Anjo's reason—whether or not it was connected with Dahno's—was good."

"So," said Toni, "we simply sit here and wait for an answer?"

"Yes," Bleys said. "I don't think it'll be long coming. My guess is they'll be back here shortly after the sandstorm ends and it's safe to get up the mountain."

Toni sat where she was for a moment, and Bleys saw she was still not satisfied. She got to her feet abruptly and picked up the tray on which the food had been brought, putting back on it the few dishes that he had lifted off.

"You've got your speeches," she said, "but I've had nothing to do except walk around the camp here in the trees, talking to people and putting in time. I think I'll get busy to Ana Wasserlied on that land-line of Dahno's, examining the plans for our leaving as much as possible, ahead of time. It won't hurt to have another mind look them over and know them thoroughly—in case we leave on the spur of the moment."

She was starting to turn away toward the door, even as he answered.

"That's a good idea," he said.

Toni completed her turn and went toward the door.

"You mustn't overestimate me," Bleys said, but so much to himself that he did not think she heard him as she went out. It was just as well. His last words had been a sudden, emotional statement that he never should have made, a naked plea for her understanding.

Chapter 15

Bleys' hope as to when Dahno and Anjo would return, turned out to be justified. The sandstorm lasted only another two days, whirling off along the mountain range to the north, as Polon had said, and taking its load of fine dust with it. Abruptly, the air was clear all along the horizon again. On that first clear day, Anjo and Dahno came back up the mountain by goat-cart—only, with something Bleys had not anticipated; a third person along with them. The third person was unconscious.

"You agreed with me when I said you wanted at least one more development in the situation here before you left New Earth," Dahno said. He had come alone to Bleys so that they could talk privately, in Bleys' personal shelter, first. The unconscious—sedated, it turned out—person had been left with Anjo in the first-aid building. "I thought with time possibly being shorter than you'd planned, you might need the pot stirred, so I stirred it."

"Be a little more specific," said Bleys. He had stood up when Dahno had first come in and Dahno had not sat down, so they were now standing facing each other.

"Don't tell me I misunderstood you," Dahno said. "You generally don't open your mind to me very much, but I haven't been concerned with politics and government so long without being able to see what you'd hoped to get done before we left New Earth. You wanted to push the Guild and the CEOs into combining to make a single enemy for the job-holders. Right?"

Bleys nodded, slowly.

"It was something that would happen eventually, anyway," he said. "But I did want to see some sign of that before we went on to the other worlds I was going to talk on, and then had to go back for the elections on Association and Harmony. All right, you were correct. Now, what did you do?"

"The simplest way to get people to do things," said Dahno, "is to tell them that the doing of them is already in progress. I just put the word out, starting with people like that lawyer I talked to on the phone from the hotel in Blue Harbor. I let drop the impression that the job-holders had already more or less combined, under your influence, and that a full-scale revolution was brewing. That, with the coincidence of the two bomb-ings—but we really didn't need them—"

"Nobody did," said Bleys.

"—As I say," Dahno went on, "all this did the trick."

He grinned at Bleys.

"It'll be true enough eventually, anyway," said Bleys, "but under ordinary conditions, if I didn't exist, it would take some time yet to build to a situation so intolerable for the job-holders that they'd threaten to erupt in open revolution. Then it would turn bloody right away. Societies have centers of gravity, just like other bodies. If that center gets too far out of position, the society rolls back in proportion, to get itself back into balance; usually in a process that involves a lot of bloodshed, as in the eighteenth-century, Old Earth French Revolution. By threatening it early, I was hoping to avoid that. But I wanted to time it just before the elections, back on Association and Harmony."

Dahno nodded.

"That's what I thought," he said. "So—it's done. The Guild and the CEOs have started drawing together for mutual support. I've got some of the evidence with me—or, rather, the evidence insisted on being taken to you. Both parts of that uneasy alliance between Guild and CEOs are still hoping they can solve this problem while using it to get the upper hand over their partner. So what you're going to hear is something agreed on by both groups, but which the Guild hopes might also give them an edge over the CEOs after you've been useful to both of them. The person I brought is an old friend of yours. Injected with sleepy-juice of course, so he wouldn't know where we were taking him."

"Old friend?" Bleys repeated sharply.

"Edgar Hytry," said Dahno. "You remember, the Guildmaster who came to see you and arranged the lunch with the Guildmasters in New Earth City."

Dahno grinned at him again.

"Look cheerful, Brother," he said. "I've given you what you wanted."

"Perhaps," said Bleys. "Let's see what comes of it before we count our winnings."

"Well, Guildmaster," he said, some few minutes later when Hytry, now out from under his sedation, had been brought, had had his blackout hood taken off, and been left alone with Bleys. "It's pleasant to see you again. How are you feeling?"

"Barbarous—" Hytry muttered, blinking at him from the chair into which he had dropped his heavy body without invitation, looking like an angry, just-awakened baby incongruously encased in a middle-aged body. "Chemicals! The word of a Guildmaster is all that's ever needed—never gave me a chance . . . "

He licked his lips, sorted his expression back into something like agreeableness, and tried to work up a smile.

"I'm all right—physically—" he said to Bleys, who sat in one of his oversized chairs, opposite. "It's just the principle . . . but that's all right. All right. I just needed to talk to you, and here I am."

He stopped, as if further explanation was unnecessary.

"Yes?" said Bleys, after a few seconds. Hytry breathed deeply.

"Bleys Ahrens," he said, in a stronger, more normal voice, "the Guilds are concerned for you."

"The Guildmasters, you mean?" Bleys asked.

"No, no—" For a moment, Hytry's face almost lost what progress it had made toward an expression of friendliness. "The Guildmasters are the Guilds, and vice versa."

"I see," said Bleys.

"As a result," Hytry went on, "we're generally in favor of the speeches and the things you're doing, and we regret the fact that you were harried by the CEO Clubs to the point where you had to go into hiding."

"Yes," Bleys murmured, "I don't suppose your Guilds have reasoned with them about that. Or are they simply too powerful for you to buck?"

"Certainly not—if we need to. But, in any case, it isn't exactly a matter of relative power," Hytry said. "I'll be truthful with you. There are certain things that are more practical than others—in essentially a political sense, if you understand. They and we share the responsibility for our New Earth. The Guild, therefore, can hardly be expected to put our whole strength on the line for a visiting preacher—"

Hytry interrupted himself swiftly.

"Philosopher," he said, "—of course, I meant philosopher, Bleys Ahrens. We have a high regard for you in the Guild. We honor and celebrate your point of view, which we feel is like the one we have fought for down the years."

"I'm gratified," said Bleys.

"Gratification was not what I was after," Hytry said earnestly. "What I said was merely a statement of fact. We'd like to be helpful to you; but, as matters are, the situation stands in the way of direct aid from us. Still, we know you need some kind of protection against the CEOs."

"I'm glad to hear all of this," said Bleys, "but how does it connect to whatever you came to talk to me about?"

"Well, Bleys Ahrens!" Hytry sat upright in the chair and slapped his knee emphatically. "I'm here to tell you that we've been searching for some way to be helpful to you; and finally, I think we've found it. It means stretching a point in our structure—in our very First Charter, when the first Guild organization was formed in a little town named Apin, over a hundred years ago. But we're determined to do it. We're willing to extend to you the rank and title of Guildmaster."

He stopped, upright and beaming at Bleys.

"Guildmaster . . . " said Bleys, with a smiling thoughtfulness.

"Yes!" said Hytry. "It has to be a purely honorary title, of course. You represent no Guild and you have no conception of the duties and responsibilities of a Guildmaster—and we don't expect you to show them, in any way. You'll have only the name. But the name, Bleys Ahrens! The name is alone enough to protect you. The CEOs would never dare move against a legitimate Guildmaster."

He sat back in his chair at last, with the contented look of someone who has labored and done well.

"I see," said Bleys, nodding. "Of course, to be a Guildmaster would be a great honor. I appreciate your offering it. But perhaps you could tell me what kind of restrictions it would put me under."

Hytry stared at him. "Restrictions?"

"Why yes," said Bleys. "I could hardly bear the name without also bearing the obligations, could I? I'd guess a Guildmaster is never just an ordinary person. There would be certain social standards and other things that I'd have to live up to?"

"Well . . . yes." Hytry's face suddenly became solemn. "Over more than a century, that name has earned a great deal of respect, and all of us who bear it are conscious of that respect and act with proper decorum. You would, naturally, have to show the same kind of decorum."

"Decorum, in what sense?" Bleys asked. "I assume you're talking about how I handle myself before the public?"

"Well—well, yes!" said Hytry. "But it would involve nothing I'm sure that you aren't capable of doing. You would want to show yourself as upright, honest, forthright and—ah—fully conscious of the quality and necessity of the Guild. You would appear, I mean to say, as one who is conscious of being a part of the Guild and . . . well, you know."

"Including being committed to the Guild's specific aims?" Bleys asked.

Hytry laughed cheerfully.

"Well," he said, "we certainly wouldn't like you to go around talking against the Guild's aims. That's only common sense. And, as a matter of fact—well, yes. We'd regard it as only fair on your part if you—not exactly—endorsed the Guild's point of view and aims, but made it clear that you were, let us say, proud of being an honorary member of our Guilds' organizations. At the same time, that would be to your advantage, too, of course, since it would make even more clear that you were under our protection."

Bleys shook his head, smiling.

"Guildmaster, Guildmaster," he said gently. "Don't you remember what I said to you at our lunch in New Earth City—that I had to give you people the same answer I'd given the CEOs? I can't continue to be a philosopher and speak to people out of my own convictions and my own view of the present historic moment, on this world and elsewhere, unless I stay entirely independent. To identify myself with any cause or institution would completely destroy the impartiality of any message that I could give. In other words, much as I appreciate your kind offer, I can't accept."

Hytry stared at him for a long moment, with a face showing astonishment giving way to disbelief, exhibited almost to the point of melodrama.

"I can't believe this," he said at last. "I can't believe you'd refuse a chance like this, Bleys Ahrens. Think about it, at least for a while. I don't like to say this to you; but while I, myself, and certainly a large majority of our other Guild members are strongly in favor of everything you say and do, there are some among us who doubt your good intentions and think maybe you're secretly letting yourself be used by the CEOs to discredit the Guildmastership in the eyes of the job-holders. Also, have you stopped to think how it would improve your political standing on your own world of Association, if it was known that you'd been given an honorary Guildmastership here on New Earth? Our world and yours do a fair amount of trading together, you know. You both buy our manufactured prototypes and hire our engineers."

"And I hope we'll do a great deal more of it in the future." Bleys stood up. "However, I'm afraid that taking time to think about it wouldn't make any difference in how I feel, Guildmaster Hytry. With all due thanks, I'm afraid, I can't accept your offer."

He reached over and touched a stud on the phone unit of the desk behind him.

"Anjo?" he said. "Or, if whoever is in the communications center knows where Anjo is, will you send him to me? I believe Guildmaster Hytry is ready to leave."

Hytry rose slowly, and with Bleys pacing beside him, walked to and through the door of the office lean-to. They had barely stepped onto the steps outside when Anjo came around the curve of the structure and met them.

"I'll take over from here, Great Teacher, if you like," he said to Bleys.

"I'd appreciate that," said Bleys. "Good-bye, Guildmaster, and thank you again."

"Some things are trite but also true," said Hytry, looking at him with a remarkably level gaze. "Believe me—you'll regret this."

"That's always possible," Bleys said.

Hytry turned away, and Anjo led him across to the first-aid building and through its entrance out of sight.

Bleys was about to turn back into his office when he saw Dahno emerge from the communications building and start toward him. Accordingly, he stood where he was, waiting for the other to join him.

Watching Dahno's blocky figure plowing toward him through the thin, dry mountain air, his arms swinging loosely at his sides, Bleys found himself intrigued by the fact that, without some other person near him by which his height could be measured, Dahno looked merely stocky. A little more than average height, perhaps, but not much more. At the same time, there was something of a relentless quality about the way he moved, like an armored military vehicle in action. As Dahno grew closer, however, he began to be measurable in terms of Bleys' own building and those close to it, and his height became more apparent. It had the odd effect of somehow excusing and obscuring the ponderous relentlessness that Bleys had noticed a moment before.

Bleys continued to watch him, musingly, as he came. Dahno had certainly done something very useful and deserved to be congratulated. At the same time, Bleys found himself surprisingly reluctant to do so. In the few moments in which he stood at the top of the steps, he tracked down and uncovered the fact his reluctance stemmed from an uneasiness that, useful as what Dahno had done was, he had gone ahead and done it without consulting with Bleys first.

There was the future to be thought of. Sometime Dahno might—with the best intentions in the world—operate suddenly and silently on his own, like this, again; and that time he might do something wrong, something that Bleys might have foreseen if he had been told about his half-brother's plans before Dahno put them into execution.

But now Dahno was at the foot of the steps. Bleys smiled cheerfully at him and, turning, led the way inside. They both dropped into chairs, facing each other.

"Well, now," said Bleys. "You certainly produced some results."

Dahno chuckled.

"You liked it, did you?" he said. "It just seemed the right time for it. You were busy at the time I thought of it, and somebody had already pointed out that the sandstorm was on the way. I didn't have time to talk to you first."

"Well, you were certainly right to go ahead," said Bleys. "But maybe you'd better check with me if you ever feel like doing it again, even if time is short or you have to interrupt me. I don't always get around to telling you all of what's in my mind."

"Come on now, Bleys," said Dahno. "You'll never want to tell anyone all of what's in your mind—"

"Great Teacher?" It was Anjo's voice calling from outside the entrance to the office.

"Come in," said Bleys. Anjo entered, walked up to them and stood. "Sit down. Sit down."

"Thank you, Great Teacher." Anjo took a chair. "I imagined Dahno Ahrens just told you. We heard your talk with the Guildmaster over the connection to the communications building."

"No, he hadn't." Bleys glanced at Dahno and raised his eyebrows a little.

"It's a circuit that was put in, in case you needed to talk to more people than this one structure could hold conveniently," Dahno said. "No one mentioned it to you?"

"No," said Bleys. "How do I shut off the connection from this end?"

Dahno reached out to the phone unit on the table not too far from Bleys' chair and well within reach of the long arms of both of them.

"These two studs," said Dahno, tapping them in turn with his thick forefinger.

"I see," said Bleys. He reached out and pressed both studs. They popped back up when he released them into the universal *off* position. "So the two of you heard my conversation with Hytry. Did anyone else in the communications building listen at the same time?"

"No," Dahno said thoughtfully. "As I remember, I sent the one man who was there over to the dining hall for coffee, I think. I didn't know your conversation with Hytry would end quite that quickly. He was still gone by the time you'd finished."

"Let me thank you, Great Teacher, on behalf of the People of the Shoe," said Anjo. "As for us, the only thing we ask from you is that you be yourself in whatever way you wish to be."

"I appreciate that, Anjo," said Bleys. "Well, were the two of you pleased with what I told him?"

"Just what I expected," said Dahno, before Anjo could speak again. "But Anjo may have more to tell you."

"Do you, Anjo?" Bleys turned his attention on the other man.

"Yes," said Anjo. "I'm sorry to have to say this, Great Teacher, but I don't think I can keep the radical element in the Shoe completely quiet, particularly if the word leaks out you're gone—and it seems to me that's bound to happen eventually within a week or two after you go. Could you give me any specific date on when you'll be back?"

"I wish I could," said Bleys, "but it shouldn't be more than a couple of months, your local time. We can stay in contact by interstellar mail. I can message you from wherever I am; and you can message me back through Ana Wasserlied. You have to remember one thing. What I said to the CEOs and the Guildmasters applies to your People of the Shoe as well. If I take sides—any side—I lose all value as an outside observer. I repeat, it's the whole human race that concerns me—not any one particular element, faction, or individual in it. That's the way it must be."

"I know—you said that," said Anjo, "and I appreciate it, Great Teacher. But, you know, even given the fastest ship time, it's going to take days for a letter from me to reach you and a letter from you to come back."

"That's true enough," said Bleys. "But I don't know anything we can do but live with that situation. With everything else our researchers have been able to do, they haven't been able to find a faster way. We'll just have to put up with the delays. Are there any other particular problems you expect?"

"Why, are you leaving right away?" Anjo said almost sharply.

"Not yet," answered Bleys. "What made you think I might be?"

"Just the fact that you said you might leave at any time," said Anjo. "Also, right now things are sensitive"—his voice became a little bitter—"but then, they're going to be sensitive whenever you leave."

"I can guess that," said Bleys. "But, again, there's nothing I can do about it except leave you with as many speeches as possible. Play them at the rate of one a week, and they should have something of a calming effect—on the mass of your people—anyway. I've tried to make them so that they'll give your People of the Shoe reason to wait and see what develops. I've also promised repeatedly in the speeches that I'll be back. Were you thinking things might explode the minute I'm gone, if I don't give a return date?"

Anjo sat silent for a moment. "No," he said slowly, at last, "not right off, anyway."

"That's good," said Bleys. "Because, as I say, I can't promise any particular date. It depends on too many things. You can tell your people, if you like, that I told you privately I expected to be back in two months. But don't ask me to confirm it. Why don't you spread that word, at least among your People of the Shoe?"

Anjo looked at him starkly for a long moment before he spoke.

"I wasn't going to tell you this just yet," he said at last, slowly. "But it has been reported to me by our people, both in the Guild and the CEOs, that those two groups already believe that you've set in motion the beginnings of a worldwide revolution against them. They're planning to anticipate that by hiring up to fifty thousand Friendly troops from your Association and Harmony. I didn't say anything about it yet to you because I didn't know any of the details and wasn't able to tell you that it was something that was already not only decided upon but under way. But I think it's as good as settled. Officially, it will be the CEOs alone who are making the contract—just like a worldwide production contract. Like with Cassida. Anyway, they're going to start hiring the troops without waiting. And if they bring in even a few thousand of those, this world is absolutely going to be ripe for an uprising, all the job-holders against them both."

Bleys broke into a laugh—a comparison with his feeling about the sandstorm had come to mind—even Dahno stared at him.

Anjo looked at him with something very like suspicion.

"Did you know that was going to happen?" he asked.

"No. No—it's just that this troop business must have been behind

Hytry's offer just now," he said. "Of course, hiring troops like that was inevitable. I expected it sooner or later; and I believe you about the effect it'll have, once even the first contingent of them gets here. You should have told me this first, Anjo, before sending Hytry in to talk to me."

"The word is they're waiting only for Hytry to get back with your answer to his offer," said Anjo. "After that, they'll start hiring. As you say, it had to happen—given the answer you gave Hytry."

He hesitated.

"So," he said emptily, "your Friendlies are coming, and the revolution will happen."

"Not necessarily," said Bleys. "Those troops may be made to help your cause, instead of working against it. Don't be too quick to anticipate the worst. But a lot is going to depend on my getting back to Association in time to have a hand in making the agreement from that end. This is a matter that's going to find its decision in Friendly politics, Anjo. Leave it to me and those with me, like Dahno here. But now we've got to finish my tour on a few more worlds and get home to those same Friendlies without delay. If you want to save your World, start now on the arrangements to move us all from here to *Favored of God*."

Anjo nodded, got up and went out.

"You expected this," Dahno said.

"Patterns—patterns of history. What have unpopular rulers done since time began when they feel threatened by their own people? Hired foreign troops to protect themselves. The Dorsai wouldn't touch a contract where they acted as planetary policemen. They've made that clear for over a century. So," said Bleys, "where else could they raise fifty thousand mercenaries nowadays, on short order, and for anything less than to defend their hold on their own world?"

Chapter 16

Three days later, they left their mountain retreat; and the second day following, *Favored of God* carried them spaceward.

Five ship's-days after that, they were on Harmony, and on the second day following their arrival Bleys was having a private breakfast with Darrel McKae, Bishop of the many Repentance Churches on Association—and even a few of the same name on Harmony—as well as Chief Speaker in the Chamber of Speakers on Association, where the laws of Harmony's sister world were enacted.

" . . . you knew I was on Harmony?" McKae was asking.

"Yes," said Bleys. "That's why I came."

They were seated privately at a table surrounded by a roof garden, on the flat top of a building by the side of the ocean Harmonyites called Tranquillity—though it lived up to the name no more than most oceans in a planet's tropical zone. The early warmth of Harmony's summer was upon them, and the sky above was cloudless under the bright light of Epsilon Eridani.

Only along the horizon, the dark band of approaching clouds, touched with momentary flashes, signaled a thunderstorm an hour or so away, and the tension of invisible electricity seemed to leap and judder soundlessly in the air between the two of them. Around and below them a small city seemed, by a freak of the approaching stormlight, to cower in the unnaturally still air, for even the regular sea breeze had failed.

The city was called Worthy and had grown up around a plant to extract from the ocean minerals that Harmony's people needed badly. The plant had been a failure, but the original town built around it had survived and developed into a small, expensive seaside resort for those well off.

"Then perhaps, I should be flattered," said McKae, with a momentary effort toward a smile. There was a darkness in the skin under his eyes. "You must have been quite certain I wasn't holding a grudge against you for that time you tried to sneak into my security force."

"As I remember, I succeeded," Bleys said.

"You did succeed," said McKae. "But you didn't do any harm. So I've never had any ill will toward you because of it—aside from the fact that ill will is foolish between people in the public eye, as we two are."

In turn, Bleys smiled. "I'm glad to hear that. It was only routine just now, then—my being searched for weapons or recording equipment when I arrived up here?"

"Were you?" McKae said.

"Yes."

On leaving the private elevator that had brought him straight to the penthouse, Bleys had stepped into a tiny room with two armed guards, who had directed him into a further room with more guards, through a doorway that showed a faint regular crack along the wall and floor sides of the door frame—unmistakable sign of a scanner for unwanted objects. The guards had further hand-searched him before they turned him over to the thin, obsequious man who was now serving them breakfast, dressed in sharply pressed and clean white shirt, striped waistcoat and gray trousers.

By contrast, McKae was almost ostentatiously casual, in a wide-collared pink shirt and smoke-gray trousers. He had put on some weight since Bleys had first met him, nearly five years before. Not much, but enough to obscure his earlier almost-youthful slimness. His jawline had thickened and his face broadened, giving him something of a leonine appearance.

"Well," he said now, "I didn't know. But the search was routine—you can guess that. I wasn't told you were on Harmony, and only a few trusted people get in to me, unsearched. I'm still surprised you knew I was here."

"You're too modest," said Bleys.

"Not at all. In your case, common knowledge was that you were still on New Earth. You forget you're quite a public figure yourself, these days. I could answer that you're also being over-modest," said McKae.

"Both worlds," said Bleys, "know the next elections on Association and Harmony have been scheduled together, to see who gets the most votes for Chief Speaker on his own world. And the hopes of Harmony's Brother Williams being re-elected here—let alone getting more votes than you on Association—aren't considerable. With any reasonable switch of Harmony votes away from the good Bishop, your chances of being declared Eldest over both worlds is pretty good. It doesn't hurt that Harmony's a little upset over the shortage of funds for the new Core Tap they've been building."

McKae chuckled. "Now, you know, I never count the duties the Lord sends me until they're revealed. But even if I did have high hopes of becoming Eldest, why should that bring you to me from New Earth— unless you decided to cut your speaking tour there short?"

"No," said Bleys, "I'll be going back, sometime after the election. It's just that seeing you right now was more important."

McKae nodded. "Maybe it's a good thing the doorway checked you for weapons and recording equipment," he said. "This breakfast of ours sounds as if we're getting into areas I'd not want anyone but myself to have on record."

Bleys smiled agreeably. He did not need to carry a recorder; since he had been five years old, his memory had been able to flawlessly reproduce any conversation he took part in. Nor did he need such a recording as any kind of proof. But he would detail the talk for Toni, along with his interpretations of McKae's reactions—it would be interesting to get her reaction to McKae.

"The thought occurred to me that maybe I could lend you a hand— just to make it more sure you'd become Eldest," Bleys murmured. "As you say, counting your duties ahead of time is a foolish thing. But I know you've a few churches here on Harmony, and you'll probably be gaining more even between now and the election. The only question is how many, and how many Harmony voters will they represent?"

"Of course," said McKae, his eyes steady on Bleys.

"I was just thinking," went on Bleys, "of making a few speeches of my own on this world, speeches emphasizing that I'm a philosopher only, of course, but still speaking of the advantages—not of you specifically— but of an Eldest over both worlds again for the first time in years—an Eldest with qualifications much like yours. Young, recently and exceptionally successful as the Founder of a new Church . . . "

"I see," said McKae.

"After all," Bleys went on, "Harmony and Association have always done best led by a single strong hand. There's the remarkable example of

Eldest Bright, a hundred years ago. Our two worlds made their greatest progress for thirty-eight years, absolute, with him as shepherd of both."

"He made some mistakes," said McKae. "Still—never mind that. It's good of you to think you might help me this way. But what brings about this charity?"

"I wasn't exactly thinking of it as charity," said Bleys. "I thought you might want to do me a kindness in return sometime."

"Well, now." McKae sat back in his chair. The breakfast laid out between the two men at the table had scarcely been touched by either one of them. "Now, I feel much more comfortable. I always like to know what I might owe someone else. If I don't, there's always a little feeling of uneasiness. You understand?"

"Of course," Bleys said. "I'm familiar with that feeling, myself."

"Well, then, this has to go both ways. If you help me, I'd want to be able to show my gratitude—if it was possible. Is there anything specific you can think of now, that I might be able to do for you?"

"Yes," said Bleys. "If you're chosen, of course, you'll be in a position to name someone to the only other office that appears only when our two Friendly Worlds join in choosing an Eldest."

"You mean," McKae said. He broke off and ran the tip of his tongue over his lips. "The First Elder. The one who would replace me if anything made me incapable of holding office."

"Yes," said Bleys. "It would give you a form of double insurance; since I think I've proved that my interests don't run toward holding any working public office. In case anything actually happened to incapacitate you, I'd throw the choice of a replacement into election in the Chambers of both worlds—which is the First Elder's right, as you know. Meanwhile, however, the title of that office would give me added respect on other New Worlds I'll be visiting."

"I see," said McKae. He wet his lips again. "You know, this breakfast could stand a little wine with it." He looked over his shoulder, but the checkered waistcoat of their server was already moving toward them from a discreet distance, now almost within reach. "Some of the yellow Tresbon, I think."

"Right away, my Bishop," murmured the server and was gone.

"You'll join me, won't you, Bleys Ahrens?" said McKae, a few minutes later, watching the lightly-yellow-tinted wine poured into the slim glass that had been placed before him. "I know you're a fruit-juice addict; but even on a brother world like this the juices are bound to taste differently—and I think you'll like this—one of Harmony's best wines."

"On an occasion like this, yes," said Bleys, watching a wineglass being filled for him as well.

"You need to take it with a good, full swallow, to get the full fruitiness of it in the back of your throat," said McKae, having just done so. "So many people make the mistake of just sipping."

"I see what you mean," said Bleys. It was a cool, semi-sweet beverage, tasting very much the same as most wines of its type. Pleasant enough, but he had worked too hard over the years to put a razor edge on his mind, to carelessly let it be dulled even slightly now, without good reason. However, in this case, McKae was taking the lead; and even with the extra kilograms McKae had put on, Bleys' own size made him outweigh the other man considerably.

"Now," said McKae, watching his own glass being refilled, "to get back to what we were talking about."

"Yes," said Bleys, and paused, looking at the server.

"Leave us to ourselves, Isaiah," said McKae. They both watched the server withdraw into the elevator housing at the far end of the roof.

"As it happens," said Bleys into the momentary silence, "I've been thinking of resigning my present seat in the Association Chamber—my brother Dahno will take it over—and I'd be perfectly free to accept your appointment."

McKae poured himself another glass of wine from the bottle that stood on the table and this time he sipped, himself, rather than swallowing as he had on his first glassful.

"Yes," he said quietly, his eyes on his wineglass, "as you said, it's a special office, of course, that comes into existence only when an Eldest is chosen, anyway. There's no administrative power at all involved—you know that? Only a yearly stipend, but too small a one, I think, to make any real difference to someone like yourself, with interstellar credit coming in from your Other organization. No real duties, of course . . . "

He looked up across the table at Bleys. "But you're not expecting, I hope, that I'm going to experience any inability in office."

Bleys laughed. "I hope not, too. I'll be talking on a number of the other New Worlds, starting with those that already have organizations of Others on them; and my schedule for the foreseeable future is very tight. Aside from how I'd feel if you had to give up the office, I can't afford the time to come back here and supervise a two-chamber election of a new Eldest to fill out your term."

"Yes. I see, I see . . . " said McKae, nodding. He poured himself a third glass, "Oh, forgive me. I didn't notice your glass was empty—last I looked, it was still almost full."

Bleys watched him refill it.

"Well, now," McKae went on, "the appointment's a reasonable return for the good you might be able to do me if you speak here on Harmony in the next couple of weeks. But then—forgive me—you might not turn out to be all that helpful. To be truthful, I think I ought to win handily, even without your help."

He smiled at Bleys and drank again.

"Oh, I think you will—barring the unexpected," said Bleys. "However, you don't want to stay Eldest just until the next election on both worlds. You'd want to beat Eldest Bright's terms in office—a series of re-elections. Moreover, right now both Harmony and Association are struggling with a lack of finances. What if you could come into office and make an agreement with New Earth to hire fifty thousand mercenary soldiers from our two planets? Harmony, for instance, could see coming the funds to drive that new Core Tap they need so badly for extra energy—"

McKae had leaned sharply forward in his chair.

"Of course!" he said. "And our own Association could have a half a dozen things that it needs right now; including replacing some of our outworn heavy machinery!"

His face changed, although his body still stayed alert.

"But why should New Earth do something like that?" his eyes watched Bleys.

"Quite simply," said Bleys. "You'll want to check up on this yourself, of course, but just before I left—and in fact, the reason I left and came directly here to talk to you—was that I'd just gotten word that the Guild and the CEO Clubs on New Earth had made an alliance for the hiring of that many mercenary troops; which they'd only be able to get from our Friendly worlds, since the Dorsai are for hire nowadays only as field or staff officers—and their price is too high, anyway."

"And what would make the Guilds and CEOs do that?" McKae asked.

"I believe my going back there and going on with my talks there might have something to do with it," said Bleys. "I don't know how close a watch your people have kept on the New Earth situation; but you must know that the overwhelming majority of those on the planet—people who call themselves simply 'job-holders'—are connected under the control of a very powerful organization called the Shoe. The Shoe has assured me—their leader has assured me—that if I keep my speeches going, they can organize even more strongly behind what I say; and the result might be something very like a revolution in the situation existing now on that planet."

"Revolution . . . " McKae murmured.

"Yes," said Bleys, "the people they represent, both in the Shoe and the general job-holders, are fed up to the teeth with what the CEOs and the Guilds have done to them over the last century. Consequently, the kind of force that the CEOs and Guilds will need to stay in power will be at least the fifty thousand mercenary soldiers I mentioned, and which they can get only from us. If you win the election—from you."

McKae watched him for a moment longer, then nodded slowly. The expression on his face did not change.

"But," said Bleys, "it all depends on circumstances, the greatest of which is whether I go back there in person. I've said repeatedly there I'm against any kind of violence. But the job-holders listen to other words I say, too. In brief, if I continue to talk there, the revolution, in one form or another, is virtually certain to threaten—unless the CEOs and Guilds have power enough to put it down in its early stages. This has become critical, as you probably know, because the CEOs just recently signed a full-planet commercial agreement with Cassida."

McKae stayed still, watching him quietly.

"It's one of those fortunate encounters that happen in life," said Bleys quietly, when McKae still said nothing. "Two instances that might otherwise be unrelated become important only when hooked together. It's not that such things can't happen or don't happen—but just that it requires seeing the possibility they could happen and taking advantage of it. It just happens that my speaking both here and there could be a key to it. I was hoping that you might want to take advantage of this situation."

"You'd be heading right back for New Earth, then?" McKae asked.

"Not right back, but I'd been thinking of returning after I've spent a couple of weeks giving talks around Harmony on my own subject," said Bleys. "I've got some business right after that on Cassida and Newton for a little while. This produces a sort of convenient interlude, as it turns out, that should give time for your election and appointment of me as First Elder to take place. Meanwhile, of course, Dahno Ahrens can be running in my home district for my seat in the Association Chamber. There's no doubt he'll win if he does. He's much better liked there than I am. In fact, if it hadn't been for his help, I wouldn't have gotten that seat in the first place."

Bleys stopped speaking. The silence between them lengthened.

"Well, you'll want to think it over." Bleys got to his feet.

"Wait!" said McKae. He started to rise himself, and then the obvious awareness that Bleys would then be looking down at him from a somewhat uncomfortable difference in height seemed to penetrate him. He sank back into his seat. "It's an excellent idea. I just want to think about it for a few days, naturally. But I'm sure my final decision is going to be to go along with you on this."

Then he stood up. "To our working together in the future, then." McKae extended his hand.

Bleys enclosed it in his own.

"By all means," said Bleys. "I need to be getting back too, then."

He glanced at the sky.

"—And we'll both get wet if we stay here much longer."

"That's right. I'll be in touch shortly," McKae said.

He stood where he was as Bleys turned and walked back to the elevator housing. He did not look back. Bleys had already dismissed McKae from his mind and was thinking about Dahno, who would not be pleased.

Chapter 17

Dahno was not pleased. His normal good humor and optimism, which was as enormous as his physical self and had a tendency to swamp those close about him with his emotion of the moment—a fact of which he was aware and which he used to gain his own ends—was in one of its rare absences.

It was the afternoon following Bleys' talk with McKae; and Dahno, Bleys and Toni were sitting together in a hotel in another city, some hundred and twenty kilometers from Worthy, in the main room of the apartment that was part of Bleys' headquarters here on Harmony.

"—It makes no sense. No sense on half a dozen counts!" Dahno was saying. He sprang to his feet. "I'm needed with you; and I'll be needed more on Cassida. on Newton, if you go there first before going back to New Earth. Our Friendlies' elections are only a few weeks off. I'd have to leave for Association right now, and you wouldn't see me again until halfway through your Newton trip. And what for? All to put on a show. I can run for that seat in the Chamber without ever setting foot in our home district. You know that. It's only to make an impression on McKae. If he goes along with you, it won't be because of anything I do or don't do. You can forget something that minor—it never counts!"

Bleys had long since given up trying to explain to any other human being that there was nothing so minor that it did not have the possibility of making a crucial difference in human history if conditions favored it.

"—So what are you going to do without me?" Dahno was saying. "I don't mean just without me here on Harmony. I'll grant you, you can handle that yourself. But what about being without me on Cassida and Newton? We've always worked together: you up front in the open, and me behind the scenes, feeding you information about people so that you can work effectively with them."

"I've told you why, before this," Bleys said gently. "Much of the time, I don't know exactly what I'm just about to do. I'm working with individuals and societies continually in a state of growth and change. I have to adapt and invent as I go."

"You have to have some plans," said Dahno.

"Not that I could be sure enough about to announce," Bleys said. "Suppose, when I grew up on Henry's farm, there had been a faint, misty mountain on the far horizon; and I'd told myself someday I'd go there. But, when I finally got the chance to go, I found there were no maps. So I simply started walking toward the mountain, working my way around obstacles as I went."

He paused. Dahno had stopped pacing and was standing listening. Maybe, this time . . .

Bleys went on. "But as long as I can still see the mountain there, I know if I keep heading toward it, I'll reach it someday. So I improvise. Of course, I'd rather keep you with me; but right now I believe I need you more on Association."

"At least you could give me some kind of answer on what the connection is between this business with McKae and my election!"

"The connection is to have you as good as elected to the Chamber for Henry's district, when McKae announces he'll choose me for First Elder if he becomes Eldest."

Dahno gave a huge shrug, walked back to his float and dropped down into it. Bleys stepped back and sat down also. They looked at each other.

"All right," Dahno said. He grinned suddenly. "I can see my being useful for you in the Chamber, and you being First Elder. But how are you planning to do without me on Cassida and Newton?"

"Cassida and Newton," Bleys said thoughtfully. "They're an unusual situation. Newton's drifted into turning nearly everything it produces in its research laboratories over to the developmental centers on Cassida. And Cassida's been selling most of the developed information on to New Earth, for further development into a mass-producible product, the engineering of which can be sold to all the other Younger Worlds."

"Nothing new about that," said Dahno. "We all know it. Everybody knows."

"Yes, but the point is the three-world flow pattern of interstellar credit. It's got to the point where all three are dependent on each other. They're a chain. By now a major change in one of them could destroy that chain and wreck all three financially."

"True," said Dahno, "and the threat of a change like that could control them. But will you tell me one more thing? This *is* still aimed at the goal of putting the Others, as I started them—in spite of all the additions and changes you've made in them—on top of things generally, if possible?"

"It is," said Bleys, "and the word is 'everywhere.' Not 'wherever.' No 'if possible.' "

"Fine, then. But I'll hold you to that—" Dahno was interrupted by a chime from the communications system and Henry's voice, speaking flatly and without emotion.

"The man Barbage is here," said Henry. "He wants to see you. I asked why, and he said he had important news for you."

"Send him up," said Bleys, letting the open phone of Henry's communication system pick up his voice from the middle of the room. "In fact, bring him up yourself. I'd like you to hear whatever he has to tell me."

"We'll be there right away," said Henry's voice.

"I'm leaving for Association now," said Dahno, and he left the lounge.

It was only a couple of moments before one of the other doors slid open and Barbage came in, followed by Henry.

"Sit down," said Bleys; and they both took floats, Barbage with the hint of a predatory smile on his thin lips. Henry had no expression on his face at all. Barbage carried a small case and was dressed impeccably, as usual, in his black uniform now with the silver insignia of a captain major on its lapels; and now also with a noticeable badge that said *"Association"* above his left pocket. It could represent identification only, since being from the other Friendly world would make no difference in either his rank or his authority on Harmony.

"Well, Amyth?" Bleys said to him.

"Great Teacher," said Barbage, "I've got news of Hal Mayne for thee."

"Have you?" Bleys said and immediately regretted the slight eagerness that escaped into his voice. He controlled his features to an expression of polite indifference.

"Yes," said Barbage. "Foolishly, on entering Harmony, he used the name and papers of Howard Beloved Immanuelson, of whom we have record as a dissenter and outlaw. This allowed us to trace him back to Coby and find record of one who had worked at a certain mine there under the name of Tad Thornhill. Thornhill had left that mine just before Immanuelson arrived on Harmony and joined the outlaw command he is now with."

"He's been seen here?" asked Bleys.

"Yes," said Barbage. "By thyself, among others, Great Teacher."

There was no particular triumph visible in Barbage, and Bleys did not alter the expression on his face or change the tone of his voice.

"Yes, I know you told me of that before, Captain," Bleys said. "When I made that speaking trip to Citadel, and the authorities there thought to impress me by parading the detainees from the jail before me. As I recall, I spoke to them and then asked for their release."

"It is so, Great Teacher," Barbage said.

"And are you now telling me that Hal Mayne was one of those detainees?" Bleys held up a hand to forestall Barbage's answer for a moment. He glanced over at Toni. "You weren't with me that time, were you Toni?"

"No," said Toni. "I was on Harmony with you, but you had me out, setting up the talks."

Bleys nodded. He turned again to Barbage.

"You're telling me he was one of those?" Bleys asked. "He'd have grown into a man during his four years in the Coby mines. And that would change the boy he was when his tutors were killed. Still . . . "

"He had grown," said Barbage. "He was then"—he hesitated, an unusual action in him—"he was then almost as tall as thou art, Great Teacher. But I gather he stood in the back rank of the prisoners and bent his knees, so that his height would not show."

Bleys nodded.

"At any rate," Barbage went on, "the records show this Howard Beloved Immanuelson was one of the men in that room where thou spakest to the detainees. On Coby, as thou mayest know, there is a great deal of collusion between mine staffs and those they hire. Individual identification marks, such as eye prints or individual DNA, can be falsified to hide the true identity of any new man who is hired."

"That close!" Bleys said, almost to himself. "That close—I didn't suspect!"

"However, we know now where he is," said Barbage, and this time his voice gave away, very slightly, the emotion inside him. "We know the particular Command of revolutionaries he's joined; and, just at the moment the local militia think they know where that Command is. I came to tell thee that and find out if thou wishest to watch the process of trapping it, and Mayne with it."

Bleys frowned.

"How much time would that take me?" he asked.

"A matter of hours only, Great Teacher," said Barbage. "If thou wilt let me show thee—"

He was already on his feet and opening the case he carried. He took out a map, put the case aside and looked about to find a table on which to spread the map. He found one and looked over his shoulder at Bleys.

"If thou wilt look, Great Teacher."

Bleys rose and stepped over to look down on the map.

"Thou seest," said Barbage, "here is New Samarkand, where we are now; and these are the foothills of a mountain range, some two hundred kilometers north of us. On the edge of that range, right now, is Rukh's Command—the leader of the Command is a woman named Rukh Tamani—and to give Satan his due, Great Teacher, the Harmony Militia hath warned me she is a wary and skillful guerrilla fighter, old for her years in outlaw actions. As long as her Command stays deep in the mountains and moves often, it would take two or three companies of militia to be sure of trapping them. But for the moment they're almost in the open."

Bleys nodded.

"Yet," said Barbage, "they have needed at last to come in close to civilization for supplies. Particularly food, rods of fresh needles for their needle guns and spare parts to repair their weapons that've been worn out. They like to re-supply all their needs in one quick trip. As a result, the local Militia commander in this district right here just short of the foothills—thou seest the area I've outlined in red?"

"Yes," said Bleys.

"That is his district. In theory, his authority runs back into the mountains as far as he wants to go in search of felons. But actually the only areas he can keep steadily under control are the close foothills and the farmlands next to it."

"That's not a lot," said Toni.

Barbage glanced at her. He hesitated, opened his mouth, closed it again and turned back to Bleys.

"It's the duty to which the Militia headquarters staff hath assigned him," he said to Bleys.

He turned once more to the map.

"He hath found Rukh's Command just behind the first folds of the foothills, and he hath gradually been moving his men into position to surround them. We can take an atmosphere ship and be there in less than an hour. After that, it will only be a matter of watching an hour, or at most two, for the outlaws to be rounded up and brought in. Thou mayest be able to pick out Hal Mayne and bring him back here with you, if that's what thou wishest. But we should leave right now. I've got a Militia A-ship waiting."

Bleys looked at Barbage for a moment.

"You make it sound remarkably easy, Amyth," he said. "Have you got so much faith in this local Militia commander?"

"I would have more faith in my own troops, if I had had permission to form my own search force on Association—forgive me for mentioning it, Great Teacher," Barbage said. He stared back at Bleys, completely unapologetic. "But the Commander—a militia major, by the way—is considered trustworthy on this world. Also, he knows—and if he didn't, I've impressed on him—that this is a matter of great importance. I promise thee he will be cautious about making a mistake. If he tells us—as he hath—that he has Rukh Tamani's Command surrounded, ready to gather in, I am inclined to believe him."

"All right," said Bleys. "I'll go."

"I'll come with you." Toni stood up, and Bleys glanced at her.

"Good enough," Bleys said. "Henry—there's probably no point in your coming. I think, Amyth, Antonia Lu will be welcome to join us. My cloak's wide enough to cover both of us."

Barbage checked whatever he had been about to say at Toni's sudden announcement.

"Of course, Great Teacher," he said. "Thy cloak is wide enough to cover anyone."

Chapter 18

Their atmosphere ship, the black Militia insignia stark on its silver sides in the bright afternoon sunlight, brought them through brief white cloud and a rain shower just ending, to set them down in a sown field, some twenty meters from the gravel-topped road where some officers of the local Militia Command appeared to be in conference.

Leaving the atmosphere ship, they had to walk across the field, crushing the little green fingertips of the young spring crops just emerging from the damp-black earth—the season was younger here—in order to get to the men with officers' silver insignia on their black uniforms. There was no way to avoid crushing the plants. Bleys felt like a murderer, knowing as he did from his days on Henry's farm, how much each of these plants must mean to the farmer who had sown its seeds.

At Henry's farm, as a boy, he had helped to build little individual tents, each from one broad leaf of a non-crop plant, to protect the tender shoots from the searing noontide rays of Epsilon Eridani during the plantings of the summer.

But now they were already at the road, and Bleys was being greeted obsequiously—and Barbage with a wary reserve. The major who commanded here, the only officer with rank senior to Barbage's, was a short, broad-shouldered man running a little to extra waistline. He looked not exactly as if he had been athletic when he was younger, but as if he had had enough extra natural strength to bully most of those around him into letting him have his way. His voice was a light baritone, but sharp and authoritative.

"I'm sorry, Great Teacher," he said, "but we had to begin the roundup without you. There were indications that the Rukh Tamani Command was slipping away from us, back into the deeper foothills to the mountains. We had to take them when we could."

"Thou hast already captured them, then?" Barbage demanded sharply.

In spite of the official difference in rank between himself and the local commanding officer, he spoke as a superior to an inferior. The major did not look at him, but kept his gaze and his smile on Bleys.

"Well, it's not quite over," he said to Bleys. "We should have them gathered in shortly."

They stood together in the hot sunlight on the gravel surface of the road, waiting; a little knot of people including the major, some subsidiary officers, Barbage, Toni and Bleys. With only a few small, puffy white clouds left in the sky, the day was warming rapidly.

Toni took off her woods-jacket. She had dressed for the outdoors, and perhaps a foray into some brush or otherwise uncleared land; with boots, fawn trousers, a light brown shirt with a filmy scarf tied loosely about her neck. Her jacket, proof against scratchy twigs as well as rain, was a deep reddish brown—called for some reason obscure to those on the New Worlds, "cordovan"—now draped over her arm.

Bleys could feel the faint breeze—not dusty at all—from the slopes off to their right, which rose precipitously, thick with mature variform aspen, birch and pines. Running between the bottom of the slope and a narrow road of oiled gravel was the cropland where they had landed, with beyond it more plowed and seeded earth. This, too, close to the road, had been sadly trampled by Militia boots coming to the road from another atmosphere ship, which was parked and silent, reflecting the sunlight with a hard metallic glare.

Beyond it, Bleys could see more farmland and, somewhat distorted by heat haze, the farther tops of mountains.

It could have been a peaceful, even a pleasant scene, with the few Militia officers chatting idly in a group on the road. But there must also be armed enlisted men, who could only be now among the trees, rounding up the members of the outlaw Command.

There were such revolutionary groups on Association, too, but Bleys had never had any contact with them. They were composed of the incorrigibles from outlawed churches and individuals labeled criminals or terrorists; but most of these latter—it was an open secret—were people who had been driven beyond the law by barely legitimate or flimsy uses of that law against them, by some individual or group in power. In general, the outlaws on Association advocated a complete shake-up of the world government; no doubt it was the same here on Harmony.

It struck Bleys it would do no harm to make sure about the enlisted troops here.

"Where are your men?" he asked the Militia major.

The major nodded toward the slopes.

"In the trees, encircling the Command and moving in on them. We'll try to herd the Command's members into the open before we really close in on them. In fact, you should hear some needle guns soon, if not some power weapons as well, as the Command discovers they're being encircled."

They waited. Sure enough, after about another ten minutes or so, from the woods of the slope came the buzzing, whizzing sound of needles from needle guns, igniting their tiny rocket ends after being fired and picking up speed in midair. Then silence. Then, after a little while again, a fair amount of needle-gun noise all at once and the explosive bark of a power pistol—not a rifle, Bleys noted. A power rifle would have made a more prolonged sound.

As for the needle guns, there was no way of telling how many of them belonged to the outlaws and how many to the Militia. Needle guns . . . every farmer on Association kept them for the common plague of variform rabbits and the rare chance at other small variform game that had been imported to the planet. No doubt it was the same here on Harmony. But the guns could be used as serious weapons, as well as game-gatherers.

A moment later, the black uniforms of enlisted Militia appeared at the edge of the trees on the slope, moving into the plowed ground. But several dozen of them surrounded only three male figures, not exactly ragged as far as clothes went, but wearing garments that had obviously been mended and washed innumerable times. They herded these captives forward as if they had weapons—although they were clearly disarmed now—across the cropland and up to the major, with his officers, on the road.

At close range they began to look like a father and two sons. All were about the same height, all had the same dark brown hair, lean bodies and narrow suntanned faces, all had the same over-large seeming hands, spread by hard work.

As they came close to the road itself, the relationship showed more plainly. The oldest was a man at least in his forties; gray was visible among the brown hairs of his head, and grayish-white stubble shrouded his lower face. Of the younger two, one might have been in his twenties with a comparable but dark stubble—and the third looked about sixteen, with a beardless face.

They had the look of Old Earth northern European ancestry. The faces of all three were expressionless.

"Sorry, sir," said the lieutenant apparently in charge of the group of militia men herding the three forward. He spoke to the major, ignoring Bleys and Toni, who stood with the Commanding Officer, "but most of them must have moved out during the night. We found sign in the woods of a good-sized group having been camped there."

"What sign?" exploded the oldest of the three prisoners. "That's our woods. My boys and I know every meter of it. If there was sign there, we would have seen it. There isn't any. He's making it up!"

"Shut up, you!" said the sergeant closest to him, elbowing the man in the stomach. It was not a hard-driven elbow, but it was enough to bend him over and interrupt his breathing so that he could not go on speaking.

"If you don't mind, sergeant," said the major, "we'll have none of that."

There was, Bleys thought, an almost unctuous righteousness to his voice, as if he was overly conscious of Bleys and Toni watching.

"Doesn't do any good to lie to us," the major went on, still in the same tone of voice to the oldest prisoner, who had now recovered his breath. "The lieutenant has better things to do than go around making up evidence."

"Hah!" said the man. "As if any Militiaman would hesitate about that—"

The same sergeant who had used his elbow before moved close again, and the man turned away from him. But the sergeant only began the gesture, he did not carry through.

"Tell me, Lieutenant," said the major thoughtfully, "you took a measurement cast of the footprints of these three? Did you find them mixed in with the footprints of the others who had already left?"

"All over the place with them, sir," answered the lieutenant.

The major sighed.

"Then I guess there's no doubt about it," he said, looking at the sky regretfully for a second, as if seeking some sort of guidance from on high. "They're obviously part of the group. A rear guard left to see if we showed up to follow their friends."

He turned back to the older man.

"Was that why you three stayed?" he asked. "Be truthful now, and it'll go easier on you."

"We didn't stay behind anybody!" snapped the older man. "We've always lived here!"

"Well then," the major said, patiently, "it had to be one of you who fired on my men." He looked at the lieutenant. "Is that right, Lieutenant?"

"Absolutely right, sir. In fact, Odderly has a few stray needles in him. Nothing important. The company aide man can get them out when he comes back. Their weapons weren't very accurate."

"Show me the weapons," he said.

Two needle guns and four knives, ranging from a small folding knife to some short straight knives, were brought forward, passed from militia hand to militia hand until they reached the lieutenant, who held them out to the major for his inspection.

"None of them's ours!" said the older of the two youngest prisoners, "except the folding knives—Jed's and mine!"

"You didn't find a power pistol, among their shooting weapons?" the major asked the lieutenant.

"No, sir," said the lieutenant. "They must have hid it. Should I send some men back up for a closer search?"

"No," said the major. "Of course they'd have some well-screened hidey-hole somewhere. Waste of time"—he looked up at the sun—"and the afternoon's getting on—and we don't need any additional evidence, anyway."

He stepped clear of the group in front of him so that he could look down the road to an elm growing by the side of it, less than a half-dozen meters from him.

"That tree's got a handy limb," he said. "You can get on with it."

Rope was evidently already in the possession of the escorting soldiers, as needle guns prodded the three over into position under the branch the major had mentioned. As the nooses were placed around their necks, the oldest looked at the two beside him. The expressions of none of them had changed, but the face of the youngest, next to the older man, had paled.

"We are in God's hands, my son," said the older man.

Bleys heard a soft, sudden, sharp exhalation of breath from Toni.

"They're not going to hang them!" she said, in a low voice.

"No," said Bleys. He raised his voice.

"Major!" he said.

The major turned and looked at him.

Bleys beckoned to him, stepping back and aside several steps, so that the major, in coming to him, stepped out of easy earshot of the other militiamen and officers. Like the prisoners, the major's face was unchanged as he stopped before Bleys.

"You will not hang those three," Bleys said in a low, private voice. He looked down into the other's face, so close to his own now, and felt an ugly griping sensation in the pit of his stomach. The feeling of wildness was alive in him.

The major's face had not altered, but his brown eyes, shaded by the visor of his uniform cap, suddenly seemed to have a yellowish cast.

"If you do," Bleys went on—hearing his voice as calm as usual and feeling his own features unmoved, in spite of the powerful emotion within him—"I'll see you court-martialed within months, or even weeks, broken, and dismissed from the Militia—perhaps hanged, yourself."

There was a moment of silence in which their eyes stayed locked. Then the major turned sharply away from Bleys to face the elm and the prisoners. All three had the far ends of their ropes over the thigh-thick branch, and militiamen ready at each to haul on them.

"Lieutenant!" shouted the major.

The lieutenant held up a hand to interrupt any further movement of the militiamen ready to pull on the rope.

"Sir!" he called back.

"Turn them loose," snapped the major. "Let them go!"

"Sir?" the lieutenant called back, his voice cracking.

"What's the matter?" the major cried furiously. "Can't you under-stand an order when it's given?"

"Yes, sir. Right away, sir," said the lieutenant.

He turned to the waiting militiamen and began speaking urgently. The rope ends came back over the branch and the nooses were taken from around the necks of the three.

These stood where they were for a moment, staring at Bleys and the major. Then, at a word from the oldest, they began to walk off together across the field of emerging crops, toward the trees on the slope.

"Wait here," Bleys said to Toni and strode after them. When they saw him following, they broke into a run and were lost in moments among the shadows that began at the edge of the wood.

Bleys followed, not hurrying. Behind him he could hear orders being given to the militiamen. He reached the edge of the trees and stepped upward into the shadow among them, the sudden coolness of the shade falling upon him like second cloak.

"That's far enough," said a woman's voice; and he stopped.

He had gone no more than half a dozen of his long paces in among the trees, which by their very height and interlocking leaves had killed off the ground cover, so that the slope had a park-like aspect. But after the bright sunlight of the open land, the relative gloom among the trees made it hard to see until his eyes could adjust. It was a second or two before he made out the person speaking to him.

Slowly she came into focus, seeming to fade into visibility like some ghost appearing out of nothingness. She was a slim young woman, not as tall as Toni, but taller than average. She looked bulkier than she probably was in the rough woods-clothes she wore, the thick jacket, the work trousers and boots—all of a dark color—so that even as he began to see her better, she seemed to blend into the dimness of the woods.

A heavy holster, with its flap buttoned down on her left hip, showed the butt of a power pistol projecting forward, so that if the flap were up it would be available to either hand. But her right hand held a needle gun, its light weight making its rifle shape balance easily in her grasp, with its muzzle toward him. It could easily be fired one-handed from her hip, as she held it now, with only a touch of her finger on the trigger button. At this short range, the expanding pattern of the needles in her first burst would not miss him.

The two weapons sat severally on her hip and hand as if long custom had made them familiar with being there. There could be no doubt she was no local farmer, like the three whose lives Bleys had just saved. But it was not that obvious difference that caught his attention, so much as the sight of her face and hands.

She was black-skinned and beautiful, actually the most beautiful woman he had ever seen. Her face was sculptured beneath its smooth skin by narrow bones; and her fingers, curled around the balance point of the dull-black needle gun, were long, slim and utterly professional in their grip. The steadiness of her gaze upon him was like the steadiness of Henry's, when he looked at anyone. Authority and intelligence sat strongly on her; but it was not even this, so much, as something further beyond the physical in her, an impression of dedication, of certainty—and a uniqueness that might well be the uniqueness of courage, or even of some towering inspiration like Bleys' own dream of the future.

"What did you say to the major to make him let them go?" she asked. Her voice was clear and pleasant, but uncolored by emotion; and she spoke as someone who had the right to be answered.

"I told him their deaths would cost him more than it was worth to him," said Bleys. "In brief."

"Why?"

"There was no need for them to hang," said Bleys.

"No. There wasn't," she said. "Who are you?"

"I'm Bleys Ahrens," he said—and when she did not at once seem to recognize or respond to this, he added, "Some people call me 'Great Teacher,' although I didn't invent the name, and I'd just as soon they didn't use it. But my rule is to let people call me what they want, good or bad."

"Yes," she said. "Now I remember hearing about you. Well, I'll thank you for what you did for the Heisler family—James and the two boys, Daniel and Jedediah. None of them had anything to do with our being here for a few days."

She paused. "It's best you turn around and go back now."

"Wait!" said Bleys. "You're the leader of the Command the Militia was hunting here, aren't you? Rukh Tamani?"

His eyes were accustomed enough to the forest dimness now to see a faint smile on her face.

"I won't deny it," she said. "Go now."

"Wait." Bleys lifted a hand to stop her own going for a few more

seconds. "Have you got anyone in your Command named Hal Mayne—
or Howard Immanuelson?"

"Go!" said Rukh Tamani.

She stepped back and sideways, so that she was immediately lost to
sight behind the thickness of the tree next to which she had stood. The
smooth suddenness of the move made her seem to vanish before his eyes.

Bleys turned about and walked away.

Once more in the sunlight, he saw that the troops were already formed
in a double line and starting the march back along the road that would
return them to their trucks and, eventually, their base, while their officers
flew. The major and Toni stood by the open door of Barbage's waiting
atmosphere ship, and Toni's eyes watched him closely as he approached
them. The major also looked, but said nothing. Only his eyes, once Bleys
was close enough to see, still held the impression of a faint yellowishness
that Bleys had noticed when he had given the man his ultimatum, earlier.

"Very well, then," said the major, expressionlessly, as Bleys reached
them. He turned away from the entrance and toward his own ship, across
the field. "I'll bid you farewell—Great Teacher!"

Chapter 19

"You are connected to Bishop McKae," said the cheerful female voice.
"May we see you, Bleys Ahrens?"

"That's not necessary," said Bleys. "You've undoubtedly got a print
of my voice there that you've already checked with what you're hearing
right now. My vision tank is going to stay off as well to avoid your doing
any pictorial recording, and I imagine the one at your end will, too."

Bleys was sitting alone in an anonymous public communications room
in the spaceport at Citadel on Harmony. The room was no larger than a
closet, with barely room enough inside it for the single chair, jacked as
high as he could get it. The green-paneled wall before him held the vision
tank, at the moment an anonymous gray; and a slot below the tank for the
insertion of identification, or credits sufficient to pay for the call.

Bleys had ignored this slot. His voice had been registered automatically with Communications General on Harmony from the first time he
had visited this world. Consequently, he could have charged this call—but
there would have been a record of his payment. Cash calls paid from the
caller's end were anonymous, but he had gone even one step further toward anonymity in the public records by making the call collect, since by
law, the location and identity of callers on collect calls, were not recorded
at all.

As Bleys had expected, there had been a minimum of hesitation in accepting the charges at McKae's end. Also, as he had expected after what he had just said, the tank stayed as gray and uninformative as if it had been filled with a heavy mist. McKae would not be in the habit of exposing his face on such a call, either.

There was a pause at the far end, following his last words; then McKae's voice came on, warmly non-committal but enthusiastic.

"Well, now! This is a coincidence—I was going to call you sometime today, probably later in the afternoon."

"Later this afternoon, I'll be off-planet," said Bleys.

"Leaving so soon?"

"I've been here ten days and given eight talks," said Bleys. "Time's getting short, I'm afraid. So I'm going now. Besides, I think I've done as much as I can for you."

"Yes," said McKae, after a small pause. "I heard your talks. It would have been even better, of course, if I could have told them specifically about New Earth's possibly hiring troops from us."

"Whether or not they do, still depends," said Bleys. "That's one reason I'm in a hurry now."

There was another momentary pause at the far end.

"Of course," said McKae. "Yes. Well, I'd been holding off my announcement of you as my choice for First Elder so as not to sound too confident too early in the campaign. Since you're leaving now, though, I'd better do it in tonight's speech."

"I would," said Bleys. "I won't be around to hear you, of course, but I'll be reading about it in a transcript of your speech sometime after I've been on Cassida more than a few days. I'll be waiting for it, in fact."

He waited for McKae to answer.

"Well, good luck, then," said McKae, coming back on the line almost abruptly. "Congratulations, First Elder."

"Congratulations, Eldest," Bleys replied. "I'll say good-bye, now."

"Remember, I'll need you back in time to be with me here or on Association when I'm installed—" McKae said rapidly. "The Installation can't be held off too long, once I'm elected."

"You'll have to hold it off as long as necessary," said Bleys. "If you look at our history, there was at least one Eldest that didn't have his ceremony of office until nearly a year after his election. So there's precedent, if you need it. Just stay in touch with me, and I'll let you know when the time's right."

"I will," said McKae. "Have a good trip."

"Enjoy your election," Bleys said and broke the connection.

Later, aboard the spaceship to Cassida, once they were a good two shifts out and beyond any light-speed communication, Bleys wrote up the conversation for his memory file.

Examining the written version, he thought over the tones in McKae's voice as he had spoken. They had not given away much—but very definitely there was something more at work in the man than the normal anxiety over the immediate future. Naturally, his election was the first concern, even though it was all but assured to him. But present, also, was at least the beginning of an uneasiness about his dependence on Bleys.

There was really no way in which McKae, without Bleys, could fulfill his glowing election speeches, promising to improve the centuries-long dearth of interstellar credit on the two Friendly worlds. Marketing more of their young men of both planets as mercenary soldiers was, as it had always been, the only possible way. Neither Association nor Harmony had ever really had much else to export. Together with the Dorsai, they had originally been spoken of as the "Three Starvation Worlds."

On all three, natural resources were scanty; and none of them lent itself to the home growth of experts in any profession other Younger Worlds would need to hire—except military personnel; and the Dorsai, starting early, had chosen to take the high road of quality, there, leaving only the low road of quantity to the Friendlies.

So now McKae was realizing how dependent he was on Bleys—and not liking it. Hopefully, he would accept that worry as only an immediate concern, and not begin to entertain the suspicion of it being an opening wedge to a much greater control of him by Bleys.

Thoughtfully, Bleys fed the written records of his note into the slot of the phase-shift sheet destructor and watched them disappear, their least physical elements now spread out evenly and instantly throughout the universe.

There was another note he should write while it was fresh in his memory. It was only now that he faced the fact that he had, unconsciously, been putting off setting it down in words. A hesitation like this was a bad sign, hinting that his memory might be trying to forget something it should remember, because it opened up possibilities that were frightening or distasteful.

He took another sheet of single-molecule paper and began.

"This is a note on shipboard on my way to Cassida," he wrote. *"Ironically, it's something I'd give a great deal to talk over with Toni. I write 'ironically,' because a talk about this is impossible. I'm sure if I told her even part of what I hope, she would be shocked by the human cost—the necessary cost—of what I must do to achieve what I want for the future.*

"Some days before leaving Harmony she and I went out into its countryside, when Barbage had been told the Militia had surrounded the Command of revolutionaries Hal Mayne had joined. The Militia had not. But the trip provided me with two harsh discoveries about myself.

"The first had to do with the local Militia Commander deciding to hang three local residents, since he had failed to capture the actual revolutionaries; and Toni was hard-hit by the callous brutality of his order.

"I could tell myself it was Toni's shock that caused me to react the way I did, but that would mean lying to myself. The fact is I was not able to let the hanging take place.

"What caused me to react like that—my Exotic ancestry or the example of

my mother—doesn't matter. The fact remains that, faced with people about to be executed before my eyes, I reacted in a way that could, if it happens again at the wrong time, threaten all my plans.

"I've always told myself I'd have to face the fact that there would be a cost in human lives to achieve the change I want in human society in my lifetime.

"That has always meant, inevitably, that some must die as at least an eventual result of my orders.

"But out in the foothills of a mountain range on Harmony, I found that I was not capable of accepting an unjust execution, such as would have been a minor part of the price to be paid for what I want.

"My reaction was not cold and reasoned. It was a hot, instinctive, visceral reaction—as instinctive as one that would make me defend against some physical attack.

"I must also remember what I saw on the face of the major when I told him I would not let him kill those men.

"I know that my face, after all these years of training and practice, was unthreatening and calm. I know my voice was perfectly under control, equally unthreatening and calm. But something about me completely convinced him I meant what I said. Plainly, I terrified him.

"The important question is—how can I do what I plan if I cannot trust myself to face the cost of doing it? I could not let the men hang. But if the major had defied me, I was ready to kill him.

"There seems no solution to this, now. I won't know how I'll react until I face the situation that either makes or breaks everything I have planned.

"All I can do otherwise is continue as planned and hope. Because I will not give up my dream of what might be. Those living today will barely begin to see its promise. Their grandchildren and great-grandchildren will be the ones to perceive it—an opening out into a vaster and more understandable future. It is too valuable not to try for. At the moment, all I can do is go forward. So I will."

He sat, gazing for a moment more at what he had written. Then he picked up the two sheets he had filled and fed these, also, through the slot that would destroy them. But their destruction made no difference. The years of training had now imprinted what he had written in his memory, and the questions would not go away. They would be there, his realization of what the day had told him, along with the events of the day itself.

He sat where he was for a little longer, with not merely his body, but his mind, it seemed, in suspension. His conscience was the first part to wake, and it reminded him that he had another memory note yet to make. A note he had also put off, finding it strangely hard to put into words. But the solution to that problem, he told himself now, was simply to sit down and start writing. The words would either come or they would not. The important thing was to get it down any way he could; and perhaps that writing would itself clarify it, so that his mind could deal with it.

"I've not mentioned this to Toni," he wrote. *"I'm not quite sure why not. There is no specific reason not to tell her. The fact that it concerns another woman*

is entirely beside the point of my hesitation—I think—though, in fact, I also think the uncomfortableness in mentioning something like this would be on my side rather than hers."

He paused in his writing for a moment, considering that.

"But I must enter into my memory file the moment of my stepping into the forest," he wrote on; *"and my one glimpse of the woman who must have been Rukh Tamani, leader of the Command to which Hal Mayne—under the name of Howard Immanuelson, possibly—is now supposed to be attached.*

"What I must remember is the way I was impressed by her. It was not merely her unusual beauty. She was, literally, the most beautiful woman I've ever seen or ever expect to see. In fact, I would not have believed that such a human essence of the word 'beauty' was possible. But the remarkable thing was that the real power of it was not really resident merely in her face and body, at all. It was something much more that illuminated her. I would speak of a light glowing from within her, but that is not really a good description. What struck me so strongly was something closer to a sort of invisible, but palpable, aura about her; that I felt, even before my eyes, adjusting to the dimness of the woods, had taken in her physical appearance. If I had owned the slightest scrap of Friendly religiosity—say, the smallest part of Henry's sort of feeling in that area—I could almost have knelt before her.

"I would give a very great deal to know her better. I would not place that desire ahead of my hunger to know and speak to Hal Mayne. Try as I will, I can summon up no memory which fits my image of what a grown-up Hal should look like. It seems to me that my memory gives me the faces of all those I saw at that time—and a face that could be his is not among them. It's possible he managed to hide himself among them; but that's a farfetched supposition. The only other possibility is even more farfetched.

"Could it be that unconsciously I am afraid of finding him after all, and learning what his capabilities or potentials actually are?

"What if he is my equal, or close to it, and his role in history is to be my Antagonist—not my ally—after all?

"This, too, is unanswerable until at last we come face to face. Then I will know."

He paused again, sitting staring at the words his hand had written. Then, he went on.

"In the meantime, I can only hope that when the Harmony Militia find him, they don't damage or kill him. I don't trust Barbage. His fanaticism outruns any fear of consequences—even from me."

He did not reread this last part of his Note. His mind fled to the matter of the upcoming days on Cassida, now only a few more days of ship-time away.

There was, legally and officially, no Others organization on Cassida. Two years before, both Cassida and Newton had declared the rather large Others' organization each had to be illegal. Therefore Bleys would theoretically be without contacts there. Actually there was a small hard core of the

Organization that kept in contact as members of other, legal organizations. Toni had written to their secret leader, Johann Wilter, about Bleys' arrival—but, strangely, he did not seem to be on hand. Nor was there any sign of the cortege of limousines Toni had arranged through a travel agency, to meet them. When she asked the terminal agent waiting at the end of the disembarkation ramp about the vehicles, the green-uniformed woman shook her head.

"Non-terminal traffic is never allowed on the spacepad," she said.

Toni looked over her shoulder at Bleys, who looked back, frowning a little. This was the sort of situation in which Dahno was useful—but Dahno was back on Association, getting himself elected to the Member seat in the Chamber, there. It was quite true that ordinarily civilian traffic was not allowed onto a spacepad, on any world. But on any world people with diplomatic passports and a security need had that rule waived for them. It should have been waived in this particular instance, since Bleys was, as far as the government of Cassida knew, a member of Association's planetary government.

"This way, please," the terminal agent continued. She was a slightly overweight young woman with a cheerful round face—which now, however, was unusually solemn as she turned and indicated two young men in uniform, with the silver of officers' insignia in bands around their blue sleeves. Just beyond them was a double file of what were obviously enlisted troops in slightly lighter blue uniforms, but distinguished more by virtue of being less well-fitting and lacking other small graces of tailoring, from the officers.

One of these officers was shorter than the other and had a pale, yellowish-white face, and slightly protruding eyes that gave him a look of single-minded stupidity.

The other was a tall, lean youngster, with nose slightly askew in a narrow face and two silver arrows on his left lapel, instead of the single one his companion wore—glinting under the light of Alpha Centauri A— a sun so close in apparent color and size at Cassida's distance from it, that it was the one star under which people newly out from Old Earth felt at home. In fact, even in Toni and Bleys, Alpha Centauri A's light had seemed to wake some comfortably familiar atavistic memory, so that they had spoken of it, as *Favored* drifted in orbit, awaiting permission for landing.

However, they did not need to go to the two officers, because those were both already advancing toward them. They came up to Bleys.

"Bleys Ahrens?" said the taller of the two.

"Yes," said Bleys. "What's this all about?"

"You're under arrest, Bleys Ahrens," said the officer. "If you and your party will come with us quietly, we can avoid a great deal of bother."

"Go with you where?" Toni demanded. "Do you realize what you're doing? You can't arrest a foreign diplomat. Bleys Ahrens is covered by his diplomatic passport—"

"I'm sorry—Antonia Lu, I believe?" said the officer. "But I'm follow-ing orders. We have troop trucks over here to transport you. If you and Henry MacLean would follow the lieutenant with me to the second ve-hicle, and your escort to the trucks behind that, please? Bleys Ahrens, if you'll come with me in the first vehicle—"

Chapter 20

The trucks were heavy-duty military vehicles painted a mud-colored gray. There were two swivel seats in front, so arranged that the truck's control stick was available to either of them. Behind these seats were two more for passengers; and behind those the back of the truck, an open area with a removable weather cover overhead and two long, hinge-up bench seats, one on each side of the back section. Bleys took the passenger seat directly behind the enlisted-man driver, while the officer took the other front seat.

"I apologize for the cramped conditions, sir," said the officer, swiv-eling his seat half-around to speak to Bleys.

Bleys only nodded. An apology was certainly called for. Not only the lowness of his seat, but the meager distance between it and the two seats, ahead had forced him to sit at an angle, in order to seat himself at all, with his knees hard against the back of the officer's seat.

But he did not make an issue of it. There had been no reason why they could not have provided a vehicle with comfortable seating for him; no more than there really was for the arrest itself. Therefore the discomfort must be part of whatever plan was at work here—perhaps an attempt to suggest mere thoughtlessness on the part of those sent to pick him up.

Bleys therefore endured the situation, distanced his attention from the cramps already starting in his legs and directed his thoughts elsewhere. He could simply have stepped over into the back of the truck and made the ride on one of the hinged benches. That would have given him half the width of the truck bed to stretch out his legs.

However, in the back there were no window areas. Here he could look out through the windshield transparency and see where he was being taken.

The officer spoke to the driver. The truck—a magnetic-lift vehicle—lifted a meter above the pad and slid off across it toward an entrance ramp which sent them angling downward to an underground level.

Such entrances to a network of underground tunnels were common in most spaceports. But from the moment they reached the lower level here, a difference appeared. Their ramp ended in a road-wide empty trough, set crosswise and running off to their left. The driver entered it and began to move down the trough; but at a swiftly increasing speed that soon outpaced any speed at which mag-lev drives could normally move them.

Behind the enlisted driver, Bleys got the strong impression that their truck had been encapsulated in some invisible way, and that it was the trough that now controlled their speed. In any case, they were soon moving so fast that it was less than five minutes before the trough rose above-ground again, and they found themselves encased in a transparent—at least from the inside—tunnel, literally flashing through a large city.

Their speed was such that it was impossible to get a close look at the buildings they passed. But, taken altogether, they were interestingly different from what Bleys had seen on all other Younger Worlds. All those— even the poor ones, like the Friendlies—had metropolitan areas that in many ways were modern enough to be virtually interchangeable between worlds. If this was Tomblecity, it was entirely different from the city he had visited once before.

It was as if the whole city had been completely rebuilt since Bleys had last been here, some years back, slightly before the meeting on Old Earth that had required the taking over of the Mayne estate. But Cassidans were known for their technolust, and of all the New Worlds were in the best position with both credit and manufactories to satisfy it.

Now it appeared as if everything he had seen before had been torn down and reconstructed according to a single master plan. For one thing, all of the buildings gave the impression of being buried deeply in the ground, so that only one to six of their top stories showed.

Not only that, but there seemed to have been a general agreement about their materials and construction. The individual structures grew uniformly taller as they approached the center of the city, and then began to lose height again as the farther edge of the metropolitan area was approached.

When at last the trucks reached the last of the city proper, the trough in which they traveled branched off from the wider one they had been sharing with other vehicles, traveling in parallel channels, and their speed was reduced.

They slowed almost as quickly as they had accelerated. The feeling of being encapsulated fell away. The tunnel ended, and they drove off onto a wide paved road that led up a steep and winding route on a mountainside.

They moved more slowly on this road, but still at what would have been an extremely good pace—much faster than Bleys had traveled on other worlds on like roads.

But their speed slowed even more as they climbed higher and the road narrowed. Eventually it wound off on what seemed to be a side road; and, at the end of this, they stopped in a paved area just before a spreading palatial-looking structure, nowhere more than three stories in height but covering a large expanse of mountainside. Large as it was, something about it gave it the look of a personal dwelling.

With the exception of Old Earth, the two Exotic worlds and the Dorsai, a home so large ordinarily did not exist. Single dwellings were normally small, meager structures, or—in the countryside—farmhouses, like Henry's home on Association, though they might be a good deal larger and much more comfortable than Henry's. Otherwise, people lived in city apartments or hotel suites.

But this place was clearly their destination. The officer in front looked back at Bleys.

"If you don't mind,"—he opened the door beside him as the truck stopped—"this way out, please."

Bleys followed him into the building. Within, it was even more plainly the dwelling place of some family or individual—but a very rich one.

From the lofty entrance hall, which gave an impression of having been carved out of one impossibly huge chunk of white marble, a ramp mounted to an upper level; and this started to move the moment they set foot on it, delivering them to the upper level. They stepped off onto a deep, ivory-colored carpet, and the officer led the way through several corridors and rooms until they came at last to a relatively small room, with a large and ornate door closed in the far wall of it.

The room had no furniture. Only, a little back from the wall that held the large door, there was a cloth-sided, very military-looking booth, with green plastic framing.

"If you please." The officer gestured toward the booth.

Bleys stepped forward and into it without a word.

Inside, there were a couple of men in white, one of whom spoke to Bleys.

"If you'll be so kind as to strip, sir," he said.

"This is very foolish of you," said Bleys.

"Strip. Please," the man repeated. Bleys did so.

After a thorough search of his clothes and his person with hand-held scanners, Bleys was allowed to dress again and was led out the far side of the booth. He found himself facing the large closed door. The officer who had brought him was standing beside it.

"This way, Bleys Ahrens," said the officer. He turned toward the door, and it swung backward, open before them. Bleys walked in.

The officer did not follow. The door closed again and Bleys stood, apparently alone in a room that was only slightly larger than the one in which he had been searched. But in all of its walls but the one through which he had entered were windows—or, much more likely, three-dimensional picture screens—that together gave a panoramic view of surrounding mountain terrain, from pine-clad slopes to snowy peaks.

The room was warmer than the temperature of the rest of the building through which he had been taken—almost too warm for comfort; and at its far end, in the one empty area between two windows, stood a large fireplace. In it, a generous wood fire blazed merrily behind a metal screen. Two high, winged-back, non-float armchairs with their padded backs to him, stood solidly facing the fireplace. Bleys moved closer and saw that in one of them sat a man who, at first glance, looked in late middle age. Not yet far enough advanced in years to be called old, but barely short of that point.

The furniture and the inoffensive appearance of the seated man should have made the room seem comforting and reassuring. For some reason—possibly the more-than-necessary warmth—it did not.

"What's all this about?" asked Bleys. "Are you responsible for my being brought here?"

He walked forward and around to face the man.

"Yes, and no. But come," the man said in an age-hoarsened voice, "do come and sit down, Bleys Ahrens."

He waved a hand toward the vacant armchair facing the fire.

Bleys walked forward. As he got closer, he saw that the chair he had been offered had an extra seat cushion, so perfectly blended in color and shape to the chair that it had not been noticeable until he had been just about to fit his own long frame into it. He also took notice of the fact that the middle-aged man was using a footstool, which disguised the fact his own chair seat had also been raised with a similar extra cushion.

Bleys sat.

"What's been done with Antonia Lu?" Bleys said. "And the rest with me?"

"She's quite all right—waiting for you in another room. This is all routine, actually." The man was older than Bleys had thought at first glance, and his eyes were the first Bleys had seen that could undeniably be said to twinkle. "I particularly wanted to talk to you for my own enlightenment, without interruption by anyone else."

"I see," said Bleys. "Then let me ask you another question. How is it that against all the rules of international diplomacy, my party and I are put under arrest and brought here?"

The man's eyebrows raised. They were pleasantly graying eyebrows in a round face with a generous mouth and smile wrinkles at the corners of his eyes. Above those eyes, his hair was solidly gray and cut short; but the eyes themselves had that impression of a twinkle in them. It was only on studying him a little more closely that Bleys realized that the twinkle was not simply one of good humor, but an "I've-got-you-now" sort of twinkle.

"Arrested?" the man answered. His eyes lost their twinkle abruptly and looked shocked. "No, no, that can't be."

"That's what the officers who picked us up off the spaceship told us," Bleys said.

"They did? It's no such thing. I only wanted to talk to you. I'm so sorry! Allow me to introduce myself. I'm Pieter DeNiles, Secretary to the Development Board of our world, here. Did those officers really use the word 'arrest'?"

"That was the word," Bleys said.

DeNiles shook his head.

"The military!" he said. "They always have to overdo it. No, it was supposed to be only an invitation to you and your people, Bleys Ahrens."

"And the complete body and clothes search?" asked Bleys. "Also, no doubt, a similar search of everybody else with me?"

"That, now," said DeNiles, "is, unfortunately, a matter dictated by certain governmental procedures which I'm sure someone like yourself will understand. I'm afraid you'll just have to take my word for it that nothing personal was intended. Neither I, nor whoever searched you, really expected to find anything dangerous. But I'm legally obligated to take certain precautions."

"Legally?" Bleys watched him.

"Unfortunately, yes," said DeNiles. "I'm just a governmental functionary, actually—in actual practice, all but retired. I only advise. But since in name I'm a member of the Planetary Development Board, I'm required to be protected at all times, as if I was an elected official like the other members."

"That doesn't seem to back up the word 'arrest,' however," murmured Bleys.

"No, no," said DeNiles. "It wouldn't, of course. But the whole matter's simply a combination of unfortunate coincidences. Arresting an accredited visitor with diplomatic status—you're quite right, it's legally not possible."

"Then why are we here?"

"As I say—coincidence, misunderstanding," said DeNiles. "No, you see what happened is that in addition to being a member of the governmental Chamber on Association, you also happen to head an interplanetary organization, whose branch on our world has been declared illegal. As a result, those on the Development Board have to show the voting public that they checked to make sure this visit of yours had no illegal purpose or connection. So they chose me to be the one to make this certain; and—my deepest apologies, because the responsibility is mine—with the misguided help of the army, I seem to have bungled it. My only excuse was I did want to meet you and talk with you, and this looked like the chance."

"I see," said Bleys. However, he did not. He still had no idea what was behind everything that was happening. But he would find out. None of this since their landing could be accidental. There had to be a purpose behind it.

DeNiles was smiling again, even more warmly, now, the wrinkles deepening around his eyes. "—Though it does seem, a number of your party had weapons shipped in, in bond, to be claimed after they got here."

Bleys laughed.

"As a member of the Board here," he said, "you've got to be familiar with the fact many diplomatic visitors have security people with them who need weapons and bring them in bond."

"Oh, yes. Yes, of course," DeNiles said. "But it was one more reason for the Board to seem concerned. We really aren't frightened about what fifty-three men might do with hand weapons against our own armed forces."

Bleys smiled back at him. "I'm sure. Anything else?"

"Well—forgive me"—said DeNiles—"but there's the fact you're here to give a series of talks to our people; and from what we learned, when you did the same thing on New Earth, the result was some considerable public unrest—even a few scattered terrorist-type bombings. That does bother some of our Members. Do you really blame them?"

"I don't know," said Bleys. "Should I? It seems to depend on how seriously they take my connection with the Others and the weapons of my escort in bond, plus whatever else seems considered matters of public alarm."

"None of it, Bleys Ahrens. I assure you. We're just going through the motions here, and I took the opportunity to meet you because what I know of your philosophy is very interesting."

"I can understand your Board having the security of your world always in mind," Bleys said. "But did you, yourself, listen to recordings of any of my talks?"

DeNiles looked directly at him; for a moment, the twinkle was missing. "One."

A lesser official might have dodged answering, or lied. Bleys began to get something very close to a warm feeling for the other man. One recording would have been considered enough by a conscientious individual, interested only in confirming evidence that already had convinced him.

"Of course I'd also had a complete digest of your personal history and of everything of interest in your other talks." DeNiles said.

"Then hearing one should have been enough," Bleys answered. "If you already had a complete background on my philosophy. All my talks have the same message, though the words may vary, as I adapt to the viewpoint of the people I'm talking to. But the message is always the same. My concern is never with individual planetary societies. It's with the society of humankind in general."

"Yes," DeNiles said thoughtfully. "I remember you saying that, several times, in that one speech I listened to."

"That and other key points—they're always repeated," said Bleys. "Most important is the fact that I deal with the broadest of fronts. That's the answer for an improved humanity and a better life for us all, particularly we of the Younger Worlds. A single universal attitude, plus the self-improvement of all individuals."

DeNiles nodded, listening.

"I also point out, " Bleys went on, "that this self-improvement, which ordinarily would have come farther by this time, has been held back by Old Earth. Old Earth has always tried to maintain as much control as she could over us, covert if not overt, so that we haven't been as free to go as far and as fast as we might have, left alone."

Bleys paused, looking significantly at DeNiles.

"You must know that, yourself."

DeNiles' face and body gave no clues. Bleys' opinion of him went up another notch. A less intelligent individual would have suggested that Bleys was lecturing to him, in hopes of being taken for someone of more limited capacity than he really had. A much less intelligent individual would have felt insulted by what could be assumed an attempt to talk over his head, and burst out angrily with something like "Is this the way you do your preaching?" But DeNiles, he saw now, was seriously, even avidly, listening.

As it happened, Bleys was being thoroughly truthful—even if the truth in this case was limited—to someone who might be capable enough to listen with a view to learning. He was suddenly, remarkably, tempted to speak to DeNiles as if he was that rare thing, a highly intelligent mind all but completely free of reservations or prejudice.

"Old Earth clings to us," Bleys went on, "hoping to hang on so we'll be controllable by her in the long run. What's behind that wanting to control is fear. Fear rooted in the survival instinct of a people who thought themselves an evolutionary end product and now begin to feel threatened by what may be a new and better version of themselves. Just as the now-extinct dire wolf of Old Earth was eventually replaced by the modern wolf. With that fear below the surface of consciousness, Old Earth is driven to compete against all of us on the New Worlds."

"You're exaggerating, don't you think," said DeNiles, "in that comparison of the Old Earth people with dire wolves?"

"There's no equation, except in Old Earth minds," said Bleys. "But that kind of fear makes them dangerous to us. Old Earth's people have dreamed of the superhuman for a long, long time. The 'overman' of Friedrich Nietzsche's nineteenth-century philosophy, the unconquerable character in innumerable books and fantasies who's been part of human cultures everywhere, in myths and legends, since the dawn of time. A figure to defeat all devils. But Old Earthers always assumed this conqueror would be a refinement of *them*—not of those who'd left them for other stars, other worlds."

"Hmm," said DeNiles.

"But not on Old Earth or on any of our Worlds is there any real possibility of a superman or superwoman," Bleys went on. "Our New Worlds men and women may on average be a little taller than those on Old Earth. But the concept of a true evolutionary jump forward out here or anywhere is no more than the illusion it's always been. Society's evolving—and still has a long way to go. But the human individual isn't and couldn't if he or she wanted to. The superhuman is a dream only, just as that has always been."

Bleys watched DeNiles closely on these last words. For if DeNiles believed in the Superman, then he had misjudged the man completely as someone he could speak frankly to. But DeNiles only nodded thought-fully.

"You see," Bleys said, "I feel strongly about the possibilities—the great possibilities—of every individual human being everywhere. But they're only possibilities, if each of us is left free of outside controls and influences, including Old Earth's. That's what started me speaking on my home world of Association, in the first place—and now I'm here on Cassida to talk about it. The possibilities and the problems."

DeNiles nodded again slightly—the head movement could have meant agreement, or merely that he was listening.

"In brief," said Bleys, "I tell people we need to be aware of this fear on Old Earth and educate ourselves to understand it; and—if necessary—work to protect ourselves against it. That's all my talks boil down to, telling people to learn and grow. Humanity's got a long way to go. I only advise it, and there's no danger to the public on any New World in that."

He stopped talking and looked at DeNiles, waiting. The ball was now in the other man's court.

Chapter 21

There was an indefinable tension between them; as if they stood facing each other across a narrow but bottomless chasm, and there was a contest between them as to who should step into it first.

"You make yourself sound very commendable, Bleys Ahrens," DeNiles said after a long moment of silence. "But forgive me. Officially, it will take more of an explanation than that to be ammunition the Board can use to justify their considering you harmless."

"Why?" Bleys said.

"Well, you see," said DeNiles, steepling his fingers before him, "you've given me rather a circular argument in which your assumption that Old Earth has a certain fear proves your assumption that your talking about it poses no threat to public peace. You can be completely honest; and what you say can even have applied on your home world of Association. But what makes you think people of other worlds—and particularly our Cassidans—need this message? You seem to assume a oneness of the human race on the New Worlds that I don't see, myself. Can you name me one vital aspect all societies of our different Younger Worlds have in common, other than the ability to interbreed?"

"Certainly," said Bleys. "Credit."

"Credit?" DeNiles dropped his hands into his lap. "How can different societies interact, or individuals in a society, without a medium of exchange? The creation of credit was surely one of the early steps toward modern civilization. But to make it a basis for a rather ambitious philosophy of a future in which we're all wiser and better off should seem rather farfetched—even to you."

"I didn't say it was the basis of my philosophy," said Bleys. He was enjoying the fencing in this argument, and he more than suspected this small, frail old man was also. "You asked me for something we've all got in common. I gave you an example—all the worlds can exist on a roughly similar civilized level only because of interstellar credit and local credit."

"But how would we exist without them?" DeNiles demanded. "Do you see some kind of future that's better because, among other things, transactions between individuals and worlds take place without credit?"

"The other way around," Bleys said. "Once individuals have developed to the point where they understand that all humanity depends on the honesty and personal sense of responsibility in every other individual, credit as we know it is no longer indispensable. Useful but not indispensable. Then, nothing more than the memo of agreement should be all that's needed—in exchange for goods and services."

"Isn't that sort of memo what a letter of credit really is?"

"Not at all," Bleys answered. "Historically, money and letters of credit always had to be backed by material worth. I'm talking about memos backed only by universal trust, and I'm saying the achievement of trust like that will be evidence that improved understanding between people has been achieved. A dwindling importance of credit reserves and that better understanding will signal an advanced social attitude—not vice versa. Remember, this was an example you challenged me to produce. It's not credit and what will happen to it, it's the advance in social attitude I'm interested in."

"Then what I should tell the rest of the Board is that you're really nothing more than a sort of very religious person seeking converts?"

"If you like," said Bleys, "and if you can tell me where social science ends and religion begins."

DeNiles shook his head doubtfully.

"Well, you asked about my philosophy," Bleys said. "I'm telling you and everyone else what I see us all coming to, inevitably and eventually. I just believe it's going to come that much sooner if more people can clearly see the road to it."

"Sounds like a utopian dream," said DeNiles. "You can't expect me to simply take your word for it?"

"Perhaps you never will," said Bleys. "A great many people won't, of course. But I believe those who do will increase over the coming generations as a percentage of the race, until we finally have a humanity in which either everyone, or a sufficient majority, understands and starts to act on that trust. Then what you call a utopian dream will start to come true."

DeNiles shook his head. "I'm sorry, but my job's only with the here and now—whether the Board should let you hold your talks here."

"I know," said Bleys. "But tell me this. Can you find anything in what I've said that you really believe would be subversive or dangerous for your people to hear?"

DeNiles frowned, opened his mouth and then closed it again.

"Someone once said to me," Bleys went on, "that Cassidans lived in greater luxury than the inhabitants of any of the other Younger Worlds, even the Exotics. I suggested that he examine what he meant by luxury. I told him what Cassidans actually lived in was not the most luxurious, but the most technologized of worlds. Their most important work is developing discoveries made by the researchers of Newton and selling the developed techniques for further expansion into profitable mass-marketable processes of manufacture on worlds like New Earth. Because of that, your people are regularly in a position to buy the best of what's new, at the lowest possible price."

"I don't see what that's got to do with what we were talking about," DeNiles said.

"I tell people," said Bleys, "they can learn only by stepping back from the society they live in and the societies they see around them; and looking at those societies from the outside. If they do, they will see people may not be evolving, but the societies are. Cassida, in a technological sense, only, is evolving heavily in one particular area. It is more specialized than any other New World."

"That's been understood for some time," said DeNiles.

"Some time, but only in the latter centuries," said Bleys. "The thinking before that used to be that in a single lifetime things didn't change so much that an individual continually had to adapt."

He paused, hoping that now, at least, DeNiles was seriously and open-mindedly listening; but the Secretary's calm old face still told him nothing.

"Remember, it was the twentieth century," Bleys went on, "before space travel became a reality, with many other technodevelopments; and it was undeniable by then that humanity's personal universe was growing and changing daily, faster all the time. So fast that grandparents had trouble understanding—and being understood by—grandchildren. At first computers baffled twentieth-century grandparents. Their grandchildren adopted them easily, and fitted them naturally into their lives."

DeNiles still said nothing.

It had become time to pin down this particular grandfather-age listener, Bleys told himself.

"Now," he said, "will you admit that that sort of thing, and at least some of what I've said earlier, are matters of historical fact?"

He paused. DeNiles frowned, but he had already shown that he was someone who saw the danger of not being open to argument.

"All right," he said. "Will you agree that what you're saying is that your talks are, perhaps, subversive? But subversive only to Old Earth—not to Cassida, or any of our other inhabited worlds?"

"That's right," said Bleys.

DeNiles opened his mouth as if to say something more; but at that moment, by possibly convenient coincidence, a melodious set of chimes sounded overhead and a pleasant woman's voice interrupted.

"Secretary DeNiles," it said, "time for your walk. If you'd like to cancel it today—"

"No, no," said DeNiles. He looked at Bleys. "Would you mind walking as we talk? I always take a walk this time of day. It's part of my necessary exercise."

"Not at all," said Bleys. DeNiles was already getting to his feet.

As Bleys rose with him, he noticed how DeNiles steadied himself with both hands on the arms of his chair as he rose and saw suddenly that the other man was even older than he had finally assumed. Not merely old, but very, very old and fragile.

DeNiles turned toward one of the walls showing the cliff face of a mountain at no great distance. As he turned, a section of the windowed wall swung outward.

He led Bleys through it onto what seemed to be the top of a broad, grassy ridge, perhaps five or six hundred meters wide and something more than that in length; like a strip of meadow among the mountain peaks, forming an uplifted corridor of grassy openness that stretched to the beginning of a pine forest at the base of a near-vertical rock face.

There seemed perhaps a kilometer's width of woods in the forest before the almost dark and bare stone of the mountain lifted steeply upward, with a small silver stream leaping and bounding down from the rock, emerging from the cliff face perhaps forty meters above the treetops, and disappearing behind the trees.

They walked together slowly, Bleys holding down his own long stride to DeNiles' short steps. The air was moist and warm—exactly as the room with its fireplace had been. This uniformity gave away its hidden character.

This little bit of ideal terrain which DeNiles probably traversed daily could hardly be a natural part of the landscape, Bleys thought. The farther terrain, the stream, cliff and distant mountains, could be all three-dimensional illusions with the nearer parts built solely for the older man's pleasure and use, and enclosed by a weather-shield. What felt like small breezes barely caressed them from time to time, and the afternoon sunlight of Alpha Centauri shone down on them here with a suspiciously softer, benign illumination.

"I like to walk," said DeNiles, stepping along with his gaze fixed on the pine trees and the cliff behind them. "But I can't do. Much as I used to."

His shortness of breath was obvious, and his age and stiffness showed more now that they were moving. What was barely a stroll for Bleys was a major effort of putting one foot in front of the next for DeNiles. He worked his way forward, his gaze fixed on the trees ahead. Bleys gazed down at the slow-moving legs, then stared closely at them. He had seen movements like that before. However, neither his face nor anything else about the older man triggered any other memory.

Bleys considered the small body moving painfully beside him. DeNiles was so small and weak that Bleys could literally have crushed the life out of him with one hand. Nonetheless, Bleys felt an unusual kindling of excitement. Unless his suspicion was wrong, there was a remarkable mind and an unbendable will walking beside him, together with an unlimited amount of courage and determination.

Ahead of them, now, Bleys noticed a slight blurring of the outer edges of this ridge and the outer trees of the woods ahead. With the few steps they had taken, they had appeared already to have covered over half the distance to the trees, and the open ridge-top had seemed three times that distance.

Of course, thought Bleys; along with weather control and all other modern conveniences, this special walkway must have an illusion of extra distance built into it, for the benefit of the man beside him.

"Stopabit," said DeNiles running the three words into one short, fast exhalation. He stopped.

Bleys halted with him. DeNiles smiled upward in wordless thanks and labored a few silent minutes at regaining his breath.

"I've a question for you," he said at last, in a more normal voice. "One I thought you might like to talk about where you could see you wouldn't be overheard. I often have things to say I don't want overheard. I suppose, like all public figures, you've got a monitor in your wristpad for any snooper ear concealed within ordinary range of your voice?"

Bleys nodded and glanced at the wrist wrapped around by the cuff of his control pad. The monitor light was unlit.

"And you can see there's no place to hide a long-range listening device within practical distance?"

"Yes," said Bleys. "What were you going to ask?"

"Just one question. What changes would the evolution of society you hope for make in the case of individuals of great ability? Genius, in fact. *Proven* genius; because it's possible for many to give the signs of talent, but fail to keep producing more than one flash of what's required to prove it. What would it do to *them* as far as their still having the necessary freedom to do their work under the best possible conditions?"

Bleys considered the other man for a second. DeNiles was surely too old to be ambitious for himself, but it was a strange question unless he had some personal stake in the answer.

"I don't know," he said. "The evolution I talk about is going to take generations to mature, even under ideal conditions. But I can't see how it would affect geniuses any differently than all other individuals then concerned with it."

"I see. Thank you," said DeNiles. "We can walk on."

They walked. Bleys mused over the possible reasons for such a question.

They were almost to the trees now and the shadow of the mountain ahead, now that midday was over, was reaching from the bottom of the outermost trees across the grass toward them.

"Well," said DeNiles, after a moment. "I'll see the Board. As—"

He ran out of breath. The illusion of distance was such that they had just stepped between the first tree trunks; and the dimness of the tall, thick-topped pines was making a gloom about them.

"But"—said DeNiles in gasps—"in all fairness. I should tell you. This should be routine. For the voters. But. Anything can—"

He blundered against the side of Bleys, wordless once more. Bleys caught him by the elbow, held him upright and stopped him, so that they were half-turned to face each other.

"I'll just say a bit more myself," Bleys said. "Your Board has to realize that the throttled pace of societal evolution on our New Worlds is about to explode, into very rapid movement, like held-down springs suddenly let go. There will be large changes happening quickly, on all the Worlds; not only changing each of them, but changing their relationship to each other. I'm sure you've already noticed that New Earth's been developing technologically in all fields, including reaching out in the direction of working directly with Newton's research laboratories?"

He paused to give DeNiles a chance to answer, but the Secretary only shook his head, struggling to breathe.

"—And that Cassida is in the position of a middleman who could eventually be bypassed, if that reaching out continues. The great majority of discoveries could go directly to New Earth for development, to save middleman costs. New Earth has been slower in social evolution, but ahead in the expansion of fields of work, while you here have been essentially noncompetitive, comfortable as you were with the situation as it was, with Newton and them."

Again he paused to give DeNiles a chance to speak, but DeNiles shook his head again—breathlessly.

"Also," said Bleys, "your world has locked itself into a mold with the cream of the technology that passed through your hands. Of all the Younger Worlds, Cassida's going to have the hardest time adjusting to its future; and of all worlds, your people probably need the most to hear what I have to say."

They had stopped and stood facing each other again.

"Tell your Board that," Bleys said.

DeNiles' eyes closed; and all strength went out of his body, so that he began to slide toward the ground.

Bleys caught him and held him standing.

There was a flicker of movement to their left and right. In seconds a man was standing on either side of them, dressed in the same army officer uniforms as the one who had brought Bleys to DeNiles' home. But these were not the same kind of officer. These were larger, broad-faced and heavy-jawed. Without a word, they took DeNiles off Bleys' hands.

"You bastard!" the taller one said savagely to Bleys, just before he turned away. "You wore him out! Go back the way you came, and you'll be taken care of!"

He had caught at one of Bleys' arms as he spoke, and held it.

Bleys stopped. "You will let go," Bleys said.

It was a statement, not a question. For a moment, the officer's eyes looked up into Bleys'; then his whole face and body changed and his arm dropped away. He muttered something and turned to his companion, who was still supporting DeNiles in an upright position and who now took the old man away, up into his arms, while the taller officer followed. DeNiles, his eyes still closed, laid his head on the officer's wide shoulder like a tired child.

Bleys turned and went back across the short real distance of the meadow, back into the room with the fireplace, and found the original officer waiting for him.

"This way," he said curtly. At first he looked at Bleys with some of the same anger that the officer in the wood had shown. But that look changed swiftly to complete expressionlessness. He did not take Bleys back out of the building. Instead he led him to a lounge, where Toni was sitting, drinking tea, while Henry simply sat, not drinking or doing anything else—only waiting.

They were left there together for only a few minutes, during which they looked at each other but said nothing. Then the two original officers appeared again and took them out of the building into the same trucks. The trucks, already loaded with the rest of Henry's Soldiers, left, going back down the mountainside and disgorging them finally at the hotel which had been their original chosen destination.

Bleys had said nothing on the ride back. Henry and Toni, after their first look at him, had also been silent. They did not speak until they were safely in the private lounge of their suite in the hotel. Once there, however, Toni dropped into a chair. Bleys did the same thing, signaling Henry to join them. Toni had been observing Bleys closely.

"Well," she said to him, "you had an interesting time."

That, too, was a statement, not a question.

Chapter 22

Word came by fastest ship mail that McKae had declared for Bleys as First Elder if McKae was elected.

Word came, days later, that he was elected.

Word came in code from the Other Headquarters on Association that there was a rumor that the New Earth embassy on Harmony had approached the new de facto Eldest—not yet officially installed, but already busy at work—with some sort of proposal concerning the rental of Friendly troops for New Earth.

"Meanwhile," said Toni, "it's been more than a week now since you talked to DeNiles, and so far no word has come from this Board of theirs. Again this morning, Johann Wilter has been on the phone to me."

She, Bleys and Henry were seated together in the main lounge of Bleys' rooms at their hotel. Johann Wilter was the latest leader to be chosen by Bleys for the Others' underground organization on Cassida. Bleys had been icily practical about transferring authority as more capable people were found, particularly in view of the touchy legal situation.

"About the bills we're running up, I imagine," said Bleys.

"That's right," Toni said. "Also the reservations around this world for your six planned talks and hotel space for all our crew nearby. He says that some anonymous contributions have been coming in to the outlawed local Others organization, but not enough to stretch their treasury. They only have a couple of thousand actual dues-paying members, planetwide, because people here are afraid the authorities may decide, without warning, to start a more serious crackdown; and anyone belonging to the organization now could be in serious trouble. Shall I tell him I'll meet the bills out of the interstellar credit we have with us?"

"Hold off a little longer on doing that—and we'll continue as planned with the tour until stopped. Time's never lost, as long as the mind can work," said Bleys. "I've had these quiet days now to think over the situation; and I've come to be sure DeNiles will want to see me in action here, to see the kind of response I'll get. To say nothing of the interworld diplomatic consequences of deporting us all without waiting for me to furnish the Development Board with an excuse for doing that."

The chime of an incoming call sounded.

"Bleys Ahrens?" said an unfamiliar voice from the wall and ceiling of the room. "This is the front desk. There's a message for you here, sealed and carried by courier. Should he bring it up?"

"Yes," said Bleys. "Tell him to ring at the door to the main room of my suite. Someone will bring him to me."

The messenger came, another army officer; this time a young one, with a tanned face and his hat tucked under one arm, showing close-cropped, sunny-colored hair. In his other hand he carefully carried a sealed envelope.

"You've something to deliver to me?" Bleys suggested.

"Yes"—the officer hesitated—"Great Teacher. I have an official communication for you from the Planetary Development Board."

He held out the envelope. Bleys took it and opened it. There was a single sheet inside that was obviously a paper substitute, but gave the interesting three-dimensional visual impression of black letters cut into a tablet of white stone. Bleys read it aloud.

" '*Bleys Ahrens, the Planetary Development Board of Cassida welcomes you*

*to our World, and would like to express its pleasure at having such a distinguished
philosopher in our midst. We, with the other citizens of our World, look forward
to hearing what you may have to tell us. If the Board can be of any assistance to
you at any time, please contact us.*

"'Signed as of this date by the Secretary of the Board.'"

Below the last line was the printed name *Pieter DeNiles,* and just above
it a signature, barely decipherable in the scrawl in which it had been written.

"My thanks to the Board," Bleys said to the officer. "Anything else?"

"No, sir—I mean, no, Great Teacher," said the officer. "With your
permission, I'll leave now."

"I'll send a note of appreciation to the Board," Bleys said.

"Yes sir." The lieutenant started to salute, nodded his head instead,
turned around and headed toward the door.

"What now, then?" Henry asked, as the door slid shut again.

"We simply keep on as planned," said Bleys. "First, my talk, wherever you've set it up, tomorrow. I've decided, after my conversation with
DeNiles, to change what I was going to say here. Now I'll speak more
specifically to these Cassidans. That should interest DeNiles, in particular."

"Why do that?" Toni's gaze on him sharpened. "Are you hoping to
make some use of DeNiles, now?"

"I need to get into the Cassidan mind—into DeNiles' mind, particularly," Bleys said. "Action provokes reaction, and reaction reveals attitudes and patterns of thought."

He turned to Henry.

"Can you and Toni together take over Dahno's usual job of seeing
about setting up the equipment to do the recording, then? Not only here,
but as we move around?"

Henry nodded.

"Then there's no reason not to get started right away," Bleys said.

The scene of Bleys' speech the following day in the park of a city
named Cartusa, a thousand kilometers to the west, was a little different in
appearance from those of his outdoor speeches on New Earth and Harmony. Once more there was the small temporary building which housed
the equipment to project his image above its flat roof; and to broadcast his
words out to the individual receivers the people listening would be wearing.

The weather was good this day, and the scene was a very shallow,
bowl-like, grassy depression in an area surrounded by low mountains. The
one great difference was that the audience this time was tiny, compared
to those who had come to listen to him on both New Earth and Harmony;
less than three thousand people. But there was an audible reaction to be
heard, even inside the projection building, when his oversize, projected
figure appeared above the building's flat roof.

A gust of emotion went through him at the sound. Abruptly, he made the decision to scrap the speech he had planned—the carefully tailored speech that would both appeal to his audience and lead DeNiles to reveal himself in greater depth.

Relatively few as they were, these people outside there were those who had come to listen to him on a world which really did not welcome him, or promise to be tolerant of those who did. It was important, not only to them but to himself, that they should hear what he really had to tell them. This was the living message, the truth—something that even Henry would admit was not fed to him by Satan, if only he had some way to explain to Henry's satisfaction his decision and what he was about to do. He still could think of no way to do this; but he would feel better speaking as he had just now decided to do.

Let them believe, he said earnestly inside himself, let them listen and understand. This much, at least of me, is real and vital to them. He began to speak.

"Cassidans," he said, "you who are here already know that it's the whole human race I'm interested in; and in particular that means in every individual alive today of the race. But I've a special message for you who belong to this world; and it's not the same message I've given and will give to people on the other Younger Worlds."

He paused.

"It's simply," he said, "that for you, the struggle toward a better future is at first going to be harder than for those on any of the other Younger Worlds."

There came an audible, swelling murmur, beyond the building's walls.

"Please don't feel offended or angered by my saying this," Bleys went on, when the noise died away. "The fact that it will be harder means that in the end you may well develop further. The need for a greater-than-average strength often means that such a greater strength will develop.

"In this sense, it's no different from the physical development your bodies could gain by exercise."

Bleys paused to let these last words sink into their minds.

"Stop and think," he said. "Aren't the Younger Worlds on which people have made the most individual progress, those where they had to struggle most for the bare minimum of survival? The Friendlies and the Dorsai struggled against impoverished worlds. The Exotics struggled against a world that was not impoverished; but which, even after terraforming, possessed a climate in which only a small amount of the planet's territory was practical for human residence and work."

He paused again.

"As a result," he said, slowly and deliberately, "these peoples were all—in different ways—compelled to become interested in the same sort of inner development that I'm interested in myself; but which they needed and unconsciously reached for—to make themselves into a special people, whose skills and talents would find a special market on the other Younger Worlds. Each in their own way—Friendlies, Dorsai and Exotics—found that development, and that market; and in the process, developed not merely uniquely successful societies, but uniquely successful, individual people.

"To understand consciously how they did it, you have to stand back from both the past and the possible future; and look at both, as well as at the present, with an unprejudiced eye. If you can once manage that, you'll see that the human race has always tended to be obsessed with the problems of its own generation; whereas the instinctive inner drive of the race has treated such as only passing roadblocks on the way to survival and growth. So that in the end it has dealt with and survived them, to emerge stronger than ever, and still on its route to a greater people and a greater existence.

"These three Splinter Cultures had to struggle for what they wanted. Now you'll have to struggle, but in a different way. Struggle developed them in ways they did not foresee—not the least of which was in an emphasis on particular senses and awarenesses. To put it simply, to survive, they developed attitudes which made them stronger and equipped to go on to further struggles—no longer against their environments, but from the limitations of their own minds and bodies.

"Open your minds, then, to the ways in which human capabilities can be extended—extended to the point where the developed abilities of these people have seemed to put them beyond competition from other humans. Let's talk about that for a little while, and then let's talk about what is possible with your own struggle. For, even though your struggle has brought you to a successful society and comfortable planet, it has exercised—and given you the beginnings of—the interior strengths that you'll necessarily need as the rest of the race develops further yet, as we all move into the inevitable future . . . "

As he talked on, Bleys found himself caught up in his own words as usual. Literally, he warmed to his subject; and literally, he began to feel a response from the crowd in the sounds of it through the walls of the building around him.

Whether it was the audible reactions that were useful to him, or not, he had discovered long ago that he preferred to speak without any written preparation of what he was going to say.

The crowd was always like an actor's audience, varying from occasion to occasion. It was possible—literally possible—to feel them growing warmer, responding to what he was saying; or feel their temperature dropping as their interest flagged and pulled away from him.

This day again, as it had so far every time he had held one of these outdoor talks, he felt the warmth steadily growing—not universally from every person in the crowd, but from such a large majority of those standing and listening that their warmth swamped and all but obscured the occasional minor notes of contradiction and exception that flowed from those few individuals who would not accept what he had to say.

He finished at last on a high, hopeful note; and afterwards left the building, walking some fifty meters or so to the vehicles that waited to carry him and his own party away.

He, Toni and Henry were, as usual, surrounded by Henry's soldiers on the way out, a living envelope of trained men who kept at a safe distance those who always wanted to crowd close enough to touch him, to speak to him personally. This time, Bleys noticed, there was an additional outer enclosure of Cassidans in civilian clothes. But these moved very much like trained bodyguards, or military, and acted as a sort of double protection.

He thought little of it until he was almost at the car; and then suddenly there was a swirl in the crowd. The warm crowd voices immediately around him were suddenly torn by screams; and he saw over their heads that the swirl was moving through the packed people very swiftly as something or someone plowed in his direction. Bleys had a brief glimpse of a man naked from the waist up and wielding a massive two-edged, broad-bladed sword with both hands. People were falling and scrambling away from him on either side as he literally slashed his way toward Bleys.

He was almost upon them when his eyes suddenly went wide, then closed. The sword dropped from his hands. He fell and lay without movement. The outer envelope of apparent civilians gathered around him, and Henry's Soldiers drew tightly back around Bleys, Toni and Henry. But Bleys pushed his way through both them and the civilian guards beyond, to look down at the man.

He was a large, thick man, but not an impressive one. A generous amount of fat bulged over the front of his belt, and he had a noticeable double chin. It was not the hard fat of an athlete who might simply be carrying extra body weight, but the upper body of a man who had probably been physically lazy for some years. He was undoubtedly middle-aged, and Bleys' first thought that the civilian guards had killed him was relieved when he saw the naked chest moving deeply and quietly, although the eyes remained closed.

"You just knocked him out?" Bleys asked one of the civilian guards, who seemed to be in command and was standing directly over the fallen man. The man he had spoken to turned to him. He was a slim, wiry individual, in light gray business clothes, with a receding hairline and mousy brown hair beyond it; but he held, barrel-down, a weapon that looked like a small void pistol. He gave the very impression of athleticism that the man on the ground lacked.

"Yes, Bleys Ahrens," the man answered. His eyes looked unwaveringly into Bleys'. "He's a Hura. The psychomedicians will take care of him."

In fact, one of the mobile clinical vehicles with medicians and various kinds of equipment aboard, was already making its way through the crowd toward Bleys and the others around the fallen man.

"What's a Hura?" Bleys asked.

"Hura?" the guard answered. "It's a"—he apparently had to think for a moment—"it's short for . . . *juramentado*," he said, "an ancient word from one of the Old Earth languages. It means someone who gets despondent to the point where he runs wild and tries to kill everyone he can get close to. He's curable. The psychomedicians will deal with him. I'm sorry your occasion here was interrupted by something like this."

Beyond the man with the sword Bleys could see other figures on the ground, scattered farther back. Men and women who were plainly medicians were busy with most of them. The ones they ignored lay in complete stillness.

"Does this happen often?" Bleys asked.

"No," said the civilian leader. "That's to say, it's not common. Happens more nowadays than when I was a boy. But"—there was almost a note of pride in his voice—"we're the only Younger World where it happens."

"I see," said Bleys.

He turned away to rejoin Toni and Henry, who had followed him. Together they reached their limousines and climbed inside.

"Toni," said Bleys, some little distance in complete silence on the way back, "use the car phone, will you? Call our contact for the Other Headquarters here and see if Johann Wilter can meet us back at my suite in our hotel."

Chapter 23

"As far as I know," said Johann Wilter, "there've been huras around ever since the first colonists set themselves up on this world. I can check if you like."

Johann (he pronounced it Yo-han) was slim, dark-skinned and intense, in a city-going bush jacket, narrow trousers and boots, all of different shades of light blue. A white scarf fluffed itself into a knot under his chin in the opening between the two lapels of his bush jacket. He looked like a lightweight twenty-year-old until you met his eyes. Then it became plain he was anything but lightweight and a good ten years older. He had the steadiest gaze Bleys had ever encountered. Bleys had never actually tried to stare Johann down, on the two occasions in which they'd met before— when Johann had made brief trips to Other Headquarters on Association. But he had a feeling that Johann would die before his eyes would waver. His calm and gentle demeanor said *"Don't worry about me."* His eyes said simply *"Don't push."*

The combination of the two messages made more than a few people uncomfortable around him, but Bleys was not one of them.

Curiously enough, the ancestry Johann claimed was Chinese. Bleys had seen him direct a long, hard glance at Toni as he had come into the suite. Toni had returned it with a smile. Bleys was interested; and more than half willing to bet that Johann had decided that whatever oriental ancestry Toni might have, it was not Chinese.

"I think that's a good idea," Bleys said now. He was holding a writing pad in his lap as they sat in the main lounge of his suite; and writing on it as he talked—his hand moving independently of his words as if his mind was operating on two entirely different trains of thought at the same time. "I'd like to know as much about them as possible. Did there used to be fewer of them? Or, to put it another way, have they increased with time? Have they increased beyond the proportion you'd expect, in the general population?"

"I couldn't tell you," said Johann. "As I say, I'll check. That army-type man you spoke to was right, though, when he said that Cassida is the only world that has them."

"Army man?" Bleys said. "I thought there was something military about those extra civilian-dress guards that Henry hadn't arranged for. I'd like to know who sent them out there."

"Undoubtedly the Board," said Johann.

"Undoubtedly?" Bleys echoed. "Do the army—I mean the General Military Forces—here on Cassida belong to the Board?"

"Oh, no," said Johann. "But they do have at least one member on the Board at all times, usually two or three."

"Is Pieter DeNiles a former army officer?" Bleys asked.

"The Secretary of the Board?" said Johann. "Not as far as I know. He appeared more or less out of nowhere about half a dozen or maybe ten years ago. But he's always been in government, somewhere in the shadows. I don't think anyone knows much about him. I can try to find more on him, too, if you like."

"It won't do any harm for you to find out what you can about him," said Bleys. "But the huras are more interesting to me at the moment. Now, you've been doing a fine job of running the Other organization here. But it always was small; and the people heading up the organizations for us on other worlds have been much more successful doing extra recruiting than your group has, since I asked all of you to do it. Any particular reason?"

"Absolutely," said Johann. "We Cassidans aren't as recruitable. We're not hungry."

Bleys was deeply interested this time. His personal opinion was that Cassidans were deeply hungry—for a freedom, a status, or a relief—from something they could not name. He opened his mouth to speak, but Toni was before him.

"Hungry?" she said, pouncing.

Johann looked at her. "Most people on this World want security, and they've got it here," he said, "unless they're absolutely unwilling or unable to fit into the planet's work somehow. If they can do a nice secure job and end up a little better off than when they started out, they're happy. No one's starving for want of basic needs—even the people in the rural areas and tiny towns far out in the wilds. Even if they were, there would be government aid for them. These are the least hungry people on any of the Younger Worlds. Except, perhaps, the Exotics. But I suppose you could say that the Exotics are hungry to discover things, so it's not the same thing."

"That's curious," said Bleys. "I touched on that fact here, more or less, in my talk earlier today. Are you saying that your organization here and what I have to tell them doesn't offer to fill any need they have? Do you mean to say that, as far as you know, they've no needs at all?"

"No—not at all!" said Johann. "What we've got to offer is something all Cassidans want, if they'll admit it to themselves. Of course, as individuals, they've got other wants, too. Maybe that's why these people who turn hura go into their fits of depression and end up running wild, killing people—always with some kind of direct tool like a knife or a sword. In fact, a sword's the usual weapon. They seem to get more satisfaction from that than from using any kind of kill-at-a-distance tool, like a void pistol, needle gun or power rifle."

"Yes. But, you know," said Toni, "it was a very odd sword that man carried this afternoon. It could have been cut out of some stiff, paper-like material, except it was thicker, obviously harder, and a sort of dark brown color. But it was crude, the way somebody who knew nothing about swords might merely cut a broad-bladed, scimitar-like weapon out of a large chunk of wood."

"Oh, the answer to that is easy enough," said Johann. "That kind of weapon can be made by the common tools you'll find in anyone's home. In fact, if you have a controller hooked up to your tools, all you have to do is simply draw what you want and give the controller some specifications—say, you want edges as sharp as a razor on the part below the hilt, for example—and the machines'll turn it out for you, exactly according to your drawing and what you told it to make. What you saw today, and almost always, is of ordinary 'made' material. You probably use the generic word—what is it—'plastic' on Association?"

"No," said Toni, with a slight edge to her voice, "we call it 'made' material, too."

"Apologies," said Johann. "Anyway, there's all sorts and kinds and colors and so on, of 'made' material available for people who want to work with their tools at home. Some persons just like to make things themselves—you understand?"

"Certainly," Bleys answered. "Now, on another topic. If you've been worrying about our expenses here, don't. We'll take care of any amount your treasury can't handle. But get me as much data as possible on the huras, including anything they're all known to eat or drink—and particularly solid figures showing whether or not they've been increasing in number and proportion among the population. Also, whether the incidence of their running amok is getting more frequent. And find out everything you can about DeNiles for me."

"I will, Bleys Ahrens," said Johann. "But there probably won't be much on DeNiles. As I say, he's always been a sort of shadow figure in government. Details on him could be hidden deliberately."

"Well, give me what you can," said Bleys, "and as soon as possible. You've got all the information on the five speeches I've got remaining, so you'll be able to find me when you get some of the information."

"Yes, all of them," said Johann. "I'll get back to you with the data on DeNiles by tomorrow, and of course you can contact me at any time as you did today. I'm arranging it so that I'll be close enough so that I can get to you within minutes."

"Fine," said Bleys. "Then, I guess that covers everything for the moment."

Johann responded to the hint instantaneously and rose to his feet. He did even this with the smoothness of a trained sprinter starting a race.

"Incidentally"—he hesitated before turning toward the doorway of the lounge, and waving Henry—who had risen with him—back into his chair-float—"I can let myself out—I was just going to say that's welcome news, the fact you're going to be able to pick up the rest of your expenses. We could do it, you understand, if we had to—"

"But it would cripple you financially for quite a while, wouldn't it?" said Bleys. "Well, there's no need. Thanks, and we'll be talking again soon."

Johann went out. Bleys, who had continued writing all the time he was talking, made a few more marks and brought his stylus to a halt. He put stylus and pad aside, but passed the paper to Toni, with a gesture indicating that she should read it, then pass it on to Henry.

Toni took it, and her eyebrows rose. She checked whatever she was about to say first, and looked calmly at Bleys.

"Ah, code," she said.

"Yes," Bleys said lightly. "Commercial codes—several commercial codes, in fact. But our office shouldn't have any trouble reading it back on Association."

The message was clear enough to both of them. It had been Toni herself who had insisted, when she first agreed to accept her job with Bleys, that she go into the Other Headquarters office on Association and learn all there was to be learned there, as well as everything else there was to be learned about Bleys—she had even insisted on making a visit to the farm that had been Henry's and was now Joshua's.

As it turned out, Henry had been away from the farm on business. Toni had said to Bleys, on their drive back into Ecumeny after meeting the rest of the family, that she thought she had a pretty good idea of what Henry must be like in any case; and a later opportunity would come to meet him.

Bleys had been mildly amused at that; Henry was not to be understood simply through knowledge of his family—let alone from a single meeting with it. Judging by what he had heard of the conversation be-

tween them at the camp in the mountains on New Earth, Toni had determined to find out more for herself.

But now she had finished reading the page in code and passed it on
to Henry. Henry ran his eyes over it and then got up and took a couple
of steps to Bleys' chair and handed the sheet back to him. At the same
time, he smiled and extended his hand.

"Congratulations," he said. "That'll really set them up back on Association."

Bemused, Bleys stood up and took Henry's hands for what seemed a
proffered handshake. He knew that Henry had not learned any of the
codes Bleys had used. Nor was it like him to smile in the fixed manner in
which he was smiling now—let alone to say "Congratulations . . . " for
anything.

Enlightenment came almost immediately, as Bleys' large hand
wrapped around Henry's. Henry closed his grip on that hand with all of
his strength. Bleys returned it, smiling himself; and their friendly apparent
struggle over hand grips became obvious, not only to Toni but to whomever might be watching and listening to them over spy-equipment.

At the same time, the tips of Henry's fingers were varying their
pressure as lightly as a spider stamping its feet—so little was the variation
of them—on the back of Bleys' hand.

Over the years, the Soldiers of God on the Friendly worlds had developed a touch language, for use in conditions requiring complete silence;
and Henry had been such a Soldier.

Learning about this, Henry's two sons had begged their father to teach
the touch-talk to them; and, indulgently, he had. Bleys had learned it from
the boys when he had come to live with Henry and his sons. At that young
age, there was a definite attraction in having a secret language amongst
themselves.

So now Bleys and Henry conversed by fingertip touch under the guise
of struggling to outsqueeze each other. Henry's grip was surprisingly strong;
but, as they both knew, this was no real contest. Bleys' long hand would
have been capable of grinding Henry's knucklebones together with relative
ease, if he had seriously been putting on the pressure of which he was capable. Meanwhile, if it had been rendered into symbols, their conversation in
the abbreviated Soldier language would have looked something like this:

"*(?)*" Henry's fingers asked.

"*2 more talks. Then Newton.*"

"*(Heard.) (Ready.)*"

Their hands disengaged, Henry shaking and flexing his hand a little
as if he had lost the contest. He stepped back to his chair and sat down
as Bleys also re-seated himself. Bleys turned about and fed the sheet he
had with him into the destructor slot on the desk, just behind his chairfloat.

He turned back to Toni and Henry.

"You know, Toni," he said casually, "it's been some time since we've
had a workout."

* * *

To an outside observer, it would have seemed as if Bleys and Toni were engaged in some strange ritual dance, in which they barely touched each other in brief moments of contact. Dressed in the long-skirted exercise kimonos called *gis*, they would have resembled nothing so much as two great, dark birds, swooping and maneuvering in a limited space. This was because the workout was as much an exercise in harmony—in *ki*—as in potentially deadly combat.

Their style of encounter drew largely upon judo and the particular martial art method developed by Morihei Uyeshiba of Japan in the nineteenth and twentieth centuries of Old Earth. It was called aikido and had been extended—it would not be correct to say "developed"—in the three hundred years since—from that to what Toni and Bleys now used.

The *ki* in "aikido" was translated variously as "spirit," "inner energy," and "breath." In aikido—the way of harmonious *ki*—it included the meanings of all these words, with no conflict between them. Breathing, spiritual balance and the point from which the body's energies were directed outward, fused indistinguishably at the *hara,* or *"center point"* of the body; a spot generally just below what would normally be the position of a belt buckle on a man's pants. Their challenge was the effort of each to blend with the other's flow of *ki*, to redirect it without opposing it, and to maintain one's own *hara* while doing so.

In their ability to *center,* Bleys and Toni were almost evenly matched; but in their ability to achieve harmony with an attacker, Toni had a slight edge. It was this capacity for harmony that allowed Toni now to lead Bleys' attack, to commandeer his *ki* before his mind's intent was translated into physical action, and to fuse it with her own.

So that with a skillful use of leverage, while seeming to do no more than barely touch Bleys, Toni was able to accelerate his hundred and twenty-five kilograms of body weight across the space of the room they were in, with almost no expenditure of her own energy. Each time, on touching ground after being thrown, Bleys rolled either backward or forward up onto his feet again within an instant, and the two blended once more.

There was, in fact, no pattern and no specific length of time set for the workout. They would work together until both were satisfied with the workout; and then halt, at a point of mutual but wordless consent.

The fact that their present use of the *ki* was constructive and helpful did not mean that the same principles could not be applied very effectively in self-defense against an opponent; or even against several opponents— as Toni and Bleys had applied it in the alley beside the CEO Club on New Earth.

But, in this case, Bleys had an ulterior motive for the workout. As they exercised, they also conversed by touch. But it was a far more complex language of that nature than the one Henry had used with Bleys, to baffle unseen watchers or recorders. Still, the means were the same if the vocabulary of touchings was much larger. In Toni's case, it had been developed, added to and refined over generations by her family; where, for those same generations, teaching and engaging in the martial arts had been a common occupation.

One of the results was that Bleys and Toni silently conversed with a much larger and more practical vocabulary than Bleys had had available in his finger-talk with Henry.

"... *So Henry understood,*" said Toni, with the pattern of her bodily movements and the manner of her finger grip on Bleys' left sleeve for a moment, "*when you played that handgrip game.*"

"*Yes,*" Bleys answered in the same silent language. "*Happily, he didn't need any reasons or explanations.*"

"*But I'd like some,*" said Toni. "*Why cut the lecture tour short after only two more public appearances and go directly to Newton?*"

"*The huras.*" This name had to be spelled out since it was not in their touch code. "*I'd read about them back when I was studying Cassida; but didn't realize the implications.*"

"*Implications?*" said Toni. "*And how do they connect the huras with Newton?*"

"*According to the theory of sociological decay you've heard me talk about, each Younger World would begin to develop internal animosities, a splintering, with like-minded groups fighting with those most like them. These troubles would grow and spread first into disturbances and then violence, mounting to general internal war and eventual anarchy.*"

"*And that's what you believe the hura incidents mean here? That projection of a future still doesn't seem to connect with present-day Newton.*"

"*It's what they're headed for, however. The connection didn't occur to me either until after I'd seen DeNiles and then watched the hura incident. DeNiles baffled me at first.*"

"*Baffled you? Why? I was sure you were pleased after your talk with him.*"

"*I was. But I was also baffled by him, as a person. He was the wrong man in the wrong place or perhaps the right man in the wrong place—in a way I couldn't put my finger on. Then, after I saw the hura incident, it began to make sense.*"

They stopped communication for a moment, not because Bleys had finished talking, or Toni had heard all that she wanted to hear; but because the pattern of their exercise put them for a moment into actions where the language could not be used. They were both moving, but out of touch with each other—and the movements for the moment did not permit signals.

"*Societies,*" said Bleys when they were in contact again, "*follow the pattern of general human social development, to the extent they're in touch with it.*" He had caught Toni and held her. "*In their own society, they respond to as much of this pattern as they're aware of. But because the pattern itself is continually developing and changing—the pattern of the progressive history of the human race as a whole—they can find themselves out of tune with that. Their awareness of this is undoubtedly unconscious, for the most part, but it gives rise to an unhappiness in each of the smaller societies, which leads to antisocial behavior, grows and finally escalates into open violence and war."*

"Why does it have to escalate into violence?" Bleys had thought he had Toni firmly in a hold from which she could not escape—but she broke loose and spun away.

"Because of the intense desire of human society to adapt and grow always toward a better condition," he signaled when they were touching again. *"If you'll take a look at Old Earth history, you can see a very good example of that as recently as the twentieth and twenty-first centuries."*

"There was certainly a lot of violence there, but I really don't see the connection between that and what you call the general pattern of history."

"There are two types of wars." He had her again—or did he? *"One showing a deeper unhappiness and a greater failure to keep aligned with the general movement of the pattern; and this is also what the thinking Exotics of a couple of hundred years ago called the expected 'decay' of the Splinter Cultures. Looking back now, it's possible to see Old Earth's progress from less awareness of misalignment with the pattern to greater awareness and misalignment in the history of the twentieth and twenty-first centuries there; for that matter, you can see it between the early parts of their twentieth century alone and the latter years of that same century."*

"In what?" Toni demanded. *"It seems to me that the smaller wars of the latter part of that century were just as violent, if more limited, just as destructive if not more so, and more cruel than the large wars—even if the large wars in the first half of the twentieth century ended up killing more people."*

She threw him. He rolled in midair, landed on his feet and came back into contact with her once more. *"As I say"*—he signaled as they touched again—*"there were two different types of war."*

"Two types?" The touch of Toni's fingers somehow seemed to signal skepticism.

"Yes," said Bleys. *"Call the larger ones Type One, a war that results from a less-desperate awareness of being unaligned with the developing pattern of their times. These were what might be called political wars—wars of policy. In them, nation fought nation, or even in the case of the two so-called 'World Wars,' a coalition of nations fought another coalition of nations. The aim of the nation or coalition starting the war was to acquire domination over the opponent, not necessarily to destroy that opponent utterly. The unconscious hope was to gain territorial or other advantages within the structure of the pattern as it was freshly developing. For the victors, if you will, to position themselves better to take advantage of new trends in the pattern of developing history."*

They broke physical contact briefly and then closed once more.

"And the other type of war?" Toni signaled, just as he caught her in another hold.

"Those, usually smaller wars," he went on, *"were wars where at least one of the opposing sides had the aim of annihilating their opponents, of wiping them*

off the face of the world the two shared. The wars of policy had been fought with strangers opposing strangers. A soldier, say from Canada, could find himself fighting a German he had never met and if he had met him under congenial social circumstances, might possibly have liked and been liked by in return. The policy wars put them in confrontation for essentially what was a prize outside either one of them—the business of one being in a dominating position over the other, as one society ruling another—as Rome ruled all the lesser societies, it gradually accumulated in its empire when it was the greatest city in the Western world."

"But," Toni asked him, *"why the difference? What makes the opponents of the Type Two wars want to utterly destroy all they fight—"*

She came very close to breaking loose, but this time he held her. He was already answering.

"—If the Type One wars had been stranger against stranger," he signaled, *"the Type Two wars were against their closest neighbors and nearest relatives. The most deadly wars of annihilation were between people who were very close except for small points of difference in, say, religious doctrine—between sects of a single religion, or—on a larger scale, between one religion and another—Hindu versus Muslim, for example."*

"But you still haven't explained how either of these types of war connect with the hura we saw. What we watched was simply a single man mindlessly driving into a crowd of people he probably didn't know and killing right and left."

"But," answered Bleys, *"that's what the wars of annihilation—the cousin-against-cousin and the brother-against-brother wars come down to in the end: individuals saying to themselves, 'I can survive only if this person or these people are all dead' and then taking action to try to make them all dead. The divisions of decay here on Cassida aren't yet as apparent as they were on New Earth, where three groups are at odds with each other. Here the conflicts are below the surface and already moved into the area of the cousin-against-cousin wars. Stop and think. If I or someone else had led the people of the Shoe to a successful revolution over the CEOs and the Guilds, the people of the Clubs and the Guildmasters would have had their blood running in the streets—but this would quickly have been followed by the blood of other people, as the divisions within the People of the Shoe began to war with each other, and one after another gained an ascendancy; and legally or otherwise executed their opponents."*

"I'll take your arguments under advisement," Toni signaled, *"but why does it all mean that we've got to cut your speeches short and go immediately to Newton?"*

"Because it becomes overridingly obvious that I'm going to have to deal with all three worlds as a unit. The strength of the connection didn't occur to me, as I said, until I saw the hura incident this afternoon."

"Still, wouldn't it have been safer to finish out your speaking tour before going to Newton? You'll make them suspicious there, by appearing so early and abruptly."

"Perhaps. But there's another element that's tied in with an interworld time schedule. I can't let McKae be in office too long before I return to be confirmed as his First Elder. That position and title for me is necessary if I'm to get done what

I want to get done with the other Younger Worlds—and in particular the two
we've got in hand right now: Cassida and Newton."

Bleys had held her locked in his grip for only a few moments during
this extended period of communication. He felt as if he had her now, but
there was one question he wanted to ask.

"Is there anything about this that disturbs you? Would you rather not be a
part of it?"

"I wouldn't miss it for all the worlds put together!" replied Toni, emphasizing her unvoiced words by breaking his hold, spinning him to the floor
enthusiastically and pinning him there in a grip from which he could not
escape.

Chapter 24

Bleys found himself unexpectedly happy and pleased. In the several years
he had known her, Toni's answer to his last question—whether there was
anything in his plans that disturbed her and whether she might not want
to be a part of it—had been the first time she had really shown any of her
inner feelings. The revelation had come not just in her answer, but in the
enthusiasm with which she had thrown and pinned him.

Bleys was thinking about it again that evening as he went to bed. He
was retiring early, which also surprised and pleased him. For the first time
in a very long while—a matter of months, if not years—he was feeling like
going to sleep. The sensation was distantly familiar; and there was a solid
conviction in him that he would sleep, once he lay down.

The only question was how much less than a full night's sleep he
would end up getting after he had first fallen into slumber, before his mind
woke him. But there was no point, he told himself, in looking gift horses
in the mouth. Remembering that ancient saying, he thought with pleasure
that someday he would be on Old Earth itself for more than a matter of
some sixty hurried hours, and actually see a living horse. Perhaps he would
even ride one.

He stripped, put on a pair of shorts as usual and lay down on the
force-field bed, closed his eyes and almost instantly drifted off.

. . . He woke with the odd feeling that he had either been asleep, or
gone somewhere for a fairly long period of time and was only now returning. There was no particular reason for this feeling, but it seemed that he
had more than a little time to consider it, as he gradually began to drift
up from a state of very heavy unconsciousness into full wakefulness, like
a cork released in deep water and mounting more and more swiftly toward
the bright surface.

Before he had fully succeeded in reaching this state, however—before he had opened his eyes—he was suddenly aware of the heat of another human body close to him, and his inner alarm system brought him immediately into full wakefulness. But he lay as before, giving no physical sign he was not still slumbering, his eyes closed.

No one should be able to approach him while he slept, without his now-highly-trained heat-sense alerting him that something radiating like an adult human was within less than three meters of him.

Bleys continued to lie as he was, not moving, eyes closed, breathing as he had been breathing when he began to wake; exploring with ears and nose the identity of whoever was close—and close that person must be, for Bley's awareness of the heat radiated was telling him that he or she could not be more than a meter from him. In fact, possibly a good deal less.

Slowly, supporting information came in, partially through his ears—whoever it was was breathing softly through the nose—and had a body odor he recognized.

It was Toni, and she was sitting beside his bed, rather than standing.

Toni almost never used scent unless it was a formal occasion, and then very sparingly. But his nose had identified the familiar signature of the soap she used; and her own, slight but also identifiable, personal odor; which was of course unique to every individual.

Bleys continued to lie still, his eyes closed as he assessed the situation. The moment stretched out.

Clearly, Toni was waiting for him to wake normally; and while she was doing so, she was holding something like a book or piece of paper, that crackled faintly in her grasp.

Not even Toni should have been able to come in like this and sit down so close to him in his bedroom when he was asleep. He had trained himself to this as he had to the martial arts—it had been a necessary learning, if at the same time a practice in a fascinating exercise, the acquisition of a skill—or, in this case, an awareness.

Bleys had wanted heat awareness as a special warning system to protect him from any enemy who might try to creep up on him while he was unaware and unguarded. It had not been difficult training, with the help of modern technology—only time consuming.

On Association, he had found a medician who was a physiological psychologist with a specialty of positron emission tomography: the mapping of the brain centers that dealt with activities of the human body and its senses.

He had gone to see this man, ostensibly to recruit him into the Others, and led him into discussion of the problem of training a person to a higher awareness of heat sources close to him. The psychologist, a Cassidan-trained expert, had been contracted to work on Association and was intensely unhappy there, feeling that his talents were not being used properly. He was enchanted by the challenge Bleys presented to him.

The medician, whose name was Kahuba Jon-Michel, had been more than willing to explain how his specialty had grown, from the first fine needles used to probe through a living skull, to the present non-invasive process. So, while Bleys sat with a helmet-like device on his head and while Jon-Michel did various things at a console with keys, studs and dials to control the image that gradually built up in a vision tank, he talked; and Bleys, who had always been fascinated by anything he did not know, had listened and remembered.

"Now here," said Jon-Michel, tapping the now-completed image in the vision tank with a stylus, "here, where I touch the image, is your heat-control center in the brain. I can easily put a very small device in place firmly against your scalp just above it, and it will stay there, with your hair hiding it. That device can send you some kind of signal when the center begins to receive nerve signals from your body that it's sensing the presence of a heat source near you. Then you can train yourself with a specific heat source at different distances, trying to increase the distance and increase your sensitivity as much as possible."

"Good," Bleys had said.

"But I've an even better idea. Now, here—" Jon-Michel tapped another point on the image—"your pleasure center is located."

He beamed at Bleys from his angular face with a pleasant air of academic triumph.

"What I could also do," he went on deliberately, "is put next to your scalp a device—about the same size—that will make a connection under the proper circumstances between your heat awareness in the heat center and your pleasure center."

"Why do that?" asked Bleys, who, in fact, already understood what the man was getting at.

"Well, you see," said Jon-Michel, "your brain's heat center is aware that your body senses heat well before you register it consciously. That is, it can feel a lower level of heat than you would normally be aware of. With training, I believe you could increase your awareness, and so lower the threshold of heat at which you notice it consciously."

He pause to gesture deprecatingly. "Of course, there will always be a difference between what you're conscious of and what your body's sensors can detect." He shrugged. "It's a kind of threshold factor."

"And the device on my scalp?" Bleys asked, although he was sure he already knew.

"Would signal you by triggering your pleasure center the moment your heat center picked up any signal of heat your body was noticing." Jon-Michel smiled. "It would be a more pleasant training regimen than most. And although the training device is small, and generally unnoticeable—except to certain security monitors—I believe we would find that your body would quickly learn to perform for this reward, with no lasting need for the device."

"I see," said Bleys.

"By careful training," Jon-Michel went on with satisfaction, "your pleasure center can tell you—in the form not of an awareness of a heat source, but rather a sudden unexplained feeling of pleasure—that your heat center has begun to react. Your brain can, I think, be trained to do this without the need of any outside signaling system." He smiled more widely.

"I must add that you'll have only a brief moment of sensation that will seem to disappear if you try to examine it, not a prolonged sensation of pleasure that continues as long as the heat source is within your range."

Bleys smiled. The thought that an assassin might be trying to creep up on him in the dark of night, and that his first wakening and awareness of this would be a feeling of pleasure, was ridiculous.

"Oh, but it's entirely possible!" cried Jon-Michel, completely misunderstanding the smile. "I promise you I can give you a device to make the connection, and I believe you stand a good chance of training yourself to make the connection with your pleasure center work. To begin with, the device I'll give you will be one that gives only the brief pleasure sensation. But with practice, your brain will be used to making the connection, and I really believe you'll be able to do away with any sort of outside help. I say that with all the expertise I've accumulated."

"Oh, I believe you," said Bleys. "We'll do it."

So they had. Bleys had lain with his eyes closed, in the darkness of his bedroom, and a moving heat panel had approached him from distances and directions chosen randomly, while a chart was recorded of the point at which he reacted to feeling its presence by raising his hand.

Bleys opened his eyes now, lazily, for a second looking at the ceiling and the room in general, and then focusing sideways on Toni. She was looking down at him with a serious expression.

"How long have you been here?" he asked her.

"A while," she said. "How awake are you?"

It was a curious question. His instinctive response was that he would not be looking at her with his eyes open if he were not awake. But he did not say that.

"What makes you think I'm not?" he asked, instead, reasonably.

"I mean completely awake," said Toni.

"Fully enough," he said. Again, a sense of a long journey taken came back to him. "How long have I been sleeping?"

Outside the transparency of his outer wall, it was not only daylight, but looked suspiciously like at least afternoon daylight, if not late afternoon.

"Somewhere between eighteen and twenty-two hours, we think," she said. "Do you feel all right?"

He nodded, gazing at her in silence. He was not used to being astonished. In fact, he realized now, he had always secretly prided himself that his ability to think ahead to whatever might happen to him would keep him fully prepared for anything that could astonish him. But now he was caught unprepared.

Toni went on. "If you're really awake, you'd better read this."

She passed him an interplanetary-imprinted ship-letter, which had been sealed with a seal he recognized as that of the two-world Government formed on one of these rare occasions when Association and Harmony were under an Eldest. The seal had been broken and the letter had been opened. There was nothing very surprising about this, since Toni handled his personal mail, opening and passing on to him only those communications he needed to consider.

On the inside of the sealed and folded single-molecule sheet of paper, was—literally stamped and embossed in large letters, rather than printed—the message he read now.

Be advised:

BY THE GRACE AND INSPIRATION OF GOD: you, Bleys Ahrens—under the graciousness and favor of the Lord to His beloved Eldest, who speaks to you with the voice of all our people on the two blessed worlds of Association and Harmony—have been appointed to the honor and duties of the position of First Elder, at his right hand.

Accordingly, you are directed immediately to cease whatever you are presently engaged in, wherever on planet or in space you happen to be when you receive this; and immediately return to that world cherished of Our Lord, called Harmony, which it has pleased the Eldest to choose as his official residence; and there you will make yourself available at the place and moment to be chosen by the Eldest for your installation as First Elder.

Therefore, on receipt of this, you will so obey immediately and without thought to any other purpose or action. You are expected by our Appointed Eldest to be in his presence as soon as may be possible in the universe of Almighty God.

By his Hand:—

The signature below the last three words was that of McKae.

Bleys had taken in the whole letter at a glance. He read it again, more for the sheer interest of doing so slowly and savoring it, than for any other reason. He passed it back to Toni.

"What's funny?" asked Toni.

"I'm smiling at McKae's being so very much McKae," said Bleys, sobering.

"So we get ready and leave immediately?" said Toni. "For Harmony? Abandoning any more talks here?"

"Of course not." Bleys smiled again.

Toni looked hard at him. "You're not going to obey this letter? Then what kind of answer—"

"No answer. Just file this so we have it for future reference, if necessary."

Toni had been sitting unmoved all the way through this. Now she relaxed visibly. She smiled also.

"You aren't going to go at all?"

"I will when I'm ready. You didn't really think I'd drop everything and run, did you?"

"Well," said Toni, "if you want to be First Elder, or go back to Association or Harmony, ever—to say nothing of whether the rest of us might possibly want to go back someday to our homes there, you'll have to send him some kind of an answer, won't you?"

"I don't see why," said Bleys.

"No answer at all? That's really going to prejudice your position as First Elder—if you even get it after you haven't answered this letter."

"Not at all," said Bleys. "It's a first lesson for McKae. He's going to have to learn he can't give me orders. In fact, he'll need to learn, eventually, that it's going to have to be the other way around."

He smiled at her.

Toni did not respond immediately, but then a slow smile spread over her face and her face itself changed in a way he'd never seen it before. It was as if she relaxed into enjoyment—as if she had been waiting for something a long, long time, and the welcome answer had come at last.

"Go-kui," she murmured.

He gazed at her, still smiling but a little puzzled. The sounds—the words, or whatever they were—were ones he did not understand. It struck him only that they must be in the language still spoken in the privacy of her family.

"I don't understand."

"I said"—she was still smiling in that fashion that was completely new to him—"essentially, that I've always known you were skilled in many ways, but not until now was I sure that greatness was surely in you."

They were bonded together by their gazes; and he was aware that it was one of those rare moments in which he was face to face squarely with the fact that he loved her; and that the barrier he kept up always between them like an impenetrable glass wall was beginning to thin into something more like a fine mist. In a moment he would disregard it, move through it and tell her how he felt about her—and the way he thought she felt about him would become explicit between them.

But the steel will of his purpose caught him back just before he was free. Memory flooded in, of the fact that once he opened himself to any other person, the entrance produced could never be closed again; and all that he was determined to do and bring about would eventually be told to whomever it was. Something innately human in him had always felt that there was no other living person who could face that prospect but himself.

He must remain solitary, isolated from the rest of the race, if he intended to do with it anything like what he wished. And that isolation must continue. He must continually remind himself of the need for it because occasions like this would come again and again, until the end of his life— for what he intended to start would not be accomplished for generations.

Chapter 25

They were on Newton. Well, almost on Newton, because the ship was descending very slowly. Possibly, it was merely a careful descent; but in any case, Bleys and all his people were jammed in the exit lounge together with a scattering of passengers from Cassida.

One of these, with his face almost against the lower part of Bleys' chest—somehow he had evaded the Soldiers' cordon about Bleys, and Bleys had signaled Henry not to make an issue of it—was a middle-aged businessman; running a little to fat, and bald on top in such a curious way that it looked almost as if he wore a tonsure, sadly at odds with the expensive gray business suit that attempted to disguise his weight by its tailoring.

"We ought to be down soon, don't you think?" he said anxiously, trying to see either around or through Bleys' body—a manifest impossibility—and out the nearest window at the ground below.

"I think so," replied Bleys.

"I just hope we're down soon," the businessman said, nervously. "I've got a very important appointment with a lab here." Evidently, nervousness was making him chatter, any words at all to fill in the interval before the ship grounded. "I hope they're taking good care of my luggage. It's one large piece, but it holds some very, very"—he checked himself, obviously on the edge of what he thought would be an indiscretion—"papers and things like that," he wound up.

At this point, the ship touched the ground with a minute shudder; the port opened, and Soldiers began to step through it. For once Bleys held back, and Toni, passing out ahead of him from the relative dimness into Newton's late afternoon, looked suddenly and sharply back over her shoulder.

"Dahno's here!" she said.

Bleys followed her out a second later into the tinted daylight that was unique to Newton, situated as it was in orbit about Alpha Centauri B, the somewhat orange-colored star which shared its system with Alpha Centauri A—Cassida's sun—as well as with the small star known on Old Earth as Proxima Centauri. The light, unusual though it might be, showed him that Dahno was indeed here.

But it was Dahno with an unusual difference. There was none of the usual good humor or friendliness to be seen about him. It was astonishing how that cheerful face, simply by dropping its grin and hardening its features, could take on such an ominous and dangerous look.

Dahno's size, of course, helped in making him appear so dangerous. But the face was one that Bleys had seen only once before in his acquaintance with this half-brother of his. That was when Bleys had still been a child. They had met face to face for the first time, and Dahno had defined their relative positions in the known universe by knocking Bleys, half-unconscious, to the ground with a casual backhanded flip of his massive right hand.

Now that same face, and the almost belligerent way in which Dahno stood—dwarfing all those around him and with his legs placed a little wide, his massive shoulders hunched and body completely motionless—seemed not to signal anything more welcoming as they approached him. His un-friendly appearance was strangely in keeping with the reddish light; so that he could have been some early war god—Thor himself, of the ancient Norse deities, resurrected just before Ragnarok.

To be fair, Alpha Centauri A was also still to be seen here, adding to the light. But very slightly; a dwarfed, if brighter, disc off to Bleys' left, only slightly higher overhead than the bloated appearing Alpha Centauri B, now approaching the western horizon.

"This way," Dahno said coldly and briefly, once Bleys was within speaking distance. Dahno turned about and strode off ahead through the entrance of the small building behind him, leading across its narrow cen-ter—it was evidently some sort of message center and clearinghouse, be-cause other passengers than themselves were also headed for it—and out a farther doorway to where the customary file of limousines were waiting for them.

Dahno headed for the first limousine in line, and waved Bleys, Toni and Henry into its ample six-chaired rear chamber before he entered with them and shut the door behind them.

"Dahno—" Toni began, but immediately Dahno's hand was held up to stop her.

"We'll talk at the hotel," he said.

He sat back in his seat and said no more, while the rest of the lim-ousines were filled by the Soldiers of God and the whole entourage took off for the city. Nor did he speak again—nor did any of the others in the limousine—during the ride into town. Toni's face had become expres-sionless, with that particular lack of expression that could mean anything; but probably right now, Bleys guessed, meant that she was not pleased.

Bleys himself was feeling slightly amused, but inwardly examining with some interest the fact that the sight of Dahno, looking like this, had so strongly evoked the past that for a moment he had relived the sudden fierce resentment he had felt as a child when Dahno had hit him, so that for a second there he had once again been small and helpless before the towering bulk of his brother.

Henry looked as he always looked: detached, and waiting.

Not until the four of them were in Bleys' private suite in the hotel, in its main lounge, did Dahno speak again, still in the same hard, distant voice.

"You'd better sit down to listen to this," he said to Bleys. He looked at Toni and Henry. "All of you."

They sat. Dahno cupped one hand for a moment over an ear, almost as if he had reached up casually to scratch the side of his head; but the gesture was enough for the others. They were being overheard, and undoubtedly also observed and recorded. None of them moved or changed expression. Meanwhile, Dahno himself took a chair, pulled it close so that they were all seated as near to each other as Dahno's own long legs and Bleys' could be accommodated, and produced a small silver device from a pocket. He held it in the open palm of one hand.

After a moment, it began to put forth from its top a tiny bubble that swelled rapidly until it expanded, not only about Dahno but about all the rest of them. They found themselves in a lounge which had now become a shimmering blue, seen through the barrier of the almost-transparent globe about them. Then the bubble's expansion stopped.

Dahno moved his thumb on the side of the device, which separated itself from a tendril that had connected to the bubble while it was expanding, and put the small device back in his pocket. The tendril disappeared, but the bubble remained in position.

"This shield"—he circled the tip of one long, thick finger in the air to imitate the bubble about them—"is the only one of its kind outside a certain laboratory here. I won't go into how I got hold of it, because we've more important things to talk about, and don't ask me how it works. All I know is it uses phase-shift principles to provide a discontinuity that lets everything go back and forth through the bubble except the sight of us or the sound of what we're saying. Anyone spying is locked out."

Toni's mouth was opening, but Bleys spoke first.

"How can you be sure?" he asked.

"Tell you in a minute," Dahno said brusquely. "You came in on one of the regular passenger spaceliners from Cassida. It's a good thing I had a watch out for you. Is *Favored of God* here at all then?"

"It landed here three days ago," Toni answered crisply. "It came in under the name of *Spacehawk*, with false papers that show it as having come in from Ceta on a purely cargo run, even though its holding areas are still configured for passengers. It will be keeping its space on the pad here for an indefinite time, under the excuse that it's having some kind of overhaul on its drives. Actually, they'll be able to lift in a couple of hours, once they get word in code that we're on our way to them. I should call it a one-time signal rather than a code, because it will be an untraceable single-word phone call."

"That's wise," said Dahno. "So you didn't come in as a complete flock of innocents."

"Of course not," Toni said. "There's no danger of anyone from Newton snooping around and finding they don't actually have anything wrong with the ship, since any spaceship is sovereign territory of the planet it has its papers from, and can be entered only by invitation of those in charge aboard it."

"Good!" Dahno sat back in his chair a little, slightly relaxed. But his face was still hard. He turned to look and speak directly to Bleys.

"You left Cassida early, didn't you? You're here ahead of time. If I hadn't had a watch being kept for you on incoming passenger lists, I wouldn't have been notified in time to meet you when you landed. Why'd you do this?"

Bleys began to feel the first stirrings of a definite annoyance. He was the one who directed matters, and Dahno had not contested his role for years. Yet now he was firing questions like a prosecuting attorney in court. Still, there might be some reason behind all this that would justify it.

"I thought there were some promising prospects if I left Cassida when I did." Bleys kept his voice—and temper—under control.

"Prospects?" said Dahno. "No matter how good they were, you'd be better off getting on *Favored* right away and lifting off Newton."

"Why?" Bleys demanded.

Dahno chuckled. But it was not his usual chuckle; this time it was as grim as his face.

"Like you, I've got my special abilities," he said.

"I've never doubted that," Bleys said.

"No, but you've overlooked it," said Dahno. "I was never more right than when I said you'd need me on Newton. If I could only have gotten here sooner, I'd have chapter and verse ready now that would turn you around and send you out. I just had a hunch this was going to be a tiger's den for you, and now I'm sure of it, even though I don't know the details. You made a mistake when you sent me back to Association to get elected."

"I did?" In spite of himself, Bleys heard a faint, but definitely hard edge in his own words.

"That's right," Dahno said. "Because there are some things I do better than you. No one can match you at seeing what's ahead of you and working out how to take control of it. You do it better than anyone I ever knew or could imagine. But I see the present better than you, Brother. This has been *my* life—the examining and understanding of what's around me at the moment, and I see it more clearly than you do because all your attention is forward."

Watching him, Bleys nodded slowly.

"You see," Dahno went on, "what you've been ignoring in the present while you forged ahead, winning every point, making everything go the way you wanted it to, building a name for yourself on all the worlds— you overlooked the fact that our human race tends to make use of the same law you find in physics and make use of in human relations—that every action has an equal and opposite reaction. The people you push, so they'll push others of the race around to suit your purpose, gradually create a counter-force to your push; by people who disagree with what they hear from you. This can vary from out-and-out opposition to simply not wanting to go along with you. But every person you move has an instinct to push back; and it grows in them like mud piling up on a spade—

"—What I'm saying, Bleys"—Dahno interrupted himself almost harshly—"is that whether you know it or not, you need me to see in the area where you're blind, or at least don't see well. I saw opposition building against you back on Association; and in McKae, and in the Chamber on Association. Henry's parish that elected you once, and that just elected me, doesn't love you at all now; and most people there disagree with the most reasonable arguments in your speeches—simply because *you* made them. The same thing is true on Newton. I've seen things you probably have missed. I've found out things you'd never have known. Because one of my abilities is to slip between the cracks and read what people wouldn't ordinarily want read by someone else."

"Go ahead, then."

"To begin with," said Dahno, "we've got a branch of the Others here, nowadays, after all. A good-sized branch, but mostly underground."

"That's interesting," Bleys said.

"The organization we had here," said Dahno, "was made illegal. The powers that be aren't witch-hunting past and secret members, but those who were or are members aren't attracting attention to the fact, because that would force the power structure to take notice of them—which could be fatal for every one of them. Just knowing that much should tell you something."

"What's that?" Bleys asked.

"Simply, if you thought New Earth had a tight social situation and Cassida a tighter one, you'll find both were wide open compared to this world. Every laboratory from the smallest to the largest here belongs to an Institute. Every Institute, and every lab, is at swords-points with every other one. They go through the motions of alliance and friendship; but it's always with daggers ready behind their backs, or a plan to take advantage of an alliance for their own profit. The result is, in the whole population, everyone's at dagger-points with everyone else; and, further, nearly everyone's an active spy, spying on the rest to survive."

"How did you find this out?" asked Toni.

"I went looking for a Newtonian who plainly was hiding some personal secret he didn't want known," Dahno answered flatly. "Then I cultivated him and learned enough to track down what kind of secret it was, and used that much to blackmail him into telling me about his relationships with his lab-mates and the relationship of his laboratory with others. From there I followed a chain upward and inward until I'd located the laboratory that made this secrecy device—meanwhile getting a picture of how this planet is run and by whom."

"All this in a couple of weeks, at most?" Toni asked. "You couldn't have gotten to Association, spent even three or four days there, and been

back here in time to have more than a little over two weeks on Newton.
How could you do so much in such a short time?"

Dahno looked at her with that grimness that seemed so new.

"I'll tell you how. The urge to spy goes nicely hand in glove here
with the hunger for shop talk—trade talk, if you prefer—so, there have to
be social meetings, which become an open market for the trading of secrets—and everything else that goes on under the surface here."

He paused again. "Enough background?"

"Very useful background," said Bleys. His own touch of temper was
under control now. "Go ahead. Say what you want to say."

"All right, then," said Dahno. "The minute I got off the spaceship
for Association, I began to give out the general impression that you and I,
Bleys, had had a parting of the ways; and that was why I was going back
to our home world, while you continued your tour. Naturally, I refused to
go into any detail, but let anyone watching know that I was fuming inside
over the way you'd treated me and looking for a way to get back at you."

"Considering the way you've always presented yourself to people everywhere," said Bleys, "I'm surprised they'd believe that—after all these
years you've been so goodnatured and easygoing."

"I cultivated a different attitude." Dahno grinned a little. "You saw
how I was looking at you when you first stepped off the spaceship? That
was my expression for public consumption."

"Effective," said Bleys, "but I'm interrupting. Go on."

"I'll do that. In a few words, I left them all thinking I'd planned to
get to Newton before you and do what I could to make things difficult for
you."

"You haven't done that?" asked Toni. "I mean, as part of building
your cover here?"

"I only gave the impression; that's all. All that was needed. The situation here didn't need much help from me. You've all been not only
observed, but controlled, right up to this present moment."

"By whom?" Bleys asked.

"The Laboratories Review Council," said Dahno. "It controls things
here the way the Board controls things on Cassida."

"I haven't seen any signs of control," said Henry. "Though they could
have been recording us from the time we stepped off the spaceship. Antonia Lu made the reservations herself, didn't you?"

He looked across at Toni.

That's right," said Toni. "I picked the limousine service and this
hotel as our destination, as the best place for us here in Woolsthorpe."

"Woolsthorpe," Henry echoed. "It's a strange name for the capital
city here."

"Woolsthorpe, in England back on Old Earth in the seventeenth century," said Dahno, "was the birthplace of Isaac Newton. As far as your
choosing limousines and hotel, have you ever had a professional magician

offer you a deck of cards and make you choose one he wants? It's called *forcing*. This hotel and the limousines were offered to you that same way."

"So this is not just any hotel?" Bleys said.

"No," Dahno said. "Remember the Bastille in Paris, on Old Earth—or the Tower of London in England? Well, this is the same thing. Hotel, fortress, a maximum-security prison for important people. A place under the thumb of the Laboratories Review Council—and that's a den of tigers for you, especially. Did you realize that you're on the same floor and probably no more than a hundred meters from where the Council holds its meetings?"

"No, I didn't," Bleys said.

"Well, that's where you are," said Dahno. "Only don't try to walk over and take a look at it. You could get into a bank vault easier than you could into that part of the building."

"There's still a chance that somebody might use a negative-matter bomb to wipe the whole building and most of the city off the map," said Bleys. "Someone who didn't see any farther than the destruction of whoever's in control here."

"They'd have to get into position to launch the bomb," said Dahno, "and from underground, on top of the earth, above it—or out beyond atmosphere for a good astronomical unit of space—all approaches are under surveillance."

"Not if they have this sort of bubble around them," Bleys said.

"But that's just the point," said Dahno. "No one—even the Council, has it, yet—"

A bell chiming somewhere in the walls or atmosphere of the lounge interrupted him. A soft, apologetic but attention-demanding, bell. Dahno reached down to the object at his feet, and put it into one of his suit pockets. The blue bubble vanished from around them. Only then he spoke.

"What is it?" he asked.

"A messenger from the Laboratories Review Council begs admittance to the lounge in which you are presently sitting," said the voice, as apologetically as the bell that had announced itself a moment before.

Dahno looked at Bleys, and Bleys nodded.

"The Great Teacher Bleys Ahrens will see him now, then," said Dahno. "Provided the message is short, since the Great Teacher is occupied at the moment."

"It's only an invitation. It can be delivered briefly," said the voice. Dahno looked at Bleys, who nodded.

"Come ahead," said Dahno.

A door to the lounge slid open. Not the door from the corridor, nor yet the one to the lift that came directly to this suite from the ground floor; but a door giving entrance from an adjoining room; and there entered, not the apologetic young man that the voice had seemed to indicate, but a tall, thin man in his fifties, with a long face that time had set in lines of severity, and wearing a black suit with a short jacket that was almost a uniform.

The atmosphere of the room changed with his entrance. Henry had swiveled his float about to face the newcomer. Dahno's face was back in the lines of grimness and anger that it had worn at the spaceship terminal; while Toni, who had not needed to move to face the door through which the man entered, had apparently not moved at all. But Bleys noticed the slight appearance of white below the iris of her eyes, which signaled her "white face."

"I'm Bleys Ahrens," said Bleys, who had rotated his own float to face the man, as he heard the door opening.

"Then it's to you I'm to extend the invitation," said the thin man in a formal voice. "The Laboratories Review Council would appreciate your seeing them tomorrow in their quarters in this building, at an hour convenient to yourself, preferably mid-afternoon."

"Mid-afternoon?" echoed Bleys. "Let me see, then. Suppose we say at sixteen-thirty hours—or four-thirty, P.M.—if you're using the Old English standard here."

"Sixteen-thirty hours will be satisfactory," said the tall, thin man. "Someone will come tomorrow before that time to conduct you to the meeting place. The Laboratories Review Council appreciates your compliance."

He turned and stalked out.

"And that's it," said Dahno, after he had reset the blue bubble of the security device. "Take my advice. Let them do without you, tomorrow. Make that code call and head for *Favored* right now."

"I know it's good advice, on the basis you see the situation, Dahno. But I'm not just dealing with Newton alone. I'm working to gain control of a three-world group—five-world, if you count Harmony and Association—and it's like capturing a python. I've got the three meters from its tail forward tied down; but the meter and a half of its front body and head are still free. This is my job for life, and I can't take any steps backward; but you don't have to stay and go down with me if I lose, Dahno—" he looked at Toni and Henry—"or any of you."

They both started to speak, but Dahno got his words out before them.

"Never think I'll leave you, Brother," he said. "I'm having more fun with you, whether it's Hell or Heaven. But I'll remind you of one thing. The invitation you just accepted was the equivalent of a Royal Command Appearance, on this world that's the den of the tigers I was talking about. You may end up getting what you want here. But be warned. You'll be playing with their dice, which will be loaded against you. I don't think you'll escape being clawed."

Chapter 26

"I'm Sean O'Flaherty," said the young man in the white uniform with the blue piping on sleeves, lapels and trouser seams. "I'm a Council intern, and I've come to guide the Great Teacher to the Council now for their meeting. My first name's spelled S-E-A-N, by the way."

"S-E-A-N?" Toni said. "Not 'Shawn,' as pronounced. I see. Another Scottish name."

"Irish," said Sean.

"Oh, Irish, of course," said Toni, so warmly that Sean, eighteen years old, fell in love with her at once.

"But," said Toni, "you're forty minutes before the time of the meeting. If the Council Room's in this hotel, which we were given to understand, it can't take you more than five minutes to walk there. He's in conference right now, and can't possibly be ready to go for another half an hour. You'll have to wait."

"I don't mind," said Sean.

Bleys and Dahno had been listening to this interchange, for it was Dahno with whom Bleys was presently in conference. The blue bubble was up around them; and, true to the promise of its maker, air, sound and everything else was coming nicely through it—only their conversation was being cut off from anyone outside by the shimmering surface of the bubble in all directions.

"Toni's been a little different lately," said Bleys, returning to what they had been talking about. "Ever since I told her that I had no intention of obeying McKae's orders to come back to Harmony immediately. She has this quality of lighting up inside—you've noticed?"

"I've noticed."

"It evidently confirms something she must have been thinking about what my ultimate aims might be," Bleys said. "I haven't told her, as it happens, just as I haven't told you or anyone else about my future plans. I'm sorry I can't take any of you into my confidence about them. A large part of the reason is that I have to decide how I'll do something just before I do it."

Bleys tried to keep any trace of guilt out of his voice. None of the reasons he was withholding the information would sound really complimentary to the person he was withholding it from. Henry would find his ultimate aims blasphemous—a literally Satanic infringement on the powers of the God Henry believed in. Toni, he was afraid, would find him less than the person she had been able to work with so far—perhaps turn from him in disgust. And Dahno would read in it a contempt for all human beings—including him—and Bleys firmly believed that Dahno could not bear contempt from anyone, least of all from him.

"That's all right as far as I'm concerned," said Dahno. "It's the way I'd work it myself. I never tell people where I'm aiming, either."

"I think, to a certain extent, it's been all right with Henry and Toni, also—for the present, at least," said Bleys. "Henry's obviously waiting for some signal that I've either gone completely into what he calls 'Satan's hands' or broken free of them. But with Toni, I never knew exactly why she was content to put up with not knowing—but I begin to imagine a possible future for me; and for some reason my taking a firm stand in ignoring McKae's orders to come back immediately confirmed it. I wish I knew what she thinks she saw or understood."

"I've no idea," said Dahno. "But if she's happy for the present, why don't you just accept that and go with it—since you have to build things as you go."

"You're right," said Bleys.

He returned to the topic they had been discussing when they had heard the interchange between Toni and Sean O'Flaherty.

"You were promising me," he said, "that the Council couldn't possibly already have the secret of this bubble, and possibly a way of listening through it. With the powers you say they have, I'd think they'd be able to learn any secret that any laboratory'd have on this planet."

"That's the point. There are always some ways in which power is limited," Dahno had answered. "The one principle on which this whole planet stands is that you can sabotage the work of other laboratories, kill its workers, attack it politically in every possible way—but the one thing you must never do is attempt to find out its current secrets. That's because those secrets are not only the lifeblood of every lab that exists here, but the lifeblood of the planet itself."

"I understand." Bleys nodded.

"Because"—Dahno went on—"otherwise, there'd be anarchy here on Newton. You'd have people from one lab kidnapping workers from other labs, questioning them—and they have all sorts of means available for that—until all secrets were revealed. And that would threaten the whole structure of scientific research this planet depends on for its bread and butter."

That explanation was simple enough, Bleys thought, but ultimately pragmatic and possible. A society had to be built upon at least a few generally-accepted agreements. This certainly could be one of Newton's. And surely they would believe that if they stole knowledge from each other, it would make it easier for outsiders to steal from them—and *that* would threaten the livelihood of the entire planet.

Of course, it would be only a principle—a socially fixed point—but what Bleys worked with were either such fixed points in a planetary society, or what that society's people considered fixed points.

"Now," he said, "about my talks here on Newton—the first is two days from now. What can I expect?"

"Well," said Dahno, "for one thing, you'd better think in terms of talking to a small audience. You're used to speaking to thousands. Here you'll be lucky if you have fifty or sixty people."

"Now, that's interesting," said Bleys. "Why so few?"

"You remember I said yesterday," answered Dahno, "that the Others, here on Newton, don't want to draw attention to their membership. A great many of them just don't want it known they've ever been Others. So it'll only be the braver ones—the rebels and risk-takers—and some government spies, of course, who'll come. Not that that means your words won't be carried quickly by those there to everyone else who ever was an Other. In fact, your speech will be available, eventually, word for word, to the population here at large—anyone, that is, who'd be interested in what you said. There may be as large an invisible audience out there for you as you got openly on New Earth. But we've no way of counting them right now. They don't want to be counted."

Bleys chuckled.

"Any objections, then, to talking to such a small group?" Dahno asked.

"I can't think of any," Bleys answered. "The very fact there are so few will point up a good deal of what I've been saying all along: that is, it'll give me a chance to emphasize some points I've made all along about our problem with Old Earth—by hinting that the same sort of blindness applies on this world."

Dahno glanced for a second, almost suspiciously, out through the blue sheen of the bubble, at the now-azure lounge about them.

"I thought you were sure that the Council didn't have the secret of this device," said Bleys. "The Council didn't have it, and no one else did."

"That's what I said," Dahno answered. "All the same, it doesn't do any harm not to mention anything that you'd like to be absolutely secure about. I wish you were in my position and could move around among these people without being seen the way most people see you—five meters tall and floating in midair—so they'd be as relaxed with you as they've been with me. Though"—he added—"admittedly, with those I could get any useful information from, I'd already put each in a position where they didn't have much choice but to tell me what I wanted to know."

"Yes," said Bleys. "Henry seems to be under the impression you actually used blackmail. According to him, that may not be an official sin but it's certainly a Godless thing to do."

"I let them infer it—that's all. Anyway, I'm never going to please

Henry with how I do things," said Dahno, and for a second they grinned at each other. "But the point I was making is that you're going to get an audience that's all of one certain type of character. Knowing that, is it worth your talking to them?"

"I've been thinking about that point," replied Bleys. "Actually, I think I can turn it into an advantage."

"How?" asked Dahno, bluntly.

"It's just an idea at the present moment," Bleys said. "Let me think about it a bit."

He rose to his feet. "I'd better meet this guide the Council sent me. I got the impression that the Council wants to see me alone. I think in this case I won't test them by trying to bring either you or Toni to the meeting with me, the way I did with Toni at the CEO Club on New Earth."

"I think that's wise," Dahno said. "It's been pretty clear from the start they want you to themselves. In any case, remember those claws I mentioned. Keep your eyes open and your guard up."

Chapter 27

Bleys saw that Sean O'Flaherty was a lean young man, a little like a younger and much less fanatic version of Amyth Barbage, the Association Militia officer.

One thing was very clear. He was not easily awed into social behavior by having Bleys stalking along beside him. From what he now said, he had spent his half-hour wait talking to Toni, presenting himself as agreeably to her as she had become agreeable to him.

Now, however, he and Bleys had left both the suite and Toni behind, and he was guiding Bleys toward the Council. He had no one left to talk to but Bleys; and, clearly, what he very much wanted to talk about was Toni. But lacking any knowledge of her relationship with Bleys, he was also clearly feeling blocked, to a certain extent.

As far as Sean knew, Bleys could be Toni's lover, employer or even a close relative; and many of the comments he much wished to make to Bleys now about this magnificent woman might turn out to be unwise.

However, the urge to talk still plainly moved him; and accordingly, he spoke almost as soon as the door to Bleys' suite was closed behind them, the words bubbling out of him as if he had been a bottle of sparkling wine just uncorked.

"Possibly I should introduce myself more fully," Sean said rapidly.

"I'm an Accredited Council Intern—of course, that's why I was sent to bring you. You're an Honored Visitor, Bleys Ahrens—but of course, you know that."

"Am I indeed?"

"Oh, yes. Otherwise they'd have simply sent an ordinary Council Intern. I know Antonia Lu introduced me to you. But my name is spelled S-E-A-N, a little differently than it's pronounced."

Even with most of his mind concerned with meeting the Council, Bleys smiled to himself. It was unusual, on one of the New Worlds, that anyone's name could attract attention; since most people carried names that announced a mixture of different heritages. This name was an exception; but from what he had already learned about the people on Newton, it was a common exception there, as it was on the Dorsai and in areas on some of the other New Worlds. In the case of Newton, it was evidently a point of social pride to have exactly the sort of name that might be encountered back on Old Earth. On most of the Worlds it was not unknown for families to cling to ancestral names; but on Newton the compulsion seemed unusually strong, as if by this they could identify themselves as being above the other New Worlds and very much still on a level with those on the rich and populous Mother World.

"So I understand," Bleys answered.

The greater part of his attention was concentrating on observing his surroundings and working to deduce from them what he could of this world's present social pattern and its weaknesses, as well as his own situation here.

They had started off down a hotel corridor empty of other people and appearing even wider than it actually was. Bleys decided this was partially so because of the unusual decor. The walls on either side of them were not recognizable immediately as such, resembling rather floor-to-ceiling banks of mist, though solid enough to a casual touch of Bleys' finger.

These were interrupted at intervals by obvious doorways closed by ordinary brown doors. But Bleys had already been given to understand that a simple technical order, sent from a desk or wrist keypad, could cause such an entrance to vanish into the mist-wall around it; so that no access at all was to be seen—if someone within did not want to be disturbed.

Otherwise, the walls were pleasant in their own right. Through them moved, faintly, all the colors of the rainbow, in a calm, slow, steady progression; so that the eyes were not invited to focus for any length of time at any one point. Only, at one place there was what looked like a shallow indentation in one wall, which Bleys had been told signaled an opening to another corridor, branching off at right angles.

In the indentation, the mist was darker; it was impossible to tell how far back that corridor ran, or what it might open into.

Bleys pondered possible advantages of this unusual architecture and found none. None, but perhaps the desire to appear technically advanced and ostentatious. On the debit side, there was the danger of turning into one of the semi-hidden side corridors and running into someone coming out.

Come to think of it, however, he told himself, there were probably technological fail-safes of some kind, that would keep people from colliding in such a way.

Since leaving the main lounge of his suite, he and O'Flaherty had proceeded past a number of the rooms belonging to it. They now came to a turn that should, according to his reckoning, be the corner of the building; and Bleys saw before them a shorter and narrower hall which ended abruptly in a further mist-wall.

Hurrying on his shorter legs to get a half-step ahead of Bleys, O'Flaherty led the way right into the mist and vanished.

Bleys followed, and stepped into a hallway that was entirely different. Suddenly he heard the heels of his shoes and those of his companion rapping noisily on the uncarpeted floor in something very much like a tunnel; for the walls and ceiling were now of bare concrete. Moreover, there were neither windows nor three-dimensional pictorial displays, let into them; so that it seemed as if they had suddenly begun to traverse some service area of the hotel.

" . . . I have to say that I was very much impressed by your Antonia Lu," Sean was saying at last, in desperation; since Bleys, with the greater part of his mind occupied, had failed to rise to any of the leading statements Sean had been putting forth continuously as they walked, to start Bleys talking about Toni. "I didn't feel right about asking her directly what her position was, the position in which she works for you. She's not your secretary, I suppose?"

The last words came out on a slightly higher note, betraying hope. If Toni was no more than Bleys' secretary; and particularly if Bleys had no interest in her, or relationship with her beyond her duties in that job, then it just might be that he, Sean O'Flaherty, might possibly . . .

"She's one of the few people who work with me, rather than for me," Bleys said, "so the things she does cover a wide area, too wide for any one title, even if such a title existed. Like a few other people around me, what she does only she could do."

"Oh," said Sean, still uninformed and obviously disappointed.

An awkward silence—at least on Sean's part—fell between them. Luckily, however, the tunnel-like hall they were in was not long. They came to an ordinary heavy, brown, metallic-appearing door, set in the wall at its far end. Sean opened it and they passed through—again into a totally different kind of passage.

This was a long, high, wide and pleasant stretch of the building—almost too wide, in fact, to be called a corridor—with tall and broad three-dimensional views set along its walls, so that now they seemed to be looking out through windows at solid ground, level with the surface Bleys and Sean walked on, although Bleys knew very well that they were over twenty stories in the air.

The scenes were all pleasant, mainly of lawns, carefully trimmed trees, hedges and flower beds, all matched by plants growing in earth-holding areas just inside the false windows, so that this part of the trip became like passing through a home on one of the Exotic worlds, where his mother's people had been in the habit of building habitations in which it was hard to tell whether you were outdoors or still within walls.

The ceiling, at least double the height of the ceilings in the suites Bleys and his people occupied, was vaulted and apparently of stone—or imitation stone—colored a blue like that of an Old Earth sky. The walls were paneled in what seemed to be warm brown wood. The floor was covered by something like darkly-rich, thickly-growing grass with earth below it. A greater contrast to the concrete tunnel they had just left could not have been imagined, and it was overwhelmingly obvious to Bleys that the contrast was deliberate.

He and Sean had walked in silence about a third of the way along this hall when the world around him made a sudden violent and brutal turn, that for a moment destroyed all sense of orientation he possessed.

"You're all right, Bleys Ahrens?" Sean asked.

The feeling had been similar to—but much greater than—the physical and emotional disorientation which comes when someone who believes he or she is moving in a certain direction in an unfamiliar city suddenly realizes that the movement had actually been in a totally different direction than he or she had thought. A feeling as if the whole city had, soundlessly and suddenly, been lifted up, swung about in a complete half-turn and set down again.

Bleys' unexpected emotional reaction had been one of abrupt, powerful and instinctive fear and helplessness.

But Bleys' body had been schooled to the point where it didn't hesitate; and since the feeling had come upon him before he could react, his body had automatically kept walking. He was abruptly aware now that Sean, still keeping pace with him, was staring at him.

Bleys made himself glance at the young man.

"Yes," he said.

Sean was silent for a moment, then burst out again.

"I only ask," he said, stretching his legs to keep up with Bleys—who without thinking, had now given his long legs their usual stride, so that Sean had been forced to a half-run to keep up. Realizing this, Bleys now shortened his steps and reduced the pace.

"—because the first time people pass the portal back there, it usually disturbs them more than a little—quite a bit, actually. In fact, Bleys Ahrens, if you'll forgive my mentioning it, since we stepped through the portal, your face looks a little pale."

Bleys glanced down at him with a warm smile. "Does it indeed?"

He might not be able to control the blood vessels of his face; but he could most certainly control the organ tones of the voice with which he had worked so hard for a number of years now.

His tone of slightly contemptuous amusement, with a kindly smile, was effective enough that he could see Sean rethinking his belief that Bleys had been shaken—as he actually had been—by the passage through what Sean had called a "portal." Sean's control of his own facial expression, for someone with only the life experience of his lesser years, was good; but he could not now completely disguise his own reaction from Bleys, trained to observe small changes like the dilation of the pupils of the eye and complete control of the face around the corners of the mouth.

"Well, that's good to hear, of course," Sean said swiftly. "You'd be surprised. Everyone else I've seen go through for the first time, reacted. The first time I went through here myself, I was with a good friend of mine—he's an Intern, too, but only in Messages rather than in Council Service. I was hard-hit myself, but he was really knocked about. I thought he was going to faint for a moment. Of course it's bound to be different from person to person; and in the Council's Service we don't think of the Message people as being particularly strong—strong in self-control, that is. Actually, there's some reason for thinking that. The way the Message people are chosen . . . "

Bleys noticed with inner humor that, even though his life experience might be relatively short, Sean had already discovered one of the tricks that Dahno used to perfection. This was not to stammer, or in any way show confusion, at the unexpected; but simply to become very voluble, pouring out words—any words—that would serve to lead another person away from any suspicion that he was at a loss in handling a situation.

With Dahno, this reaction slipped easily and imperceptibly into any one of his established patterns of conversation, so that it was not noticeable to anyone who did not know him well. Sean was not yet proficient at it. The increased rapidity of his speech, and his sudden flow of chatter on the subject of Messenger Interns as opposed to Council Interns, was too obvious. But the technique was still designed to give the person talking some time to collect his thoughts and work his way back to safer topics.

Bleys had, in fact, already moved most of his attention once more away from Sean. He had more than a guess at what the "portal" had actually been.

In the early days of phase-shifting, as it was used by interstellar spaceships, each phase-shift any human experienced had exacted a heavy toll—emotionally, mentally and physically. There were drugs that helped, but only partially.

Nowadays there were better drugs which, taken before a trip, were a full body and mind defense for however many shifts might be experienced. But ordinary passenger-carrying spacecraft were normally careful not to exceed a prudent limit in any twenty-four hours of ship-time; or even approach that limit too closely, since people varied in reacting to the shifts.

On his first trip with his mother between the worlds of two different stars in the human-inhabited region of space, the very young Bleys had deliberately delayed taking his medication until after the first phase-shift, simply because he wanted to experience the feeling of the shift.

So he had; and his instinctive human reaction had been one of extreme fear and panic.

The sensation Bleys had just now felt, passing through the "portal," had been almost exactly what he had experienced as a child when he had made his experiment.

What he and Sean had just now passed through was certainly some form of phase-shift discontinuity—but a very limited one to disturb him so little, now that long training had made his senses so acute. Sean had undoubtedly been medicated against its effects. In fact, the younger man was probably habitually under the influence of medication to protect him if he had to pass the "portal."

The phase-shift was undoubtedly the Council Room's outer "gate." Such a mechanism, designed to move spaceships light-years at a jump, by "redefining" their position with regard to the surrounding galaxy, could be set to effectively dispose of an intruder, just as the slot on his desk disposed of his sheets of paper, permanently. Or it could be set, as this one was, to give a "gentle" warning.

He and Sean, Bleys guessed had been moved only half a pace forward, or perhaps only millimeters of distance. But, it occurred to Bleys, such a short trip could well act to give the Council a certain advantage, in dealing with a visitor shaken out of his normal composure. . . .

Sean had fallen silent.

It was just as well. Bleys' mind was only peripherally concerned with his guide. The rest of it was all taken up with his speculation on what he might encounter in this meeting with the Council.

This meeting could be his first real test. Real or not, it was likely to be the sternest test he had met so far.

What he had done with the Others organization, both on the two Friendly worlds and other planets he had visited, had been to build on and change their direction somewhat, working on what Dahno had originally created almost as a sideline, in the exercise of his political genius.

Dahno was an obvious genius. Bleys had merely accepted that fact when he had been younger; but, as he grew up, a question had presented itself to him frequently. Why had Dahno chosen such a small use for his talents, in being simply a political manipulator? Like their mother, he had been content to influence only those people immediately around him, whose actions impinged directly upon him and his life. It was inconceivable to Bleys that anyone with such ability should not aim at a larger goal.

However, that was Dahno; and it was Dahno's business, not Bleys'. Bleys had learned a long time ago that it was impossible to understand people completely—as impossible as it was to change them deeply once they were adult, or anywhere near to being adult.

His problem now was not with Dahno, but with the shape that historic social decay had imposed on the people he was about to meet.

All the worlds had shown the classical signs of that social decay Exotic thinking had predicted. All, that is, except Old Earth, which was, so far, largely unreadable by him, as far as its present direction of historic movement was concerned.

As also the Dorsai and the Exotics were, for other reasons. He would necessarily be concerned with them all, eventually. Socially, the Exotics and the Dorsai were hopeless candidates for the type of influencing that he had hoped to use with the rest of the New Worlds. The people on them were simply not vulnerable to what had worked for him so far on New Earth and Cassida. He was beginning to think that Newton was a question mark.

But the difficulty in knowing that much was that it was not much help. Even being sure of that much did not give Bleys any clear idea of what he might encounter in the next few seconds.

The words "the next few seconds" were still in his mind as they passed out of the long hall with its large window scenes and went through a cream-colored door into what seemed to be essentially a blank, gray-walled lecture amphitheater.

It brought back to mind a picture he had seen of an Old Earth class-room of several centuries ago; with the seats in rows rising toward the level on which they had entered, so that the first seat of the top row brushed against his left leg as he came in, and all attention was designed to be focused down to a circular area, well lit, with a long flat table and a spot of light beamed onto it so that it was the brightest place in the room—a place where a lecturer or instructor would stand.

The chairs were unpadded, wooden and almost primitive. Once more, a greater contrast to both the hall he had just left and the concrete tunnel-like stretch before it could not have been more deliberately made.

Sean led him around the curve of the back row of seats, through another door—green, this time—and they stepped into a lounge. A lounge that, except for the fact it lacked a fireplace and a real or artificial fire blazing behind its fire screen, was a somewhat larger duplicate of the main lounge of his suite here; and those in most of the other hotels in which he had stayed on this trip and others.

Its window wall had a door opening on a balcony like the one outside his bedroom—but larger. Its door was ajar at the moment, and the afternoon air from outdoors was making a small stir in the staler, filtered atmosphere of the room.

"Bleys Ahrens!" said a brisk, slim, elderly man, getting quickly to his feet from his padded float. "Good, that's all, Sean—you can go now. Bleys Ahrens, let me introduce you to the rest of the Council here."

"The rest" were five in number, making six in all, the others seated in the same sort of padded armchair floats that the speaker had just left;

and not one of them, thought Bleys looked the way a research scientist might have been expected to look. More like—as individuals—a sulky author, a librarian, the owner and operator of an exclusive shop selling high-fashion clothing at outlandish prices to rich women customers, and so forth . . . anything but World decision makers.

The man doing the talking was gesturing around the rough circle in which they were seated.

"Right next to me here, Bleys Ahrens," he was saying, "is Council Member Georges Lemair."

He indicated the man who had struck Bleys as looking like a sulky author. He was a little over middle New Worlds height, but slightly overweight; in his mid-forties, with red hair, he looked as if he might be outspoken.

There was a don't-give-a-damn attitude about him; and in spite of the fact that he was dressed in the formal fashion of tight jacket and ankle-length pants—his pants were not flared at the bottom, as was common among people of his generation on most of the other New Worlds nowadays, but ruler-straight from knee to ground—he looked untidy.

The man on his feet was still introducing.

"Sorry, I probably should have introduced myself first. I'm the current President of the Council. My name is Half-Thunder—of the Phase Physics Institute. Oh, and I should probably have mentioned that Georges Lemair is of the Institute on Atmospheric Chemistry."

"Honored to make your acquaintance," Bleys said to Lemair.

"Honored to make yours," Lemair said indifferently.

"—and this is Din Su, of the Mathematics Institute." Half-Thunder was moving on around the circle, and Bleys stepped with him. Din Su was a woman in her fifties; plump, unremarkably dressed, with an almost-comfortable, grandmotherly appearance, except for an incisive look about her which Bleys found interesting.

"Honored to make your acquaintance," Bleys said.

"Honored to make yours, Bleys Ahrens," she replied in a comfortable voice that matched her appearance rather than his impression of her incisiveness.

"And this is Ahmed Bahadur," Half-Thunder stopped before a float holding a man who sat very straight in his chair.

"Honored," he said, with a touch of hoarseness in his voice. He was a tall, old man, patriarchal in appearance; and he sat broad-shouldered, upright, but at ease. He answered as easily as Din Su had done, white teeth gleaming in his ample gray beard—but gleaming apparently without humor, or perhaps with an automatic rictus of a smile that meant nothing.

"Ahmed Bahadur is a researcher in the Biological Variforms Institute," Half-Thunder said.

"Honored," said Ahmed Bahadur, again, in his rusty old-man's voice.

"Honored," said Bleys.

Half-Thunder moved on.

"And this is Anita delle Santos of Human Engineering."

"Honored, Bleys Ahrens," said Anita delle Santos. She was small, blond, pretty and strangely fragile-looking; but the impression she gave was one of powerful concentration on anything to which she turned her attention—which at the moment was Bleys.

Bleys replied pleasantly and was moved on to the last person in the circle, almost back to Georges Lemair and an empty float that had been obviously prepared for Bleys, since it had been positioned higher above the carpeting than any of the others, so that it afforded ample legroom. It was interesting, Bleys thought, that none of them seemed concerned about the fact that they would be looking up to him. It argued an unconscious sureness of themselves.

"And this," Half-Thunder was saying, stopping beside the fifth person, "is Iban. For personal reasons she uses only one of her names. I'm sure you'll understand. Iban is Systems Institute."

They were all a little too sure of themselves in this situation, Bleys thought. It would do no harm to jolt the situation a little and see what the results would be.

"Honored," said Bleys, and fired his first gun of the meeting in the form of a question. "Very honored to meet you, Iban. What are your other names?"

Neither Iban herself nor the others gave any large or obvious signs of disturbance. But the question was calculatedly impolite, and Bleys was aware of a slight, but general, stiffening around the circle.

Iban, however, looked back at him without a change of expression on her narrow-boned face under very black hair. She was wearing a simple, almost austere dress of deep-ocean blue.

"As Half-Thunder told you," she said calmly, "my other names are personal. For your information, Iban is a tribal name for the Sea-Dyaks of Old Earth."

Strangely enough, while the name "Sea-Dyaks" rang a faint bell in Bleys' mind, he found he knew nothing in detail about that particular people, tribe, or ethnic group. But he was sure that they had been from the oriental area of New Earth—and Iban, like Toni, did not look oriental. She was slight-boned and not so much pretty as beautiful, in a knife-like sort of way. She looked almost as ready to bite as speak.

"Thank you," said Bleys with a smile. "It's kind of you to explain."

"Will you sit down, Bleys Ahrens?" said Half-Thunder, now, just behind him. "We have a float for you here. As it happens, one of our number was unable to be here today. I hope it's adjusted to your comfort."

Bleys turned. It was possible, but not likely, that they would have had a chair identical with all the rest made for him, hastily, in order to give him the impression that he was merely filling the seat of an absent member. He stepped back and sat down. The seat was in fact just the exact height off the floor so that his legs were comfortable; and the interior of the chair, between its arms and back—which was adjustable in any case—had been expanded to accommodate his longer limbs and body.

"Well now," said Half-Thunder, who had reseated himself in his own float, "you're comfortable?"

"Very," said Bleys.

"Then, if you'll excuse me for a second," said Half-Thunder, "we'll say nothing for a moment while I set up a shield."

He touched a stud on his wristpad, and a blue bubble began to grow from the arm of his chair, expanding until it surrounded all of them right to the walls of the room and the entrance to the balcony.

Having reached the walls, the bubble stopped growing. It was identical in appearance with the security bubble Dahno had produced. Either Dahno had been lied to, or else one of the unbreakable rules necessary to Newtonian society was not all that unbreakable where the Council was concerned. Half-Thunder took his hand from the wristpad.

"A security device," he said to Bleys. "We want to make sure that none of the Council's deliberations are ever made public; and it's impossible for anyone to spy through this particular shield."

"Sensible," said Bleys.

He gazed about at them, trying to put his finger on the common quality among them that was alerting him.

Their faces were perfectly calm; and, with the exception of Lemair's, politely friendly, but otherwise revealing no information about their inner attitudes or thoughts. None of them showed any signs of tension or animosity. Nonetheless, there was that common element in them all that had triggered all his defensive instinct. He had not felt like this before, not even facing the CEO Club on New Earth—or even facing Pieter DeNiles. They were like DeNiles, but much more actively inimical.

It was not so much that quality in them that concerned Bleys right now. He had expected sooner or later to meet up with people like this, even a group like this, organized and united in their attitude toward him. What was concerning him was the quality in them that was signaling itself to him through one of his senses. But he had heard nothing in any voice, no sign of tension, nothing in the way they spoke or their appearances—

Then it came to him. It was in the way they all looked back at him. Steady and all curiously alike. Their eyes of all colors—from the very dark of Iban's to the ice-blue of Georges Lemair—but all, all those eyes examined him in the same way.

They weighed and measured him. They sliced him up into small transparent slices to be examined on the screen of a microscopic camera in the mind of each. He had not moved them in the slightest degree by his deliberate impoliteness to Iban. They were—as they obviously had been from the moment he had entered the room—remote, deliberative and absolutely sure of themselves.

"Have you seen our *Symphonie des Flambeaux*, Bleys Ahrens?" asked the motherly Din Su.

Bleys looked at her agreeably. But, as she spoke, his mind was racing. The question itself was innocuous. The *Symphonie des Flambeaux* were indeed considered one of the several Wonders of the Worlds—even including Old Earth. Until the claim became ridiculous in the last century, Newtonians had been in the habit of insisting that the *Symphonie des Flambeaux* ranked first among all such wonders, ahead even of the Final Encyclopedia.

The breath of the air through the partly open door to the balcony cooled the side of Bleys' face that was toward it. Din Su's question, apparently harmless as it was, was still also the opening gambit of the Council's talk with him, and merited study as much as a Queen's-pawn to Queen's-pawn-four opening in a chess game between master players. The piece moved was one of little power, the move could be simply an automatic one; but in the hands of such a player it could also indicate a dangerous pattern of attack.

If so, it was a pattern Bleys must deduce, make plans to oppose and be ready to meet.

Chapter 28

"Not yet, I'm afraid," Bleys said. "As you probably know, I just got here. I haven't had time. But I'll be seeing it tomorrow. I wouldn't want to miss seeing at least one performance."

"So," said the light tenor of Georges Lemair. The mathematician himself had not stirred, or the expression of his face altered. "Sight-seeing as well as work—is that the kind of trip it is?"

Bleys looked at him pleasantly.

"No," he said. "Work only. From my point of view, the *Flambeaux* are an index of Newton's development. I've made quite a study of your past and gone to some trouble to decide what I want you to do in the future."

The ambiguous words were said so lightly that they took a few seconds to sink in, even on this group.

Then Half-Thunder leaned forward in his float. "Are you by any possibility suggesting that you yourself might have some influence on the future of our world?"

"Well," Bleys answered. "I have already, of course; and I don't see why I shouldn't continue."

There was another small silence.

"Is this man completely sane?" Iban asked Half-Thunder.

"As far as we knew," Half-Thunder directed both his answer and his attention to her.

He turned back to Bleys. "Or perhaps this is some kind of joke, Bleys Ahrens?"

"Why should you think it was a joke?" Bleys asked.

"If you really need an answer to that question," Half-Thunder said, "we'll assume your sanity—which I'm not surprised that Iban questioned—and simply say that you're about as far from having any influence on this world as somebody in a cage in the other end of the universe."

His voice had risen—but only slightly—on the last few words. He paused, then went on with perfect calmness.

"You're not only not in a position of influence here. The Council has brought you before us to tell you we're going to have to take some measures with you. Apparently, you have come here under the cloak of diplomatic immunity to disturb our citizens with this nonsense about your Others."

"You must be mistaken," Bleys said. "This is a speaking tour only. Naturally I make it a practice to be available to the local Others when I'm on a world where there are some. What else would you expect?"

He shrugged his shoulders in the face of their silence.

"My talks," he continued, "have nothing to do with you or the Other organization, but with the future of the human race itself. Newton's population is part of the human race, so what I say applies to it as well as to everyone else. Of course, that population can choose not to listen. But I think some may, in times to come."

"You admit it, then?" Iban said. "You're here to disturb our society?"

"I admit what I say." Bleys looked half-humorously at her. "If you want to put some sort of different construction on my words, I can't be responsible for that."

"Oh, yes, you're responsible," said Georges Lemair.

"Georges is quite right," Half-Thunder said. "All the more so because you're here on a diplomatic passport. Our Council here, looking at the whole pattern of your behavior—not only on our world but on the others you've visited, and on the two Friendly Worlds from which you come— find it adequately clear that you're here only to try and upset society on the most valuable New World the human race possesses."

Bleys laughed.

"You think it's funny?" asked Anita delle Santos, her words coming all the more cuttingly from her apparent fragility and delicacy.

"I'm afraid so," Bleys said. "Here you are, the senior—essentially a responsible and ruling—body of what you call the most valuable of all New Worlds—though I can imagine some other New Worlds disagreeing—and still, you seem to have dreamed up some sort of cloak-and-dagger farce with me as the chief actor. I wish you'd explain to me just how something like what you're imagining could be going on under cover of my talks about all the race on all the worlds?"

"I think you know as well as we do it's not a farce and how you have been doing it." Half-Thunder looked around the circle, which responded with a murmur of agreement from the rest sitting there.

"In any case," he went on, "it's quite clear that with the help of your older brother, you first set up the nucleus of a subversive organization on as many worlds as you could. Here on Newton, you weren't able to set it up as well as you probably wished; but there are some weak people among even our good researchers who've been attracted and influenced by your notion that the human race in general needs only to throw off the yoke of Old Earth—a yoke that's nonexistent, of course; I think you know that as well as we do—and remake itself according to your own notion."

He paused. Bleys merely watched him. When the silence had lasted more than a moment, the older man went on.

"Having set all this up, you're now going around lighting a fuse to these groups and the general public on each of the Worlds. What surprises all of us is that you also seem to have a fair amount of intelligence. How you might have expected Newton to stand for this—this open and bare-faced sabotage—simply because you come here with a diplomatic passport, perplexes us all. I can only hope that intelligence of yours extends to the point of understanding that we're simply going to disregard your diplomatic immunity, if necessary."

"That'd be unwise," said Bleys. "The New Worlds exist by financial interdependence; and that, more or less necessarily, requires a host of commonly accepted conventions. That includes the ancient convention, brought from Old Earth originally, that accredited diplomats are given consideration on another World they're visiting, as if they were still on the soil of their native planet."

He looked around at them, smiling. "Violate that convention, and there's no reason why all the other connections and agreements shouldn't also break down; and that would be disastrous to all of us."

"I know casual public opinion on most of the worlds runs that way," said Half-Thunder. "But it overlooks the fact that Newton has been moving into a position where it's the one world that's vitally important to all the rest."

"Vitally?" said Bleys.

It was Georges Lemair who rose to the bait.

"Without us, none of the other inhabited planets have a common technology!" His voice was loud.

"Aren't you assuming quite a lot?" Bleys murmured. But Lemair was going on without listening.

"If we cut off connections with them all, tomorrow, they would all end up going different ways at different speeds, falling apart—back into savagery. Meanwhile, our World and those with us would go on advancing scientifically and technologically into a brighter and ever more advanced condition, with a larger and larger understanding of the universe. We'll be an empire, eventually, in which Newton, of course, will make decisions. For all. In fact, we're practically there now."

"I see," said Bleys. "I imagine you've already made plans, too, for your own manufactories, like they have on Cassida; for medical research units and teaching units, like they have on the Exotics; and military training, like that found on the Dorsai—wasn't it a Dorsai, Donal Graeme, that brought Newton to surrender, a century or so ago?"

"Those worlds have already taken their specialties as far as they can go. We already know as much as they do," Lemair answered.

"I see," said Bleys again, soberly.

He did indeed.

In fact, he suddenly understood, almost certainly, more than they intended him to, and possibly more than they understood themselves.

One of the evidences of social decay predicted for the New Worlds had been a drift into a form of megalomania, in which each planet's people began to think of themselves as not only living on the best of the New Worlds, but the one world that, in the long run, must outpace all the others.

He had been prepared to meet this form of collective semi-insanity, but not this soon; and he had always expected—in fact, assumed—that the first indications of it would be armament building, construction of an armed force that hoped to take over the other Worlds by force.

Old Earth had once hoped to militarily conquer the Dorsai World. But Old Earth had been unexpectedly defeated—not because of a military genius; not even by the best of her fighting people—but by the non-combatants of the planet. Since then, such dreams had been discounted.

Clearly these present Newtonians expected to make their conquests by other and less violent means, most likely commercial ones. But that still meant that this Council could be in deadly earnest after all, with the announcement of its plan to disregard his diplomatic immunity. If they really wanted to arrest him, there was little he or Henry's Soldiers could do to stop them.

As yet, between the worlds, Bleys was still a small fish. These people on this Council did not fully realize it, but McKae would certainly not risk any real break in relations between the two Friendly worlds and Newton simply because a Friendly government member had been mishandled there. McKae had neither the character nor the temperament for such a determined move.

He would probably do as little as possible, secretly pleased that Bleys was the member mistreated—not realizing that Bleys had already made enough of an impression on Harmony and Association, at least, that if he went down, McKae would shortly go down as well. Friendly voters had long memories and strong opinions.

All this went through Bleys' mind very quickly, so that he hardly paused before speaking to Half-Thunder.

"Even supposing you wanted to risk committing such an unheard-of act as disregarding my diplomatic immunity; and possibly even do something more than deport me—though it's hard to imagine what—"

Half-Thunder smiled as he interrupted.

"I can tell you specifically what we intend. We intend to bring you to trial here under our laws for attempted sabotage. I won't cite you legal chapter and verse; but under our system, conviction on that charge could make you liable to a death penalty."

"Which, of course, would be carried out immediately," said Bleys, with a tinge of irony openly in his voice.

"I've no doubt it would be carried out immediately," said Din Su in her comforting, motherly voice. "I'm sure we'd all feel relieved if all the New Worlds were free of your tendency to trouble people."

"Haven't you overlooked one thing?" said Bleys. "If you tried me in the face of all international custom and agreement, then executed me, you'd be making a martyr of me. Look at history. Not only our history on the New Worlds, but all the history before that on Old Earth. Martyrs tend to be remembered and sanctified. Their philosophy tends to make more converts after their death than they made themselves, alive."

Half-Thunder shook his head, smiling. "Our situation here has a different precedent in history. Do you remember the observation someone once made, that Carthage was recorded in history as the villain in its conflict with Rome—but it was Rome who wrote the history? Soon we here will be in the position of Rome. We'll write the history."

"I see," said Bleys. He sat back on his float. "Then you'd better get busy with your legal and diplomatic moves. Because, as it happens, I believe in what I tell people. I don't consider my life anywhere nearly as important as my message."

He looked around at them all.

"Not my life," he said, "not the Others' organization, nor anything else. All that's important is the future of the race. I can hardly claim I'll enjoy the prospect of my death; but I realize it's something that, in spite of what you say, is going to do more for my message and more for the human race than probably anything my words could do while I was alive."

Grimly now, he smiled at all of them.

"Perhaps," he said, "I should even thank you."

Not only was Bleys telling the truth—what he actually believed in—but his words were delivered with all the trained power of his voice and person that had carried conviction on so many other statements to so many other people. The Council members hearing him might be trained and experienced in many ways; but they were not experienced auditors, skilled in warding off the emotional influence in the voice that now spoke to them.

Even if they had been, it was still the truth—all but the last few words. Within himself, Bleys believed sincerely that the end toward which he worked could be achieved only if he stayed alive and continued to work for it. But there was little likelihood that they would be able to separate that one grain of difference from the rest. Moreover, by this time Bleys was completely convinced that if this was actually what they aimed at, there had been little sense in their bringing him before them, simply to shock and frighten him.

Clearly, they had meant to shock and frighten—but only as a step toward something further; and it was that something further for which he now fished with an attitude mostly truthful, but partly false.

"A very brave attitude," said Half-Thunder, after a moment. "But, in any case, no matter how many other people think you're a martyr, on the other Worlds—and there's little likelihood of that getting out of hand here on Newton, while Old Earth is not really concerned in this—it will actually make no difference to how we guide our own world."

"Are you sure?" Bleys asked. "You might find my martyrdom may make converts who'll be strongly opposed to you; who'll make things difficult for you when you come to try and lead all the other New Worlds."

"We already *do* lead all the other New Worlds," said Anita delle Santos.

Bleys glanced at her briefly, but returned his attention to Half-Thunder.

"I'm not talking about what you can do, particularly with the hard sciences," said Bleys. "I'm talking about your trying to be in a position to give orders to all the other New Worlds. As an ultimate goal, there could be difficulties in reaching that, if enough people on other Worlds hold a philosophy that doesn't agree with yours."

"What gives you the idea that Newton has any interest in giving orders like that?" Half-Thunder asked.

"Isn't that what the best end up doing?" Bleys said, innocently. "Being the most powerful? In a word—dominant. All and each of you."

This time, small tensions and small movements in those around him gave away the fact that he had taken the conversation into a sensitive area. Very likely they had not officially or even unofficially discussed how power would be apportioned among them if and when Newton became the world ruling all other New Worlds. But that was the obvious end toward which they were heading. All of them had to have been able to taste the power of rulership in their minds, and that was a particularly attractive taste to some personalities.

That question of future authority raised a large point of potential trouble between those here. Bleys had brought it out into the open; meanwhile giving them reason to move on to the unspoken proposal he expected from them—the carrot and the stick he had encountered on New Earth—but with a difference. This business of ignoring diplomatic immunity and putting him on trial for his life could hardly be a preamble to such a proposal. He was waiting for one of them to get to it.

Bleys had guessed that one would be Din Su—and it was.

"I'm interested," she said. "What makes you feel there is any great number that will even remember you, let alone think of you as a martyr?"

"They came in the upper tens of thousands—I believe we had close to eighty thousand people there one day on New Earth, when I spoke," said Bleys. "That was a World that had never seen me before, but heard what I had to say only on recordings. That indicates something to me. Doesn't it to you?"

"It indicates something," said Din Su, "whether it's what you had in mind or not, I don't know. Interest like that is largely unmeasurable. Any unusual event or six-day wonder will attract a crowd."

"Close to a hundred thousand people?"

Instead of answering him, Din Su turned her attention to Half-Thunder.

"You know," she said to Half-Thunder, as quietly and as unconcernedly as if she and he were alone in the room, "we did talk about making some other use of him."

"You aren't saying you believe these claims of his?" said Half-Thunder.

"Oh, they're inflated, of course," said Din Su. "Even if he was serious about being willing to die for his philosophy, he'd still have reason to want to make us think that his following was as large as it could be. But he's got what some writer or other back on Old Earth once called 'a dangerous eloquence.' We might find a use for that eloquence for our own concerns and purposes. What do you think?"

"Hmm," Half-Thunder said noncommittally. He looked around at the others in the circle, who looked back but said nothing.

"Well," said Half-Thunder, with a touch of irritation in his voice, looking around the circle again, "tell me what you think?"

"I don't care," Georges Lemair growled. "Whatever the rest of you want."

"How could we be sure he could be kept under control?" asked Anita delle Santos. There was something artificial and rehearsed about the way she asked it.

"Oh, there are ways," Half-Thunder said. "You remember we've set up that kind of control with a few of our own people here. Remember?"

After a second, Anita nodded.

"I say put him on trial and execute him," Iban said. "Why take chances?"

"Sometimes, my dear," said Din Su, "the chance is worth taking."

At first Iban looked as if she would answer. Her lips parted, then closed again. She sat silent, looking hard at Din Su.

"Well, now," said Din Su, "I think we'll be pretty safe in making use of him." She looked at Bleys.

"Do you understand what we're talking about, Bleys Ahrens?" she asked.

Bleys smiled. In fact, he almost grinned at her.

"I can guess. You want to use my ability by having me adapt my philosophy to what you want people to be brought to believe. Am I right?"

"You see," said Din Su to Half-Thunder. "He's extremely intelligent. It would be a shame to waste him."

"Possibly you're right," said Half-Thunder. "*I* don't think so, but if everyone else does . . . "

They all looked at Bleys.

"You might consider asking me what I think about this," Bleys said to them.

"It really doesn't matter what you think," said Half-Thunder, in the gently soothing tones with which he might have spoken to a child. Half-Thunder and Din Su, Bleys told himself, were almost certainly the controlling elements in this Council. If the two worked together, the Council would probably go their way. Nonetheless, Georges Lemair was scowling, and Iban had a frown that made her look even more carnivorous than she did without it. Nor did Anita delle Santos looked pleased.

If they were all acting, it was good acting. But then, with people like these, such acting capability should not be surprising. Bleys thought he would lose nothing by prodding them a little more.

"Oh, but I think it does," he said. "You see, I'd no more prostitute my message to save my life than I would to avoid a martyr's death. My message is my life."

"You see," said Iban. "He's unusable."

"Not at all. Not at all," Half-Thunder answered in a tone almost as soothing as the one he had directed toward Bleys. "I don't think he understands the situation, for one thing. For another, there are always ways by which these matters can be guaranteed. But, in a way, he's right. It won't work if we don't have his willing cooperation."

He turned back to Bleys. "To begin with, Bleys Ahrens, you have to understand that none of us want you to distort what you call your message. That much about you is really harmless, after all."

Bleys smiled.

"I know you don't think that," Half-Thunder said reasonably. "But from our point of view it's so. It can be considered irrelevant as far as Newton is considered. At present, the villain of your scenario is Old Earth. We've no quarrel with that. We'd be happy to have Old Earth go on being the target of hatred by the inhabitants of the New Worlds, though we here understand the Mother World better. But you see, if we just let you go on as you plan, you might later on want to identify us and our sciences with Old Earth's pursuit in the same direction—for example, with the scientific accomplishments claimed for the Final Encyclopedia."

"I thought what you were concerned with was my disturbing your people now by coming here and talking," Bleys reminded him.

"Oh." Half-Thunder gave a small wave of his hand. "That was the immediate reason we decided to do something about you. But it's the future that really matters. Now, if we could be sure you'd confine yourself simply to what you call your message, and your blaming everything on Old Earth, then I think we'd feel comfortable letting you go around talking as you want—even here on Newton."

"That's interesting," Bleys said. "I won't bother to repeat that I never intended to speak evil of Newton or any other New World, in any case. I talk about the New Worlds as a social unit; and my vision of the future has always been, in a word, more spiritual than political."

"You don't see any objection, then, to working with us?" Din Su asked, softly.

"So far you haven't given me reason for any," Bleys answered. "As for one cropping up in the future, I can't see where my interest in the race really has a great deal to do with yours. I tell people only what I've come to believe and leave it to them to either find that information useful, or not. If they do, it may help. If they don't, it's their own loss. Trying to do anything more would be going beyond the proper territory of the philosopher."

"Well," said Iban, "he wants to live, after all."

"He's eloquent, yes," said Half-Thunder. "But, more to the point, he's agreeing with Din Su's suggestion. But I wouldn't trust him not to change his mind in the future. I say, just put a potential restraint on him and see how he reacts."

He looked around at the other Council members. They all nodded.

"What sort of potential restraint?" Bleys asked. "I've warned you that I don't intend to alter my message—"

But even as Bleys spoke, softly against the underside of his forearm, which was lying on the armrest of his chair, through his shirtsleeve and formal jacket, he felt what seemed like a touch of a cool finger for an instant. Then it was gone.

"The health of our Council members, you see," Half-Thunder said, "has to be of the utmost concern to our World as a whole. So a medical-response element is built into the arm of each chair-float here—in case of some sudden physical emergency. I'm sure you understand what I'm talking about."

"I understand," said Bleys. "How long do I have?"

"I said he was intelligent," Din Su murmured.

"Twenty-six to twenty-eight hours from now—until roughly tomorrow at this same time," Half-Thunder answered. "Actually, I'd suggest you come to us a good three or four hours before your limit for a second application—the antidote, as it used to be called, in cases like this. Otherwise, while another application will save your life, you may spend an uncomfortable time for a matter of hours first. If you go beyond that limit, you could still probably be saved as much as another ten hours later, but you'd be—perhaps I should say—quite sick, for a period of time that would vary in length according to the delay in getting the antidote to you— and possibly lingering aftereffects."

"So," said Bleys, and he kept his voice perfectly even, "I'm already a captive of yours?"

"We'd rather think of it as just giving you a day to think over our offer," Half-Thunder said. "The option of martyrdom is still open to you, of course; although since we've already decided on this course of action, if you don't agree to work with us, we might simply withhold the antidote and let nature take its course."

Chapter 29

Sean O'Flaherty was waiting to guide him back. Once more, he kept up a steady chatter. But if anything, now, the Council Intern was a little more polite than he had been when he had escorted Bleys to the Council.

It was as if, in his eyes, some of the grandeur of the Council had attached itself to Bleys. Sean seemed, in fact, to be somewhat astonished that Bleys himself did not feel ennobled and uplifted by having rubbed shoulders with the Council's exalted members; and he urged a superior attitude on Bleys, even as he emphasized the inferiority of his own position.

"... I told you you were important," he said, among other things. "It's only the important people they get together in the afternoon for. Ordinary meetings, like the one this week—there's only one a week, you know—are held in the evening. That'll be tonight, but apparently they're going to stay overnight themselves and hold another special meeting for you again tomorrow. I've never known that to happen with any one person—three meetings in a row!"

Bleys assured the younger man he would do his best to appreciate the honor done him.

He was less obliging, however, when they got to the door of the main entrance to his suite. He politely but firmly denied the Intern's eager suggestion that he take advantage of the fact that since he, Sean, was here, he ought to step in and thank Antonia Lu for being so kind to him during the time he had to wait for Bleys, earlier.

Sean allowed his disappointment to show, but made no effort to push the matter. Bleys left him outside the door and went in.

Inside, the entry lounge was deserted, but the door to the private lounges and the private rooms beyond and his own personal bedroom and others was open—but he could hear no sound. He walked on, and in the end lounge, he found himself staring at the outside of a blue bubble.

Even as he looked, it expanded around him; and he found himself now inside it, now able to look through its surface; and in the company of Dahno, Toni, Henry—and two strangers whom he did not recognize.

The group had apparently been talking, all standing together. They broke off to turn and face him.

"What's this?" he asked.

"Interesting matters," said Dahno. "Everything in and on this planet is known to anybody who wants to know, within hours, if not minutes—"

"Not anything said by people protected by my discontinuity," said one of the two strangers. He was a thin, half-bald young man with a few hairs sticking untidily out of his nose and ears. Incongruously, he was wearing blue sports clothes, as if he had just been out for a run or some kind of athletic game.

Dahno lifted a calming hand that loomed so large in comparison with the weedy speaker that it seemed it must throw him into shadow; and might indeed have if there had been a central source of light instead of the even illumination coming from the ceiling and all the walls.

"Granted, inside his discontinuity," Dahno went on to Bleys. "Bleys, this is Will Sather"—his finger indicated the young man who had just spoken—"and Kaj Menowsky, a medician, native Newtonian with Exotic internship."

Kaj Menowsky was a shorter, trimmer man. He had very black hair, very black eyes and a bright aggressive look to him.

"Honored," Bleys said to them briefly before turning back to Dahno. "And if Kaj Menowsky is willing, this saves the trouble of looking up a medician for me. Dahno, you're about to explain why they're here."

"They want to join us," said Dahno, "and there are some rather good reasons for letting them do so, I think. Will Sather, here"—he nodded at the man with the nose and ear hair—"is the creator of the security bubble which we're using. He's learned two things through his individual grapevine. One is—against all Newton's customs, laws and order—the Council has stolen the secret of his device. The second is, he also seems to have a pretty good idea of what they planned for you. We'll have to wait and let you tell us what the Council actually said and did, of course."

"Thank you," Bleys said.

"No thanks needed," Dahno answered cheerfully. "But, in any case, he's got the secret of his device still with him; and he's willing to make us partners with him in it if we'll take him with us—oh, he's been an underground Other here, in any case. So is Kaj. Because of what Will Sather thinks the Council may have done to you, he offered Kaj the chance to join him in joining us. All he asks is that we protect him and eventually get him and Kaj safely off Newton. In return he'll work for and with us as long as we want him. Kaj's offered his services too."

"What does Will Sather's grapevine tell him the Council planned for me?" said Bleys.

"He thought they would try to make you their captive, one way or another; and that they've almost certainly either done this by now by using drugs, or used drugs to reinforce any agreement you made to work with them. That's why Kaj Menowsky is along. He's a medician with a specialty in the type of drugs they might have been using."

"Actually," said Kaj in a brisk, light baritone, speaking very quickly and crisply, " 'drugs' isn't really the right word for what we're talking about."

"I suppose," said Dahno. "Anyway, we can go into definitions later. Bleys, what did the Council do with you?"

"The grapevine wasn't too far off," Bleys said. "I was first told that they were going to put me on trial for sabotage, disregarding my diplomatic immunity—"

"They can't do that!" said Toni.

"They could, but I don't think they really wanted to face the cost of it. It was only their way of softening me up to begin with. When I gave them a lead in a slightly different direction, they came through with an offer to have me continue my speaking on the various worlds, but under conditions that favored them; and to make sure of this, they injected me with something they told me would begin to affect me in twenty-six to twenty-eight hours, but I should come in four hours early to play safe . . ."

He ran through what had happened in a few brief words.

"Do you feel sick now?" Toni asked quickly.

"Not at all," said Bleys. "The impression I got was that I wasn't supposed to notice any change, for at least twenty-six hours, which would put me to a little later than this time tomorrow; and they ended up saying they'd meet with me again tomorrow afternoon, just about the time I'd be paying attention to the effects."

"I thought so." Kaj Menowsky rose to his feet. "I'd better have a look at you right away. I've some portable equipment with me, and the sooner we know what we're up against, the better. As I said, 'drugs' probably isn't the right word for what they introduced into you."

"Yes," said Bleys, "and, understandably, I'm interested in being treated as soon as possible. However, there's something else first. I'll have to ask you and Will Sather to step into one of the other lounges for a few minutes, while the rest of us discuss something privately. You don't need to have any doubts about our taking you with us. But you don't really belong to my special comrades, here; and for the moment, you'd better consider yourself just as passengers being carried along with us. Toni, will you take them into one of the other lounges to wait while we talk?"

"This way, if you don't mind," Toni said to them. Dahno opened the bubble and, with a glance at Bleys, she led them off.

"What's this now?" Dahno asked.

"We'll wait until Toni comes back," said Bleys. "Ah, here she is. I think I'll sit down, and the rest of you had better sit down, too. I'm still feeling perfectly all right—but let's sit down anyway."

"Dahno," he began, looking at his half-brother. But Dahno winked at him, reaching into his trouser pocket at the same time.

"I'm way ahead of you," Dahno said. His big hand came out half-closed, hiding the small device; and a moment later, the blue bubble from it began to enclose them.

"Thanks," Bleys said as Dahno put the device back in his pocket. "I'll make this as brief as I can, because I want to see that medician. Essentially, what the Council did was throw a threat at me first—"

In as few words as possible, he told them of his meeting with the Council, this time giving them more of his interpretations of the meeting.

"So they actually did drug you," Dahno grunted.

"As the medician said," said Bleys. "What it means is that we have less than my twenty-six hours in which to get very busy."

He turned, and his float turned with him as he faced Henry.

"Henry," he said, "you remember that when you first came to me on Association to help me, I said that you were the answer to something I had been very much in need of? And you remember I said that what I might want by way of a protection unit, was really a small Strike Force?"

"I remember," Henry said.

"Well, now we're really going to use your Soldiers as that Strike Force," said Bleys. "I'm going to give the appearance tomorrow of being an ordinary tourist, visiting the *Symphonie des Flambeaux* for a performance in the afternoon. Somehow you've got to pick me up from the *Symphonie*, without attracting attention, armed and ready to fight our way, if necessary—"

Dahno grunted again. "It'll be necessary," he said.

Bleys nodded.

"—fight our way to the spaceport; and to *Favored of God*. Better get in touch with them, Toni—as soon as we're through talking here."

Toni nodded.

"All right," Bleys went on. "The Council won't want to make a public affair out of this, but they'll undoubtedly try a number of undercover ways of opposing any attempt of mine to escape, even though I've got this whatever-it-is in me. So, that means you, Dahno, and possibly you, too, Toni, are going to have to check into a number of situations, including the layout of the *Symphonie* auditorium, its entrances, exits and anything else that we'll need to know, and all places and ways they may use to try and stop us, once they know I'm on my way. As I say, their efforts are going to have to be discreet; so we have that and surprise as an advantage. As for the actual use of our Soldiers, that'll be your department, of course, Henry; and I'll leave it in your hands."

"There's not a lot I can do, Bleys," said Henry, "until I have some idea of what kind of opposition we're likely to run into, how it'll be armed and what kind of tactics it'll use—its advantages and disadvantages."

He looked across at Dahno. "Can you get me information on that?"

"I think so." Dahno frowned. "In fact, I may be able to get more than you'd guess. A tight society like this has its own kinds of vulnerabilities. For example, tight as Cassida was, it would have taken me four or five days, there, just to find who was the best person to tell me what the likely best available security device was. Here, it was a matter of three hours and half a dozen conversations."

"All right, then," said Bleys. "You each know what you're after. Why don't you go ahead with it? Talk it over with each other, and so forth. We'll get together in about three hours here for dinner and see where we stand at that time."

"And now, Bleys," Toni said, "you'll see the medician?"

"There's no hurry. I've got the twenty-six hours at least, even if those people on the Council weren't bluffing—and considering my diplomatic status, a bluff is quite possible—"

"Hmm," said Dahno, looking doubtful.

"I need to re-think this whole Newtonian situation; and since I usually do that best when I let my unconscious work on it first, I'll leave the situation to you three for the moment."

He got to his feet. "So I'm going to take a nap. We'll talk again in a few hours at dinner. Then the medician can check me out."

For a moment, Toni looked as if she might argue with him, but she said nothing.

They dispersed.

While Bleys was an ordinary insomniac as far as night sleeping went, and often lay with his mind galloping faster and faster until finally it drove him from the bed—in his afternoon naps, he usually dropped off as soon as he closed his eyes.

This time, happily, was no exception. He lay down in his bedroom with the door open to the balcony so that the afternoon breeze came through; but with the window wall dialed to obscurity, to the point where the room was in a night-like gloom. Lying so—it seemed—he merely blinked his eyes.

A blink only—and he opened them on a small, interior sense of pleasure, to see Toni coming toward his bed. His mind still held the tag end of a dream that had been about her; so that he was not surprised to see her there and smiled up at her.

"It's dinnertime," she said, "and we're all together with things to tell you. Are you ready to eat with us?"

"Right away." Bleys shrugged off the last heaviness of his nap and swinging his legs over the edge of the bed as he rose to a sitting position.

In the dining room, the table-float had been reduced to a size suitable for just the four of them, and the meal was already on the table. As they sat down, Bleys saw Henry's lips moving silently and realized that Henry was saying his own private prayer before the meal. For a moment, it brought back memories of his first meal at Henry's farm and himself as a boy; and then the memories were swept away by other concerns, and they had all begun to eat and drink.

The late-afternoon light of Alpha Centauri B came through the window wall and filled the room with a warm but revealing light that emphasized the fact they were alone.

"Oh, almost forgot." Dahno put down his large goblet of wine and reaching into his pocket. A moment later, the blue globe of discontinuity that made them private enclosed them once more.

"By the way," said Bleys, "where are those two volunteers that showed up—Will Sather and Kaj Menowsky? Is someone seeing to it that they're fed and taken care of?"

"I've got a Soldier with them to make sure they have everything they need. Toni gave them a lounge with an adjoining sleeping room at the far end of your suite here," Henry answered. "All right, Bleys?"

"That's fine," said Bleys. "I'll see that medician—Kaj—Kaj Menowsky—as soon as possible when we're through here. Did he object to my putting it off until then?"

"He wasn't happy about it," Dahno said. "I had a little talk with him. The sooner the better, on general principles, he says; but a proper diagnosis calls for equipment we haven't got and don't dare try to get for fear of alerting the Council. The ship's clinic will have the necessary equipment, above and beyond the few things he's carrying with him, to build you an antidote—only he called it a 'counter-antagonist.' Eat your dinner and let us catch you up on present information. Then you can have your examination."

"Good," Bleys said. He was, in fact, both hungry and thirsty. He began to eat and drink even as he waved his hand at the rest of them. "Go ahead, then. Tell me what you've found out and whatever you think I ought to know."

The three looked at each other.

"You start, Dahno," Toni said.

"All right," said Dahno. "Bleys, I've already briefed Henry. There are actually four different, armed outfits the Council could put into action to stop us, if we try to move you off-planet. The first and most available is the undercover squad of the city police. But the Council may not want information about us to be circulating in the Woolsthorpe police force, from which it could easily leak into the public news. The news media is controlled by the Council, but that control is so automatic, and so self-censoring, normally, that in this case the information might not get censored before it was made public."

Bleys nodded.

Dahno went on. "The second bunch are the Lab Security Inspectors, who have their headquarters here. They're actually a paramilitary outfit that normally operates in uniform—and I doubt the Council would want people in uniform going against you in the public eye—away from that eye would be different. Of course, they could send them in in civilian dress; but again, they're a large and semi-public body, and it'd take time to get them out of uniform and into action. More likely are the Woolsthorpe police Special Squad. That's actually a number of individual small squads—any number of which, however, are trained to be integrated and used as a single larger unit. Also, they're particularly trained in city fighting. Henry agrees that they're the most likely opponents to run into—and probably the first we'll see."

He stopped.

"Well," said Bleys, after a second's silence, "you mentioned four."

"Sorry," said Dahno. "So I did. In addition to the three I just mentioned, there are the Council Guardians. Specially trained individual security people, belonging to the Council alone and having the job of protecting and guarding the Council members and the people of its various subsidiary units. These could possibly be sent after us fastest, but they're not trained to fight as a coordinated military unit. Oh—and there's the spaceforce barracks units—that makes five, not four—Woolsthorpe is Headquarters for Newton's Space Force, such as it is; and they've got barracks here for the regular military units that act as subsidiary troops and guards for the Council, itself. But these last are pure space-and-surface military; and the least likely, Henry thinks, to be used against us. They simply aren't trained for guerrilla fighting, and most of their weapons will be far too powerful, from the Council's point of view. In other words they might get us, but they could also visibly damage parts of the city or spaceport, in the process."

"I see," said Bleys. "And Henry, what do you think of all this?"

He looked at Henry.

"I think as Dahno has told you, Bleys," said Henry, "I've got a clear idea of what will need to be done—" he glanced at both Dahno and Toni, then back at Bleys—"thanks to the help of these two, and what they were able to find out."

He glanced at Dahno and Toni again.

"So, if you don't mind"—they both nodded, and he turned his attention back to Bleys—"Bleys, you'll do nothing, except let yourself be carried along. In this case, you're in the same situation as Dr. Kaj Menowsky—I should say Medician Menowsky—and the blue-bubble inventor. You'll be a passenger we're getting safely on to the spaceship."

He stopped and looked at Bleys sternly.

"I understand," Bleys said.

"Good," said Henry. "The afternoon performance of the *Symphonie des Flambeaux* runs late in the afternoon, so we'll be into twilight almost from the time we pick you up and well into darkness on the way out to the ship. That will help. The Soldiers have a large advantage in fighting at night—that should be useful against the sorts of Newtonians Dahno tells me could be brought against us. You go to the *Flambeaux* with Toni, and she'll take you away just before the end of the performance. Do what she says and leave the auditorium with her. The two of you will be picked up in a driver-controlled vehicle, driven by a Soldier."

"*One* driver–controlled vehicle?" asked Bleys.

"One," said Henry. "Each Soldier will have his own task and go about it separately, including picking up a vehicle for himself and perhaps one or two others, depending on the job of each. They will each perform these tasks at points far separated in the city, after seeming to be just putting in the day wandering around and enjoying themselves. The vehicles will be stolen; their alarm systems and any outside control connections put out of order, so that they are completely free to go anywhere. It's necessary that we don't gather all our people together during the first stage of the escape."

"Fine," said Bleys. "It's your department, Henry. If you think that's best, we'll do it. But you plan on us all getting together at some point or other?"

"Yes," said Henry. "Now, there are four points where they are most likely to try to stop us. One is just where we'll be coming out of the inner-city trafficways onto the main spaceport route. The next: well outside the city, at the highway bridge over the river Da Vinci. By the time we hit the bridge, though, it should be dark enough so that while they'll have had a chance to set up a roadblock, we'll have the night to work in."

"Correct me if I'm wrong," said Bleys. "But I'd think any military, paramilitary or even ordinary security unit would have facilities for lighting an area they wanted to defend; lighting it so brightly that there wouldn't be much darkness for any opposition to take advantage of."

"That's right," said Henry. "Still, we're going to be moving as fast as we can, and hoping that they won't have time to set up the kind of lighting and other equipment they might usually have with them. They'll probably have some ground-level lighting; but, within limits, our Soldiers can take care of that."

"I see," said Bleys. "Go on, Henry."

"Once past the bridge, the next best point for them to set up a road-block is going to be at our entrance point to the spacefield area. We can theoretically come in by any entrance to the spaceport pad—and you know how much ground it covers—which should mean they're going to have to cover all possible entrances and therefore spread thin whatever forces they have available. That, along with a diminished but still-useful darkness, is our advantage as far as getting onto the field goes."

"Do we know where *Favored* is parked on the spacepad?" Bleys asked.

"Yes." said Henry looked briefly at Dahno.

"Nothing to it," said Dahno. "I just called spaceport general information. An automated system told me where."

"They won't know exactly what we're headed for on the pad, at first," Henry said, "but they'll start to pinpoint it, the closer we get. As soon as they know what sector of the pad, they'll be able to cluster a makeshift—but maybe effective—defense there, to keep us from getting past them.

This will be the last opposition we'll have to crack before we can get to the ship; and when we do, we'll face opposition. They'll have force waiting to stop us even while we're taking off. Dahno tells me, legally, they'll have to leave us alone once we're off the pad and headed into space; and once in space, we can phase-shift beyond their finding. Don't need to waste time talking about that. Now, go and see Med Kaj and have him examine you, Bleys."

"I'll do that." Bleys frowned slightly. "But—forgive me, Uncle— you've given me a lot of general information but no specifics at all. Have I suddenly become someone not even my own people trust?"

Both Toni and Dahno started to speak, but Henry's voice cut through theirs.

"This is my responsibility. Bleys, in this case, that's what you've become. Kaj's told us about what was done to you. While the main purpose of what the Council put in you was to kill you if no antidote was given in time, there was undoubtedly something else: an added regular drug—to make you an informant."

"Informant?" Bleys frowned.

"A chemical, that would make you talk," Toni explained. "It's been known for centuries that there's no such thing as an actual truth drug. But there are drugs that will make you talk uncontrollably; the way someone who's drunk might reveal more under the influence of alcohol, say, than they would if they had been sober; only much more effective. The person might even babble things he wouldn't ever normally want whoever was around to hear. Imagine the drunk-talk tendency multiplied, to where it's a compulsion."

There was a moment's silence.

"You see, Bleys," Henry said, in his immovable tone of voice, "if you know my plans in detail and you're taken by the Newtonians, the Council could find out nearly all—if not all—you know, along with the assignments of all of us—including my Soldiers. And I have a duty to protect those who fight for us, where I can."

His last words came out with the same calm but unyielding finality in which he announced all his decisions. But Bleys, looking at him, saw in the tiny wrinkles around his eyes, the same signals of a pain he had seen once before. It had been shortly after Bleys had been sent to live with Henry on Association; a time when Henry had found it necessary to beat his oldest son because he believed it a father's duty to do so.

But the fact he had done this had almost destroyed Bleys emotionally. He had been brought up by his mother, a native of Kultis, one of the twin Exotic worlds, where they believed that to willfully cause any pain—but particularly physical pain—in another human being, was not only the worst of crimes; it was essentially unthinkable—unimaginable.

Blindly, muffled in an unfamiliar nightshirt, Bleys had tried to go to his slightly older cousin. Henry had intercepted him; and with an understanding beyond that of Bleys, had stopped him gently, turned him around and sent him back to his own bed. But it was then that Bleys had seen the pain he saw now and the stern will that leashed it, in and around Henry's eyes.

But this time the pain was not for the other, slightly older boy—his cousin Joshua. It was for Bleys himself.

Chapter 30

Bleys stood in one of the smaller lounges of his suite, with Kaj Menowsky and three tabletop machines, which surrounded him, viewing him from three separate angles with the irritable red eyes of their on-lights. In this modern day and age, he had not been required to strip in order to be viewed from the uppermost hair on his head to the skin on the underside of his feet, with these parts and everything in between examined in three dimensions of microscopic sections.

The machines tolerated clothes by ignoring them. However, they were quick to object if he so much as twitched a muscle. They each complained about the movement immediately, with a sharp beep the moment sight was lost of whatever had been under examination—and now had to be found again.

"They'll get it eventually," Kaj said. "But every time you hear a beep, they have to go back and start over to find it. The less you move, the quicker the examination will be over."

Kaj was abstractedly reading a series of hieroglyphics that clicked out on a tape from a fourth machine that evidently gathered and condensed the information from the three observing Bleys.

The medician's words were like something pointed and sharp jabbed into Bleys' back. For someone who had trained himself as strictly as he considered he had, they struck him as very close to an insult.

He told himself grimly that he should be able to stand absolutely unmoving for any reasonably necessary period. He had simply been careless until now, letting his mind run free and his body take care of itself during this examination. But from now on . . . *I am a statue,* he told himself. *A statue of pure and solid marble all the way through. That is what the machines will find. Marble. Unmoving. And my time sense will be compressed, so that however long I have to stand still, it will seem like only a few seconds more to me.*

Bleys closed his mind down on what he had just thought and achieved it. The machines did not beep anymore . . . time had no importance until Kaj spoke again.

"Well, that takes care of it," said a voice, waking Bleys to an awareness that the red lights on the machines had gone out. Kaj went on, "It's pretty much as I thought. The Council piggybacked a compulsive-talk drug—which won't be hard to identify and neutralize—on the back of a genetic invader—set to attack your DNA; almost certainly the result of the attempts here and on Old Earth to re-create some of the animal forms that were lost through human hunting or pollution caused by early modern technology and the population explosion on Old Earth. I can't do anything about either intruder until I've got the facilities of the ship's clinic on your space vessel. But now I know where to look and what to look for."

"That's quite a bit to find out, isn't it, medician—what's it been—half an hour?"

"A little longer than that," said Kaj. He tore off his strip of hiero-glyphics, folded its length into a reasonable package and slipped it into one of his jacket pockets. He gestured at the devices, their eyes now a dull, uninterested gray. "These did the work for me. That's one thing. Another's that, pretty much as I expected, the Council didn't show much imagination in what they picked for you. The babble-drug's a standard one, and its variforms are limited. Given that much, it's merely a matter of working down the list of possibilities until I find the one they used. The genetic intruder, which will be some alien—alien, that is, to you; perfectly normal human-style DNA otherwise—is going to call for a little imaginative detective work. But, as I say, nothing I didn't expect."

"How could you expect anything at all, specifically?" Bleys asked curiously. "By the way, I still feel fine."

"You probably will, right up to within an hour or two of its effective deadline—which may or not be the time they gave you. You might begin to feel something before the deadline, but the sensation ought to be slight. But you'll go downhill rapidly after you pass the time limits. By that time we'll hope to have you in the ship, and I'll be able to make you more comfortable, as well as start doing something about what I believe needs to be counteracted. As far as expecting anything, it's a matter of knowing what's convenient under the conditions and physiologically possible."

"You say they put some sort of DNA invader into my body?" Bleys asked.

"Call it a fragment of DNA. But a living something that can attack a vulnerable area of your own natural system and convert it to something else, similar but inimical or destructive to you, personally."

Bleys was tempted to ask the medician about where this fragment of alien DNA would have come from and how it would work. His insatiable hunger for information prompted him strongly; but outside the wall win-dow of the lounge the last light was already gone from the sky, and he had an appointment to keep that Kaj must not know about or delay him from keeping.

"But you did say you're feeling fine now?" Menowsky was asking, a little sharply.

"Certainly," Bleys answered. "And didn't you say I shouldn't feel anything until the deadline?"

"You shouldn't, as I say," Menowsky said. "But it never hurts to check these things. If you notice any change in how you're feeling, let me know immediately. Immediately. I understand we're all leaving for the spaceship tomorrow sometime during the afternoon. Do you know if I'll be in the same vehicle you are? I understand there may be some trouble getting to the ship."

"We're pretty sure there will be trouble," said Bleys. "No, I don't know if you'll be in the car with me. Would you check with Henry MacLean on that, and explain why you need to be with me, if necessary? The arrangements on this are up to him. He's the one who will make the decisions."

"I absolutely should be with you," Menowsky said.

Bleys looked at him closely.

"Medician," Bleys said slowly, "how sure are you that I'm not going to feel the effect of what's been put in me for some hours yet?"

"As sure as I can be! But no one can be a hundred percent certain when dealing with something that tinkers with basic elements in the human body, each one of which is individual."

"Then you're saying the chance I'll need you is nothing more than a statistic? That makes you think you ought to be with me? Or is there something more that makes you sure—for instance, the information you've just gotten from your machines?"

"As a matter of fact, there is. I'd made a pretty good guess at the sort of drug they would use even before I first saw you, from what I know of their use of medical elements and the techniques they've used in the past. I thought they'd use it on you—one more evidence of their stupidity."

"Stupidity?" Bleys repeated. "They looked intelligent enough to me."

"They *are* intelligent, in their own areas," said Kaj. "And they're all fine—even brilliant—scientists, if not the real, rare breed of universe-beaters, any of them. But they're stupid in their dealings with people. Being on the Council has done that to them. Authority does it to the best of humanity. It makes people arrogant and indifferent. Someone who uses any part of medicine purely to gain a personal end has lost most—or all—of his or her humanity. They become at least part-tyrant; and the longer they stay in power—and most of those people you saw have come back again and again to their Council chairs for some years—the more they become complete tyrants, until they're no better than those ancient Old Earth rulers who used to torture or murder at will."

Kaj had an odd, crisp way of talking. Not angry, in any way, but as if he was quite prepared to be angry if anybody else wanted to start an argument or fight; and this message managed to make itself heard in the way he spoke.

"All right," said Bleys.

"I'm glad you see," Kaj said. "I've seen a number of very good people destroyed by them, and now, finally, with you, I'm going to rob them of someone they want badly."

His voice had not risen at all, but his eyes had grown even darker, like invisibly burning coals.

"Could that be why you volunteered to come with Will Sather?" Bleys asked.

"One of the reasons. As for knowing, I knew you were here, and I knew them. It was bound to happen."

"All right," said Bleys. "Simply tell Henry that you and I agreed I'd want you with me. I'll leave now. I've got an appointment. Get your machines packed away, and I'll turn off the security bubble."

On his way back to his own private room, Bleys had to pass through a number of the rooms of his suite, any one of which Henry, Toni or Dahno might have been in—but none of them were.

It was still early in the evening, local time, about eight P.M.—twenty hours. They were, he thought, probably about the business of preparing for the attempt to reach the spaceport tomorrow; and those preparations had taken them out of the block completely. But it was time that he was getting to this other matter he had called an appointment.

An appointment it was, but one which the other parties had no suspicion of his attending. It was the Council meeting Sean O'Flaherty had mentioned as he and Bleys came back from the afternoon's Council session.

Bleys' own private lounge was a corner room, last of the long row of connecting chambers that made up this expensive suite. Two of the walls were transparent from inside, so that he could view almost a hundred and eighty degree spread of the city lights in the dusk around and below him.

He had used the control pad on his wrist to keep the lights in the suite from turning on before he entered. Once he was through the door, he locked it behind him with another three-fingered touch on the pad, and waited. Gradually, his eyes began to adjust to the illumination that the city lights outside gave the room.

The long, rectangular space was shadowy and dim, but everything in it was clearly visible. In fact, with a little imagination, he could imagine it as bathed in soft moonlight—although neither of the moons of Newton were in the sky at the moment. The general glow of the lights outside made a strange but adequate substitute.

Bleys stood there a moment longer, thinking about his trademark cloak. He wanted to be impressive, but it was impractical; so he contented himself with his dark dress suit, including the red cummerbund presently fashionable on Newton. Its outside end was fastened to the layers wound underneath about his waist by a heavy, ornate clip, just where a belt buckle might have been. He moved.

By the glow of the city lights, Bleys walked to the doorway in one window wall which opened to the balcony there that gave a view along the flanking side of the building. He could now look directly toward the balcony belonging to the Council meeting room. He and Sean had made a turn at the start of their walk from his own lounge to the Council Room.

But that had been because they had started from the main lounge, now behind him. From here, the way to the Council balcony was straight ahead.

A cool evening breeze laved his face and hands. He could not remember whether or not he had noticed this coolness of the night air when he had made his way along the side of the hotel in Ecumeny, that night when, wakeful, he had been driven to get as close as possible to the stars that had been his talisman from the beginning of memory. A night in which he had indeed been alone with them, until the people watching him from below had caused him to climb farther around the corner of that building.

Bleys remembered now how he had made the corner turn, with a reckless, swinging pivot on one foot that he had never tried before. No such turn would be necessary here. The climb should be a simple matter. He had already checked the possibilities. With the exception of his own suite on this floor, the building he was now in, unlike the one on Association, did not have balconies above balconies, with ridges midway between them, around the sides of it, as support for his toes and fingers.

But it had, in fact, something better for his need. Undoubtedly for reasons of architectural appearance, each of the top three floors here—of which his floor was the middle one—were stepped back, each from the one below, by a good twenty centimeters. So that he could travel along one of these step-backs as if he were on a ledge, twice as wide as one of his feet.

Even more useful, these three top, stepped-back stories each had a decorative panel along the building side from the lip of each step-back and extending down a full meter and a half. They had the appearance of marble, several centimeters thick, a width of gold-streaked white stone, with carvings completely through them, wide and deep enough to be handholds. Each panel, from street level, gave the illusion of an ornamental cap on the step-back to which it was attached.

One of these step-backs ran directly below his balcony. He could step out on to that, and walk easily to the Council Room, holding on to the panel reaching down from the step-back above, and climbing over the intervening balconies on his way.

He had seen that sort of ornamental false cap before, when he had been a child, still with his mother, on one of the large private estates at which they had stayed for a while. The panel had been called a "fluted fascia," in architectural terms.

In that past time, at one rich estate where they had been residents, he had used the holes of the carvings in the fascia to climb up from a garden into an open first-story window. He had been a great deal lighter then; but still, as he remembered, the fascia had been a firm part of the wall to which it was attached. It was unlikely these panels would not be anchored as firmly.

Bleys turned around and went into his sleeping room, next to the lounge. Stepping inside, he let the lights turn themselves on only after the door had closed behind him, so that no gleam would show in the lounge.

He touched the controls on his wristpad, and the farther wall opened up to display his wardrobe.

Bleys crossed to it, picked out a pair of dark gray trousers and a long-sleeved, black shirt. His face would be to the outside wall of the building once he was on the ledge. There were gloves in the wardrobe, but he did not want anything between the sensitive skin of his fingers and whatever he was holding on to.

Feeling a sudden desire for a shower, he took off his clothes. It was a need of something symbolic to wash away the earlier part of the day from his mind, leave it clean and empty, ready to deal with the climb along the ledge. He stepped into the shower cubicle.

He touched the stud on his wrist control pad that should have brought a grateful small torrent of water cascading down on him. But instead, the cubicle seemed suddenly to swing sickeningly around him; so that, reflexively, he thrust out both hands against two of its opposite walls to keep himself from falling.

Abruptly the cubicle was normal again. Except that his skin now felt as if he had been wiped all over by something cool but dry, that had tingled slightly for a moment, but left him feeling unnaturally clean—as if he had been scraped over every inch of his body by the feather touch of a blade sharper than any ever invented. For a moment, he tensed in every muscle; then he realized that this hotel in its opulence had installed supersonic cleansers, something he should have expected in such a place. He was almost surgically dirtless, more so now than water could ever have made him.

But cleanliness had not been the reason he had decided to shower. He had wanted the feel of water washing away everything but his present single-minded purpose. Moreover, his years of self-training in sensitivity of his sensory reactions had made him unnaturally acute; and this kind of supersonic stimulation, mild as it was supposed to be, had destroyed his sense of balance momentarily. He looked at his wristpad, saw the possible alternate signal lit, there, and touched it.

Water, automatically set to his body temperature, poured down upon him. He turned his face gratefully up into it.

He stood for several minutes, letting the flood inundate him. Then, feeling remarkably refreshed and new, he punched the wristpad again and a waft of warm, desert-dry air flooded upon him from the walls of the cubicle, drying him.

He left the cubicle, dressed in the dark clothing and went about transferring the contents of his pockets to his fresh clothes. The shower had worked its symbolic as well as its physical effect. Even the unpleasant moment in which he had lost his balance was unimportant now. By inter-world law, he knew, these cleansing cubicles were not supposed to have supersonic cleaners set high enough to be uncomfortable for any normal person. But, in that area, he was no longer normal. He would be careful to use the water option from now on.

Dressed once more, Bleys hesitated for a moment over the wide five meter band of cloth that was the cummerbund, then wrapped and pinned it again around his waist. If by chance he was caught doing what he planned, he preferred to appear a slightly insane hotel guest, rather than a prowler.

Back in the dimness of the lounge, he brought from one trouser pocket the small device, lost in his hand as it had been in Dahno's, which produced the blue privacy bubble. He had borrowed it from Dahno at the end of their talk, earlier, with this climb in mind. The device's controls were simple: a single stud, placed to slide in a groove, with three positions—one for *off*, one for *on*, and a third for *hold*.

Bleys slid the switch to *on*. A bubble began forming around him, growing and enclosing his whole body. He realized then that it would keep on growing unless he stopped it and slid the stud even farther forward to *hold*. The bubble ceased growing. He thumbed the switch back to *off*, the bubble vanished, and he stepped once more out on to the balcony, after putting the device back in his pocket.

He had trained himself to measure distance by a nearly automatic counting of his strides; and he had counted them both on the way to and from the Council meeting room. Now, looking along the side of the building, he estimated the room's balcony to be distant some three-quarters of that side; and indeed, at a distance, he thought he could identify the precise balcony.

Bleys glanced around the dim, empty lounge. No one was likely to come looking for him for some hours at least. He looked down. There were only a few vehicles on the trafficway. The sky was clear. Neither one of Newton's moons had risen, but the stars were brightly visible.

He put one hand on the top railing of the balcony and stepped over it with his right leg on to the step-back that ran beneath. On this climb he would travel facing the hotel wall, which would make the trip even easier. He reached up with his right hand and hooked his fingers into the cuttings of the fascia above him.

Bleys hesitated, one hand on the balcony, one on the fascia.

Both balcony and fascia were cold and hard to his touch. The trafficway was far below, and it, too, would be unyielding, cold and hard. The night air about him now felt colder, though the evening could hardly have cooled so quickly.

Bleys looked at the stars. They seemed remote, now, at their full astronomical distance; not only from him, but from each other. They no longer reached out to him like old friends, warming and welcoming in their community. They were specks of alien illumination, nothing more.

He looked along the way he would go, and an uneasiness niggled at him. It did not seem reasonable that a body like the Council should allow even so unlikely an access to their private meetings. It would not be difficult, even for someone noticeably shorter than he—given only a good tolerance of heights—to approach them secretly. Perhaps even this way was booby-trapped . . .

Then he realized it was the prospect of the climb itself that was making him hesitate. Earlier he had taken his ability to do so for granted, as he had climbed the wall of the Association hotel; but possibilities, both good and bad, were now thronging into his mind, and it came to him suddenly there was something missing here that had been in him at that other climb.

There he had been—not "berserk," that word from the Old Earth language of the time of the Vikings. Perhaps "fey"—another old word which could have a number of meanings, but all connected with an awareness of the nearness—or chance—of death.

Some definitions for it had been "timid," or "cowardly." But neither of those had been right, then. Then it had been an adventure almost joyful, like looking forward confidently to a fight with a dark warrior. A test, preliminary to a greater test.

But whatever it had been then, it was not now. He felt very human and limited. He had never feared heights. He had merely been aware of them. But he was very aware of this one. An anger at himself kindled in him.

That fear had to go. Lost far back in the mists of earliest childhood had been the decision. He would never be able to accomplish what he hoped if he ever let himself be afraid.

He stepped over the balcony with his other leg. The wall of the building, with all its transparent window-walls, stretched out before him, The windows were all dark, as he had counted on their being, with their occupants out, at this Newtonian dinner hour.

Bleys went forward, sideways, like a long-legged crab, climbing over the balconies in his way. As he went, his tension relaxed. Now, there was nothing but the step-back beneath his feet and the fascia in which he set his fingers. His long practice and exercise of self-control took over. Only he and the building existed.

He went forward, calmly—until, without warning, some inner alarm bell sounded, and he stopped.

It was nothing obvious, not a response of his trained sensory system. But it was a definite feeling, real but unexplainable; like that awareness called the "loom of the land," that for centuries described sailors' awareness of an unseen shore, out of sight still below the perfect, unbroken circle of watery horizon.

He pushed his forward foot farther, cautiously feeling for any change in the surface beneath it.

But there was only solid surface as far as his toes could reach. He pulled his foot back and slowly advanced his body, then stretched out his arm, sliding his fingers over the incised surface of the fascia, until they were farther out than his foot had been able to reach.

Abruptly, his fingertips slipped over an edge into emptiness. He looked at the apparently continuous surface there; and his fingertips now seemed buried in the marble.

He stretched forward a little more and looked closely, finding the line of division between reality and projection. It was perceptible here, as with any illusory image, seen close up. In daylight it would have been immediately obvious. Now there was no more question about it.

Clearly, past the line he recognized, there was no more fascia, only the three-dimensional illusion of it. The illusion was all the more effective in this dim light from the city below. If the fascia became unreal, then the step-back space beneath him . . . he leaned as far out as he could and slid his front foot forward over the step-back surface, gradually moving his body forward also.

The step-back stayed solid. It continued solid as far as he could stretch. But there was no real fascia above it. He brought his foot back. Suddenly the step-back seemed to have narrowed to half its width. If he tried to go on without the fascia to hold on to, and the step-back unexpectedly also became illusion—he looked ahead toward the balcony he had picked out as that of the Council meeting-room. There was only one other balcony left between him and it.

Fear and uncertainty were bad companions. It was easy to tell himself that there would be other ways of getting the information that he hoped to overhear once he had reached the Council Room; but it would be a retreat, and he had promised himself he would never retreat. If he did it once, he was afraid he might be tempted to do it again—and again, and his life would end with his goal still out of reach.

Bleys thought back to his earlier climb, and his use of *ki*, to anchor himself to that building so that instead of being up against a vertical wall, he had felt as if he lay on his back on a flat surface, looking up at the stars.

He had done it once. He could do it again.

The thought was like a clean wind blowing away the fog of emotion that for a moment had threatened to conquer his sense of purpose.

Kioshizumeru, he thought to himself.

The Nipponese term for what he would do calmed his mind. Training began again to take over. His attention left the step-back and the fascia, concentrating on the *hara*, the centerpoint of his body. He gathered himself back into that single point, just above his navel; and it was like returning to a solid base from which all other things could be seen in proper perspective, in their true dimensions. An inner peace flowed out through his body. He began to imagine his *ki* as carrying all his spirit, concentrated now into his *hara*, deep into the wall before him and anchoring him there. It reached out, and his perception of the wall tilted at his will, not back to a perfectly level surface, as on Association, but at an angle in which he felt himself lying comfortably on it as on an inclined plane, a slope not steep enough to let him slip downward easily.

Bleys took his hands from the fascia and stretched his arms out on either side of him, the palms of his hands flat against the surface of the wall. His feet moved him sideways over the ledge supporting him.

He moved up to and over the next balcony, jutting up and backward at an odd angle; stepped down once more to the setback, with his arms outstretched and his palms against the building; and moved once more toward the last balcony, that would connect with the Council Room. He could hear voices now, through the half-open door to the final balcony; the talking audible, but the words still unclear. He let the wall return slowly to the vertical.

Bleys felt his weight once more on the step-back below him. The balcony was only an arm's length away, the voices raised in argument were now understandable—and suddenly the ledge was as nothing beneath his feet. Without warning, the same sensation of vertigo that had nearly brought him down in the shower struck him again. But this time many times stronger, killingly stronger. All at once the world spun around him, and all his sense of balance left him.

Chapter 31

The timeless moment passed—and he was still on the step-back, still pressed against the wall surface, with his arms outstretched and his palms flat against the face of the building, but a full step further on.

His body had ignored the disturbance of his inner ear, which should have toppled him from his footing; and obeyed instead the command of his trained mind.

For a minute, Bleys simply stood as he was. It had been a simple but nasty little trap for anyone who had managed to get this far without the fascia to hang on to. He had simply been lucky in having used *kioshizumeru* when he did. But the balcony that was his goal was only a couple of steps away now. He moved to it and climbed over the railing onto the balcony itself.

Bleys was able to hear the voices clearly, now, coming out through the half-open door with the filmy inner curtain that also blew outward in pleasant, ghostly fashion into the night air, under the pressure of the hotel's air system—feeding cleaned, cooled atmosphere at a slightly higher than outdoors pressure into the room.

Close up now, Bleys could see only faintly through the wall itself, that had been opaqued from the outside, but was lit and transparent from within. He stood back from the doorway, back where wall-end and balcony met. From there, even looking from the night darkness at an angle through the partly open balcony door, they would not be likely to see him—even if one of them looked out.

There was of course, the problem of getting safely back, unnoticed, to his suite. He could not now go back the way he had come. He was physically as strong as when he had started, but there was an exhaustion in him from the tension of the climb and the near-thing of the sonic trap.

In any case, Bleys had come here by this route to spy on the Council. He forced his mind away from all else and fastened all his attention on the conversation in the lounge.

For the first time, he realized they were not using the blue bubble phase-shield for secrecy. He had brought along Dahno's small device, hoping to make it touch and merge with one that the Council would be using, so that effectively they would all be in the same bubble, and he would be able to hear what they said. It had been unnecessary.

Plainly they felt more secure in their evening private session here than he had expected. Kaj had said it was not the most brilliant of their professions who sat on this Council.

Now, glancing through the fluttering gossamer curtains moving in and out through the doorway with the airflow from inside, Bleys could not only hear their voices—one had an odd sound—but see them; if not well, at least clearly enough to recognize that all he had met this afternoon were there. And there was also the interesting addition of one extra person, possibly the source of the odd-sounding voice. Whoever the new member was, he or she was seated farthest from Bleys and could not be seen fully from Bleys' angle of view through the balcony doorway.

"I should never have let the rest of you talk me out of it," Half-Thunder was saying, his voice pitched higher and more angry than it had been while Bleys was with them in the afternoon. "I said then and I say now, it's ridiculous to delay, on some wild hope of his usefulness to us in the future. We didn't even really need to talk to him this afternoon. We should simply have taken care of him right away. It's straightforward and easy enough. I already had everything arranged."

"It's foolish not to explore all possibilities," said Din Su's placid voice. "We agreed on that sometime since. Now, what the rest of us have already decided just needs finalizing; and we only need you with us, so we have the required six votes on it. Any original arrangements you've made shouldn't make you close your mind to the considered opinions of the rest of us."

"You don't have to scrap what you've set up," said Ahmed Bahadur. "We can hold your arrangements ready for another day or two, can't we?"

"Of course, of course!" Half-Thunder said. "But that's not the point. Of course it's ready, and can be kept ready to go at a second's notice."

"Any given individual can fail to behave as predicted, and we might wind up getting a too-public mess out of it," said Anita delle Santos.

"Nonsense!" said Half-Thunder, with something very like a sneer. "That's what you tinkerers would believe, naturally. Good theory, perhaps. But for practical purposes, I tell you the man I picked for the job is completely under control. He not only has the proper genetic and social background, but I've got him thoroughly conditioned. I do mean thoroughly!"

"Any human individual can betray you on the best of programming," murmured Anita delle Santos.

"Of course. As I say, Human Engineering would guarantee you'd believe that," said Half-Thunder. "So, you're really saying it for the record, aren't you?"

"Think what you wish," she said.

"Yes. For the record, and for the people back in your own Institute," said Half-Thunder. "But we don't need political remarks, we need a decision. We need action. All I'm saying is, I was against what you did with Bleys Ahrens; and in spite of the fact I ended up giving in to you just before we met him, the interview confirmed everything I'd thought. He's too dangerous to play games with. I'm saying that strongly, and having had a few more hours to think about it, my opinion's confirmed."

"Five-to-one, still, then," Din Su said. "Since I assume Georges will vote with the rest of us in the majority. Isn't that right, Georges?"

"I think Thunder's got some reason on his side," said Georges Lemair, "but yes, I'm with the rest of you."

"Yes," said Din Su. "Then, if Thunder's determined not to go along, maybe the Gentleman would care to give us an opinion that might fulfill our six-vote requirement?"

The one additional person in the room shifted position slightly, and Bleys got a clearer look. It was instantly clear why the odd voice had rung a faint bell in his memory.

Someone else's legs were still between his angle of vision and the lower half of the unknown's figure. But the upper part of the body Bleys saw was wearing a dark blue jacket with a neck-scarf beneath it that could have been worn equally reasonably either by a man or a woman. Where the head of this person should have been, however, was the same sort of blur that had hidden the identity of the two people brought to speak with him on New Earth; both of them Others, but one also a member of the CEO Club and the other a member of the Guildmasters. Here, too, the blur was concealing an identity.

"That's a request I've had made to me a number of times by earlier members of this Council," said the unnatural voice. "I'll give you the answer I gave them. In spite of the fact that I've theoretically had to accept a full membership in this Council to be part of its deliberations, I stipulated from the beginning that whatever I said would be restricted to the information I bring and my opinion about its usefulness. I wouldn't—and won't—exercise any of the regular prerogatives or duties of a Council Member. You're all going to have to settle this among yourselves."

There was a long moment of silence inside the lounge. Bleys could imagine the look of smug victory on Half-Thunder's face.

Then Din Su's voice spoke again, still placid, still gentle, still un-changed. "I'm afraid, then, you don't leave me any alternative. I'm going to need to call for a re-election of the Council; and of course the topic to be aired will be the matter of you, Half, being the only one who disagrees with the rest of us."

This time the moment of silence was very brief.

"You won't do that!" Half-Thunder said. "You'd be putting your own neck on the chopping block, as far as re-election was concerned—to say nothing of the necks of everybody else who agrees with you here in this Council. I don't think they'll thank you for that."

"Oh, I don't think the rest have a lot to worry about. I know I'm not worrying," Din Su said. Bleys had never appreciated before how utterly deadly such an apparently gentle tone and manner of delivery could make a voice. The threat in her words was multiplied by the total lack of threat with which they were uttered and the quiet certainty of her voice.

She continued, "The other Council members voting with me for re-election on this question are simply doing our duty to steer Newton in the direction it has always gone, with due caution and concern. The Institutes' members electorate will understand that none of us wanted to fall into the trap of a quick-and-easy—but possibly dangerous—solution. It is my duty I'm doing, isn't it, Gentleman? If I remember the Directives, the one that's concerned here says: '*Any Council member who feels it his or her duty has the right to call for a general re-election of all Council members, to test whether the consensus of opinion within the Council reflects the best aims and ends of Newton's immediate purposes and ultimate destiny*' . . . Did I quote correctly, Gentle-man?"

"Perfectly correctly," said the voice from the blur above the tightly suited shoulders Bleys could see through the doorway.

There was a sudden silence in the Council lounge.

"Din Su's right, you know, Thunder," said Anita delle Santos, after that moment. "We're all of us just doing our duty. You know as well as the rest here that the main direction of this Council's actions have always been to steer Newton into a position of power over the other New Worlds—not merely silent, but acknowledged power; and as we've said, right here in this room, Bleys Ahrens plainly has something like the same dream, only for himself. But there's a great difference between the careful actions earlier Councils have taken in that direction over the past century and what one person can do in just a few years with a clever tongue. He's not that dangerous to us. Compared to all we've done and what we are, he's no real threat. On the other hand, he might be useful. I repeat, he's not that dangerous."

"You've said all that before," Thunder snapped. "I'm sick of the blind lot of you."

Bleys could just make out through the doorway Thunder's movement as he jumped to his feet from his float.

"—And if my views are going to be disregarded continually by this Council, what am I doing sitting around with the rest of you?" he said bitterly. All at once, he was striding toward the doorway out onto the balcony.

There was no time to think it over.

Chapter 32

Bleys stepped forward, himself, in two long, swift, strides passing through the doorway into the room and stopping. Almost within his arm's reach, the approaching Thunder checked abruptly. Bleys smiled pleasantly at all of them, and they all stared back at him; but with quickly schooled faces on which there was no expression, least of all that of astonishment.

"I apologize for breaking in on you like this," Bleys said pleasantly. "I'm just cutting through your room here out into the hallway on my way back to my own suite. I'm sure you understand."

"Of course, Bleys Ahrens," said Din Su, almost without hesitation, in that unvarying voice of hers. "You're certain you know your way back?"

"Quite certain."

In the continuing silence, Bleys walked on around their floats to the doorway by which he had left the lounge the last time. He stepped through the door as it slid open before him, clearly opened by one of the members—probably Din Su he thought—and, as he stepped through, it slid to again behind him.

But before it closed completely, he heard the first of the words breaking the silence from the room; they were from Half-Thunder.

"Didn't I say he was dangerous?" Triumph rang in Half-Thunder's voice, followed by a fractional moment of silence only—but a silence with no dissenting voices.

Thoughtfully, Bleys turned and headed back toward his room.

He had had no choice but to brazen out his having been on the balcony—how long, they would have no way of guessing. It was possible, of course, that his own cheerful treatment of the matter as nothing out of the ordinary, and Din Su's apparent agreement, meant that they would not alter their plan of not taking any sudden action about him, simply because he had had a chance to overhear at least part of what they had said.

Normally, any such governing body would react immediately. In fact, if it was up to Half-Thunder alone, undoubtedly he would be pressing studs on his control pad right now and giving orders. But, in this instance, Bleys guessed the Council, as a whole, would not.

The Members would have to be too much aware of their personal reputations for responsible decisions, to say nothing of their commitment to the Council's long-standing plan which Anita delle Santos had mentioned. In short, they were not likely to go off half-cocked, if only because they were too used to looking before they leaped.

He thought of supporting reasons. The long-term ambitions of Newton had been no secret on the New Worlds for over a century—had been obvious since the Exotics of Mara and Kultis had ceased to dominate the New Worlds with their interworld mercantile power, during the last century. Being intelligent themselves, the majority of the Council Members would be very conscious of Bleys' own intelligence; and assume that he probably had already guessed the general aim of their main interest and actions. Therefore he would have heard nothing surprising to him out there on the balcony; though clearly they would not guess how he planned to turn those ambitions of theirs to his own advantage as he had, in fact, already been doing with similar social ambitions on the Friendlies, New Earth, and Cassida.

But Half-Thunder, in his instinct to act, had been right for reasons they did not suspect—and Half-Thunder himself probably did not realize consciously.

Of course, once they knew he was making a break for the airport and fighting through any opposition in his way, the fat would be in the fire. They would realize that Half-Thunder had been justified, if for deeper reasons than any of them had guessed—but by that time it would be too late for Thunder's plan.

Still, while there might be only a slight chance of some threat against him in the hours between now and the *Symphonie* performance, it was time for Bleys to reconsider his actions between now and the time when *Favored of God* would carry them safely into interstellar space.

Accordingly, Bleys went back to reconsider those actions, and lost himself in the intricate fascination of juggling the characters and situations that his escape would require.

Engrossed as he was, and braced for its happening, he was disturbed only temporarily when he walked through the point in the high-ceilinged hall where the phase-shift once more transported him nowhere—though a portion of his mind did register a momentary, uncustomary flare of anger at this unnecessary discomfort.

Bleys passed onto and through the section of bare concrete hall; and it was not until he stepped through its farther door into the last relatively short leg of normal hotel-type hallway, leading to the right turn that would leave him finally facing the first door to his own suite, that his mind was suddenly awakened from its musings. As the door to the earlier section clicked shut behind him, all illumination of this final stretch of hall went out, leaving him in complete darkness.

He stopped, his senses at once alert. Then, almost in the same instant, he backed up a step and put his hand behind him to touch the emergency *open* button of the door he had just passed. The stud depressed, but the door did not open. He tried his wrist-controls—with no success. Whatever had locked it was beyond most customary controls.

He breathed out softly. Almost reflexively, he moved forward again silently, sidling against the left-hand wall of the hallway, so that he would have room behind him in which to back up and maneuver. Then, once more, he stopped and reached out, feeling with all his senses for any information they could pick up through the utter darkness. His mind raced over the situation, hunting for understanding and searching for possible courses of action.

So, he had overestimated the calm reassurance of Newton's ruling minds. Either the Council had decided to act immediately after all; or, perhaps, Half-Thunder had activated his own plan defiantly, possibly even secretly. Overhearing Thunder's words from the balcony, Bleys had assumed the other man was talking about the legal action the Council had used as a threat in the afternoon. But this looked like some action that would be more direct, and physical.

Instinctively, now, Bleys felt the urge of a trapped creature to start swiftly toward the far end of the corridor, to get out at that end since this was locked behind him. But a moment's thought made it obvious that if this end was locked, the other would be, too.

Bleys' mind swept back and forth over the situation, searching for understanding and possible courses of action. If this was what Half-Thunder had arranged for him—he checked in mid-thought. There was something not right about the way his mind was working. He could not put his finger exactly upon what he sensed; but his reasoning power seemed both slowed and showing a tendency to think in circles. He had been about to repeat the whole train of thought he had finished a second before.

Concentrate, he told himself. Clearly, his reasoning had skimmed over the situation in very superficial fashion, when it should have been digging in, looking for loose ends in Half-Thunder's plan that he could turn to his own advantage. Angrily, he made the effort to concentrate.

Down the corridor some distance ahead of him, Bleys heard a latch click. His straining ears heard a door open and the sound of someone brushing through that opening.

Bleys did not hear the door close again. But after a few seconds in the silence of the darkness, he heard a barely audible, rhythmic panting, like that of a man with a hoe chopping at something noiselessly—and it was coming slowly but steadily toward him along the wall of the corridor at Bleys' right hand, as he faced toward the sound. The panting could now be heard to be accompanied by the voiceless susurrus of something swung through the air. Both sounds were working their way toward him.

Bleys suppressed another unusual, powerful rush of animal panic and closed his eyes. He exhaled deeply and *centered*. He opened his eyes on the darkness again. His elbows pressed lightly against his rib cage as the reflexively tense muscles in his neck and shoulders relaxed. His knees flexed, settling his heels firmly to the floor, bearing his weight evenly on both feet.

Mind followed body into the dreamlike harmony from countless hours of practice for physical contest. His senses reached out, sharp now, separating the sounds approaching him into their separate meanings.

The scuff of a sole at the far end of the corridor . . .

A syncopated footfall . . . *heel and toe. Not the gliding slip-step of a trained fighter.*

But that regular, repeated sound—*the faint swish of whatever was flailing the air.*

Near at hand, Bleys could feel the quickly fading residue of heat from the earlier illumination of the walls. That heat still masked any other source of thermal energy, but the technology was established and reliable. The heat would be gone, enough not to interfere, in a few more seconds.

Scuff . . . *swish-swish.*

The sound conjured the image of a blind man swinging a cane.

No, not a cane. Something else.

Bleys let his mind sink deeper into meta-awareness, liberating memories long submerged.

A Japanese word rose to the surface of his mind—two words—*bokken* . . . the wooden sword . . . *katana* . . . "the sword that cuts from heaven to earth" . . .

Clearly back to his mind came the image of his tutor's long, sad face, abruptly eclipsed by darkness and the feel of the blindfold against his own forehead, leaving him with blended music of sword and breath, and the distinctive sound that was the signature of the sword as it cut the air. "*The tip of the sword moves faster than sound, Bleys Ahrens. It leaves a trace of vacuum in its path, and the surrounding air rushes in like thunder in the wake of a lightning stroke.*"

—*Swish-swish.* Not the crisp hiss of a focus cut . . . but prolonged . . . whispery . . .

The remembered image of his tutor dissolved into another—one of a man batting at a swarm of gnats.

Bleys felt his body turn in trained response, a few degrees to his right. He felt a perceptible moving heat source now. Whoever was coming was drawing nearer along the wall opposite the one against which his left shoulder was pressed.

Bleys waited for the next step of the other toward him, to cover any sound from his own soft-soled half-boots. He eased himself around so that the left wall now was now hard and flat against his back, his heels against its base above the carpet.

Sound   approaching.   *Scuff/slap—swish/swish* . . . *swishhh* . . . pause . . . *scuff/slap—swish/swish* . . . *swish* . . .

The beat of the sound brought back the memory of his tutor's words. *"As the tip moves toward you, the pitch rises, like the sound of an oncoming air-car. When it moves away, the pitch falls."*

The rhythm was broken for a second. Then continued.

The darkness lost importance. Sounds, heat and memory were building together a clear mental image.

...Average New World height for males. Tip of sword making a figure-eight—left to right ... Likely two-handed grip, but if so, the sound is too even ... A trained swordsman would make a drawing cut on each down stroke. The sound would vary—left cut from right cut. An untrained man, flailing with the sword, rather than using it.

Bleys stepped away from the wall, let his feet glide toward the sound. Slipping along close to the wall at his left now, silently.

No more than three paces now from the oncomer.

Swish/swish—left, right. —Left, right.

Bleys moved to his left again—the oncomer's right. Two steps ...

Swish—cut to the left—scuff/slap.

The sound and heat came closer, moved past Bleys. Reek of sour sweat ... and Bleys turned to follow, silent upon the carpet, breathing shallowly.

He was now behind the moving, panting figure.

Swish/right hand ...

The sword tip-sound came up close over the assailant's left shoulder as he shifted his body slightly, beginning a downswing to the right. Bleys' left hand arced over the man's head and followed his mental image of the sword arm.

There was no grunt of surprise as Bleys clamped his hand around the man's right wrist. The assassin tried to jerk Bleys' hand away, and Bleys went with the movement, pivoting on his heels to his left and bringing up his right hand to join his left. He dropped to his right knee, still gripping the man's arm as if Bleys himself were delivering a sword-cut. It was *kote-gaeshi*, one of the most effective throws in aikido.

On the practice mat, Bleys would have thrust his arms out, propelling his opponent forward and allowing him to roll out of the throw; but his hands now moved as if they had minds of their own.

In the darkness of the corridor, instead, Bleys drew them down and inward. The attacker flew over his back and directly head-down toward the floor.

He released the wrist and elbow he held a fraction of a second before the attacker's head struck the floor, with all his body's weight behind it.

Suddenly the silence was complete. Only the stale smell of sweat ...

Bleys' long fingers reached out, found and probed beneath the man's collar. The warm flesh under his touch gave back no pulse.

He away took his hand. It had been a perfunctory, almost a ritual examination. The man's neck had taken the full weight of his body, accelerating through an arc of decreasing radius before striking the floor. A gust of feeling moved through Bleys. He felt nothing in himself. But why had he killed? It would not have been necessary.

For a second, his mind was back on Harmony, when he had stopped the Militia major from hanging the three farmers.

Bleys straightened, swiftly. Now, after the tension of concentration in darkness, his mind was clear and sharp-edged. Quickly he went down the corridor, feeling along the side the attacker had come down, until his fingers slipped into the empty space of an opened doorway from what must have been the assassin's room.

He entered it. Within, the lightlessness was as complete as it had been out in the hall.

In the dark, Bleys turned and felt about on the wall at the left of the door for the general emergency alarm required in public buildings. He found the stud for it and pressed it.

A bell began to clang loudly, in the room and in the hall outside. A voice spoke loudly from the room's ceiling.

"This is an emergency, but there is no immediate reason for alarm. Will all guests please evacuate this section of the hall. This is an emergency . . . "

It went on repeating. Beyond his own opened door, Bleys could hear the sound of many other doors opening automatically. He stepped out again into a hall where the lighting was on and every door open. More important, the locked barriers at each end of this row of rooms should be unlocked.

He glanced briefly at the body of his would-be killer. Its head was at a brutal angle to its shoulders. A crude, plastic, homemade sword, like the one Bleys had seen dropped by the man running amok on Cassida, lay a little distance from the right hand of the body on the floor. The body itself was that of the rather portly businessman from Cassida who had tried to start a conversation with him on the spaceship as they were landing on Newton. Bleys still felt nothing.

No one had come out of any of the other open doors. Of course. The Council would have made sure that this particular stretch of hotel corridor was unpopulated; except by the one man primed or conditioned by Half-Thunder to run amok and kill Bleys, in what should seem to be an unfortunate accident. As crude and direct a solution to Bleys as a Council problem as the blast of sonics had been planned to be. No wonder the Council's other members had resisted it.

But the alarm was still sounding. Abandoning any appearance of ordinary movement, Bleys ran to the far end of the corridor, went through its now-open end and along a short stretch of corridor.

The alarm stopped sounding.

The silence came like an unexpected shock. But Bleys had turned the corner and was at the doorway of his own private lounge, now—happily closed, like all the doors of his suite. He pressed the stud on his wrist control pad, stepped through the opening door and let it close automatically behind him. Inside, he pressed the stud that turned on the lights and dropped into one of the oversized float chairs.

Reaction, at last—a hollow feeling of shaky exhaustion formed like a blue bubble inside him, flooding him with a sensation of weakness he could never remember sensing before. Bleys felt emptied out, a shell of himself; and besides that, he, who never had headaches, had the threat of one now just above the space between his eyes.

Growing up through all this, though, was an emotion like the relief of a hunted wild animal that had safely regained its burrow, even though it still heard the hounds of the hunters baying close by.

For a long moment, Bleys gave in to the reaction; then, with a surge of will, he thrust it from him. His mind began to work, picking up speed on a new tide of excitement beginning deep in him, but now rising.

He had actually chosen very carefully the order in which he would go and speak on the first three worlds. New Earth had to be first, Cassida had to be second and Newton had to be third. This order, because they must necessarily represent an escalation of the opposition he would face among the powers that controlled each world.

And so they had. But something also had happened—something not entirely unexpected, but something he had been not counting on at any particular time. Just as it was impossible, in any practical sense, to be lucky all the time, he had reasoned, so it would necessarily be impossible to be without luck all the time.

Somewhere along the rungs of the ladder of things to be done, which made up the outline of his plan, there would be unforeseen difficulties— like the unbelievable temerity of the Council, in injecting him with whatever the substances had been. He would have to deal with that situation quickly, now. But the point was, just as unfortunate things could happen, the fortunate could, too.

He had been on the alert for such an eventual gift of luck; and now it had happened, with the attack upon him in the dark. The attack itself had indeed been crude; but the Council must have voted unanimously for it after he had left the room after walking in from their balcony. The vote of the anonymous member with the blur for a head would then not have been necessary.

But it was that same anonymous member who now fascinated Bleys. He had reasoned that as his opposition became more and more capable, eventually he would find someone in a controlling position who was unusually capable, a kingpin worth conquering or recruiting.

The individual who had hidden his identity with the head-blur just might be such a find. But just now there was no time to think about that. First, right now, a quick change in immediate plans was necessary.

He punched the private, shielded call numbers on his wristpad, for

Toni, Henry and Dahno. They were numbers that did not change, even when they went from world to world—automatically picked up on his landing and made part of whatever communication system existed on the world they had come to.

"I'm calling you all," he said, keeping his voice casual, into the pickup on the pad. "What with everything going on today, I haven't had a chance to talk about our schedule for tomorrow. In my case, I want to make that afternoon concert of the *Symphonie des Flambeaux*. But if you're close, give me a tone, and I'll expect you all here within a few moments."

He dropped his arm with the control pad on to the chair arm beneath it and leaned back, closing his eyes. Within seconds of each other, three separate chiming notes sounded from the walls around him.

"Good," he said. "I'll be waiting."

"—You're all here. You must all have been in the hotel, then. That's good," he said a few moments later when they were assembled, guarded by the blue security bubble and seated in floats around him. "I was afraid at least one of you might be out."

"The three of us were having our own meeting," said Henry.

"Of course," Bleys said. "Now I'll tell you what's happened since I last saw you."

Briefly in simple words, he told them of his climb along the wall, his escape from the balcony of the Council, and his meeting with the amok Cassidan who had been conditioned to kill him. They listened in silence.

"I don't think," he said when he was finished, "we can wait for tomorrow to make our break. Henry—is it possible to try to break out starting right now?"

The other two glanced at Henry.

"Yes," Henry said. "But all our plans are based on picking you up from tomorrow afternoon's *Symphonie des Flambeaux*. If you're sure you want to start now—"

"I do," Bleys said.

"Then we don't have time to arrange a new pickup point for you. You know there's also a performance of the *Symphonie* at twenty-three hundred and thirty hours tonight? You could make that, and we can shift schedules accordingly to pick you up from it. Toni goes with you, in any case."

"Then that's what we'll do," Bleys said. "Now, will you tell me the details of how you're going to pick us up there?"

"No," Henry said. "A lot of our people are going to have to make plans as they go along. Also, if you want to start now, we haven't time. I still need to get a number of the Soldiers out of the city ahead of us. They're still here because they weren't expecting to go until tomorrow. But I can start them moving in the next fifteen or twenty minutes, casually.

Or even shortly after you've left with Toni for the *Symphonie*. Dahno and I will be going in separate directions, to rendezvous with the rest of you later. Let Toni tell you what to do. She knows the plan."

"All right," Bleys said. He looked at Toni, and she smiled at him. Strangely, for the first time since the lighting had gone out in the hallway, he had a sense of safety, with her here. He smiled back. A warmth flowed between them.

Chapter 33

"*If this is your first visit to the* Symphonie des Flambeaux—" Bleys read to himself with some difficulty from his copy of the brochure that had been handed to both him and Toni as they came into the auditorium to find their seats for the performance.

It might be the dimness of the place, but for some reason he seemed to have to strain to keep the letters of the words in focus. The small threat of a headache was still with him.

"*—You may feel both the auditorium itself and the unlit Torches of the Flambeaux in the stage area seem rather utilitarian and unimpressive, considering the reputation of this great artistic achievement. Rest assured however, that this impression will vanish once the Flambeaux are lighted and the performance begun . . .*"

Bleys paused to glance around him. He and Toni were in excellent seats in the front row of one of the small private boxes that took the place of the first ten ranks of seats in the amphitheater—ranks which rose by steps behind the boxes and occupied some hundred and forty degrees of the semicircle that was the auditorium itself.

The remaining forty degrees was filled by the stage area, on which the slim shapes of the unlit Flambeaux stood like stiff soldiers of black metal.

Both stage and auditorium did look utilitarian and bare. Probably deliberately so, in order that the program would seem that much more exciting by contrast.

Bleys returned to reading the brochure.

"*Again, for our first time guests at the* Symphonie, *perhaps a few more words of information.*

"*The* Symphonie des Flambeaux *is literally a symphony; the creative, disciplined effort of that great composer, artist and writer Mohammed Crombie.*

"*The composition of it was his lifework; and into its realization has gone a technology developed by the best minds of Newton.*

"*It should be understood by those in the audience that what the 'Dance of the Flames'—which you are about to see—has been sculptured to do, once the torches have been lit, is what all successful great works of art manage to do: supply the listener, viewer or reader with material for that person's own creative imagination.*

"Just as the reader, reading a great work of fiction will begin to 'live' its story as if he or she were a part of it, so any performance of the Symphonie *becomes a life experience, unique to the person watching.*

"What the viewer sees is built by that person's own creative imagination; and what he or she sees will never be experienced by anyone else, now, in the past or in the future.

"Therefore, the best way to enjoy what the Symphonie *has to give, is to simply let the flames absorb your attention. Let your mind go free to build whatever it wishes, from their light and movement.*

"That way you will not only be making the best use of Mohammed Crombie's great artistic genius, but your own as well.

"A hint to those who may think this process difficult: simply watch the flames and let yourself be taken over by them.

"Humans have gazed into the flames and embers of open fires for thousands of years; and even if you have never done this yourself before, you will find this sort of watching comes naturally to you. Just abandon all else and give your full attention to the flames."

The last few lines printed on the brochure seemed to be lost in the white background of the page they were printed on. Bleys looked up to see the lighting was being turned down. At the same time, in the increasing gloom, the Flambeaux awoke. Small blue flames, flickering into red, came to life at the tops of the torches on the stage.

The light continued to dim until the stage and auditorium were in near-total darkness. The flames grew until they were as tall as the torches themselves. Their increasing light seemed to intensify the gloom around and below them, hiding even the torches themselves, so that what the eye fastened on was only flames.

Bleys watched, conscious of an unexpected anticipation, mingled with a touch of wariness. Everything about the design of the auditorium, the pattern of the torches on stage, and the lighting dimming as the flames grew, seemed to suggest the *Symphonie* would produce its effects by a form of hypnosis.

He was a bad hypnotic subject. He had known this ever since he was very young. An Exotic medician, brought in to relieve him during an illness, had tried to ease his discomfort with hypnosis and found it did not work well with Bleys.

"You're fighting me," he had told Bleys gently. "Just relax and let your mind follow where I lead it."

"*I am* relaxing!" said the unhappy five-year-old Bleys. "I'm not fighting—I'm really not. All I want is to feel better. But I'd really like to know what it feels like to be hypnotized."

"I see," said the medician, the Exotic gentleness still in his voice. "That explains it. What you're doing is trying to stand aside with part of your attention and watch yourself being helped. But with what I'm doing now, this won't work for you. You can't stand apart and watch. You just have to relax and let what will happen, happen."

"I . . . can't!" Bleys wailed.

Nor could he. The medician finally had to give up and give him a chemical form of relief, which was very much against what the Exotics stood for in medicine.

Since then, Bleys had run into a number of instances of his innate resistance to hypnotism. His whole life, it seemed, had necessarily concentrated on being able to stand back and observe—not merely himself, but everyone and everything in the universe.

On the other hand, he had become excellent in the use of hypnosis on those who accepted it; to the point where the proper tone of voice, the proper body attitude and movement on his part, plus a slight flash of the red lining of his cloak had become enough to focus the attention of an audience.

Toni, Dahno and Henry—he had found out by testing them all when they were unaware—were not good hypnotic subjects either. Henry, in particular, was a stone wall where any hypnosis was concerned. So, possibly not surprisingly, was Amyth Barbage.

Bleys had come to suspect that all Faith-Holders, True and Fanatic, were resistant; and many, perhaps all, Dorsai as well. Also, he suspected trained Exotics could also be resistant or not, as they chose. Other people, individually, varied in their susceptibility.

But now, as the flames began to move in intricate dances, Bleys found himself relaxing. Here was no hypnosis. This was something laid out before him, for him to pick up, make use of if he wished; and that was all. He remembered the words of the brochure about the thousands of years people had stared into the flames of fires and the glowing embers below them.

It had been one of his secret occupations in the days when his mother, who as an Exotic could not bring herself to use any form of physical punishment, would confine him in his own bare bedroom, where there was nothing to read, nothing to play or work with, nothing to do.

What she had overlooked was that in many of the bedrooms that were his over the years, there had been a fireplace and a fire within it; often a real fire—if only for cosmetic purposes. So he had spent many happy hours losing himself in dreams he found within the flames, and in the phantasms generated by the red-white, glowing embers of the half-consumed firewood.

So it was easy now for him to do the same thing with the torch-flames before him. There were intricate, almost hidden—but varied and repeated—patterns, to their movements, shapes and brightness. They varied, like the waxing and waning colors of burning embers, as moving air brought them more or less oxygen for combustion. These variations became rhythms that slipped into his dream, and seemed to move it to a drumbeat felt but not heard, marking time with his pulse, at a little more than fifty strokes per minute.

The drumbeat grew in Bleys' mind until he began to hear it like a single voice; and the fabric of future history and his part in it unrolled before him in the firelight of his mind.

He looked at his plans for his future and the future of the race, twined together; and it seemed that he saw them more richly, more fully imagined than he had ever seen them before. A fever of planning was unexpectedly on him. His mind raced; and things that he had thought of only in general began to develop specific parts, so that his mind expanded to a voice that at last seemed to be singing actual words . . .

> *Hear them talking, hear them laughing*
> —drums at my command.
> *Put an end to talk and laughter*
> —drums at my command.
> *Drum them running, running to me*
> —drums at my command.
> *Drum them into ranks and squadrons*
> —drums at my command.
> *Drum them armed and into armies*
> —drums at my command.
> *Drum them drunk on dreams I dream them*
> —drums at my command.
> *Drum them last to a greater people,*
> *But*—Drum them first to war!

The drumbeat and song rang in his head as background images in his mind. Now Hal Mayne was before him, and the two of them were seated across from each other at a small table, just beginning to find common ground . . .

A touch brought Bleys back to the present; the darkened auditorium and the flames broke away, became a thing apart. Retreating from him and carrying his personal dream with it.

The touch was Toni's. He turned to look at her in the gloom and saw she had one hand slightly raised, her slim index finger beckoning him. She rose and left the box; and he followed, but with the uncomfortable feeling of someone torn abruptly from something deeply engrossing. He would have given anything, at that moment to have explored further the imagined conversation with Hal Mayne that the magic of the *Symphonie* had kindled in him.

But now Bleys put all such thoughts aside and concentrated on the immediate moment. The first thought that came to him as they went up and out of the auditorium, along the aisle barely lit by small floor-level lights at the end of the rows of seats on each side, was that the Council would surely have watchers here. Some of them would be sure to notice Bleys and Toni leaving, and take action to keep them under observation.

Then he realized that such action would call for a routine, rather than an emergency response. One of the ways in which Newton aped Old Earth was in the customs of its social groups. Most of these had been long forgotten even on Old Earth—like the present Newtonian practice of a man accompanying the woman he was escorting for the evening to the door of the ladies' restroom. Then waiting outside until she should reappear again, to escort her back to her seat.

It was a protective, ancient custom, as unnecessary on Newton as it had once been necessary in certain areas of ancient Old Earth; but it might be assumed by any watchers to be the reason Bleys and Toni were going out.

Someone would undoubtedly follow to see whether this was the case. But—the following would be routine up to the point where the follower did not return. He wondered whether he should let Toni go ahead and stay behind to take care of whoever might come along to investigate. But Toni forestalled him as they left the auditorium for a side passageway.

"Stay with me," she said, as if she had read his thoughts.

She evidently knew her way. They made several turns, going down short lengths of corridor; and on a final turn found a tall, broad-shouldered man in his thirties with blond hair. One of Henry's Soldiers, waiting for them. He smiled when he saw them.

"Go ahead," he said. "Don't worry about anyone behind you. I'll take care of that. You'll find someone farther on to take you the rest of the way."

Toni nodded. They went on. Turning another corner, they almost ran into Sean O'Flaherty.

"It's all right!" Sean said hastily, as they stopped abruptly. "I'm with you. I'm an Other!"

Pride sounded in his last three words.

"Dahno will tell you about me," he said. "Come on now. No time to lose."

He led them quickly through several more corridors, through a couple of doors, and down a short ramp. The Soldier they had passed earlier caught up with them just as they emerged into the city's night. Newton's larger moon was well up in the sky. The *Symphonie* had been underway longer than Bleys had imagined.

"Only one man followed," the Soldier said to them. "I handled him."

A long blue limousine with magnetic levitation floated around the corner of the auditorium, on the trafficway that circled it, almost the moment they stepped outside. It had probably, thought Bleys, been some rich person's toy before being stolen.

It stopped before them. The back door opened.

"Go ahead," said Sean. "Tom and I'll follow in another vehicle."

They stepped into the spacious rear compartment, with two rotatable armchairs, and floatseats for six more people. Two men were visible beyond the transparent division, in the control cabin, both Soldiers.

The limousine closed the door by which they had entered and floated away from the auditorium, slipping out on the exit to the main city trafficway. It gained speed.

As they pulled away, Bleys turned on the viewing screen in the back section of the limousine, setting it to look back at the spot they had just left. He saw a battered gray van pull up to pick up both Sean and the Soldier, Tom. It was also a magnetic-lift vehicle; but, like most commercial vehicles, it would probably be badly underpowered for reasons of economy. In any case, the limousine soon left it out of sight behind them, once the luxury vehicle left the interior ways for the high-speed city trafficway.

Bleys' mental map knew this particular ribbon of road as a belt-line route looping the inner body of the city. At points there were turnoffs to the Great Trafficway leading to the spaceport; but the limousine passed the first one they came to at full speed, and instead—a little farther on— turned on a down ramp that led them back into the city.

Here they followed a route that seemed to make little sense. They would travel some distance down one way, turn off at right angles for a short distance, then back again to their original direction; only to turn again farther on, cross over and head back in the opposite direction. The limousine had slowed once more to city speeds, and occasionally it dropped almost to a walking pace as they slid slowly past a particular location.

But each time Bleys could see nothing of importance at the spot; only an unoccupied corner or a dark, closed store in mid-block—occasionally a doorway into one of the tall buildings. But no one was ever there waiting for them. It struck him that Sean's hurry earlier had been unnecessary. The headache between his eyes, that had vanished as the Flambeaux lit, was with him again.

But this trip was all in the hands of those around him. He had resigned control to Henry. He caught sight of Toni sitting back in the limo's other armchair, watching him. He could, of course, ask her to outline the plans to him, even now. But she would undoubtedly refuse, and he did not want to show concern at not knowing.

He sat back in his chair and closed his eyes, but he did not feel capable of sleep. From time to time he lifted his eyelids slightly for a moment. But each time all he saw was Toni in her silence. However, after a number of changes of direction that made a ridiculously complex and meaningless diagram in Bleys' now-instinctive mental-mapping process, his exasperation got the best of him.

"As long as we're just riding around," he said to her, opening his eyes fully, "why don't you fill me in on the plans you, Henry and Dahno made for getting us safely to the spaceport and on board?"

"The medician said to refer all questions to him," Toni said.

"I'm not asking you about my health," Bleys said—and was surprised at the tone of his own voice.

"Kaj made a point that any questions should be to him, first," Toni said. There was the slightest of hesitations. She went on. "That was why Henry dodged your question about the plans, back in the hotel."

"You mean"—it was an incredible thought. Henry never did such things— "Henry misled me deliberately?"

"No," answered Toni, slowly, "he told you the exact truth. Just, not all of it. Kaj wants you to rest as much as possible, Bleys."

"I don't know what the concern's all about," said Bleys. "This Kaj Menowsky seems to be acting more like a stage magician with a bag of tricks than any medicians I've had to do with before this."

"He's very good," Tony said. "Dahno said the Exotics offered him a chance to stay and practice on Mara, when he got through his internship."

"Well, that's a recommendation. But I always understood the patient came first." Even to his own ears, Bleys sounded unreasonable.

"I think that's what he's doing with you—putting you first," said Toni, quietly. "Ahead of all the rest of us and anything else, for that matter."

Bleys sat back again in his seat. He closed his eyes and once more pretended to sleep. Damn the headache.

Surprisingly, he did drop off; and evidently for some considerable period, because when he woke, it was slowly and from a deep heaviness of sleep. The limousine had finally come to a halt.

Bleys opened his eyes fully and sat up to look out. He felt dull-witted and stiff-bodied, as if he had slept for a week. They had stopped in a lighted parking area before a food-display store, one of the convenience-places where the city's inhabitants could examine eatables on sale before ordering them for delivery. However, both the men in the front seat were still there; and a moment later the door on Toni's side opened, and Dahno stepped in.

"Forgive me, Toni," he said. "But would you take one of the movable seats? I'm going to need that larger one you're sitting in."

"Of course." Toni moved. "I was expecting Henry."

"He's riding with the two sections of his Soldiers that left early. Any others not with him or us will be out right now, making false attempts to escape at other exit points."

Dahno sank into the large chair and sighed.

"I've been sitting on a packing case in the back of a truck," he said to them, then swiveled his armchair to look directly at Bleys. "And how are things with you, Brother?"

"Fine," said Bleys. "Never better."

"Glad to hear it," Dahno said. "Things could get a little difficult later. We all ought to be feeling our best, now."

"How close are we to the exit point we're using?" asked Toni.

"Close," said Dahno. "We should be there—"

He broke off. The limousine had just started to pull out from the parking area. It headed toward the nearest trafficway; and, once on it, began to move fast—this time disregarding the city speed limits.

"We'll attract attention, moving like this," said Bleys, looking out as the limousine slid swiftly past the other traffic.

"Doesn't matter," said Dahno. "From now on, timing's important. We haven't any time to waste."

"So Sean O'Flaherty said when he met us in the auditorium," Bleys said. "He said you'd explain him. Explain what?"

"Oh, I simply told him you might be a little suspicious of the fact he claimed to be an Other, while you'd met him as an Intern for the Council," said Dahno. "But he actually is one of the local Others. I talked to some I trusted, earlier, and asked them to recommend someone—preferably one of our Members—who was already accredited to the Council. They came up with him; and he turned out to be a good choice. He was one of our Members who successfully amended your personal history in the Council's files. But do you know what, Bleys? I believe he's got a touch of hero worship where I'm concerned."

Bleys nodded, unsurprised. For some years now, Dahno had taken over the responsibility of planting false and confusing accounts of Bleys' earliest years in official files on other worlds; full of elegant false details, including his age at the time he had come to live with Henry and his two sons on Association.

But probably not even Dahno realized that while these spurious accounts would probably work in all data archives, the exceptions would eventually be seen through by the Final Encyclopedia and the Exotics' information-gathering service. It was the Exotics Bleys planned to keep his eye on. They would never go along with his plans; and, while their beliefs would prevent their taking any direct personal action against him, historically they had found ways around such restrictions.

Then the thought of Dahno's last words made him smile.

"Is this the first time that's happened to you, Dahno?" he asked.

"No," said Dahno. "But I can't remember when the worshiper was Sean's caliber. Don't let his chattering mislead you; he's one of the most capable recruits I've seen in any of our Other groups. For the moment, he thinks I've got all the answers. But he'll grow out of that."

Bleys had been watching the street behind them in the still-lit vision screen of the limousine's backseat. He had seen three other vehicles—two kinds of van and one passenger car, none of then particularly new or otherwise remarkable—follow them out of the store parking area.

Now, as he watched, another car—a low leaf-brown electric vehicle which showed a remarkable turn of speed for the wheeled conveyance it was—was keeping up with them, having just come from one of the side 'ways to join them.

"Toni told me the medician said I wasn't to ask anyone but him about your plans to get us to the spaceport," he remarked.

"Oh, that," said Dahno. "There's nothing to that. The plans are much what you heard from Henry in advance. We'll probably run into some opposition at three points—"

"Henry talked about that," Bleys said.

"—Three points," went on Dahno, evenly, "along the way to the spaceport, no matter what route we take; and we may have to smash our way through one—or two—or all three. But that's to be Henry's and the Soldiers' job, not ours. You know everything but the details, and the details are going to be controlled by what we run into at those three points. The first is just coming up—the exit from the city to the spaceport Great 'Way—and the one river crossing, where we've got no choice but to go across a bridge. Then there'll be the matter of the perimeter of the spaceport itself; and possibly trouble right up to the moment we're actually inside *Favored of God* and off the pad. Once we're no longer touching ground, it's not likely the Newtonians will really dare break the Interstellar conventions by bringing in ships to force us down again. Frankly"—he looked at Bleys and chuckled—

"I don't think they think you're worth it—the kind of trouble that would cause them with all the other Worlds at once," he said. "No, Kaj Menowsky just thought that you shouldn't be stressed more than necessary until he had a chance to check you over, on the ship."

He chuckled again.

"You do have a tendency to want to take charge of whatever you get involved in."

There was a certain amount of truth in that, Bleys thought, and it was typical of Dahno to talk himself into a righteous position in any discussion. Bleys looked in the screen and saw yet another nondescript vehicle closely following them. Like the others, it was keeping up. The limousine must be holding its speed down to stay with them.

The main trafficway broadened; and there were few other travelers on it at this time of night—or morning. He looked at his wristpad. It was after four A.M. local time.

He looked again in the screen. They would be reaching the spaceport trafficway shortly—and very soon now Newton's sun would be rising.

Chapter 34

A single musical note sounded from the speaker in the back section of the limousine. They slowed, out of the passing lane to the parking strip at the nearer edge of the trafficway, and came to a stop.

As they did, they approached another leaf-brown wheeled vehicle exactly like the one Bleys had seen join them earlier.

This conveyance was stopped well away from even the lane of least speed, and its body-shell had been lifted up and well clear of its motive unit above its frame and related working parts; so that altogether it reminded Bleys disagreeably of a cadaver in a morgue, half-dismembered by an unfinished autopsy.

Three men were standing around the power unit, staring down at it, talking and apparently, from time to time, doing things to it.

The driver of the limousine got out and strolled over to the other vehicle. He joined those standing there and they talked, peering in at the drive unit for a few moments. Then one of the three who had been standing there turned and came to the limousine. It was Kaj Menowsky.

The limousine door across from Bleys was opened for him—evidently by the man who had been riding beside the driver. He stepped inside and took a floatseat, which he turned to face Bleys diagonally across the back space of the limousine.

Bleys looked back without a smile. Kaj did not seen in the least disturbed by the lack of a friendly welcome, if indeed he noticed it.

"How are you feeling now, Bleys Ahrens?" he asked.

"I feel the way I always feel. Fine," said Bleys. It came to him he could hate this man with his eternal questions.

"Good," Kaj said. "Keep as quiet as possible between now and when we get to the ship. It will make things easier both for you and for me if you're disturbed as little as possible by whatever's done around you."

"I'll do my best," Bleys said, still unsmiling.

He looked away from Kaj as the front door of the limousine opened and the driver got back in. They lifted from the parking surface and pulled back into the traffic lane. There, they picked up speed rapidly, caught up with and began to pass the vehicles that had been traveling with them.

Kaj said no more. Soon they were back in the lead. As their driver lessened the vehicle's speed and held his position, the phone in the back compartment sounded again, suddenly, this time with a brief snatch of melody, a series of notes that sounded as if they might have been from some ancient folk tune.

"Code." Dahno looked at Bleys. "Nothing too hard to break, but they won't have time enough to do anything like that before we're in position. It's Henry. He says he's with Teams One and Two, and they got out of the city before the exit blocks were set up—"

He was interrupted by what sounded like a longer playing of the same or a similar melody.

"He says, barricade at the exit to the spaceport trafficway ahead," announced Dahno. "But trafficway police, only—needle guns and stunning weapons. His two teams will make a diversion as soon as we're in sight, then blow an opening in the barricade where it crosses the passing lane. All our vehicles to come through together, with this limo in the middle. Other vehicles on each side of it and in front and back as shields—"

He paused. Another burst of melody.

"Try to get all vehicles through, but don't stop for any disabled. Once through, our first six vehicles, not counting the limo, should peel off farther down the road and set up a line of defense for his two teams already in place beyond the barricade. There shouldn't be a problem. We've got power weapons. All the police have are needle long-guns and hand weapons. Once pursuit's stopped, the vehicles already through will join us; and we'll head together for the next point of opposition."

Dahno stopped talking. A few brief notes sounded.

"Next point should be the Da Vinci bridge. We can expect heavier weapons there."

All their vehicles were close together now, on a long curve empty of other travelers. The dawn of Alpha Centauri B was not yet showing. The barricade was suddenly in sight, extra lighting making it starkly visible in one bright area.

Fifty years ago, it might have been no more than a double row of trafficway police cars. Now, even with the brief time at the disposal of the police, there was a chest-high, meter-thick barrier wall across the entire trafficway, bonded to the surface below it; and with a gap wide enough for only a single car to go through it in the center lane. The limousine was approaching that gap at two hundred kilometers an hour, and the other vehicles were running with it.

"Teams One and Two had better act in time," Dahno said softly as the barrier wall rushed at them.

But just then the end of the wall at the single-vehicle opening exploded before them, and a space the width of four vehicles appeared.

Dahno chuckled harshly. "Henry must have a power cannon small enough for a couple of men to hand-carry—at least."

"Yes," Toni agreed.

In almost the same instant, two of the other magnetic-lift vehicles had speeded up and dodged in front of the limousine, while other vehicles of the group moved in solidly around the limousine, leaving it just barely room to steer. In what seemed like the same instant they were through the gap, there was a brief glimpse of vehicles and rubble beyond—and then they were headed up the open trafficway beyond, with what sounded like a storm of hail hitting on the windows and sides and even the roof of the limousine.

"Needles," Dahno said unnecessarily.

"Yes," Toni said evenly. "I think Bleys knows they won't penetrate the body of this limousine."

Bleys had not known. He was suddenly very aware of how little he knew about actual shooting outside of gallery practice, in spite of his younger years when some of the members of Henry's church—the one that Bleys needed to attend with the rest of the family so as not to attract attention on worship-days—had gone out to be Soldiers of God. But his church itself had never been attacked seriously, except by youngsters with relatively harmless weapons; and the local church sergeant-at-arms, who had a power pistol, had only used it to scare them off.

Bleys felt a passing twinge of unusual and painful inferiority to Henry and all his men. But it was a brief sensation. The headache had become almost an old friend now, and a dullness in him seemed to suck up all his energy.

Now that the momentary excitement of passing the barricade was over, he was slipping back into what was almost an indifference. It was possibly the long night, almost without sleep, but Bleys had a feeling as if what was happening was taking place outside a transparent capsule in which he sat, apart from it all; no more connected with the action going on beyond the wall surrounding him than if what he saw and heard was only something projected for viewing.

The rain of needles diminished as they pulled away from the brightness of the barricade area. Gazing into the vision screen set in the bulkhead between their compartment and the control cabin, he saw it showing a view of what was behind their limousine, with the gap torn in the barricade receding rapidly. Close behind them, their own vehicles were following, with the wheeled cars coming last, lurching and bouncing as they passed over bits of rubble thrown widely by the explosion of the barrier where the bolts of a power weapon had hit it.

It was ridiculous, Bleys thought annoyedly, that a century had gone by with no one improving the range of the power weapons in atmosphere. Some small improvement to make better use of their tremendous destructive power. A power rifle would not need to have the amazing range of the needle guns, where every needle was effectively a miniature self-propelled missile that would keep going until its propulsive back end used up its fuel. But it would produce a remarkable difference if power guns could be made effective at more than a hundred meters or so from their target.

Four undamaged police cars, evidently most of those that were left workable, could be seen in the glow of the lighting from the blockaded area, setting out in pursuit—a brave, but probably useless action. They were all magnetic-lift vehicles, and their capacity for speed would undoubtedly be at least as great as that of the limousine—probably the fastest of the transportation in Bleys' party—but they were making no real effort to close the gap between themselves and the last of those before them.

Fairly obviously, they were following only so that they could send messages ahead about the numbers and doings of the group that had just passed them.

As Bleys thought this, the power weapon that must have torn the hole in the barricade fired again, tearing up a wide strip across the trafficway behind the vehicles in Bleys' group, but well ahead of the pursuing police.

The police pulled off to the side, stopped and got out, to simply stand and watch, as the steeply wooded slopes of the cliff beyond the turnoff began to disgorge more vehicles, as undoubtedly stolen as the limousine and those with it. These joined with those about the limousine. Soon they were all far enough off so that the cars and men behind them had dwindled to dots.

The road broadened and curved away before them again.

"How do you feel now, Bleys Ahrens?" Kaj asked. Bleys was aware of the medician's fingers lightly holding his left wrist, the middle fingertips pressed against the blood vessel that was throbbing there with his pulse.

"That won't do you any good." Bleys glanced down at the hand holding him. "It takes more than something like that to speed up my pulse."

Kaj let him go without comment.

"You didn't answer my question, Bleys Ahrens." he said. "How are you feeling now?"

"Just the way I felt the last time you asked me," Bleys said.

"Good," Kaj said. "If you do feel yourself getting tense, in particular, let me know—immediately. It's a tricky business treating anyone who's been dealt with the way you were; but I've got a short-acting chemical sedative here if you find tension or excitement beginning to run away with you. Try to avoid both."

"I'll do that." Bleys turned to Toni and Dahno. "How far to this river crossing?" he asked—and realized instantly that he should have known that himself. He did have that earlier crossing in his mind's eye now, but it was not very clear. It had been afternoon, then; now it was night—though now the sky was beginning to lighten. Alpha Centauri B was undoubtedly just below the horizon ahead of them, and a first paling of the sky showed where it would rise; while in the screen he could see that behind them the sky still held the color of night. Ahead of them, the stars were already fading and disappearing.

But the bridge . . . as he remembered, its two traffic surfaces—the upper one, outbound to the spaceport, and the inbound beneath it, to the city, had been so little different from the wide whiteness of an ordinary trafficway, that the fact they were crossing water could have passed unnoticed, except for the two towers at each end. It was a suspension bridge; but with modern materials, particularly single-molecule cables with their great tensile strength, the towers could be low and fairly inconspicuous.

As far as the river and its surroundings were concerned, what Bleys remembered was that the river had not been wide; though he seemed to remember it was deep and fast moving and ran under the bridge through a cleft with steep, heavily wooded sides, at right angles to the trafficway.

Leaving the bridge for the city, before, they had gone around a curve like the one they had just taken. Before reaching the bridge on the way in from the spaceport, the 'way had curved in the opposite direction through another wooded cleft; for the river ran between two ridges, coming down from the mountain range now on Bleys' left. So the bridge itself was still out of sight ahead and would be so until they were almost upon it.

On both sides the bridge approaches were short, flat stretches cut through the earth and rock at each of the bridge ends. But the slopes on either side of these stretches had been overgrown with bushes and trees; so that they seemed a natural part of the wooded reaches sloping down on each side of the river. The spaceport-bound trafficway crossed the bridge on a level above the trafficway toward the city.

"How soon do we get to the bridge?" Bleys asked again, for Dahno had not answered. All their vehicles were slowing, and the big man was busily watching the wooded incline now beginning to rise steeply on their right hand, as the slope on the left side was also beginning to do. Toni answered.

"Any moment now," she said. "We're just about there."

In fact, just then, their limousine slowed almost to a walking pace, turned to the right edge of the paved surface and moved off it; on to the grassy verge and up the slope above, floating between the trees on its magnetic lift but dodging right and left to weave its way between the tree trunks.

Bleys saw the other air-lift and magnetic-lift vehicles following. He could not see whether any of the wheeled vehicles were attempting it, though the view behind them was artificially bright in the screen. A glance out the window to his own left, however, showed a forest still so deep in pre-dawn darkness that it was hard to see beyond the immediate vegetation.

Bleys gave up trying to see, either out the window or in the screen, and sat back in the chair. He was, he told himself, only a passenger.

The limousine, jinking right and left to find clearance to pass between the dark, gloomy pillars of variform pines, continued on up the steepening slope, until, after a few more minutes, it came out into a small clearing plainly made recently, for the fresh-colored stumps of cut trees, with the fallen trees themselves between them, were to be seen in the top-shaded emergency light set up in the middle of the clearing.

The limousine stopped. Dahno got out hastily, and the others followed him, Bleys included. Bleys stood up, stretching himself to his full height with relief after sitting in the vehicle as long as he had.

The emergency light was little more than a dim glow in front of them, not much more than a single candle would have shown; but by its illumination it outlined a number of figures reading large unfolded pieces of paper like maps; and apparently seeing very well through goggles. Bleys recognized one figure by the way he stood. It was Henry. The others had already started to move toward him, and Bleys went with them.

When they reached the group and stopped, Henry alone looked up from his paper, and Bleys saw the dark lenses focusing on him.

"I'm glad you're here safely, Bleys," he said.

At that moment, something was thrust into Bleys' hands; and, looking down, he saw that it was a pair of goggles like those the others were wearing. Night-glasses, of course, Bleys told himself. He should have realized.

"Now you'll be able to keep up with what we're doing here," Henry said.

"Perhaps it would be better if Bleys Ahrens didn't have a pair of those," said Kaj Menowsky, just beside and behind Bleys.

"Medician—" Bleys turned toward the voice. But he got out only the first word. Henry was already speaking before him.

"No. Put the night-glasses on, Bleys," Henry said.

In fact, Bleys had already put them on. Once they were in place, the scene before him jumped into view, as clearly visible as it might have been on a heavily clouded day. Henry stood less than a long step from him, and there was a difference about him that registered on Bleys immediately.

Henry MacLean had never been a particularly tall or big man; but here and now he looked larger, more impressive than any of them. A lot of it was an air of command that Bleys had never seen in him before. There was also something else that Bleys found it hard to put his finger on. It was almost as if there was an enthusiasm—what even might be called a glow of happiness or enjoyment in him—born of the present moment and the present situation.

"Come, Bleys," said Henry, turning away from the others. "I want you to look at the situation with me."

Chapter 35

Henry and Bleys moved off together into the light the night-glasses alone found for them among the trees.

They went in silence for some minutes, Henry saying nothing more and Bleys feeling no need to talk; winding their way through available openings, for the growth was even thicker here. Bleys recognized the imported variform Norway pine, intermixed with a low native bush. They stepped suddenly through a last screen of trees, out into an open space, and Bleys was blinded by the sudden glare of light against his night-glasses.

Bleys felt a hand catch his arm and stop him, while another hand pushed the goggles up on his forehead. He blinked his vision clear to see that they were now out under open sky and the dawn was actually with them, although the daystar was not up. As his vision adjusted, Bleys saw that Henry had halted him no more than a step short of falling over the edge of an almost vertical cliff which plunged to the seemingly-unmoving gray-blue width of the river at its foot.

The broad, pale strips of the two trafficways to and from the spaceport, crossing the bridge, were a little down the river to his right, with the reverse trafficway—the one coming from the spaceport to Woolsthorpe— just visible underneath the outbound 'way where they came together to use the bridge. Then both strips curved away, still one above the other in the limited space alongside the river, for a short distance before disappearing again through the ridge on that side.

As his eyes adjusted, Bleys saw that work had been done on the outbound traffic strip on the bridge.

Undoubtedly using the same quick-setting material that had been thrown up to make a solid barricade at the city exit, beehive-shaped structures which were plainly weapon-shelters had been built over holes excavated in the upper trafficway surface. The horizontal slits of the shelters' openings looked toward the city end of the bridge; and were at, or rather just above, the surface of the outbound trafficway itself.

At least four of these had been completed and others were under construction farther back. The foremost, already finished and armed, blocked the left passing lane; and the one behind that the next, speed-regulated lane. More building with the same material was also going on at the far end of the bridge, where larger structures were being erected, with half-buried, protected passageways between them.

"They look serious about stopping us here," Bleys said.

Henry nodded briefly. "Those are the Woolsthorpe Headquarters space soldiers out there," he said. "There were probably delays in getting them here, with the necessary equipment and building machinery. But since, they've been making up for lost time. But why I wanted you to look at this, Bleys, was to see whether it gave you any ideas that might help me. I've got a pretty fair notion of how to break through, but I'd like to hear anything that comes to your mind. Odds are I'll stay with my own planning. But there's a chance you'll come up with something I haven't thought of."

Bleys gazed hard at the bridge, the construction going on, and tried to put some order to his thoughts.

"I never paid much attention to military strategy or tactics," he said, more to himself than Henry. "I never thought it would be necessary. I suppose those places they're building will stop needles, of course."

"Certainly," Henry said. "It won't stop our power guns, though. We'll be able to break through those fire-shelters along the road and probably just about anything they have beyond—but it'll take a number of bolts directly on them in each instance; and every time we fire, we'll be giving away our position. Let alone the fact that to make the power weapons effective we're going to have to move closer—out into the open space near this end of the bridge."

"Yes, your power weapons—for that matter, all your weapons," said Bleys. "Where did you get them? I know we've always landed on another world with your Soldiers carrying nothing but those small fingernail-trimming pocketknives. I know you had sidearms and pocket weapons coming in, in bond. But you never got the ones for Newton, here, did you?"

"No, but the smallest knife is dangerous if you know how to use it," said Henry. "You remember what I told you, Joshua and Will, as boys, about any sharp or pointed object. But about the weapons we've got—we got them the way the Soldiers of God and the outlaw Commands on both Harmony and Association have always gotten them. From Militia depots."

"There aren't any Militia on Newton," said Bleys.

"No. But there's the regular space troops those out there belong to, permanently quartered in Woolsthorpe," Henry answered. "Remember my mentioning them yesterday? They're here to act as personal body-guards for the Council and government, if needed. They've got all sorts of weapons up to the heaviest possible—even some too heavy for use aboard space or atmosphere craft. Extra supplies are kept in the city's military supply depots; and the first thing we did was locate them. That's where most of the Soldiers were last night, getting all the weapons they could hand-carry."

Bleys looked again at the scene before him. The dawn sky had brightened even as they had stood there; and the river was now darker in color, closer to a deep-sea marine blue, rather than the slate-blue it had shown just a short time before.

The dust-grayed white of the trafficways and the bridge was in contrast with the pure new white of the fire-shelters.

The contrast stood out, even against the dark green background of the variform Norway pines and the native bushes—which had leaves very much the same color as the pine needles, except for a faint orange tinge around the rim of each leaf, making the bushes appear to glow in the fresh morning light.

Bleys studied the fire-shelters, the construction still going on behind the manned ones, and entirely off the bridge on the far side as well; and sought for something that would be worth suggesting to Henry. But his mind was oddly tired and dull. No thoughts came.

The river surface was so calm that it would have been easy to believe it was not moving. But with the slope of its bed from the foothills of the mountains to Bleys' left, its current must be stiff. Yet only some small turbulence where it touched shore showed this; plus an occasional branch or tree limb that made a slight bump in the smooth liquid surface, moving swiftly toward the bridge.

His thoughts wandered . . . like an Old Earth song . . .

> *"Mein Fader var ein Vandringsman,*
> *Ich hab' es in das Blut . . . "*

. . . Ezekiel MacLean, Henry's brother, who had claimed fatherhood of Bleys, had had a knack for Old Earth languages and had taught Bleys bits of songs and stories in a number of them.

But Ezekiel's wandering could hardly have been called happy. Perhaps, Bleys thought, if he was actually Ezekiel's son, he, too, would "have it in his blood" and be fated to wander—always the stranger . . .

Bleys made himself concentrate once more on the bridge. But his mind failed to focus, and his eyes saw no pattern in which he could look for a weak point.

"I'm not much help, Henry," he said. "Maybe because I've been up for too long a time."

Even as he said it, he remembered that Henry and all the rest would have also been up at least as long.

"—Perhaps," Henry was saying, "we can arrange some kind of shelter for you to rest in while we go about this business of breaking through here. A quiet spot in the woods—"

"No!" Bleys said sharply. "I'm fine—just no ideas for you. If you move your power weapons out in the open to use them against those fire-shelters, the men holding them are going to be sitting ducks for the ones in the shelters. In fact, I don't see any way to get at those shelters, unless you could get above them in aircraft, or somehow tunnel underneath them—and tunneling wouldn't work beyond the edge of this cliff; because there's the river; and nothing for you to fire at because the underside of the reverse trafficway would absorb the power-gun bolts. I'm no help, I'm afraid."

Henry nodded without expression. "That's all right. What you say backs up my own thinking. Do you want to wait here with me and see how things develop? Standing here, the trees around make us hard to pick out. Even if one of those space soldiers did, it would take a marksman with a needle rifle to be a threat to us. Actually, I don't think they know we're here yet."

"Henry, what actually are your plans?"

"Stand here. You'll see," Henry said. "I had the attack movements begun as soon as you showed up with the rest of the Soldiers. We should be seeing the first effects of it, soon."

He lifted the wrist holding his control pad to his lips.

"Anwar," he said, into it. "Time to start draw-fire."

"Right, Henry," said a small voice from his wrist. "Draw-fire in one minute or less."

Henry lowered his wrist and looked at Bleys.

They did not have to wait even one minute. Before that time, from various points downstream in the trees overlooking the river—and apparently never from the same point twice—needle-gun fire and a few ineffectual bolts from power guns began to sound. Bleys frowned before realizing he was doing so. The fire-shelters were beyond effective range for the power guns in the woods, and the needle guns would do no good at all unless they happened to be so amazingly and luckily accurate in their aim that the needles would go through the small weapon slits in the fire-shelters.

The fire-shelters had begun an answering fire almost immediately.

"Didn't you say that if we fired on them, we'd give our position away?" Bleys said to Henry.

"Our general position, yes, but this is just light firing to concentrate their attention here. Shots by a few Soldiers only, moving about, and no-where concentrated enough for them to be targeted by the Newtonians; unless one of our people moves back to a previous position—and my people all know better than to do that. Meanwhile, we find out what they have in the way of weapons and sharpshooters in those shelters. It shouldn't take long."

In fact, the firing from the woods was already dying down; and, even as Bleys noticed this, it stopped. Almost immediately, the return fire from the fire-shelters stopped; and a silence took its place that had something unnatural about it—as if the whole scene was somehow holding its breath.

Bleys was abruptly conscious of a pulse in his neck and the fact that he had been unconsciously counting his own heartbeats. To take his mind off them, he reached for something to say to Henry. If nothing else, he knew the difference in sound, from his practice in shooting galleries through ear protectors, between that of a hand-held power gun and a hand-powered cannon, such as the one that had blasted an opening in the barricade for their vehicles.

"Well," he said, "at least you know they haven't got any hand cannons in those fire-shelters."

"I think they have," said Henry. He paused. "You can hold the trigger button down on a needle gun and spray an area by moving your point of aim across it. But a power weapon of any size fires one energy burst at a single point and then another, again at a single point. At the range we are from those fire-shelters, a bolt from a hand cannon wouldn't be any more effective than one from a hand-held power gun. That's why they're answering with needle fire. The few power guns they're firing are simply to warn us to stay back. They'll hold fire from their heavier weapons until they can hit effectively."

"Yes," Bleys said, mechanically. His voice sounded odd to his own ears.

Henry lifted his control pad to his lips. "Begin primary attack."

The firing began again from the woods, this time supplemented by an increase in the occasional sharp explosion-like sound of hand power weapons—though as far as Bleys could see the shelters were still beyond effective range. The shelters replied. But then, unexpectedly, power guns opened up from the two cable towers at the near end of the bridge; but against the shelters, not with them into the woods. At that range, they were effective against the shelters. Immediately, there was the sound of power weapons from the Newtonian positions, but with the occasional deeper boom of hand cannons speaking against the towers.

"You've got Soldiers in the towers!" Bleys said.

"We were here first," Henry said.

"But those towers can't have a fraction of the protection in their walls that the fire-shelters have," said Bleys. "It seems to me—"

But before he could finish, the firing of power weapons toward the towers ceased abruptly; though the towers continued to fire back. The firing from the woods continued; and now Soldiers began to dart out from the woods, one by one, running a short distance into the open space, and dropping to the ground in anything as slight as a small depression, but which gave them shelter from either needles or bolts from the fire-shelters.

Still, Bleys saw one Soldier hit almost immediately, though he was already on the ground. He jerked convulsively and began rolling over and over like a child enjoying the sport of being taken by gravity down a slope. Bleys stared at him, his own body tensing as if it, too, was rolling in pain across open ground. He looked away from the man who had been hit.

Look at him, he told himself fiercely and forced his gaze back to the Soldier. But the man was already dead. Another almost-exhausted bolt from a power weapon had hit him, not with enough energy to tear him apart, but enough to pick him up and toss him some little distance away, so that he now lay huddled and still.

Another death, Bleys thought. The counting of it was an iciness in what seemed to be the hollow shell of his body.

"We must take any hurt or killed with us," he said to Henry. "The spaceship can carry them to Harmony. Then any dead can be shipped to relatives or their homes, wherever they are."

"God willing," Henry said.

"We have to take them with us."

"As we can," said Henry. "In any case, the soul of the Soldier who just died is in the Lord's hands now."

"Even," said Bleys, "if he's died for me—I, who am in Satan's hands?"

He was remembering the words, almost the first Henry had greeted him with when Henry had come to join him on Association.

"God will judge," Henry answered; and, looking at this man he had always called his uncle, Bleys saw his face as still as the naked stone of the distant mountain walls.

The deep sound of the hand cannon drew Bleys' attention back to the bridge; and he saw the nearer of the two towers now trembling, evidently from the impact of the heavy bolt. But, abruptly, the firing of all power weapons against the tower ceased as if they had been suddenly ordered to do so. The firing from the towers against the shelters continued. They were blasting away sections of the forward shelters; and meanwhile the shooting from the Soldiers in the clearing was continuing and they were continuing to move forward, while other Soldiers emerged from the wood, behind, to run, drop, rise and run again, as they all moved on toward the bridge.

Bleys stared at them.

"Look at the river, Bleys," said Henry's voice.

Bleys pulled his attention from the bridge and looked instead at the peacefully flowing ribbon of water.

"Why did the shelters stop firing at the towers?" he asked. But even before Henry replied he realized he had known what that answer was. Power weapons could not only break through the thin shell of the towers easily, but would also cut the cables inside it, the cables helping to support the bridge on that side.

If only some of these were cut, the bridge could tear itself loose. The whole section with its two freeways could fall into the river beneath. As yet only the defenders were on that part of the bridge that was over water.

"Cables," Henry had answered, even while Bleys was thinking this.

Bleys tried to focus on the river, as Henry said. The calmness of the flowing water brought him some feeling of peace after watching the Soldier rolling down the slope. Gradually he began to concentrate on its movement, again noticing the half-submerged bits of flotsam on its surface, now occasionally interspersed by an entire small tree or a section of dead tree trunk. Perhaps, part of his mind thought idly, there had been some sort of landslide farther up the river; and the debris from it was only now reaching the bridge.

In fact, Bleys now saw there were a number of larger pieces of wood, and even small whole trees, coming downriver at the moment. Unexpectedly, there was a momentary brief, small flash of light from one.

He did not connect this with the sound of a weapon firing from the bridge or the return fire from the advancing Soldiers. Suddenly his mind became more alert as he woke to a suspicion. He reached automatically for the goggles on his forehead, then dropped his hand. There was no telescopic power built into these lenses.

Bleys continued to focus as best he could on the larger floating pieces, as these came closer. His searching was finally justified by the sight of a human face and the thick barrel of a power rifle; both barely above water and among the branches of a fairly good-sized young tree, whose needle-bearing branches spread out on the water's surface. As he looked, the barrel winked again, and this time he identified the power rifle sound with the wink.

He turned to stare at Henry, who gave his momentary, quick quirk of a smile, with just the upward corners of his lips, that in Henry was what might be as much as a belly laugh from another man.

"A full advance team," Henry said.

Bleys stared back at the river. Now other large pieces of the floating raw timber were close to the upper side of the bridge itself, and he was able to pick out those that had Soldiers with them, all of them with the barrels of power rifles barely showing above the surface. They were firing from the water up against the underside of the upper section of freeway.

They would be aiming at the bottoms of the power shelters above, where the spaceport-bound trafficway had been pierced. Would these underneath shelter parts be armored? Probably not, Bleys thought. Or, if so, only lightly; to protect against power-gun fire that might carry through the surface of the trafficway and still have energy to expend, coming in at an angle against that part of the fire-shelter out of sight from above.

"Four? Five?" Beside him, Henry was addressing his wrist control pad; and a moment later there came back two small voices, answering separately. *"Six* in place." *"Seven* in place."

"Ready all," said Henry.

Bleys' attention was still on the water and the faces and gun barrels he had discovered among the floating parts of trees. The river was indeed moving much faster than it appeared. The first of those he saw in the water had ceased to shoot and, already had begun to pass from sight under the edge of the bridge's lower trafficway, as seen from Bleys' point of view.

Bleys had been holding his breath, waiting for the return fire that should come against them from the fire-shelters above.

"They're better than shooting-gallery targets, down in the river there," he muttered.

"No," Henry said.

In fact, as Bleys strained his eyes to see beyond the bridge to where the water surface again became visible, the trees and parts of trees that were appearing on the other side seemed to show no sign of anyone with them.

After a moment, Bleys identified a particular tree trunk to which he was positive he had seen one of the water-bound Soldiers clinging; and definitely no one was with the floating wood now.

Of course—Henry would have foreseen the fact they would be easy targets in the water; and he had sent them down the river anyway, knowing that the people in the fire-shelter would not fire back—could not return fire to begin with—because their hastily-thrown-up shelters had only a single opening for their weapons—in front, toward the shore where the approaching Soldier skirmishers were now almost to that point where the trafficway left land and began to travel on the bridge.

"So, Bleys," Henry said, "you weren't that far out. We couldn't tunnel to them or fly through the air, but we did attack from an unexpected quarter—and that's what you were really thinking of."

"Those Soldiers who floated down," Bleys said. "They're getting off under the bridge?"

"Yes." Henry nodded. "I've got some others of our people there, tending a rope stretched across-river, its ends out of sight among the trees under the bridge, and the bight of the rope just down under the water, out of sight. Another advantage of being here first. The rope will give teams One and Two something to catch hold of and pull themselves to shore on. They'll be coming out on the far bank; and when they're all out, they'll move up to support the attack of teams Six and Seven, who have been waiting in cover, beyond the far end of the bridge."

Bleys nodded. He felt empty and useless.

Henry's whole battle plan was clear now. In his mind's eye, Bleys saw the wet Soldiers from the river gathering, climbing the bank to just underneath the spaceport-to-city trafficway, and waiting. He imagined the Soldiers of teams One and Two waiting out in the trees. Henry was speaking again into his wrist control pad, but Bleys was not really listening.

The overall picture was still oddly unclear. It was as if the transparent shell that had continued to be about Bleys had now also closed around his thoughts, so that they were compressed; and he had only the mental equivalent of tunnel vision. His mind worked as usual when he focused down on some particular segment of their situation; but his customary grasp of a whole range of factors, that he was used to dealing with easily, was not with him.

So strange that he should feel removed and apart this way; while, at the same time, other thoughts were reminding him that he had found he himself could be deadly, with the Militia officer on Harmony and when he had actually killed the Cassidan who had been sent to kill him.

Strangely, there was still something unreal about that moment in which Bleys' arms and hands had seemed to move of their own will. It was hard to think of the man in the dark as a real and living person. But the Soldier rolling over and over on the ground had been real.

But the present remained unreal. Not like a nightmare so much as a dream. A dream without flavor and color; something he would rather put from him and forget, but could not. At the same time he knew it to be part of reality; and reality stretched ahead along an inevitable path that he had known for a long time—he simply had not known that it would affect him like this, once he was on his way down it.

"—We should be getting back," Henry was saying . . .

. . . Bleys broke free of his thoughts and suddenly was back on the cliff. The scene before him had become utterly quiet. A group of human figures—Soldiers of God only—were standing upright at the near end of the bridge, and another group on the ground beyond its far end, obviously waiting.

Bleys seemed to have fallen out of touch with events and time for a period, at least long enough for the whole business of their winning their way over the bridge to be wound up and concluded.

"Yes," he said to Henry, automatically answering the last words he remembered hearing. Turning, he followed the older man back off the edge of the cliff, through the trees, into the region where Alpha Centauri B's reddish morning light now filtered down through the branches above in rays and patches, so that it was easy to see their way without the goggles.

Chapter 36

Bleys had expected the feeling of a transparent shell about his thoughts to clear when he was back with the others and away from the bridge. It did not. He carried it into the limousine again, together with a heaviness that was almost a physical pain, all through him.

The limousine flew on, roughly a meter and a half above the pavement of the passing lane of the deserted trafficway. He did not speak to any of the others, and none of them—Dahno, Toni or Henry, who was now riding with them—spoke to him.

They talked amongst themselves in low voices, and so detached was Bleys' mind that he only heard their talk as low murmurs in his ear. Kaj Menowsky spoke to him once, and he felt the medician's fingers taking his pulse; but he did not answer, and Kaj did not insist on a response.

From there until some vague point later was lost time. Ideas unconnected with what had passed through Bleys' mind a moment before followed earlier thoughts in no pattern or sequence. It was a little like moving at random through a completely furnished, ready-to-live-in house, that was empty of other people and also completely unfamiliar; so that he wandered from room to room through unexpected doorways, finding everything different all the time, and no area having any particular importance.

Bleys came out of this state at some unmeasured time later, as the limousine abruptly began to decelerate. He glanced automatically into the viewscreen. There were the other carriers, coming to a stop behind the limousine on what was plainly a service road, running along just outside a six-meter-high wire fence that clearly guarded the edge of the pad.

Bleys started to rise from his chair to leave the limousine, but Henry—seated on one of the movable seats facing him—waved him back down.

Bleys sank back in his seat. Henry turned to Kaj.

"Kaj Menowsky," he said. "We're going in now—"

"Why here, particularly?" asked Toni.

Henry glanced at her briefly. "We could go in anywhere. Here, we're as close to our ship as possible. The point is they know we're here; they just didn't know this was where we'd stop and go through the fence. We can't do that anyway without setting off alarms. It doesn't matter. *Favored*'s less than a kilometer from where we are at the moment; though we'll probably go double that distance, dodging for cover from behind one spaceship to another as we cross the pad."

"Why should we dodge?" Kaj asked. "Wouldn't it be faster to go straight?"

Henry explained, "According to Interworld Conventions, each of those ships, is officially the territory of the world it belongs to. It would

be a violation of sovereignty for the Newtonians to go through them—or
even damage them accidentally—in hopes of getting us. So we can use
them for cover."

"I see," Kaj said.

"Yes," Henry said. "We'll start, riding as few vehicles as can carry
everybody, but we'll probably have to abandon them shortly and split up
in groups. Our Team leaders and sub-Team leaders have smoke guns,
which we'll use to hide us as we make our run between the ships. We can
also use them to hide which group Bleys is with, since it's him they really
want. The rest of us don't count, except for being in their way. I'm telling
you this to give you necessary background. Now, everybody out!"

They followed Henry out through the door on the far side of the
limousine, next to the fence. Bleys was last out and, stepping down onto
the uneven ground, he stubbed a toe and stumbled slightly. Dahno's hand
caught him by the elbow and steadied him.

Henry and Kaj were suddenly in front of him.

"How are you?" Kaj asked sharply.

"I've got a headache, and I haven't slept for two days," Bleys said.

"Nothing else?"

"If there was—"

"Never mind all this." Henry's voice cut coldly across both of theirs.
"Bleys, how much strength have you got? Can you do everything you'd
usually do?"

Answering Henry was a different matter.

"I'm probably not in top shape. No." Bleys said.

"Yes," Henry said. He turned to Kaj. "Medician, you're to give Bleys
the strongest stimulant you safely can, whatever will keep him as close to
peak performance as possible, for the next hour or so."

Kaj Menowsky's face altered—only slightly, but the alteration was
noticeable.

"No. It would be the worst thing for him right now."

"If we don't get him to that spaceship alive," said Henry, "it won't
matter whether the last medicine he had was the worst thing for him or
not. He'll need to run for his life. He may have to fight for his life. For
that he needs strength. All the strength he normally has, and then some."

"Still—" Kaj was beginning when Henry interrupted him.

"There's something else," he said. "If I'm killed or badly wounded
before we reach the ship, who's going to lead my Soldiers? There's only
one other here I've trained them to follow without question. Bleys. Lead-
erless, no one here may reach *Favored*. If you won't help Bleys right now,
you may have all the lives around you on your conscience."

"What about Dahno Ahrens?" Kaj asked. "Or Antonia Lu?"

"Not my best sport," Dahno said lightly. Toni said nothing, but she
looked at Kaj and did not need to speak.

"Toni, forgive me," Henry said. "I don't doubt that in some ways
you're the next best qualified to lead. But Dahno shares something with

Bleys. Because of his size, he's easy to see. And that's a help to my Soldiers. It also means he shares Bleys' disadvantage of being easier to target than the rest of us. But the aim is to get Bleys to the ship alive, even if no one else gets there. We can't do that and protect Dahno at the same time. But if Dahno's put out of action, my Soldiers will turn to you."

He looked at Dahno. "Meanwhile, if Bleys and I go down, it'll be up to you, Dahno."

"I was afraid you'd say that," Dahno said.

"Medician?" Henry said, for Kaj still had not reached for the small case he had been carrying with him since he stepped into the limousine for the first time. Now, however, he did. He searched in it for a minute with one hand and came up with a small, stubby blue-white cylinder. He was already in front of Bleys. He reached forward and pressed the cylinder against the back of Bleys' right hand.

Bleys felt something like the light touch of a finger. Then the cylinder was taken away and tucked out of sight again in the bag of tools.

"Give it fifteen minutes," Kaj said.

"Toni, you go with Team Two. The closest one forming there. Dahno, Team Three, next over," Henry ordered.

He raised his voice to the Soldiers, now all standing outside their cars.

"All right!" He raised his voice. "All teams, move out as planned. Team One, follow our van."

They all moved. Bleys found himself on the wide front seat of a broad van; seated next to a door with Henry beside him on his left and the driver of the van at Henry's left. Clearly determined to stay close, Kaj was in the body of the van just behind him. There was access from there to the front seats, through an entrance apparently built for people not more than a meter and a half tall.

But Bleys did not want him to come forward. Whatever Kaj had given him, whatever had been in the little stubby blue-and-white metal cylinder, was already beginning to take effect, and he felt as if he was waking up from a confused nightmare. His mind was sharpening, and his body was coming alert with energy and strength.

"Go!" Henry said to his wrist control pad. Somewhere behind them, a power rifle blasted twice, vans from among the convoy of vehicles that had brought them here drove through a wide gap in the fence on to the pad, Soldiers not only inside them but clinging to their tops and outsides wherever there were handholds.

Gazing through the transparency of the van's forward wall, which would have been a simple glass windshield on a poorer world like Association or Harmony, Bleys could see the broad expanse of the pad. It was almost uncomfortably bright now, under a large sun, high enough in the sky so that its reddish tint was effectively invisible.

Across this wide, flat space, the parked spacecraft looked closer together than Bleys remembered. Now, with his mind coming awake again, he was thinking to some purpose.

"Henry." Bleys turned his head to look as he spoke. The calm face next to him turned to meet his, and he was suddenly aware of the smell of sweat from the driver. There was no such tension-odor about Henry. He was as quiet and serene as if they were all going on a picnic. "Henry, just how will the Soldiers react if anything happens to you?"

"They've been told to look to you. No hesitating," said Henry. "Also, you know Carl Carlson?"

"He's the older Soldier with our group—Team," Bleys said. "Tall, thin, clean shaven? I know him."

"He's in this van, in the back," Henry said. "He knows my plans. He'll be close to both you and me. In case anything happens to me, he'll answer your questions if he can. Also, he'll fill you in on what I've told him about covering this last stretch to the spaceship. Don't ask him about that now. Keep your mind clear, and don't worry him until it's necessary."

Their van was past the fence and weaving among the parked space-craft already.

"I don't see any signs of opposition yet," said Bleys, looking ahead at the pad. It seemed to stretch to the horizon; but the true horizon, he saw, was hidden by other spacecraft.

"When it shows up, they could be coming at us from all directions," Henry said. "But we ought to be able to cover maybe half the distance before they can get any opposition to us here. When we do, we abandon the vehicles and start splitting up into different groups."

"Could the Newtonians have put pressure on the standby crews of the parked craft, to call them the minute anyone sees us?" Bleys asked.

"Have to locate us first," Henry said. "Remember, there are thousands of craft here in this one parking area. Also, there's no reason any crew would do that for them. In fact, I think any request like that is not allowed, either, according to the Conventions."

They were passing between two very closely parked spacecraft now. There was as little as thirty meters between them. The other vans of their Team were behind them. A single chimed note sounded simultaneously in the wristpads of Henry, the driver, and others in the van's body behind them. The van stopped suddenly.

"Out!" Henry ordered. "Team Two's hit opposition."

Toni. Bleys moved his mind resolutely away from any thought of her. They were all getting out of the van, and the vans behind them were emptying, too.

Someone—Bleys did not see who—fired off a smoke gun. A brown cloud, very like the fringe of the dust storm Bleys had looked down a mountainside at on New Earth, enclosed them and the side of the ship against which they stood. He breathed in smoke without thinking, but it did not seem to irritate his throat or lungs.

Still, Bleys felt a sense of relief when Henry pulled from his pocket a small canister with a squeeze trigger handle. He squeezed it, pointing in various directions around them, and whatever was in the canister cleared a cave-like open space, the area of a good-sized room, around them. Visible now to Bleys were Henry, Kaj and the driver, together with half a dozen Soldiers. As Bleys watched, these turned and ran to the edge of the clear area, dropped to the ground, and lay as if looking out under the smoke, where it came down to the pad.

"The clear will hold four minutes. After that, we can spray again, if we have to. Carl"—Henry said to him—"Carl? Good you're still with us here. Give Bleys that extra smoke gun and spray pump."

Carl Carlson, particularly recognizable to Bleys because of his graying hair, reached into a belt-pack at his waist and brought out the two items Henry had called for. He passed them to Bleys silently.

"Carl, who has the power cannon?"

"Jim Jeller and Isaac Murgatroyd, Henry."

Carl gestured toward a point in the cleared space behind Henry. Henry turned. Bleys stepped aside to see around him and made out two more Soldiers, on their feet, with the awkward and heavy weight of a portable power cannon balanced on their shoulders.

Bleys knew that, in theory, one man could fire it by himself. But he would almost have to fire it from the ground or from some other solid rest. It was two meters in length and weighed almost as much as either of the men now carrying it—an awkward, angular chunk of gray plastic and metal and black handgrips. Under actual battle conditions, it came to Bleys from some early reading, the weapon should be held and fired by two men together. But they would need to be on their feet, with the gun balanced on their shoulders as it was now—and they would necessarily have to be erect and motionless with a strong grip on the weapon.

"Good, keep them with us," Henry was telling Carl. "Bleys, there's probably three hundred shots in your smoke gun, but only about two hundred clearing sprays in the pump-spray. The spray's our own Friendly invention, by the way."

Bleys stared at him, because Henry had given one of his sudden rare, brief smiles.

"The Militia used to use smoke guns against us, and we came up with this out of our own kitchen chemistry. These Newtonians aren't likely to know about it—too locked into their gadgets. It gives us an edge."

Bleys looked around him. The men lying at the edge of the smoke had power pistols in their hands, needle rifles slung on their backs.

"Why not power rifles?" Bleys asked.

"At the short range between parked ships, pistols are handier," Henry said.

As he spoke, one of the men they looked at tilted his pistol up and fired into the smoke cloud on an angled, upward slant.

"He's firing blind," Bleys said.

"No," Henry said. "The smoke won't hold down on a surface hotter than the air around it, so there's a clearing between the top of the pad and the bottom of the smoke. It's not enough to do anyone on the outside any good, but our men can see out at legs, wheels—whatever's there. When they see a pair of feet, they simply aim through the smoke at where the body should be above it. It's a trick you've got to work to learn, but you finally get the feel of it. Most of my Soldiers are good enough so the smoke cloud might as well not be there. But the fact that he's fired means someone's caught up with us now. Carl, have you shown Bleys the map?"

"Not yet. Here it is," said Carl. He had already pulled out a tightly-folded piece of paper. Once he started unfolding it, it flattened out perfectly, without creases. A one-molecule sheet. On it was an odd diagram with little elliptical shapes and different paths starting from beside one such shape and going in different directions to other shapes, only to come together again at a final ellipse, close to the right-hand edge of the page.

"The circles are spacecraft like this one." Carl struck with his fist against the side of the spacecraft where they stood; a hollow, ringing noise sounded from the hull. There was no response inside the ship. They were, Bleys noticed now, only a few steps from the entry port, which was shut and obviously locked.

"They're just keeping their skirts clean, inside," said Henry. "The Newtonians don't dare fire into our smoke for fear of hitting the ship. Go on, Carl."

"The lines here"—Carl pointed—"are the general routes the different Teams will try to take, to confuse whoever's come against us. Our line's the green one. We'll move to this next ship, and from there to the next. See?"

His finger indicated one of the central zigzag lines.

"If we hit opposition, we can break right or left to join the routes of the Teams moving nearest us. There's an extra power pistol and needle rifle here for you, if you want." Even as he spoke, he was beckoning two of the men lying about the circumference of the cleared area to them. The two got up and ran back to stand with them. "Do you want them?"

"No," Bleys said. "—Yes! I know how to shoot at targets, at least."

One Soldier lifted the slim shape of a second needle rifle from one of his shoulders and the other unstrapped an extra power pistol in its holster from around his waist. They fastened these on Bleys. The Soldier with the power pistol grinned up at Bleys for a second, when it turned out that the belt went around Bleys' waist and buckled at one notch less than it had around his own.

Meanwhile Carl Carlson was holding up his own wrist control pad, studs gray-green against the black of an imitation leather.

"You want to set your control pad to *Where*," he was saying, "and I'll touch-transfer point my data to your wristpad, so that you'll have everything there."

Bleys nodded and touched the proper studs on his wristpad. An area the size of his little fingernail lit up like a small screen with the image of a simple meter, a curved line divided at regular intervals by black cross sections, and a needle pointing to a center point above which was something that looked something like a "W," but was actually Old Earth's ancient Greek symbol for Omega, the last letter in the old Greek alphabet and meaning "*end.*"

Now Carl touched a stud on his wristpad. The needle of the meter wavered for a second, then centered a little to the right of the centerpoint.

"The needle points you along the route our Team's got laid out for it on the map. If you join another Team, it'll switch to their route," Carl said.

Needles from needle guns firing outside the smoke cloud had begun to ricochet off the pad, either through the smoke or just short of it, into the cleared space. No one seemed to be trying to shoot with power weapons from outside.

"Time to move," Henry said.

They went up along the side of the spaceship. One of the Soldiers in the lead, followed by the two carrying the power cannon, was spraying a narrow but clear path for them through the smoke toward the front of the ship. They passed around its bow, the wide observation transparency there now blacked out, and around to the other side, still in the smoke.

There was a short pause while the Soldier with the spray gun went forward to have a look at things beyond its obscurity. He came back, nodded and they moved out of the smoke into clear air; and a pad showing nothing but silent closed spaceships.

"Go!" Henry said.

They all ran toward the farther ship that Henry had indicated with an outflung hand. Bleys ran almost without effort, his mind reveling in its alertness.

They reached another ship. Smoke cloud again, Soldiers down and peering out under its bottom edge as they all caught their breath.

Kaj Menowsky was close beside Bleys, and Bleys noticed that he was not breathing at all heavily after their run. Obviously he was in good physical shape himself. He had no power pistol or needle rifle; but then, almost no Exotics would touch weapons; and many Exotic-trained medicians from other New Worlds also refused to do so, as a matter of principle.

A Soldier peering under the smoke looked back at Henry and made pushing motions through the air with one hand toward the space beyond the other side of the vessel.

"Go!" Henry said, pointing.

They went. They reached one more ship without trouble, then another, and even one more with no sign of opposition. A corner of Bleys' mind began to worry that the groups Toni and Dahno were with might have drawn all the Newtonians' attention from Henry's group.

He looked at Henry; but Henry was already indicating several of their Soldiers. One of them was the woman who had been part of their original group when they had left the vehicles.

"—All the way out!" Henry was saying.

The three—no, four—Soldiers ran in different directions toward the four ships nearest to them. They took varying times to reach their goals, and the first three to arrive peered quickly around a ship's end and signaled back with the same pushing motion of one hand that the Soldier peering under the smoke had used a short while before.

The woman was the last one to reach her ship, which was the farthest away. Indeed, she never reached it. Before she got there, Bleys heard the hollow boom of a power gun. She was struck and thrown through the air some small distance, to fall and lie still as a cast-aside rag doll.

Bleys made an instinctive step in her direction, but Henry was speaking again.

"The other way, then! Everybody!"

And once more they were running—and, as suddenly, with no transition whatsoever, Bleys found himself once more inside a smoke cloud, pressed up against the side of yet another ship, with needles ricocheting through the smoke at them. As ricochets, the needles no longer had the power to go through the side of the spaceship, but they were still dangerous—if not lethal—to human bodies.

Bleys saw that at least two of the men had already been hit. One had an arm dangling uselessly; the other was bleeding from high on his head, his blond hair now stained dark in the sunlight by the blood from what could be merely a scalp graze, or something more serious. But he was on his feet.

"Move!" Henry circled his hand in the air and pointed back along the side of the ship they were up against.

They moved, Henry first, clearing the path with his spray gun, followed by the two Soldiers still carrying the power cannon, and Bleys, with all the rest, behind them.

They went back along the silent side of the ship, in the narrow lane through the smoke, around the back end of the ship and finally past the thick edges of the massive plates that directed the thrust on which the ship relied in atmosphere for its landings and takeoffs into space.

"Scout," Henry said, and a Soldier dodged past Bleys, the power-cannon carriers and Henry himself to venture into the smoke ahead.

"Clear," his voice came back.

They moved, and in a moment they were out in the open air. Henry was pointing at another ship off to their right, and they ran.

They were all taking their pace now from Henry and the cannon carriers behind him, who were going as fast as they could. Bleys felt as if he was actually running at his top speed; though he knew he was not—nowhere near it. His feet pounded on the surface of the pad, and his lungs heaved as if he were at the very limit of his exertions; but none of this was true. He simply could not go ahead and leave any of these with him behind. It had been bad enough to leave behind the Soldier woman he had just seen die.

They were almost to the ship Henry had indicated. They were closest to its bow end, and Henry turned slightly to his left to circle out around it. The others caught up and they went around it in a body.

—And ran almost body to body into a group of Newtonian space soldiers, each with a power rifle and a needle rifle slung from their shoulders.

Henry, the cannon carriers and the rest of the Soldiers had instantly dropped to the pad. Bleys was a second late in seeing what they had done and following them and in that moment he felt a sudden impact on his left side. But by that time he was down on the pad. Around him, the Soldiers had their power pistols out and were using them. The Newtonians were dropping.

Almost immediately Henry and the others were getting back to their feet again and holstering their guns. There had been only a few, late return shots from the men they had run into—and all of those were now dead, lying scattered singly, or in small heaps on the pad. They had been taken by surprise; and Bleys suddenly realized that probably these military spacemen had never actually been in a firefight before. It had been almost like an execution.

More dead. Bleys tried to keep his mind from counting.

"Go!" It was Henry again.

All about them, there were only ships and pad, no movement. But Henry now had them running toward one more, farther ship.

I will not count, Bleys said to himself. He had the sudden wild feeling that they were not so much progressing toward the unseen goal of the ship that actually waited for them, as running and re-running over again the distance between the last ship behind which they had taken shelter, to the ship just beyond it; and then somehow starting all over again to run the same distance under the same urgency—and suddenly everything was different again.

He was once more in a smoke cloud, once more beside a ship, but this time he had the feeling it was not the ship they were running for a few minutes before. This time he had the feeling that a longer length of time had passed. Needles were coming in, but Henry held them all where they were. Again, whoever was firing at them were deliberately firing into the smoke cloud at an angle so that the needles would ricochet through whatever position they might have within the smoke cloud—dangerous to them, but harmless to the ship against whose hull they were now clustered.

Some of the Soldiers, he saw, were down; some moving, some not.

One of the fallen was Henry.

Everything went strange to Bleys for a moment.

Chapter 37

"No, I'm all right," Bleys said.

The sensation of strangeness cleared, like tunnel vision expanding once more to normal range.

"Henry!" Bleys started to move toward Henry, but felt himself checked by a grip on his right arm. He was about to break loose when his mind also began to clear. He looked to see the face of Carl Carlson beside and looking up at him.

Bleys was still clearheaded and strong, but there was a sudden cold rage in him; and instead of dominating it and pushing it from him as he normally would, he let it grow.

It was a rage at his life that had given him a lonely childhood, had made him different from other children; set him apart and isolated, belonging neither to the child world nor the adult world that had separated him from everyone else.

He looked past Carl again at Henry.

This, at least he would not let happen; and if life had already robbed him of Toni and Dahno, he would find some way to make life pay. But if nothing else, Henry and the rest of those with him now would not be taken by Newtonians. He would get them to *Favored*—even at the cost of his life's plan.

"Bleys Ahrens?" Carl was saying. "Are you really all right? Can you hear me?"

"What makes you think I'm not?"

"I thought you were fine, up to a minute ago," said Carl. "I was saying—we can carry Henry and the Soldier who can't walk. Henry's only wounded, but I don't know how badly. Hit in the body. It's up to you now. Tell us what to do."

"Where are we?" Bleys asked. "How far to *Favored?*"

"Almost there," Carl said. "If it wasn't for the smoke cloud, you'd see it. It's straight ahead, looking from this ship's side. They're firing at us from the left of it. To our right, the only way between a couple of other ships is blocked by two cannon wagons that came up. Jeller and Murgatroyd took our hand power cannon and knocked them out. The wagons're still there, but nobody's been dodging out from behind them; and there's no fire from that direction."

Bleys glanced around; and saw that the power cannon, as well as the two he had seen carrying it, were not in the cleared area.

"Where are Jeller and Murgatroyd?" he asked.

"Either just inside or outside the edge of the smoke, I think. A little to your right as you go directly out. They haven't come back."

"Our power cannon's with them?"

"Yes, Bleys Ahrens," Carl said. "Do you want me to send someone else out to bring them back with it? The chances aren't good, if Jeller and Murgatroyd were needled and the cannon's lying out, clear of the smoke now. Whoever goes can put more smoke out to cover picking it up, but if they do, all the shooting is going to zero in on their area; and their chances of getting back, particularly with the hand cannon, are up to God alone. Shall I send someone?"

Bleys' mind had put aside his rage now, but his decision remained. His thoughts flowed rapidly, concisely and capably. The situation was clear, complete and in his hands.

"Not yet," he said. "You say we can carry our wounded? All of them?"

"I think we can carry all, Bleys Ahrens. It will slow us, though; and if we make our run in the open, I don't think any of us have much of a chance of getting to *Favored*. We'll try it in a smoke cloud, of course, but we're still going to lose people."

"Why?"

"The needle gunners. I'm not sure why the fire from the two power-gun wagons is dead. But just the needle gunning from our left, even with with us moving in the smoke, is going to take half of us out. Some, maybe all, of the other Teams are there already; but they can't come out again and help us, not without compromising the ship's extraterritoriality, now *Favored*'s given them sanctuary."

"Right," said Bleys. "But we can't stay here. So the only chance we've got is going in a smoke cloud for *Favored*. So, go. But I want that hand power cannon. I'll carry it. I can carry it alone."

"Bleys Ahrens—" Carl began, with a note of protest in his voice.

"That's it," Bleys said. "Now tell me a few things."

"Yes," Carl said.

"How long will one of the smoke cans keep putting out smoke, if you pump it up, hard as you can, then tie the handle down so it keeps spouting?"

"Oh"—Carl hesitated—"at best guess—two, three minutes."

"And how much smoke would it put out in that time?"

"Oh, a lot," Carl said. "Several times the smoke we've got here—no, more than that. Maybe enough—yes, added on to the smoke here now, it could cover all the distance between us and *Favored*—"

"All right," said Bleys. "How much of that smoke would hide the side of *Favored* with its entry port? Its full length? Half its length? How much?"

"Full length," said Carl.

"Fine," said Bleys. "Get me two more canisters. Do we have any line?"

"Line?"

"Yes!" said Bleys. "Line—rope or the next best thing to it. I want to measure the distance to the edge of the smoke. And get an eye-estimate of the distance from the edge of our cloud to *Favored.*"

"No, no rope, or anything like that," said Carl. "But I can have a Soldier crawl out through this smoke, staying well down on pavement to the smoke edge; and he can see under it to *Favored.* We've got several people pretty good at estimating distance."

He turned away from Bleys and raised his voice slightly.

"Merivane!"

A thin young Soldier with black hair looked up and scrambled to his feet at the edge of the smoke cloud where he had been lying, peering out at the pad.

"Merivane, we need to know how far to *Favored.* Use your own body length to measure. Have you got a way of marking one body length at a time, as you go—or something you can put down so that you can look back and see where your head was when your feet are level with where your head was before you moved?"

Merivane stared for a moment, then plunged his hands into a trouser pocket and came out with perhaps twelve miniature white cubes with black specks on them.

"Dice!" Carl stared at them. "Where—"

He checked himself. Merivane grinned, closing his hand around the cubes.

"Remember, Carl?" he said. "I'm not a Friendly."

"That's right." Carl looked at Bleys. "He's from Ceta. Merivane, have you got enough of those—*things?*"

"A dozen, anyway," Merivane said. "It can't be that much a distance to the edge of the smoke."

"Crawl out at an angle," Bleys said to him, "and come back straight. That way you leave the cubes where they are and you can count them— don't pick them up on your way back—don't expose yourself, just get close enough to see, take a good look at our own ship, and give me your best estimate of distance to it—wait a minute."

He turned again to Carl.

"How good is he at judging distance?"

"He's one of the very good ones," Carl said.

"Good. Go, Merivane," Bleys said.

Merivane stepped to the nearest edge of the cleared area in the smoke, dropped to the surface of the pad, left a die and crawled out of sight in the smoke. Bleys watched his feet disappear and looked back at Carl. "There'll be enough clear space down there for him to look back and see the die he left?" he asked Carl.

"Yes, Bleys Ahrens. But you asked about line. We haven't got any, as I said. No rope or anything like that. I can't think of anything we could use, either."

"Then tear up clothing. Make strips; tie them together. Tear up underwear, if you've got nothing else. I don't imagine anyone here is wearing single-molecule underwear?"

"No." Carl brightened. He turned to two Soldiers who had been standing by through the last few exchanges of words, took the smoke canisters they were holding out, passed them to Bleys.

"Are these pumped up? Come to think of it," said Bleys, "is there some way to pump them up and tie the handle down, without having them spew smoke right away—some sort of shutoff?"

"There's a safety," Carl said. He took back the canisters, turned to the two men and handed the canisters to them. "Tear up your undershirts. Make a rope or string of them by tying them together. Then put the safety on, pump the canisters up as far as you can, tie the handles down—and bring them back to us, to Bleys Ahrens."

The two took the canisters, turned away and took off their shirts.

And Bleys turned again to Carl. "Soon as Merivane is back, get everybody ready to make a run for *Favored*. If he can give us a good idea of the distance, you can probably tell me how much time you think it'll take us to get there, carrying Henry—"

Bleys broke off and looked around for Henry, finding him lying on the ground, with a couple of Soldiers kneeling beside him. Henry's head was propped up on his own rolled-up jacket. Bleys forced himself to look away again. He turned to Carl. "How badly is he hurt?"

"Needles in his left leg. Can't walk," Carl said. "Also, he's been hit low, right side—the opposite side from where you've been hit, Bleys Ahrens. By the way, you've lost blood. How are you?"

"Forget me!" Bleys had no time for the wound. So far he felt nothing where the needles had entered. "It's unimportant."

Carl said, "The only trouble is, about that hit on the side that Henry took—with these ricochets, we're not sure it didn't come in on an upward angle, and maybe into a lung. He's not coughing blood, but he's not able to move, and it's just as well he doesn't try."

"All right," Bleys said. "Now, remember, carry all wounded with you when you go. It'll be slow, but take them."

"We'd do that anyway, Bleys Ahrens," Carl said.

"Fine." Bleys turned away from him suddenly. "Merivane! You're back. How far to the edge of the smoke cloud?"

"Nearly eight of my body lengths," said the young Soldier. "I'd guess fifteen meters. Carl, the power cannon's just inside the smoke. Old Jeller and Murgatroyd are lying by it, just in the smoke, but they've both been done."

"I'd figured that," said Carl. He turned to Bleys. "Now what?"

Bleys hesitated. But Merivane had gone out and back successfully; and his doing it again would save Bleys time if he lost his way in the smoke.

"Thanks, Merivane," he said. "Do you think you can get me the power cannon? Have somebody help you."

"I can bring it myself," Merivane said stiffly. He turned and went. Bleys stood, thinking. Carl waited.

"All right," Bleys said. "Carl, get everyone together and ready to move. I'll tell you when, and you start out with everyone else, together, wounded and all, spraying a smoke cloud around you as you go. Meanwhile, I'll have already started a diversion. Thanks, Merivane."

"What kind of a diversion, Bleys Ahrens—and can't a Soldier do it?" Carl was frowning. "And shouldn't I be told what you're planning?"

"No. The hell with that! You just get everybody together, go to the smoke's outside edge, and when you're due to move, get going! Fast as you can—don't pay any attention to me. Just get everybody to the ship, quick as you can."

"I think I've got a right to know—" Carl was beginning.

"No, and keep your voice down. I don't want Henry to know I'm going until I'm gone. You've got just one job: to get everybody to the ship. How long to get ready to go? Because I'll start as soon as you're ready."

Bleys looked down at his belt. The two canisters, their handles bound down by strips of white undershirt, were already hooked to the belt supporting the holster of his power pistol. He had forgotten all about that pistol. It was rather foolish to weigh himself down with it, if he had the power cannon, but a waste of time to take it off now. He heard Carl's voice answering.

"I've already signaled. We'll be ready to move in thirty seconds."

"Then I'm ready, too—wait," said Bleys. "I was about to go off half-cocked. Get me a good three meters of underwear strips. I want to make a sling."

"A sling?"

"Never mind. Just get me the strips," Bleys said.

With the strips in hand, and with the help of a knife borrowed from Carl, Bleys doubled two meters of the underwear strips to make the sling's ends, cut off the remaining length of cloth, double-folded the leftover end to make a socket pad in the middle of the strip, and used the sling strip to tie each end of the pocket pad to it. He took one of the smoke canisters from his belt to fit it into the pocket of the sling.

The canister was small enough to be hidden in the closed hand of an average man. It fitted the pocket well enough—and, even if it had not, Bleys remembered that on Old Earth, in Europe, they had used slings as late as the seventeenth century to throw hand grenades.

The sling had not been easy to master. In Bleys' first attempts, the missile had gone in all directions of the compass; but he had finally become a marksman with it—mainly out of his irritation that he had not been able to learn its use more quickly.

It flung its missile after whirling it in a vertical circle, with the two ends in one fist, and the missile in the pocket, until speed was built up. Then one of the ends would be released just at the time when the missile would fly in the direction it was aimed. That took practice—but Bleys had learned.

He tucked the ends into his belt and nodded at Carl.

"Good," he said. "Give me a minute to reach the smoke's edge—then the rest of you go."

He left without waiting, plunging into the smoke with the heavy hand cannon balanced in his left hand, then dropping to the ground, and starting to crawl forward along the line of dice that Merivane had left.

Bleys found that it was easier to drag the hand cannon by its muzzle end. Even so, there were problems. The pistol at his waist dug into him; and his cape—he was so used to wearing his cape, he had forgotten he had it on, but it would be more trouble than it was worth to try to take it off now—entangled his elbows as he crawled.

But he found he could see better than he had expected, though the smoke hovered less than a hand-span above the surface of the pad. Just back from the outer edge of the smoke cloud he stopped; and lay, listening to Carl's group move out through the smoke cloud.

Bleys watched in the direction of the sounds they made. A moment later, he saw smoke blossom to his right from the outward face of the cloud, expanding across the open area of the pad toward *Favored of God*. From where he lay, he could see the bottom of the ship resting on the pad and the lower half of its open entry port, with someone standing in it who, from the size of his legs, was Dahno. There was also someone else, whom he hoped was Toni, and two other people.

Carl would be bringing his group along well behind the front point of the growing smoke cloud that was being sprayed. He saw sparks coming up from the pad beside the cloud, the sparks of needles from Newtonian needle guns being bounced in off the pad.

Bleys closed his mind to the images, the thought of whom the needles might be hitting—Henry among them.

Already, he could no longer see *Favored*'s entry port. The new smoke, still settling, barred his view. But he had a momentary glimpse before it also hid the two disabled power-cannon vehicles to his right, opposite the needle riflemen. The vehicles were silent and one listed a little to one side.

The two original carriers of the hand cannon had given their lives to take the vehicles out; but there was no firing coming from that angle. Maybe they had been intended merely to block any view of the gunfight from that side. Now, even if the vehicles fired, their bolts could go beyond the smoke cloud, into their comrades on Bleys' left.

The enlarged smoke cloud already covered half the distance between Bleys and *Favored*. It was time for him to move. As the smoke got closer to the ship, the attackers would concentrate on an area just before the entry port, to take out anyone trying to reach it.

Bleys looked left, for the source of the needles, and saw two orderly ranks of white-uniformed figures some thirty meters off, wearing space soldiers' cap-helmets and lying prone, legs spread openly on the pad, firing needle guns. Long guns—rifles.

Leaving the hand cannon lying at his feet, he fixed the image of the Newtonian riflemen clearly in his mind's eye, then stood up in the smoke. Keeping the vision sharp in his mind, he put one of the smoke canisters into the pocket of his sling, thumbed off its safety, and whirled the sling in a vertical circle beside his body before letting it go—not toward the Newtonians, but toward the visible, forward part of *Favored*.

The underside of the ship's hull curved in toward the pad below it, and the canister, he hoped, would land, bounce, or roll beneath it; hopefully ending up where needle fire could not destroy it.

Bleys dropped flat again.

The canister had not quite reached *Favored of God*, but the safety he had thumbed off before putting it in the pocket had already set the canister to pouring out a thick cloud of smoke that was rapidly swelling outward now in all directions—including up along the ship's side, forward beyond the entry port.

As soon as the new cloud reached halfway to the bow, Bleys rose. He ran forward, carrying the hand cannon and with the sling once more tucked in his belt, moving in Carl's smoke cloud until he could duck across to his own out of the needle gunners' sight.

Bleys was alone now, with no slower runners to hold him back. He ran as he had been trained, a "floating" run, the weight of his upper body leaning forward slightly and the thrust coming down his back through thighs and calves directly to the balls of his feet.

He was conscious now only of the smoke around him, that he must stay within for his own safety—the need to travel in a straight line and the utmost exertion of his energy—his heaving lungs, his pounding feet. Instinct, plus practice of running in total darkness in some of his training sessions, warned him of the loom of the spaceship not far in front of him, and he checked his speed just in time to keep from running full tilt into the side of *Favored*.

Even as it was, Bleys' body struck the side hard enough to send a hollow booming through the ship; and Dahno's strong voice immediately called from his right—he had deliberately veered left toward *Favored*'s bow in the smoke, which had spread while he was running through it and was now well forward of the entry port.

"Hello? Whoever you are—the entry port's back here. This way!"

Bleys would have liked to have called back to ask if they had Carl with the rest of the Soldiers and Henry, safe; but he had neither breath nor time to spare. He knew he was ahead of Carl's group. They would need protection. At all costs, he must stop the storm of needles when all the riflemen would concentrate on the area of the entry port.

He stumbled along the side of the ship, away from the port, toward the riflemen and *Favored*'s bow, breathing the smoke in deep gasps and feeling grateful that it did not interfere with the oxygen his hungry lungs wanted. He was dragging the hand cannon now and brushing one hand along the hull of the ship to keep himself beside it as he moved.

Bleys came to a little clear space, like a small room in the smoke, and saw that beyond it the smoke was thicker. He must be at a point where a bubble of clear air from the entry port had been pushed toward the bow by the spreading smoke of the canister he had flung with the sling.

He had gambled on this as a possibility; but it had been a gamble, only. He felt a brief surge of hope, which vanished at the thought of what was still to be done.

Bleys dropped and began to crawl, dragging the hand cannon. Shortly, the small aperture of clear air between the bottom of the smoke and the pad gave him a clear view of the needle gunners.

There were anywhere from twenty to thirty of them, all still lying with military exactness, their legs spread, each needle gun firm on a swing-down support under each barrel, firing steadily into the smoke behind him.

He counted. There were thirty-two, more than he had guessed. But he had them all firmly in a mental image as he rose to his feet, lifted the heavy cannon to his shoulder, and leaned both his body and the butt of the weapon against *Favored*'s hull to steady his aim.

For a moment, something in him almost refused what his will ordered. He thought of Henry and closed his eyes to picture exactly the remembered positions of the needle gunners.

His forefinger came down on the firing stud of the power cannon, his hands aiming the cannon through the smoke, starting at the closest end of the line, pressing the button again and again, going to the one end of the visualized gunners' line, then back again. Down and back once more, and again—until the explosions of his cannon ceased, leaving him half-deafened, with a depowered weapon.

Bleys forced his finger to release the firing button. His throat was raw. He had been screaming something at the gunners as he fired—what, he could not remember now. He got down once more to look below the smoke cloud. He saw piled rubble that had been spaceport pad where the gunners had been. Nothing else was to be seen; but there was no more sound from that location, no more needles coming toward the space through which Carl would be bringing—or had already brought—his people.

Slowly, he stood up again.

He felt something like a cramp in his groin, and his trousers hung with an odd heaviness from their waistband. Looking down, he saw the fabric darkened from the crotch down the inner side of each trouser leg—and for the first time he felt the dampness of the cloth.

He could not go back to the entry port like this. The image of the Bleys Ahrens he had worked years to build could not go back looking so.

He dropped the hand cannon, stripped off his trousers and his shorts; and flung them under the curve of the hull. The lower-hull blasts of the ship's atmospheric drive would destroy them on takeoff.

Suddenly aware of his extreme weariness, Bleys picked up the hand cannon once more by the end of its heated muzzle and wrapped his cloak closely around his lower body and legs. Feeling his way blindly along the hull with his left hand, he fumbled back along the side of the *Favored* until he almost fell into the entry port.

Fingers were prying the barrel of the cannon from his fist.

"Hand's burned—" he heard Kaj's voice saying.

Bleys' fist opened. The barrel came free. He felt nothing. Underfoot, the ship's deck seemed to tilt and waver.

"He's lost a lot of blood," said Kaj. "Quick—to the clinic!"

Dahno picked Bleys up in his massive arms, as if he had been no more than a man of ordinary size. Someone else dropped the power cannon. It clattered out of sight behind them as he was carried off by Dahno. Toni was beside them and Kaj going ahead, snapping at people who did not get out of the way quick enough—on down through the corridors of *Favored of God.* Even as they went, he felt through Dahno's arms the tremble of the deck underfoot as the atmospheric engines woke and the ship lifted from the pad.

Chapter 38

Somewhere in the process of being carried away by Dahno, Bleys lost track of events. It was some indefinite time afterward before he was aware of being awake again. He was lying in a bed in a darkened room. In the gloom, he was just able to make out someone seated on a chair beside him.

"Toni?"

"It's me," she said warmly. "I'm here."

Her hand closed about his. It was very comforting. Bleys lost touch with everything again.

When he opened his eyes again, it was on the same room. There was a little more light, but not much. He could just barely make out Toni, still seated near the bed on which he lay, but not quite as close as before. Kaj Menowsky stood over him.

"You remember me?" Kaj asked.

"Of course," said Bleys, "medician—Kaj Menowsky," he added in case there should be any doubt left about the state of his memory.

"We're in space, aren't we?" he went on. "Headed for Harmony? If for any reason we're not headed for Harmony, the master of the ship should be told directly to change course and head there."

"We're in space, headed for Harmony," Kaj said. "How do you feel?"

"Feel?" For the first time since he had awakened—or whatever he had done to come out of wherever he'd been—Bleys paid attention to his body. "My side hurts. But that's not the important thing. I feel—" he searched for a proper word—"ugly," he said at last.

"Can you be more specific?" Kaj asked.

"No. It's a general feeling . . . body and mind. My head's fuzzy . . . foggy; and my whole body feels as if there's something out of order with all of it."

"Yes," Kaj said. His fingers closed on Bleys' wrist, the tips on Bleys' pulse. "If you were a piece of machinery, how would you describe this general feeling?"

"I'd say"—Bleys thought for a second—"I feel as if I've been hit by a hammer big as a truck. Everything's jarred out of alignment; some parts broken, maybe . . . if that makes any sense . . . "

"Yes," Kaj released his wrist. "That's pretty much what I expected. You said your head's fuzzy. Is it clear enough so you can answer a question?"

"Do the best I can."

"All right," Kaj went on. "You've been having blackouts, haven't you?"

"Blackouts?" Bleys' mind had to reach to make the word connect with his moments of sudden transition from being in one place to being in another, particularly during his run toward *Favored of God*. "Yes. Is that what they are?"

"It's the normally used name for them," Kaj said. "They're to be expected, now and in the future, following too much stress. That's why I hoped you'd have as little stress as possible getting to this ship. Now, if you're up to it, I'm going to give you a general idea of what you'll be facing in the next week or so. All right?"

"Yes," Bleys said.

"Good. I didn't tell you earlier because I didn't want to add to your stress during the race to get aboard—since nothing could be done anyway until we were here."

"Thanks, but next time tell me."

"That's usually the medician's decision," Kaj said.

"With me, it's mine," Bleys said.

"I see. Well, as I was about to say, I've killed the genetic opponent that was placed in your body. What's left of it will gradually be excreted in time, in various ways.

"What's going to stay with you for an extended period are the results of the tremendous damage you've had from the shock of the intrusion into your system and the attempt to change it over to agree with the opponent—all made worse by the stress you underwent before I could deal with it, here. The blackouts are the body's defensive action, once you relax from whatever emergency overstressed you. They are aimed at getting you to avoid stress. So avoid it from now on. It may mean you'll black out. You follow me?"

"Yes," Bleys said. "Go on."

He thought grimly that there was no way he was going to be able to avoid stress.

"Very well. The fact you're able to talk with me now means that I got rid of it in time, and eventually you're going to go back to being what you were before it was forced upon you. But your body's had a severe general shock, and complete recovery can take up to a matter of years. Some elements of the damage will linger, though the worst ought to be over in the next two or three weeks. But for those next few weeks, it'll get worse before it gets better. You'll run a high fever, and you may hallucinate. For the present, don't worry about getting better. I give you my word you will. Just ride it out."

"Don't you mean, tough it out?" Bleys asked.

"Essentially. But the important thing you need to remember is that all this that will be happening to you is unnatural; and, in the long run, transient—temporary. Eventually it will pass, though it'll be uncomfortable for you at times in various ways for—maybe even some years. But, one by one, the unnatural reactions will drop off; becoming first more and more infrequent, shorter and less troublesome—"

Kaj's voice seemed itself to becoming distant and slightly higher in pitch. Also, the room seemed to be getting dimmer. Bleys could no longer see Toni, and Kaj, right beside him, was becoming hard to make out.

"I may be blacking out again now," Bleys said or thought he said, though he seemed to hear his voice, also strangely distant now, and slightly higher in pitch, "but it's happening gradually—and it always was over in a flash before. I'd suddenly find myself sometime later . . .someplace different . . . "

"—However, you're an unusually capable person, Bleys Ahrens." Kaj was speaking. "It may be that you can utilize, or learn to utilize, that natural creative ability that the Exotics, three hundred years ago, finally proved was in everybody. So it's there in you, to speed your mending, or help alleviate the symptoms of recovery, if you'll reach for it. If you can put it to work to help you, you'll either get well faster—or what you suffer won't be as bad. But remember that while it's a powerful force, it's not worked from the conscious part of the mind, but from the unconscious—"

"Did I black out for a moment just now?" Bleys asked again; but Kaj was going on, his voice getting thinner and more distant, as if Bleys had never spoken at all.

"—You'll have to develop a communication between the conscious and the unconscious. But I think you might manage that. Some people do. Only, you'll have to find your own way of doing it."

"I know. I've already done that."

"—But it won't be easy, and it may take years. Now, I'm going to be able to help with some of the purely physical pain. But in all other situations, where the pain's connected with your suffering from the mental damage, I won't be able to help; because what I'd give you ordinarily for physical pain, in the case of damage like this, would hamper your body and mind in dealing with the damage yourself, the way you should . . . "

Kaj's words were becoming indistinct; and he himself was, to all effect, lost in the darkness of the room. Bleys concentrated, trying to make out what he was saying.

" . . . Remember what I've said . . . "

"I will," said Bleys. But then he stopped trying and went off into nothingness—carrying with him, however, the surprisingly valuable information about universal creativity that Kaj had just given him.

It was hard for Bleys to believe that he had never realized—never known or never heard—that everyone, everywhere, was creative.

This was information of shining worth. Bleys held it to him as he went away into nowhere, determined to cling to it from now on. It was an understanding he could put to use in making all of his plans work. It could be made into a symbol for everyone on all the New Worlds—a symbol like the supposedly "golden" eagles that Napoleon Bonaparte had given as standards to the troops in his armies, derived from the eagle standards of the ancient Roman legions. If Kaj had offered to pay all of Bleys' interstellar expenses for the next six years, the medician could not have given him any greater gift.

Several times after that conversation, Bleys had come awake briefly; but he could remember nothing said or done then, and nothing at all of how long the awake periods might have lasted. Then came a time in which he was sure he was awake, although otherwise nothing was very clear.

The ugly feeling that Bleys had been conscious of lately had escalated in him by this time to the point where it was either a pain, or so comparable to a pain that it was impossible to distinguish between them. He was conscious that his side where it had been wounded by needles was also hurting. But that pain was so drowned in the general feeling of *wrongness* filling his whole body that it was impossible to separate the hurting from the rest. He was also aware of a high fever that made his head swim like a drunken man's.

Under all this, his thoughts still worked, but in no useful fashion. They hopped like a grasshopper with its nervous system out of control, going nowhere crazily, but going continually. He tried to concentrate on his surroundings, and for a moment did so. Toni was still beside him, and the room was as dim as it had been before. There was just enough light from the ceiling, the walls and the floor so that he saw her as through a heavy mist that blurred any sharp outlines—but recognized her anyway.

"Was I talking?" he asked her hoarsely. "I thought I was talking . . . "

"A little." Toni placed a wonderfully cool hand on his forehead.

"It's hot in here," he said and was shocked to hear his voice come out fretfully, like a child's.

"You're feverish," said Toni. "But there's nothing to worry about. Nothing at all. Just relax."

"What was I saying?" Bleys asked.

"Nothing important," Toni's voice flowed soothingly through him, like water. There was something compelling, almost hypnotic about it. *But I'm not a good hypnotic subject*, Bleys thought, and then another small voice from some corner of his mind seemed to say—*but that was before. Is it different now?*

"I need to know!" Bleys' voice still sounded petulant. "What was I saying?"

"You were talking about Henry's farm." Toni's voice reached inside him, coiled about the core of his discomfort there, and soothed it. "Rest, my Bleys. Rest."

And he was gone again. When he woke, he was in a different room—more spacious, but still a room—with a bed, and a float armchair beside it in which Toni sat, the familiar dimness of lighting turned down almost to complete darkness. He had been moved physically. If he had been on the spaceship before, he was there no longer.

"Where am I?"

"Harmony," Toni said. It was exactly as if this word followed the last words he could remember hearing from her before the darkness that had just ended.

"Yes," he said, "well—that's very well . . . " But then his voice went on as if it had a life and will of its own. " . . . *This is where I wanted to come. The loose ends have to be tied up here before I go back to New Earth. There's no time to waste. The trouble with pulling all the threads together is the knot has to be tied at a certain place; and I have to know where I am when the knot is tied. And there's McKae to deal with first. Drinking . . . the man's addicted to alcohol now. The signs were there, even years ago. I knew . . . "*

In dawning horror, Bleys found his voice going on and on, beyond his control, the words tumbling out of him. Toni sat beside him, unchanged, saying nothing. His words seemed to divide and flow past her—as if they were water and she a rock in its streambed. But she must be hearing and understanding; and these were things he had wanted to tell no one, least of all her, for fear of driving her from him with a truth about him so unbearable she would not be able to endure him . . . and still his voice went on . . .

"What am I saying?" Bleys cried out suddenly, interrupting himself by sudden wild determination. Immediately, Toni's hand and voice were soothing him again. But now he could not drop back into the silence, but stayed awake and went on talking in spite of himself, in spite of every effort he could make to stop; until exhaustion finally brought sleep—and the sleep, for the first time, brought dreams.

The first dreams were merely of the run on the spacepad to *Favored*, over and over again; particularly the moment in which he had lifted the hand power-cannon and destroyed the Newtonian riflemen.

But these dissolved finally into shapeless dreams, formless, swirling masses of color or floods of important information, pouring at him too swiftly for his scrambling mind to catch and order them. Then they began to be interrupted by occasional flashes of pictures—a glimpse of the female Soldier being power-gunned into the air—the darkness of the hallway where he had stood listening to the oncoming sword movements of the amok Cassidan—a close-up of the face of the Militia major back on Harmony when he had told the man that he would not let him hang the three farmers, as he had planned.

Gradually, these flashes grew longer and began to resemble real dreams, in that they covered short passages of time that moved, for brief moments, coherently; and were part of the chain of dreaming that had a sort of logic connecting its parts together.

He was back pacing his private lounge in the Other building on Association, fiercely impatient to be off on his speaking tour, but waiting for one last indication that it was time for him to go. This time, however, for a moment he caught sight out of the corner of his eye of an ancient book left open on one of the room's float-chairs and partially covered by his cape, where he had tossed it from him on returning to his suite. But the cape had covered one page only and the other showed the image of a gyrfalcon, head upright and turned sideways, beak closed and fierce, eye cruel.

Only a glimpse, and he paced on. But the image stayed in his mind and suddenly it seemed he fell through the image into a prehistoric moment in which a Tyrannosaurus rex *was being attacked by an enormous gyrfalcon.*

The gyrfalcon had begun the attack. It dove and dove at the dinosaur's head, slipping by the gaping, massive-toothed jaws and hammering with beak and balled claws at the dinosaur's head—and the dinosaur weakened, began to try to avoid it, and finally fell to lie still . . .

The flash ended, and another took its place. *He was one of a group of archaeologists excavating prehistoric wolf bones. They were the bones of the dire wolf, a precursor of the modern wolf, and he and another archaeologist were examining the skull.*

"Look how small the brain space is, compared to a modern wolf," the other archaeologist was saying.

"Yes," he heard himself saying. "No wonder the new form displaced them . . ."

The flash ended in a jumble of colors and meaningless shapes and sounds, only to be replaced later on by another flash, and a little later another . . .

But, even in this state, his dreams were meaningless. He moved about worlds, he looked at stars, he spoke to people—but there was no sensible reason to its parts. Any one dream bit was unconnected with those before it.

At last these gave way to what might be real dreams; in the sense that he knew what was happening from a dreaming standpoint, even if they followed a natural dream-like, reasonless pattern. Most of these were forgettable—he went places, he saw things, but they added up to nothing in particular. Then finally he came to his first full, coherent dream.

It came at a time when the dreams, interspersed by the periods of talking, began suddenly to be interrupted by what must certainly be blackouts; which for some reason gave him a growing inner certainty that he was stronger, gaining the upper hand at last over what had made craziness out of everything he seemed to have been seeing, feeling and thinking.

He was a sandstorm. He had been at some earlier time a large cyclonic windstorm over water, over a large body of inland water. Now he had moved over land and weakened; but in weakening he had picked up hot sand from the stretch of desert sand that bordered the body of water here. Now it was a wall of sand, and he was carrying it forward, the heat of the sand replenishing the chemical engine of his atmospheric structure that powered him.

He gained power. He picked up more sand and became a mighty sandstorm. Then darkness came and once more he weakened; but he had not died completely when the sun rose again; and again his strength revived with the day—and grew even greater. So he continued, growing and moving, broadening and widening over a larger expanse of land away from the water.

He was conscious of something in him like a mindless but all-consuming hunger to conquer. The land was before him. He would cover it, would own it, would pick up its surface, grind it and cover it with grains of the ground-up surface. He went on and on until mountains loomed before him; and a terrible rage was born in him, as he found he could only climb a certain distance up the mountainside. But he could not stop trying; and so the rage within him grew and grew even as he became weaker and weaker—only slightly at first—but then more so, as he began to burn out his strength against the mountains.

But he could not stop. He was not built to stop . . .

. . . And there was a blackout.

He was back in the room with Toni.

"*. . . Evolution. Adaptation end of evolution.*" he heard himself saying. "*The old form, too highly specialized to a specific environment, begins to die off as that environment changes. A new form, better adapted to the changed environment—or, even better, an environment in a continual state of change, takes over. Prehistorically . . .* "

He was dreaming again.

He was newwolf. He was Band-father—first-ranked male in a pack of early modern Old Earth wolves—Plan-Speak-Hunt People—who were supplanting the older evolutionary lupine form: the oldwolves, or *dire wolves*, as later Old World archaeologists would call them.

In the shadow of the young maple trees and the thick brush of the hillside, he looked down on the open floor of the valley below, at the open area a hundred feet or so down, where the dire wolves were already through their forenoon sleep, in preparation for the coming night of hunting. They slept, some who were friendly lying close to each other, even making small clumps—others scattered singly about at a good distance from all other sleepers.

By the Band-father's right shoulder stood Next-brother, the second-ranking male of this pack of newwolves, first among those not Band-father, but who carried their tails straight as ranking members of the Band. By his left shoulder stood Band-mother, the top-ranking female of the new-wolves; and mother, in fact, to many of the Band. None stood ahead of Band-father.

Like him, those with him looked out on a black-and-white world; but the air reaching their spread nostrils was rich with a multitude of nose-*tastes*—"scents" was too pale, too meager a word to capture the fullness of a newwolf's world of smell.

Strong upon it was the wolfish *taste* of the oldwolves down below. They were larger than the newwolves; their bones were heavier. They were able to hunt large prey like the hairy mastodon. But future archaeologists, finding mud casts of their brains inside their fossil skulls, would note that their brains were smaller than those of the new-wolves.

The eyes of Band-father and the others noted and read each tiny movement of each other and the dire wolves below; and when Band-father turned to them at last, he read by the flick of an ear, the smallest movement, the narrowing of an eye—those tiny signals from them, that the other newwolves understood and agreed.

It was decided. He turned, they all turned, and began to trot back to their own packground.

Even as he dreamed, Bleys—the human Bleys—was telling Toni about it; Toni and anyone else in the room.

He could not help himself.

—It was noon when they got back to the packground and the Band was gathered together. Excitement was high. Band-father went back and forth among his children, his brothers and sisters and their children, touching noses, receiving their signs of obedience—gripping their noses in his jaws as some Roman legate might grip the forearms of his soldiers in approval before a battle. Gradually, the understanding amongst them all grew, an understanding that passed from one to the other, not in symbols, but simply by a chain of smaller actions and gestures—nose touching, nose bites, slight movements, the whole language of the new people—for they did not think in symbols, but in images of scent and sound and sight and emotion, all joined in a patterned community of understanding that replaced what could not be said in words.

This afternoon we hunt the oldwolves and drive them; as we hunt and drive the meat-animals that are our prey—in a two-pronged attack, by two part-Bands. I will lead one part-Band. Next-brother will lead the other.

Then Bleys moved even deeper into the dream, no longer conscious of saying aloud what he was experiencing—to Toni or anyone else. Only, for a moment before he was submerged . . .

"I thought you ought to have a look at him," something in him was barely conscious of Toni saying.

"Yes," Kaj said. "You were right. . . . "

But Bleys went deeper, leaving them . . . lost now completely in the dream.

He *was* the newwolves' Band-father.

Chapter 39

Band-father, in the wildness of his dreaming . . .

. . . I am with my part-Band, running. My ears stand tall and breathe the voice of the west wind. My straight-held tail is groomed by claws of low branches as it streams proudly behind me. My ear flicks back, and the distinctive footfall tells me that Band-mother is in her customary place, protecting the flank of my windward side. We have crossed the fast water and skirted the place of fiery rocks since Next-brother left with the boldest of pups-now-two-snows-old and the bent-tail hunters of the other part-Band.

Band-mother and I with my suckle-mates, each as full-grown and strong as I, seek the oldwolf Band-father and his oldwolf, dominant straight-tails. They will be in prized places of sleeping.

Next-brother, with his part-Band nearby will wait in silence. He will not break cover until he hears bones and teeth. He is a newwolf. His companions will obey him. They are newwolves.

The sun is bright, but the world is still black and white. There is gray shadow, but very little, because the sun warms my back and shadow-brother-who-runs-with-me when the sun shines, is under my belly, hiding from the light. When the sun is lower, he will run beside me. The wind speaks to my nose. A blackwing cries to us of food that needs no killing. She would share. Band-mother growls softly, warning the others to pay no heed. Deadsister-daughter snorts. They need no warning. They are newwolves.

The trees here are small and closely packed. The earth still smells sharply of burn when I scrape away the leaves. The heavy underbrush is good cover, but we have no need of cover. The oldwolf smell is still faint. We circle around the brush and leap the fallen logs, half-charred. The others are behind me. The day is warm . . .

. . . I, and those with me are very close to the oldwolves now. Their band-scent is the many scents of separate individuals. We move quickly.

Suddenly I have two wolves inside me. Part of me is Watcher, part Mover— but over both I am still single, still Band-father. Trees rush toward my part-Band and pass out of sight behind us. We are no longer just running. Legs gather beneath us and send us forward in great bounds.

We break from the trees; and in the wide clearing before us—looking not unlike ourselves—the oldwolves are beginning to stir. From the shadow of the large boulder near the middle of the clearing, a great oldwolf rises and stretches and looks incuriously at us. Several others look at us and growl softly and look back at this crook-tailed oldster.

He is their Band-father.

He is mine.

Watcher-in-me casts an eye about the clearing as Mover increases the length and power of his leaps toward the oldwolf Band-father. The other oldwolves are no longer looking to him for lead-signals. They are rising and fighting. But they are scattered. Band-mother accepts a challenge, then dodges an oldwolf's charge while Deadsister-daughter sinks her teeth into the challenger's hindquarters. Then both dart away.

The oldwolf Band-father braces himself and takes Mover's charge on the shoulder and his jaws close on the back of my neck. Mover-in-me has been too sure of himself. I have been Band-father too long to be careful enough. But Mover-in-me is faster than any oldwolf, and the season of green grasses and plump calves has been better to us than to those we fight, for the great beasts they hunt are ever scarcer. My neck is thick with fur and heavy with fat. The heavy jaws clamp down on my thick neck-hair and hide, and Mover-in-me snaps my teeth on oldwolf's foreleg to crush its bone. The oldwolf falls, dragging me down with him, never loosening his grip. Lying beside him, Mover-in-me breaks his other front leg. We roll to our feet and tug. The oldwolf has strong jaws, but he cannot dig in with his broken legs. I tear loose.

Other oldwolves are coming from the trees at the far side of the clearing, loping toward us. They are many, they are young and they are proud. They will let us kill their leaders. Then they will challenge us, drive us off or kill us, and become themselves leaders of the oldwolves.

They are young and foolish. The Band is the source of life.

Mover sidesteps a charge and plunges away as Watcher sees Next-brother and his companions charge suddenly from hiding in a tangle of brush. They charge the younger oldwolves who wait to win and lead their Band. Two of the oldwolves stand bewildered, their attention shifting back and forth from the battle before them to this new threat.

They die where they stand; for all but their strongest and bravest turn away from the charge, having seen me and my part-Band winning against their older leaders; and Next-brother and our eager young wolves with the taste of a kill strong in their noses take down those who linger.

—Too late, the others turn, but now Mover and Band-mother and our other companions have disengaged from our first attack and joined Next-brother among the newcomers.

Bite . . . feint . . . check . . . dodge. Mover is the one in control of me now.

It is too much for the remaining oldwolves. They break and flee. Mover would follow, but Watcher holds him back.

The oldwolves will not return. We have hurt them too much. When the snows come again they will die, for the great long-haired ones they hunt are too few, and the oldwolves are not swift-footed and quick-bodied enough to bring down the fleeter meat-beasts, as we can, to feed their young.

I howl deeply, and the newwolves gather at my signal. We lope back toward the shade of the trees. Shadow-brother-who-runs-with-me stretches out, far ahead of my feet, his nose to the horizon . . .

Gradually, still running in his mind, Bleys slipped out of the dream and back into the room, the dim room with Toni and no one else.

Still full of strength from the fight, Bleys started to sit up in the bed, but could not move. He was held. His arms and legs were fastened some-how to the edges of the bed so that he could not move.

Wildness flooded him.

"Why am I held?" he shouted at the face of Toni, close beside him.

He felt her hand stroking his forehead.

"It's all right, it's all right," she said.

"Take them off!" he shouted. *"Take them off!"*

She reached for her wrist control pad, and the restraints fell away from his arms and lower legs. He almost dropped back into unconsciousness in relief; and when he came fully to himself again, she was gently and sooth-ingly, rhythmically wiping his face, neck, naked shoulders and upper body with a cool, damp cloth, and he was gradually relaxing, gradually, gradually, gradually . . .

—Again, there was a long time of chaotic dreams . . . then, finally, a dream that came clearly once more.

He dreamed he was having a conversation with the young Hal Mayne, whom he had finally found.

The boy sat cross-legged, like a lean young Buddha in lotus position, on something like a dais. High enough so that, seated as he was, his eyes were level with those of Bleys, who stood talking to him.

The room they were in was shadowy and cool, to the point of being almost cold. Hal Mayne had something like a blanket, of some indeterminate color—Bleys could not tell which, the room was so dim—draped around his shoulders. This cloaked him. It was impossible to say what he was wearing otherwise.

They were in earnest conversation; but that was not going properly, from Bleys' point of view. Hal Mayne was at odds with him. Their talk had come to the point where the youngster seemed almost to be pronouncing judgment on the adult Bleys.

"—Why can't I make you understand?" Bleys found himself saying.

"Because your language isn't understandable," Hal answered calmly. "You don't speak to me in normal human language. You are Other.*"*

The boy had pronounced the last word as if it had been an identification name, like Dorsai, *or* Friendly.

"No, no," Bleys was saying. "The Other organization is only that, a means to an end—a good end."

"*Good or not,*" said Hal, "*it's got nothing to do with what you are. You are* Other."

"*Why do you keep saying that? Is this a joke—as if to say I come from a race of aliens?*" Bleys demanded. "*I'm talking Basic, and I'm human as you are.*"

"*No,*" said Hal. "*Of course you aren't alien. You're human, but individual—as all we humans are different from each other. So you're the only one of your kind. The* Bleys-Other. *It's always been so for you. Always, you've thought of yourself as the only one of your kind, even with your mother. Your mother knew this, without understanding it; but that was one reason she felt toward you as if you were a changeling. She feared you. Think back. You've always known this. You were not so different as a child; but step by step as you grew, you grew toward being* Other. *You made yourself* Other. *Soon you'll have forgotten you were anything else. You'll live only to turn the human race into* Others *like you, so you won't be alone anymore. But that can't be done, even by you.*"

"*How do you know about what I was like as a child? What do you know about my mother?*" Bleys demanded.

"*I know because I'm unique, like you, and like every other human born since the race began. But I know you for what you are; and one of my duties in the always-evolving pattern of history is to stop you from destroying people in trying to make them into what they were never meant to be.*

"*Because you work for that, I know you for the antagonist you are. I know the destruction that could come; and that you lie, even to yourself when you tell yourself.* What I plan will not be bad."

"*You and I know better . . .*"

The dream lost itself in darkness, and Bleys slipped into different sleep. Not the disturbed slumber he had almost become used to; but honest, deep sleep. When he woke, all things seemed different.

The pain in his side was gone. The feeling of *wrongness* was gone. Only a deep, abiding sadness was left.

There was more light than before in the room. He could see his surroundings clearly, now; although the one window wall of the room—he had clearly been right when he thought that he was in a hotel room—was lightened only partially. It was like coming back to life.

Bleys could see everything within the walls of the room quite sharply and clearly. Toni was leaning over him, shaving him with a small razor, undoubtedly of Newtonian concept and Cassidan design, but one which was familiar to him as it was to millions of people on the New Worlds— it burnt the sprouting beard off at a tiny but measured distance above the skin and felt merely as if his face was being stroked. Toni must have done that daily, during the time he was ill.

Then Bleys became aware of Kaj looming behind her; and as soon as she was done, she moved out of the way. Kaj himself moved closer.

"How are you feeling?" Kaj asked.

"Good!" Bleys said. "How's Henry?"

"He's fine. He and Dahno will be in to see you in a few days. But I asked how you felt."

"I've been sleeping. Real sleep."

"I believe you," Kaj said. "You've made a good recovery. Better than I expected, even given your excellent health to begin with. You must have harnessed your creative ability with a vengeance."

"Harness"—Bleys checked himself—"you know, what the Council hit me with must have begun to affect me a lot sooner than twenty-four hours later. I remember now not feeling right as early as when we were driving to the spaceport."

"They lied to you, of course," Kaj said. "They wanted you to feel you were even more helpless than most people poisoned that way. I didn't warn you because I didn't want to suggest—"

"I'm not particularly suggestible," Bleys said.

"No," said Kaj. "But I didn't know that then. Medicians have to play safe."

"How long was I out of action?" Bleys asked.

"Counting from the time you came aboard *Favored of God*, a little over two weeks."

Bleys gave a long sigh of relief.

"Only that? It felt like eternity. That's good. I don't have the time to spare for being sick. But at least I'm well now."

"I wish I could agree with you," Kaj said. "But maybe you remember my telling you that the effects of this would linger. You're still going to have occasional episodes of what you've gone through, these past two weeks, including finding yourself talking uncontrollably, and blackouts. There may be other elements, too, that have been going unnoticed so far, but which you'll discover as the large effects fade. But if you keep the positive attitude—or whatever it is that's brought you back this much— you'll eventually get rid of them all, and you'll greatly shorten the time wrestling with them. Let me just give you a couple of words of caution— stay optimistic. Stay confident."

Bleys smiled. "I was born optimistic and confident. In fact, I can't imagine being anything else. And thank you, medician, for all you've done—even though I don't know what it was. Without your help it'd've been a lot worse."

"Any medician could have helped you," Kaj said, almost shortly. It was the closest Bleys had ever seen the medician come to betraying any emotion.

"Well, thank you anyway," Bleys said. "Now I'll get up—"

He raised his head and started to raise his body; but Kaj's hands stopped him and gently held him back, pushing him back down.

"Move very slowly," Kaj said. "Move fast and you'll find yourself getting dizzy, perhaps even blacking out again, or having some other of the symptoms you've just been having."

Kaj turned toward Toni. "Help me here. We'll prop him up on pillows gradually till he's sitting; then, if he's all right with that, then we may let him try to sit on the edge of the bed. Tomorrow, perhaps, he can stand up, and eventually try walking."

"Tomorrow?" Bleys said. Kaj ignored him.

In the end, they did it just as Kaj had said. It was four days before he walked across the room with one of them on either side, but with neither holding onto him as he went.

"You see?" said Bleys. "I'm fine."

But the truth was, he was not. He had not become dizzy. Nor had he blacked out. But his whole body felt weak and strange. He would not admit it, but he was glad when they steered him once more to the bed and he sat down on the side of it.

"Now, I suggest you rest for a while, then try sitting up, standing up and walking again, and alternate between rest and exercise that way for a day or two." Again Kaj turned to Toni, who now was right beside him as they stood looking down at Bleys, seated on the bed, his head almost on a level with theirs. "You'll be able to help him, won't you, Toni?"

"Of course," Toni said.

So she did. She not only helped, she dominated the process of his getting used to being on his feet and moving around again. So he took it more slowly than he had intended. It was not quite two days—but a good thirty hours or so—before he was moving around on his own.

Again, secretly, while his whole being struggled against the slowness of this, Bleys was grateful every time he could return to the bed and lie down. His strength had indeed been at low ebb; and now, while it was coming back swiftly, by the time he had done some few physical things, he was ready to rest, if not sleep.

But his determination to get himself back to moving normally was so strong that finally they went twenty-four hours around the clock, with only naps at intervals. It was only when he realized Toni could have slept only while he was napping, that he noticed how tired and drawn her face was; and realized that, while putting himself to the limit of his strength, he had also been pushing her to the limit of hers.

"How did you manage to stay by me all those earlier days?" he asked.

She smiled. "I had a small bed brought in. When you were unconscious, I slept. There was a monitor on you that warned me when you woke up."

"And you did that for over two weeks?"

She smiled again, if somewhat wanly.

"Kaj said the fewer people you had contact with during the worst part of your illness, the better. I told him it had to be just me."

Bleys understood—suddenly, as if with a touch of clairvoyance. By being here alone with him she had made sure no one else heard what he was saying. Whatever effect his fever and drug-driven words had had on her, she had understood how much he would not have wanted anyone else hearing them.

Bleys shook his head. He could not think how to thank her for her understanding. Maybe in time he would.

Unbidden, like a serpent slipping into an unguarded corner of paradise, came the thought that—however—*she* had heard; and she must have realized how that might pose a problem to him. Silently, he thanked the God he did not believe in for the fact she could not know what his real concern about her hearing him had been.

"I think I'd like to take a shower," Bleys said as lightly as he could. "Don't you want to get away from me now? Go off by yourself and sleep, if nothing else?"

"No, that's not necessary"—Toni broke off and shook her head, then smiled once more—"I could sleep. Yes, I could really sleep."

"Well, then, go to sleep. If I need you, I can call you. If you're doubtful, hook up that monitor to me again. I imagine it's something I could walk around with?"

"As a matter of fact," she said, smiling, "it's still attached to you. It's quite all right; you can take a shower with it. The water won't hurt it."

Bleys nodded and watched her as she turned toward the door.

"You're sure you feel all right now?" Toni paused and looked back as the door slid open when she was within the length of one step from it.

"I feel perfect," Bleys said. "Go ahead."

She went out.

The door closed behind her, and he gazed at it for a long moment. There was too much to think about right now, he thought. He would have to face what those weeks of hearing his soul poured out might have done to her. In spite of her undisturbed appearance, she had heard him, and they must talk about that, eventually.

Bleys moved restlessly about the room. He could not imagine his future without her now. She had become a vital part—not only of his plans for coping with it, but his plans for holding himself to the stern, necessary line of his plans. He must do what he had set out to do—control, one way or another, of at least all the other New Worlds—and even that would be only the beginning.

Deliberately, he shut the problem out of his mind, turned, and walked through a half-opened door into the attached bathroom.

He was wearing only the shorts that he normally slept in. They were clean shorts, however. It occurred to him—and he put the thought from him again almost immediately—that Toni would have needed to have done much more than merely sit and listen. She had been his nurse in all ways, not merely soothing him when he woke, but taking care of him in what must have been less pleasant ways.

Inside the bathroom, Bleys stepped to the mirror over the sink, running his hand over his jaw unthinkingly to make sure his face was shaven smoothly all over. It was, and he dropped his hands to look at his upper body and see what two weeks of idleness might have done to it. But he was hardly changed. The muscles of his arms and torso certainly felt more slack, because of the strength he had lost, and the food he had not eaten for two weeks. Only now, it occurred to him that Toni or others must have gotten at least some liquid down him to make it possible for him to survive that long, and they may have found some way of feeding him in the process. If so, it had happened during the periods of darkness and dreams. He had no memory of it.

Bleys looked again at his face, and for the first time really saw it. He stood, staring at himself.

The handsomeness of features, of bone and flesh he had been born with, that he owed to nothing but his genes and which he had turned to use, like an actor, in projecting his tall cloaked image effectively to his audiences—was still there, but different.

It had been through the fire of his recent experiences and been changed. What he saw now was a face, the bones and skin of which were all as before, but which now seemed to project a permanent difference.

It was as if he had become an *Other* in the full sense of that word. As if, as actor, he had actually become the character he displayed.

Perhaps it was not the sort of thing that those who saw him from the audience, or on a casual basis would notice as a difference. Only someone who knew him well might realize how the darkness that had been always lurking in him had broken down the wall between itself and the rest of him. So that he and it had become one, melted together.

Toni must have seen it happen, all through his time of blackout and compulsive talking, and all the physical and mental change that the Newtonian poisoning had put him through. She must understand now, not only his reasoning, his purposes, his goal, its cost—but how he had allowed it also to make itself a part of him. He had shaped it—and it had shaped him. She, of all people, must know him fully now. Yet she had stayed with him. He did not understand.

Bleys' intention of taking a shower was no longer important. He turned from the mirror and went back into the bedroom—only to catch himself up shortly as he saw Toni there, standing just inside the door, with the door itself shut behind her.

"Toni!" he said. "You came back!"

"I had a feeling"—she looked deeply into him now, he thought—"you might need me for something . . . so I thought I'd just step back and see."

He met her gaze with his own.

"Toni, do you want to leave me?"

For a moment she did not answer. Then slowly she shook her head.

"No," she answered.

Chapter 40

"I heard you were back on Harmony," McKae said. "But it was just a general rumor, nothing specific. Then I investigated and found you here, but you hadn't got in touch with anyone. I thought you'd call me as soon as you were free. I suppose you had some private business to deal with first. You know—I was expecting you sooner, but that's not important now . . . "

His voice ran down. Bleys sat still, looking gravely at him, from the chairfloat which had been set to a comfortable height for him, before he got there—almost certainly when he had finally called to say that he would be coming.

They sat in McKae's office in Harmony's government building. A special office, larger even than that the Chief Speaker on each Friendly World ordinarily occupied. One of two identical offices, each in the Chamber building on either Harmony or Association. An office to be opened only when an Eldest had been elected.

This one, on Harmony, occupied one full end of the government edifice. It was actually three rooms: an office, a reception room, and a private lounge. But the walls between them could be caused to disappear into the ceiling at the touch of a command from McKae's wrist control pad. Right now the walls were down, and they were in the office—which, interestingly, was the smallest of the three.

They were alone. The humidity and temperature were up slightly in the office, so that there was something of a hothouse atmosphere. The effect of the melding of his ultimate purpose and the darkness within him was still with Bleys. It had not been until he came in and saw McKae's eyes fasten sharply on him that he realized he had never thought the man a close enough observer to see the difference in him. But clearly McKae had, and the awareness of it had clearly brought a sudden change to the new Eldest's original plans for this meeting.

Now McKae got to his feet suddenly, still talking, and walked to a large cabinet molded into the structure of the wall at his left. He opened it and took out a couple of bottles of the same yellow wine that Bleys had seen him drinking before, along with two tall, ornately decorated and fluted glasses. He brought these close to his desk, set them down on the desk top and moved his chair around the corner of the desk, so that there was no furniture between them.

Still standing, he beckoned Bleys to bring his seat forward to the desk.

" . . . We have to celebrate our getting together." He smiled with an obvious effort. "Things've been going well—very, very well. But I'm glad you're back. There are other things to be done, and I'll want your opinion on them—though, of course, the final decision will be mine.''

McKae was pouring the wine into the glasses, watching it rise in them as if he was engaged in some delicate chemical experiment. He filled them full—in fact almost over-filled them, but stopped just in time—and set the bottle, now one-third empty, back on its base and picked up his own glass with hand that showed only a faint tremor as he lifted it to his lips.

"Here's to our being together again!"

He drank off half the wine in his glass and set it down on the desk top. He looked at Bleys.

"You didn't drink," he said.

"In a moment, maybe," Bleys murmured.

McKae had continued to stand. He opened his mouth, then closed it again.

"Why don't you sit down?" Bleys said.

McKae sat, staring steadily at him.

"As I say," he said, "I've been looking forward to having you back. I need your counsel in many things. I need you available." His voice was stronger now.

"You've got a great many people to counsel you," said Bleys. "I'll be glad to give you the benefit of my advice, though. In fact, I'll be in touch with you regularly. As it happens, I'm going to have to leave Harmony again, almost immediately; and I'll be gone a while. I'm due back on New Earth. I suppose you understand I arranged the conditions there that caused the CEO Club and the Guild to get together so they could hire our Friendly soldiers? By the way, how many of them are already there?''

"I hadn't known—why, as a matter of fact," McKae said. "I'm not sure . . . I think more than half of them. That's right. They wanted fifty thousand in all and I believe we've already shipped something like thirty thousand with all the necessary equipment and supplies. No, as I say, I didn't know you actually had a hand in making them ask. How did you?''

"Put pressure on them from several different areas in their society," Bleys said. "The most important was through an opposition group called People of the Shoe. They'd been a problem to CEOs and Guilds anyway, but it was with the popular support and attention I gave them that they began to look like a serious threat. My part in things there wasn't too different from the way I helped your election as Eldest.''

There was a moment of silence.

"By the way," Bleys went on, "did you follow my advice of making the contract on the Dorsai model, in which the troops are under the orders of their own superiors, only?''

"Yes," McKae said. "It's sewn up all the way around, just the way the Dorsai contracts read. The New Earthers can only ask the Expedition's superior officer to do what they want. He'll consider the request, decide if it's practical, decide how the troops will go about doing it if he orders them to; and they'll move only on his orders, not those of anyone from New Earth."

Bleys nodded.

"But I still wish you'd told me beforehand you were going to do what you say you did on New Earth," McKae said.

"No need," Bleys answered evenly. "My work there is entirely aside from yours here."

McKae was still watching him closely. Barely glancing aside to do it, he topped up his own glass, raised it to his lips, and drank again—not quite as much as the first time, but a noticeable amount.

"I remember your telling me that the CEO Club and the Guild would be wanting to hire the troops from us, just before the election," McKae said, slowly.

Bleys nodded again. "Of course. And, of course you were able to make good use of that information in your pre-election speeches," said Bleys. "You did a good job of giving the impression that only you could bring about that hiring, and the large influx of interstellar credit it would mean to Harmony and Association, in payment."

"Yes," McKae said. "But still, I would have liked knowing you had a hand in it."

"There was no need for you to know then," Bleys said.

There was another moment of silence between them.

"And there is now?" McKae said.

"I think so."

McKae looked at his wineglass for a long moment without saying anything. Then he almost seemed to shake himself like a man coming awake.

"In any case," he said, "we can't have any talk of your leaving shortly. As I say, I need you here to counsel and advise me—" he smiled thinly— "that's what the First Elder is supposed to do for the Eldest, you know—counsel and advise. It means the First Elder has to be at the Eldest's elbow all the time."

"As I said a moment ago"—Bleys' voice had kept its unvarying calm—"you've a great many people around to counsel and advise you. But I won't stop telling you what you should do. You'll hear from me regularly on that, as I said, from wherever I am."

"If you aren't at my elbow—" McKae stopped to drink thirstily from his glass, almost emptying it; and automatically, it seemed, his hand went out to refill it again from the bottle that was now rapidly becoming empty. "—You can hardly be considered a First Elder. In fact, in that case there would be no point in your continuing to be First Elder."

"I think there is every point in things staying the way they are," said Bleys, "for your sake."

"For my sake?"

"Yes," said Bleys. Their eyes met again. "Remember the weight that the promise of income from those fifty thousand troops had, in getting you elected. A powerful factor. You're Eldest now, but there's the matter of your staying Eldest. Wouldn't you want to hold the job for a lifetime, like Eldest Bright did, a century ago? There are all sorts of possible factors; and I expect to be changing the interstellar situation—to which, as Eldest, you'll have to respond. Conditions could work against you as well as for you. You'll be wisest to do what I tell you when I tell you to do it."

McKae reached for his glass with a hand that this time trembled visibly. He gulped and set the glass down so hard that a piece chipped off its base.

"Are you threatening me?" he asked harshly.

"Of course," Bleys said.

The silence stretched tight between them. After a few moments, Bleys got to his feet.

"I see," he said. He turned and started toward the door of the office.

"Wait!" McKae called. Bleys turned back. McKae had refilled his glass again and already had it at his lips. He put it down on the table, holding it to make sure it did not tip over because of the missing piece in its base. "If I—if I give you your freedom to go when and where you want, and you simply speak to me when you want to," he said jerkily, "things will be all right?"

"You'll be fully protected," said Bleys. "And, after all, that's the most important thing. I believe you'll make a good Eldest for Harmony and Association—with my help. In fact, you should stay Eldest for a long time. You might even break Eldest Bright's record."

He smiled reassuringly.

"Yes." McKae had been staring at Bleys, as if he had become limited to the point where he needed to lip-read what Bleys was saying, as well as hear it. He looked down at his glass, staring at it, and went on. "Then it's settled."

"Yes," said Bleys, "it's settled. I'm glad we agree."

"Oh, I agree!" McKae drained his glass and put it back on the table. It fell over on one side.

He looked up at Bleys.

"I'll be in touch with you," Bleys said, and turned toward the door.

"Wait!" McKae's voice rang on the walls of the room behind him, and Bleys turned. McKae pointed with a shaking finger at Bleys' still-full glass. "Aren't you at least going to drink to it?" His eyes stared at Bleys a little wildly.

"Oh, yes," Bleys said, softly. He took three long strides back to the desk, picked up his glass and drank it empty. "To your long life and long tenure as Eldest."

He smiled again at McKae. McKae reached for the bottle without looking for it, poured what was left within into his glass and drank it off. Then he also smiled. As Bleys turned once more to leave, the new Eldest began to laugh—harsh, unhappy laughter; and the laughter went on as Bleys reached the door, which opened before him and let him out.

"Barbage is here to see you," Toni said to Bleys, as he stepped back into his suite in the hotel to which he had been brought from the *Favored of God* and in which all those with him were now also quartered. "He came a couple of hours ago, but said he wouldn't go until he'd talked to you."

"Good," said Bleys. "I'd have gotten in touch with him if he hadn't come. Has he got any special news?"

"I think so," said Toni, "but he didn't want to tell me. He wants to tell you, in person. Anyway, he's in the second lounge over."

"All right," Bleys said. "By the way, you know I've just come back from seeing McKae. I told him that I was going to have to leave shortly for New Earth, and I decided on the way back here that probably it'd be a good idea if I left as quickly as possible—both to drive the lesson home to him and to make sure I'm back on New Earth as soon as possible."

"So it's back to New Earth, then?" Toni said.

"Yes," he answered. "I'd like to get off without too much delay. The only problem I can think of might be that I'll want as full a complement of Henry's Soldiers as possible; and I know he gave those who wanted it some time off. They may be scattered all over this world, or even a few gone to Association to see family. But let's get as many together in the next few hours as we can and try to take off in the next twenty-four hours or so. Would you call the *Favored of God* at the spaceport and see if it could lift in that length of time? If necessary, I could wait a little longer, but I'll hope to get together at least half of Henry's people by then—"

"You aren't forgetting, are you," said Toni, "that most of these Soldiers don't have any particular place to go? They either don't have families, or they've been separated from them for so long that they've lost connection with them. I was talking to Henry and got the impression that most of his Soldiers are still right around Citadel here—or not too far from it. I imagine Henry could get nearly all of those ready in twenty-four hours."

"If he can, good." Bleys hesitated. "How many—"

"We lost or left behind thirty-three of them."

"Thirty-three!" Bleys sat down abruptly.

"Henry's found others to replace them," Toni said.

"Good," Bleys said mechanically. "More than half. How many of those were left behind?"

"Alive, and left?" said Toni. "We don't know. At least five."

Bleys sat still. After a long pause, Toni spoke again, gently.

"You'll want to say something to Henry about them. Don't, now. Later, maybe."

"Yes," Bleys said. "I understand."

He sat for a moment more, then stood up.

"You said the second lounge over has Barbage waiting?"

She nodded at a door in the wall just behind her and a little to her right. Bleys started toward it.

"Do you want to come along?" he asked.

"As I said, I think he wants all the effect of telling his news to you himself, and in a one-on-one atmosphere."

"Why don't you listen in on our talk, then?" said Bleys, as the door opened before him and he went through it. "That way you can tell Henry or Dahno, if there's anything to pass on; and I won't have to rehearse it to them, or you."

"All right," he heard her say behind him. He stepped into an empty lounge with a sea-green motif, its window wall ablaze with the early afternoon light of Epsilon Eridani. He passed through it into the next lounge, the walls of which were stark white and the furniture upholstered in gray imitation leather. Amyth Barbage stood alone in the room, upright with his back almost against the window wall, his hands behind him, his legs spread a little apart as if he was in a position of command. In his black, perfectly tailored uniform against the strong illumination from behind him, he looked almost like a figure painted upon the wall.

But the wall dimmed abruptly, the moment the sensors in the room read Bleys as turning to face the strong outdoor illumination; and Bleys was able to see the details of Barbage's face and the sudden change in it at the sight of him.

"Great Teacher—" Barbage began—there was the most momentary of hesitations, then a slight change in Barbage's expression. Almost, he smiled. "Great news! I have Hal Mayne for thee!"

The words had all the ring of a sentence meditated and rehearsed. But that was a matter of indifference to Bleys. Not so the hesitation, followed by the alteration in Barbage's expression. Like McKae, he had clearly read the difference in Bleys; but, unlike McKae, the change in his face was toward an expression of fierce glee, clearly welcoming what he saw.

Bleys stepped over to take a chairfloat and sat down in it.

"That's good news, Amyth," he said quietly. "Tell me more and sit down yourself."

Barbage clearly would rather have stood. But he came forward and sat, very erect, his back not touching the back rest of the float, squarely facing Bleys. From the greater height of the seat of his own float, Bleys looked down at him. But in the same way that it had always seemed impossible to look down on Henry, so it was also impossible to look down on Barbage. Like Henry, he seemed immune to considering anyone else greater than an equal, at most.

"He hath been captured in the local air-and-space terminal in Ahruma as he attempted to escape," said Barbage. "I have him safely for thee, in Ahruma, in a cell in Militia headquarters there. Also, I have on the roof of this hotel, a craft waiting to take thee to him."

"You say he was captured?" said Bleys, still speaking calmly. "How?"

"It was known he was in the area of Ahruma city," said Barbage, "and a watch was kept for him. Some of our Militia were in the terminal; and a man with them named Adion Corfua, who would know him on sight, identified him. There were only five militiamen, but they blocked his escape while more Militia came from farther in the terminal and enclosed him. They took him."

"I see," Bleys said.

He yawned. He spoke ostensibly to his wrist control—but actually to Toni, listening to what had just been said. "If anyone wants me, I've been taken to Ahruma by Amyth Barbage," he said. "They've a man identified as Hal Mayne there, and I want to look at him. I'll be back fairly quickly—"

Bleys broke off, looking at Amyth.

"How far away is Ahruma?" he asked. "How long would it take to get there, let me talk to Hal Mayne for perhaps half an hour, and then get back here?"

"No more than two hours, Great Teacher. Ahruma is the better part of this continent away, but I have a Militia air-and-space craft that can get thee there and back quickly."

"How's the weather there?"

"Moderate, as here."

"Then we'll leave right away," said Bleys. To the wristpad and listening intercom, he added, "I should be back in two hours—wait here a moment, Amyth. I'll be right back."

He left the room, going back through the doors and the intervening lounge to the one where Toni was.

"A private word," he said to her, as the door from the lounge closed behind him. "What other ships of which we—the Others, that is—own a share are in the spaceport here at Citadel now, besides *Favored of God?*"

"I'd have to check," said Toni. "I know the *Burning Bush* is also in, and there may be a couple of others."

"Good," Bleys said. "*Burning Bush* will do, if *Favored* isn't available. I'd like to travel without other passengers this time if we can; and I want to send a couple of messages ahead of us to New Earth. You'd better send them by the next ship lifting for there—one message to the People of the Shoe, simply telling them that I'm going to be back. Say in about six days, their local time from now; if we leave as soon as we can here—"

"And the other message?" Toni prompted after a second, for Bleys had fallen silent, his mind galloping ahead to the literal meeting with a flesh and blood Hal Mayne.

"Oh, yes," Bleys said. "The other message goes to whoever the commanding officer of the Friendly forces is on New Earth. This will be their top classification for 'secret.' Tell him we may have some trouble with the New Earth authorities when we land; and we'd like a competent body of military, ostensibly merely as an Honor Guard, to meet our ship when it lands and protect us in our hotel afterward. Can you think of any problem

Gordon R. Dickson

in getting those messages off in the next few hours? There must be other ships lifting from here for New Earth before midnight."

"I'm sure there are." Toni's fingers were busy on the studs of her wrist control pad.

"Good," Bleys said. "I particularly want the People of the Shoe to leak the news that I'm going to be there, so phrase that message accordingly. But the Commander's message is absolutely top secret. Nobody but he should see it. Sign it from me officially as First Elder."

"I can't imagine any problem," Toni said. "You're on your way to Ahruma then, with Barbage?"

"Yes. If I'm delayed I'll let you know."

"—And the outlaw Command Hal Mayne was with?" asked Bleys, as he and Amyth Barbage were re-entering the atmosphere on their flight to Ahruma, after their Militia ship had made a sharp half-loop up clear out of the atmosphere and then back down in again, to slow to atmospheric speeds at the spaceport of their destination. "Did you get them?"

"We did not, Great Teacher," Barbage said.

He sat stiff-backed and upright, opposite Bleys, across a small, round table in the heavily upholstered, if tiny, lounge of the militia craft they were in. In front of Bleys was a glass that had been re-filled with variform apple juice twice, while Barbage had drunk none from his.

"I'm surprised that Hal Mayne was separate from them," Bleys said. He watched Barbage closely.

"We will get him to tell us," Barbage said. "Only those strong in their mistaken Faith have ever succeeded in not speaking when we require it. Those such as the one who barred the way of the Militia troops close behind the Command Hal Mayne had been with; troops which would have captured the Command, undoubtedly, if it had not been for this Old Prophet who barred their way—and indeed killed more than a dozen of them before they could work around behind him and kill him—it was in a wooded area."

"Old Prophet?" echoed Bleys. "One of this same Command, you mean?"

"Yes," Barbage answered. "One of Rukh Tamani's Command. Would it had been Rukh Tamani herself! But this Old Prophet was one who had held to blame the Militia for the death of his wife many years before and been an outlaw against us for all that time. He was old and wise in combat; and stubborn, as I say, in his mistaken faith. His name was Child-of-God."

"You knew him?"

"I knew the names of many with Rukh Tamani, though I had never seen them," Barbage said. "Him I had seen. It was when I had been on Harmony before, serving as an exchange officer with a local Harmony Militia group. The Group I was with then caught up with the Rukh Tamani

Command in the mountains, and there was a small interchange of cone-rifle fire—"

"Cone rifle?" Bleys said. "I know needle guns and power guns, but I've never heard of cone rifles."

"Thou hast never seen how the needles are packaged for putting into the rifles?" Barbage asked. Bleys had, but said nothing. "The point of one needle fits into the hollow at the back of the one before it, so that they form together like a rod, although each one comes off separately for firing. Because of the indentation at the back and the point at front in each, they look each like a small cone; and in fact that shape aids their stability in flight, once they are fired. Needle rifles, therefore are sometimes called cone rifles on our own two worlds, which God has blessed."

"I see," said Bleys. "But you were telling me how you happened to see this Child-of-God."

"Yes," Barbage said. "It was Hal Mayne himself who disarmed me, and held me at rifle point. I defied Child-of-God, when he came, in that he should get any information from me. He recognized me as one of the Elect and knew therefore what I said was true; and so brought his own rifle around to kill me—but Hal Mayne knocked it out of line, so I took the chance and escaped."

"Why did Hal Mayne stop him?"

"I know not. Nor does it matter. There was a chance to escape and I took it. But I remembered the Old Prophet's face—dark, lean and ancient, a scar just in front of his right ear. It is long training with me to remember the faces of any of the Abandoned of God. Therefore I recognized him in death, even though he was broken apart by the power guns that finally ended his troublemaking. But he had managed to slow pursuit of the Command enough so that they escaped. But they will be found. Always, in the end, we find and catch them."

The angle of descent of the spacecraft abruptly steepened, and there was a moment before the apparent equilibrium of the lounge had compensated and they once more felt as if they flew level. Barbage looked out the section of hull that was presently on transparency, beside him.

"In fifteen or twenty minutes, I shall have thee at Ahruma Militia headquarters; and within minutes after that thou shalt see Hal Mayne."

The Militia headquarters in Ahruma had trafficways—local trafficways, but wide ones—on all five sides of it. The mag-lev vehicle that brought Bleys and Barbage in from the spaceport, at top speed for the streets and with its siren roaring, approached from the back; and going up along one side toward the front and main entrance of the headquarters, it slowed enough so that Bleys could see a traffic entrance into one side of what had appeared to be the solid building.

The entrance gave access to a sort of courtyard in which Bleys saw a couple of mag-lev vehicles, painted Militia black; a doorway and near it a loading dock—obviously a back entrance for the delivery of supplies, and possibly the discreet delivery of prisoners. There were no known outlaw groups in any of the major cities, as Bleys understood it; but there were the Cliques of the so-called Disaffected, who had contact with and aided the outlaw groups passing by the city.

For a moment Bleys considered the question of whether these outlaw groups and the Cliques would pose a problem for him once the Friendlies were well under his control through McKae—then put aside the idea. Altogether, both types of dissidents were a fraction of the populace; and the Militia, who acted as local police all over the planets, were strong enough to handle the problem, or at least keep it within some bounds.

The Militia could never cooperate with the Disaffected; there was too much history behind them for that. They were hated in their own right for their interference in interchurch warfare and their brutal handling of any who fell into their hands as suspects.

Within, the Militia Headquarters at Ahruma was like any military or paramilitary headquarters on any of the New Worlds. A place of offices and corridors, with self-cleaning walls and floors, bright lights and an air of industry—which might be actual or just an appearance. The cells to which they eventually came, however, were several flights down from the level of their entrance.

Here the lights were just as bright, but the corridors, in spite of their yellow dye and bright lights, had a more sterile look; and Bleys thought he smelled the odor of disinfectant as they went along them. The doors were blank, with little Judas windows which could be opened only from the outside.

At one of these, Barbage halted, and the headquarters militia man who had been preceding them tapped out a code on the entrance door, stood back as it slid into its niche in the wall, and let Barbage and Bleys go past him into the cell itself. He entered behind them and the door closed automatically, locking again.

Chapter 41

Bleys had ducked his head automatically as he stepped into the cell; but the ceiling, though low, was enough for him to stand upright, so he straightened again. The cell was brightly lit—if anything, over-brightly lit. The sudden glare, combined with his straightening up, kept him from looking directly at the cell's occupant immediately. When he did, he saw that Hal Mayne was lying, obviously asleep or unconscious, on a narrow bed against the wall just to his right; and as he turned to look at Hal squarely, Bleys got one of the few deep shocks of his life.

This was not the boy of his fever-dream, the youngster whose image Bleys had been carrying in his mind all these years; in spite of knowing that Mayne must have grown and aged in the years since he was fifteen.

This was a half-starved but still obviously powerful man, with coarse black hair and several days' growth of black stubble on his strong jaw and lower face—and tall—very tall. *He's as big as I am!* Bleys thought, still in his moment of shock.

Hal's feet and his lower legs from the calves down projected beyond the foot of the bed on which they had fastened him; and suddenly, it was as if the figure Bleys saw lying there, was more than human; was both a giant and something beyond ordinary humanity—so that he was not only bigger than life, but had something greater than human about him, like the power of the ancient Greek Sibyl of Old Earth. So that for an instant the fear touched Bleys that the bearded lips might open; and a voice tell him something that would destroy all the plans he had laid out for himself, turning him aside and sending him off in a different direction—and what had been said to him would stay with him forever, so that he would never find his way back to what he had set out to do in the first place.

Only then, in the glaring light, Bleys saw how they had tied him down; with cords drawn so tightly that they sank into the scant flesh of his wide-boned wrists, and into the fabric of the worn bush trousers covering his long legs. Immobile . . . as Bleys himself had awakened to find himself after the fever-dream of wolves. He felt again the restraints on his wrists and ankles; and for a moment Hal and he were one.

His stomach turned over. He looked away from Barbage and the Militiaman jailer. In this moment he could control his voice but not his features; and, above all, it was Barbage he did not want to see his face—in a rage even greater than the Militia captain had seen, the last time Bleys had been on Harmony.

"Get a medician!" he said.

"Great Teacher—" began the Militiaman, shocked.

"Silence!" Barbage snapped. He already had his wrist control pad at his lips and was speaking into it. "This is Captain Amyth Barbage. The medician to Hal Mayne's cell. Immediately!"

"Forgive me, Great Teacher," he said to Bleys—but with no real apology in the words—lowering his arm. "I should have thought thou mightest have need of him. He will be with thee in a moment."

Barbage turned his gaze burningly upon the Militiaman; who literally shrank back against the wall, opened his mouth as if to say something, then closed it again.

"Good," Barbage said softly. "The word I spoke was '*silence.*'"

"Ah—Medician," said Bleys, when the man arrived, literally within seconds. He must have been close by, in spite of what Barbage had said.

He was a short man in civilian clothes, with a worried look on his pinched face, under graying sandy hair. A small box like the one Kaj had carried was in one of his hands. He glanced at Bleys with concern and apprehension.

"I want to talk to this prisoner," Bleys said calmly to him, "but he's unconscious. I'd like him roused—gently. I want him to feel comfortable— no matter what's wrong with him—during the time I'm talking to him."

The worried look on the face of the medician deepened.

"He's got pneumonia," the medician muttered, stepping to the bed-side. His one hand felt Hal's forehead, went to his pulse; then as quickly left it again. He began opening his box.

He took from his equipment box a small bronze cube with a stud in the bottom. He placed the opposite end of it against the sleeve over Hal's left arm, just above the biceps. He touched the stud once. Then he put the cylinder back in the box, closed it and stood back, looking at Bleys.

"It'll take him a moment or two to come completely to his senses," he said to Bleys.

"All right," said Bleys. "You can go now."

Barbage's gaze burned now on the medician, who turned and left. Bleys hardly noticed the sound of the cell door opening and closing behind him.

"That's better," he said. "Now take those stays off him and help him sit up."

Barbage and the Militiaman moved to obey.

Bleys' mind was still occupied in trying to encompass the shock he had felt on seeing Hal there. Like most unusually tall or short men, Bleys ordinarily forgot his difference in size, except where it became a problem with those around him, or some other inconvenience resulted from it.

He could remember one night in his bedroom at Other Headquarters on Association, coming awake slowly as he usually did and reaching out, half-asleep, to turn off the ceiling image of what was now a bright morning sky overhead. He had turned it on the evening before to show him the nighttime starscape that he always liked to have above him during his hours of rest or slumber.

In his drowsiness, he had fumbled, and turned the ceiling to a mirror surface instead—and had been suddenly startled, looking up, to see his own length in the bed, a bed made to the same dimensions as that which Dahno had caused to be made for himself.

He had just recently, then, reached his full height; but for the first time he *felt* it, where before he had merely been aware of it. All at once, a number of things had rushed back, little moments in which he had reached for something in the last year or so and been rather pleasurably surprised that it easily within his grasp—though anyone of average New Worlds' height would have had his fingertips far short of it.

It was with something of the same unexpected awareness he had rec-ognized Hal Mayne's growth, now. But in the case of Hal it had triggered a shock—and something almost like an ancient flash of animal rage in him.

It had been only momentary—felt, instantly controlled—and probably he would have begun to put the memory of it from him by now, if he had not wakened from his dream of the newwolves, to find himself fastened as he had seen Hal tied down, just now; and if that memory had not still burned in his soul like the mark of a recently applied red-hot branding iron. Now, however, he made an effort to erase both memories from his mind, as the eyelids of the figure now sitting up on the bed fluttered and opened, and the eyes of the prisoner focused on him.

"Well, Hal," Bleys said softly, "now we finally get a chance to talk. If you'd only identified yourself back in Citadel, we could have gotten together then."

Hal did not answer, but the concentration of his gaze was all on Bleys. And, as full awareness came back into that gaze, so Bleys saw also a steadiness come into it, as he clearly recognized Bleys.

He must have known me when he was among the dissidents paraded before me, last year in Citadel. But unless he'd heard my name, how did he recognize me then? He could not have seen me on the terrace where his tutors were killed—or could he?

So Bleys thought, inside himself. The expression on Hal's face had not changed. It was as still as the face of Toni, whenever she had gone into the expressionless appearance that signaled that she was completely relaxed, completely unfocused, ready and capable of meeting anything. But Bleys felt a sudden, reasonless fear that the hopes with which he had come here could be dead before he and Hal had even spoken.

A float-chair had been placed by the bed, and Bleys sat down on it. For all of Hal's expression, half-masked as it was, but recognizable to Bleys, and which possibly meant that he also had had some training in the martial arts—probably from one or more of his tutors—the young man was still young, Bleys reminded himself. Perhaps Bleys could reach him by talking to him as if he was still not fully grown, and the reflexes of youth would help to make him hear.

"I should tell you how I feel about the deaths of your tutors," Bleys said. Never had he put more feeling into his trained voice, reaching with it to relax and reassure Hal, and at the same time carry conviction into the very depths of Hal's mind. "I know—at the moment you don't trust me enough to believe me. But you should hear, anyway, that there was never, at any time, any intention to harm anyone at your home. If there'd been any way I could have stopped what happened there, I would have."

He paused.

Hal said nothing. Bleys smiled, a little sadly.

"I'm part-Exotic, you know," he said. "I not only don't hold with killing, I don't like any violence; and I don't believe ordinarily there's any excuse for it."

Still there was no response from Hal. No change in that expression of his.

"Would you believe me," Bleys went on, "if I told you that of the three there, on the terrace that day, there was only one who could have surprised me enough to make me lose command of the situation long enough for them to be killed?"

Again he paused, and still Hal was silent.

"That one man," said Bleys, "made the only possible move that could have done so. It was your tutor, Walter, and his physically attacking me. That was the single action I absolutely couldn't anticipate; and it was also the only thing that could get in the way of my stopping my bodyguards in time."

"Bodyguards?" Hal repeated.

His voice was weak, so husky that Bleys seemed to hear it from a distance. But there was a hard note in it, nonetheless; and once more it touched Bleys with his strange feeling of something on the instinctive animal level between them—an echo of his fever-dream—like the voice of someone more powerful, more implacable and *right*, than anyone should be, answering him.

"I'm sorry," Bleys said. "I can believe you think of them in different terms. But no matter what you think, their primary duty there, that day, was only to protect me."

"From three old men," Hal said.

"Even from three old men. And they weren't so negligible, those old men. They took out three out of four of my bodyguards before they were stopped."

"Killed," Hal said. There was no particular inflection to his voice. It was as if he merely corrected a minor incorrect statement. Bleys nodded slightly.

"Killed," Bleys said. "*Murdered*, if you want me to use that word. All I'm asking you to accept is that I'd have prevented what happened—and could have if Walter hadn't done the one thing that could break my control over my men for the second or two needed to let it all happen."

Hal looked away from him, up at the ceiling. He said nothing for a moment; then he spoke.

"From the time you set foot on our property," he said, "the responsibility was yours." He sounded weary.

He closed his eyes against the brightness of the lights overhead and Bleys looked sharply at the Militiaman who had shown him and Barbage the way to this cell.

"Lower that illumination some more." The Militiaman moved to do so. "That's right. Now leave it there. As long as Hal Mayne is in this room, those lights aren't to be turned up or down, unless he asks they be."

On the bed, Hal opened his eyes again. The light in the cell was now more comfortable even to Bleys' eyes. Strangely, in the reduced illumination, Hal seemed even larger, even more—something greater than human. Bleys felt an emptiness in him that was almost a feeling of despair. He spoke again, still trying.

"You're right, of course," Bleys said. "But still, I'd like you to try and understand my point of view."

Hal's eyes came back to Bleys' face.

"Is that all you want?" Hal asked.

"Of course not." Bleys still kept his voice pitched low, but as persuasive as possible. "I want to save you—not only for your own sake, but as something to put against the unnecessary deaths of your tutors, for which I do feel responsible."

"And what does saving me mean?" Hal's face was still without expression; his eyes watched Bleys.

"It means giving you a chance to live the life you've been designed by birth—and from birth—to live."

There was a fraction of a pause before Hal answered, but so slight that if Bleys had not been listening and watching closely, he would not have noticed it.

"As an Other?" said Hal.

"As Hal Mayne, free to use his full capabilities."

"As an Other."

For the first time, there was a slight crack in the barrier of disbelief which Hal had placed between them; a crack that Bleys thought might be exploited. Hal obviously had been given some information that exaggerated the abilities of the Others as they now were—either that or else this bearded, half-starved young man before him could see into the future to what Bleys intended the Others finally to be. Yes, that crack might be exploited. At least, it was worth trying.

"You're a snob, my young friend," said Bleys, a touch of sadness in his voice. "A snob and misinformed. The misinformation may not be your fault. But the snobbery is. You're too bright to pretend to a belief in double-dyed villains. If that was all we were—myself and those like me— would most of the inhabited worlds let us take control of things the way they have?"

"If you were capable enough to do it," Hal said.

Bleys felt a sudden apprehension. It was not possible that somehow this young man could be anticipating the future—Bleys' plans and everything he hoped to do. But Bleys was now committed to trying to exploit the crack he thought he had discovered; and, in any case, he would have to continue in that way for a while, so as not to make Hal suspicious.

"No." Bleys shook his head. "Even if we were supermen and superwomen—even if we were the mutants some people like to think we are— so few of us could never control so many unless the many wanted us to control them. And you must have been better educated than to think of us as either superbeings or mutants. We're only what we are—what you yourself are—genetically fortunate combinations of human abilities who have had the advantages of some special training."

"I'm not like you." The response from Hal was almost automatic.

These latest words came, when they came, with something close to disgust in them.

"Of course you are," said Bleys, keeping his voice in the same tone, calm and reasonable.

Hal's eyes moved past Bleys to look at the headquarters Militiaman and at Barbage. They dwelt on Barbage.

"That's right, Hal," said Bleys, glancing in the same direction. "You know the Captain, don't you? This is Amyth Barbage, who'll be responsible for you as long as you're in this place. Amyth—remember, I've a particular interest in Hal. You and your men are going to have to forget he was ever connected with one of the Commands. You're to do nothing to him—for any reason, or under any circumstances. Do you understand me, Amyth?"

"I understand, Great Teacher," Barbage's eyes went past Bleys, and he looked at Hal with eyes as unblinking as a snake's as he spoke.

"Good," Bleys said. "Now, all surveillance of this cell is to be discontinued until I call you to come let me out of here. Leave us, both of you, and wait down the corridor so Hal and I can talk privately—if you please."

The enlisted man looked as if he couldn't believe the order, and wanted to object; but as he started to move, Barbage, never looking away from Hal, closed his hand on the other's black-sleeved arm, thin fingers sinking deeply into cloth and arm. The enlisted man froze.

"Don't worry," said Bleys. "I'll be perfectly safe. Now go."

The two of them went, and the door locked behind them.

"You see"—Bleys turned back to Hal—"they don't really understand this; and it isn't fair to expect them to. From their standpoint, if another human gets in your way, the sensible thing is to remove him—or her. The concept of you and I as relatively unimportant in ourselves, but as gathering points for great forces; and in a situation where it's those forces that matter . . . that's the thing essentially beyond their comprehension. But certainly you and I ought to understand such things—not only such things, but each other."

Bleys waited.

"No," Hal said. There was another long pause and then he spoke again. "No."

"Yes." Bleys looked down. "Yes, I'm afraid I have to insist on that point. Sooner or later, you're going to have to face the real shape of things in any case; and, for your own sake, it'd better be now, rather than later."

Now Hal was looking away from Bleys, at the ceiling.

"All practical actions are matters of necessity in the light of hard reality," Bleys went on. "What we—those who are called the Other People—do, is dictated by what we are and the situation in which we find ourselves; and that situation is to be one among literally millions of ordinary humans, with the power to make our lives in that position either heavens or hells. Either—but nothing else. Because the choice isn't one any of us can avoid. If we fail to choose heaven, we inevitably find ourselves in hell."

"I don't believe you." Hal looked at Bleys once more. "There's no reason it has to be that way."

At last, thought Bleys, he could be showing at least a touch of uncertainty. Perhaps it was still possible to lead him—talking to him as a voice of experience, speaking to the youth he still almost was.

"Oh, yes, my child," Bleys said softly. "There is a reason. Apart from our individual talents, our training, and our mutual support, we're still only as human as the millions around us. Friendless and without funds, we can starve, just like anyone else. Our bones can be broken, and we can fall sick as easy as ordinary mortals. Killed, we die as obligingly. If taken care of, we may live a few years longer than the average, but not much."

He paused, hoping for some reaction from Hal, that would tell him whether his words were striking home or not. But Hal merely lay there, watching him with those gray-green eyes.

There was a need in Bleys—almost a savage hunger—to make the man on the bed understand. This young man whom he knew could understand if he wished, but either was not getting the information that would allow him to, or was refusing to listen. But Bleys had based everything up 'til this moment on his belief that Hal would not be someone who either could not—or would refuse to—understand. He went on speaking.

"We have the same normal, human emotional hungers for love, for the companionship of someone who can think and talk our own language. But, if we should choose to ignore our differentness and mold ourselves to fit the little patterns of those around us, we can spend our whole lives miserably; and probably—almost certainly—we may never even be lucky enough to meet one other being like ourselves. None of us chose this, to be what each of us is."

Again he paused. Again, Hal had not moved or changed his expression.

"But what we are," said Bleys, "we are; and, like everyone else, we have an innate human right to make the best of our situation."

"At the expense of those millions of people you talk about," said Hal.

"And what sort of expense is that?" Almost without conscious will, Bleys' voice grew deeper with his effort to push a feeling of the sincerity of what he had to say across to Hal.

"The expense of one Other borne by a million ordinary humans is a light load on each ordinary human. But turn that about. What of the cost to the Other: who, trying only to fit in with the human mass around him, accepts a life of isolation, loneliness, and the endurance daily of prejudice and misunderstanding? While, at the same time, his unique strengths and talents allow those same individuals who draw away from him to reap the benefits of his labors. Is there justice in that?"

Bleys threw the question at Hal like a challenge. But Hal still did not respond. It was not as if he was refusing to listen or absorb what Bleys had said. It was rather as if he stood back, waiting for a case still to be proved.

A strangely mature, even old reaction. By the time Bleys had been twenty, he had been in Ecumeny for several years, immersed in the politics that was Dahno's life, his time full with self-training for the future he saw before him—not yet in detail, but in general shape. While Hal had been a sheltered boy growing up, until he had run for what he thought was his life on the death of his tutors, and gone on from there to bury himself among the miners on Coby, a closed-in world with little to offer; and from there to the nearly-as-limited, one-point-of-view environment of the out-law Command of this Rukh Tamani.

Yet something in the way Hal lay, watched and listened was like that of a person even older than Bleys—appearing to absorb and weigh what Bleys said, but finding that so far it had not proved its argument. However, there was no place for Bleys to go except forward with that argument, so he did.

"Look down the long pages of past history at the intellectual giants, men and women alike, who've moved civilization forward while struggling to survive in the midst of lesser people who innately feared and distrusted them. Giants, crouching daily to keep their differences from showing and arousing the irrational fears of the small ones around them. From the beginning of time, to be human—but different—has been dangerous; and it's been a choice between the many who could carry one lightly on their combined shoulders and the one who must carry the many all alone, with his or her much greater strength, but staggering under the proportionately greater effort; and which of those two choices is fairer?"

Hal's eyes had focused with his last words. Something like an intuition came to Bleys. Perhaps the mental image of a giant crouching had gotten through. Hal's words, coming a second later, seemed to back up this feeling.

"Why crouch?" he said.

"Why crouch?" Bleys smiled, tolerantly, but secretly also with a touch of hidden relief. "Ask yourself that. How old are you now?"

"Twenty."

"Twenty—and you still ask that question? As you've gotten older, haven't you begun to feel an isolation, a separation from all those around you? Haven't you found yourself forced, more and more often lately, to take charge of matters—to make decisions not merely for yourself, but for those with you who aren't capable of making them for themselves? Quietly but inevitably taking charge, doing what only you realize has to be done, for the good of all?"

He waited. When there was no word from Hal, after a moment, he went on.

"I think you know what I'm talking about. At first, you only try to tell them what should be done; because you can't believe—you don't want to believe—that they can be so helpless. But, little by little, you come to face the fact that while they may do things right under your continual coaching, they'll never understand enough to do what's necessary on their own, each time the need arises; and so, finally, worn out, you simply take over. Without their even realizing it you set things in the path they should go; and all these little people follow it, thinking it's the natural course of events."

Bleys paused; hoping, as always, for a response from Hal. Speaking as he was doing was like walking along the edge of a precipice. It would be very easy to trigger whatever notion of responsibility to the rest of the race Hal had absorbed, particularly from the tutor who was Walter InTeacher, the Exotic.

It would be easy for Hal to misjudge what Bleys was trying to tell him, taking it only as an arrogant display of wanting to dominate all other people. But—so far he had trusted to Hal's perception to understand that this was not what he was driving at. Perhaps he could simply tell him so, although not in direct words.

"Yes," Bleys said strongly, "you know what I'm talking about. You've already known it and started to feel the width and depth of this gulf that separates you from the rest of the race. Believe me when I tell you that what you now feel will steadily grow deeper and stronger as time goes on. The experience your more capable mind acquires, at a rate much faster than they can imagine, will continue to widen and widen the gap that separates you from them.

"In the end, there'll be little more kinship between you and them, than between you and any lesser creature—a dog or a cat—of which you've become fond. And you'll regret that lack of real kinship bitterly, but there'll be nothing you can do about it, no way to give them what they'll never be able to hold—any more than you could give an appreciation of great art to monkeys. So, finally, to save yourself the pain that they don't even know you feel, you cut the last emotional tie you have with them; and choose instead the silence, the emptiness and the peace, of being what you are: unique and alone, forever."

"No," said Hal. It may have been the drug the medician had revived him with, but he spoke like someone considering a problem at a great distance from it. "That's not a way I can go."

"Then you'll die." Bleys tried to keep his voice cool and rational. "In the end, like those who were like us in past centuries, you'll let them kill you, merely by ceasing to make the continual effort necessary to protect yourself among them. And it'll be wasted, all wasted—what you were and what you could've been."

"Then it'll have to be wasted," said Hal. "I can't be what you say."

"Perhaps," said Bleys. There must be some doubt in the boy; it was simply not surfacing in his voice. He rose to his feet, pushing the float back with his legs. "But wait a bit yet and see. The urge to live is stronger than you think." He looked down at Hal.

"I told you I'm part-Exotic. Do you think I didn't fight against the knowledge of what I was when I first began to be aware of it? Do you think I didn't reject what I saw myself committed to being, only because of what I am? Do you suppose I didn't at first tell myself that I'd choose a hermit's existence, an anchorite's life, rather than make what then I thought of as an immoral use of my abilities?"

He paused, possibly for the last time, but now not waiting for an answer; but wanting his final words to sink into Hal's mind and work there.

"Like you," he said slowly and expressively, "I was ready to pay any price to save myself from the contamination of playing God to those around me. The idea was as repellent to me then as it is to you now. But what I came to learn was that it wasn't harm, it was good that I could do the race as one of its leaders and masters; and so will you learn—in the end."

He turned and stepped to the door of the cell.

"Open up here!

"It makes no difference," Bleys said, turning again while footsteps sounded in the corridor, "what you think you choose now. Inevitably, a day'll come when you'll see the foolishness of what you did now by insisting on staying here, in a cell like this, under the guard of those who, compared to you, are little more than civilized animals. None of what you're inflicting on yourself at this moment is really necessary."

He paused.

"But it's your choice. Do what you feel like doing until you can see more clearly. But when that time comes, all you'll have to do is say one word. Tell your guards that you'll consider what I've said; and they'll bring you to me, out of here to a place of comfort and freedom and daylight, where you can have time to set your mind straight in decency. Your need to undergo this private self-torture is all in your own mind. Still, as I say, I'll leave you with it until you see more clearly."

Barbage and the enlisted man unlocked the door and swung it open. Bleys looked one last time into Hal's eyes, as he lay unmoving on the bed. Then he turned away and walked off, into and down the corridor, without looking back. He could hear his own footsteps, and then those of Barbage and the enlisted man, as they re-locked the door and followed after him. It seemed he could hear the pocket of silence that remained behind in the cell.

Chapter 42

"*Favored of God* was still here and not tied up in any way," said Toni when Bleys returned to his suite in the hotel in Citadel. "She can lift in eight hours. With no passengers and a cargo type of run, she can make it to New Earth in three ship's days. She can lift with all of us aboard with six hours' notice and make the trip in four to five days without any danger of shift-sickness among our people; unless some of them are unusually sensitive to phase-shifting. But none of them showed any signs of that on our earlier trips to New Earth, Cassida and Newton, so they don't think there'll be any problem."

Bleys nodded.

"Dahno and Henry could leave right now, if it's necessary; and we've located all but five of Henry's present Soldiers of God—oh, and *Burning Bush* was just about to lift. Its master took both your messages, in sealed envelopes. He'll hand-carry them himself; one directly to the Commandant at Friendly military headquarters there—your First Elder seal on the envelope should get him to the military commander. The other one, to the People of the Shoe, will go to our New Earth Other Headquarters, for Ana Wasserlied's attention only. Again, since it's plainly from you, I don't think that'll be opened by anyone else."

"Fine!" Bleys said. "Outside of the unexpected, then, we're as good as on New Earth already."

The unexpected did not happen. When *Favored* settled in its place on the parking pad of the New Earth City spaceport, the Friendly expedition's Honor Guard was already drawn up ready to receive them as they stepped out of its exit port.

Certainly, Bleys thought as he watched them through an observation transparency in the disembarking lounge of the *Favored of God*, the Friendly soldiers were going magnificently through the motions of being an Honor Guard; although there were also certainly far too many of them to really hide the fact that they were something more.

The Friendly Commander must have assigned something close to a full regiment to meet them. Limousines were just outside the exit port of the *Favored of God* as she landed; and once Bleys' party were in them, they drove slowly down a long avenue between two double rows of Friendly Soldiers, who brought their weapons to the salute as Bleys' limousine passed. At the end of the double rows, an orderly arrangement of military vehicles was waiting; and these moved out—preceding, following and flanking the limousines as they made their way into the city, to the same hotel that Bleys had been in before.

Clearly, Bleys decided, the Expedition Commander had detailed his best troops for this duty. He made a mental note to talk with that officer as soon as possible. He could possibly see him or her the following morning—he checked himself. Since he was First Elder now, the Commander should come to him, rather than vice versa. He would have Toni send a message setting a time.

"Toni's told me that neither the CEOs nor the Guilds have tried to reach me so far," Bleys said to Henry and Dahno, mid-morning of the next day, as she and they sat with him in one of the lounges of his suite. "That's as I expected. Neither one would want to seem anxious. On the other hand, the longer I stay here doing nothing, the more they're going to worry I'm getting something done out of their sight. Meanwhile I've asked the Commander of the Friendly troops if he'll be good enough to call on me—"

A tiny chime sounded from Toni's wrist control pad. She touched a stud on the control pad, so that the message came to her by bone conduction from her wrist directly to her inner ear, rather than from the auditory device that would have sounded the message into all their ears. Bleys, however, stopped speaking until the message was over and he could have her attention again.

Toni smiled, listening. Her lips moved briefly, inaudibly, as she answered the message sub-vocally; and—still with a smile—she looked at Bleys. It almost never happened in real life that anything happened at the exact dramatic moment which would be ideal from the standpoint of stage management. Bleys had in fact stage-managed a few such happenings for his own purposes in the past; but this time it had happened of its own accord.

"He just got here," said Toni. "He's waiting for you, next lounge."

"Right on time!" Bleys glanced at the chronometer on his own wrist-pad. Dahno laughed.

"That's the military mind for you," he said, still chuckling. "It would never happen in politics."

"I'll leave you temporarily and talk to him," said Bleys. "We'll finish off this conference after he's gone; I won't be long. Why don't the rest of you listen to our talk over the intercom? Toni—would you have somebody send in something in the way of refreshments for us?"

Toni nodded, lifting her wristpad to her lips again. Meanwhile, Bleys had gotten to his feet. He stepped over to the door, which slid back before him, and passed through. A middle-aged man in a black uniform, only slightly different from that of a Militia officer but with the twin-worlds insignia of a general officer, rose from one of the padded floats in the room as the door closed behind Bleys.

"First Elder—or should I address you as Great Teacher?" he said.

"Either one," said Bleys, waving him back into his float and taking one himself. "It makes no difference."

"In that case, First Elder," the officer said, "I'm honored by your invitation to visit you. I'm Marshal Cuslow Damar, by God's favor and appointment of the War Departments of Association and Harmony, in command of our troops contracted here to New Earth."

It was a thoroughly formal self-introduction, but there was nothing stiff or even formal about the man. He was somewhat under average height, slightly thick-waisted, but if overweight, not by much; and he moved easily as if he was still in good physical shape. His hair was straight and brownish-gray, combed back and relatively short. His face was round, calm, pleasant and unremarkable. About the only thing about him that would have made him stand out in any crowd were his eyes. They were a pale blue—not the ordinary pale blue of eyes, nor yet the blue of any precious stone, but the smooth, water-polished flat blue of matched pebbles picked up from the streambed of a shallow, swift-running creek.

Those eyes were neither friendly nor unfriendly, neither commanding nor yielding; and the man seemed completely at ease, completely in control of himself and not at all bothered to be talking with a titular superior such as a First Elder.

"I'm pleased to meet you, Marshal Damar," said Bleys. "We ought to be getting something to drink and nibble at in just a moment or two. I wanted to thank you for the Guard of Honor. I was glad to see it—and impressed by the men and officers. They looked an unusually fit and ready body of soldiers."

"They were mainly cadre," said Cuslow. "I thought, since you suspected there might be some disturbance between the ship and your hotel here, it would be best if what met you were experienced troops. Troops that would know what to do—if the unusual occurred."

"Yes. I guessed as much; and I appreciate it—" Bleys broke off as Toni brought in a tray, with an assortment of small eatables and two tall wineglasses, with bottles both of fruit juices and New Earth wines on them. She smiled at Cuslow, as she set the tray down on a small table-float and pushed it through the air to within reach of both of them. But she said nothing, turning immediately and going back out of the room.

"I don't believe I know the citizen's name," said Cuslow, looking at the door that had closed behind her. His blue eyes came back to Bleys. "I'm right, aren't I? She *is* from either Harmony or Association?"

"Association," said Bleys. "Her name's Antonia Lu."

"Yes." Cuslow nodded. "I remember that name now, from the information furnished me about your party."

"Did you bring along a copy of the agreement under which our troops are here? I wanted to have it with me."

"Here you are, First Elder." Cuslow produced a several-paged document from an inside pocket of his uniform jacket and passed it over to Bleys. Bleys glanced at it, nodded and put it aside on a float-table nearby that had nothing else on it.

"I'm glad to have that," he said. "How many soldiers do you actually have on New Earth right now?"

"I'm ashamed to say I can't give you the exact number," said Cuslow. "In excess of thirty-eight thousand. Ships should be landing in the next few days with at least four or five thousand more. Was the exact number important to you, First Elder?"

"Only in one way. You said you expected several thousand more in the next week. How long before you have the full fifty thousand?"

"I'm afraid that getting the full complement is going to take some time yet—a matter of three or four months at the very least," said Cuslow. "You know how the draft works. Both our worlds divide their occupied landmasses into areas, and we draft from each area in turn. It's set up so that, theoretically, by the time we reach the last area in turn, a new generation of sixteen- to twenty-year-olds will have grown up. So, in theory, we can keep drafting steadily, and there will always a new generation ready to tap for basic training. However, after those chosen for draft are called for training, it takes roughly three months to train them before they're ready to be shipped away on contract. If they aren't shipped in a reasonable time, they need at least a four weeks' refresher course. Ordinarily, the system works very well."

He paused and looked at Bleys.

"I can see it does," Bleys murmured.

"But in this case," Cuslow went on, "New Earth's sudden need for fifty thousand soldiers—not necessarily experienced, but trained—has made for a very large contract. Also one including, on our side, a number of demands that usually only the Dorsai make and can get an employer's agreement on. We assumed, of course, that New Earth's need was both urgent and severe. But, a call for so many troops exhausted our pool of trained and quickly refreshable soldiers, as well as those about to finish their training. We're now at the point where we're going to have to wait at least a couple of months for further additions to our strength here on New Earth."

"I understand," said Bleys. "But do you think, with the strength you've already got here, you could handle most situations that might come up?"

"No doubt of it," Cuslow said. "I'd be surprised if they've got even three-quarters our number of actual military, spread out over their whole world. It would take them a month or more to get even those all together, and longer than that to train them to work together. The only way they could create any kind of troublesome force in less than a month would be by combining military and paramilitary forces, right down to the local police. And such diverse groups would just get in each other's way."

"Would they?" Bleys asked. "Why?"

"They'd have no experience in operating as part of a unified force," said Cuslow. "And, in addition to whatever jealousies or other problems there could be between them, sheer misunderstandings are enough to cripple any joint effort. By the time they got any kind of an effective opposition group set up, we'd have whatever situation there was completely in hand. In short, we'd have put ourselves in a position where it would take a trained force of at least double our strength to reverse the situation."

Bleys smiled. Cuslow smiled back, slightly. It was not the quick quirk of Henry's smile, but it was very like it.

"You mustn't judge our military by the militia on our two home worlds, First Elder," said Cuslow, in a slightly lower voice. "I say that privately, for your ear only; but please be reassured on that point. If something like our own Friendly Militia were opposing us, we'd go through them like a knife through soft goat cheese—even if they were comparable to us in having uniform weapons and with a unified command, plus all the equipment we have that they don't."

"I'm very pleased to hear that," Bleys said. "Well, now, I've something I wanted to ask of you—a rather small matter, but an important one. I'm going to be having a meeting here some time in the next few days, and there's a group I'd like to bring to that meeting. Their situation's like the one we were in, when we landed at the spaceport."

"I see," said Cuslow. "You mean local authorities might make the mistake of interfering with them?"

"Yes. I'd like them picked up by an escort of your troops at Other Headquarters here on New Earth, whenever I give you the word that it's time to bring them to my suite here. Of course, I suppose that means you're going to have to have soldiers standing by around the clock, because I don't know exactly when the meeting would be held; and your notice would simply be a call from one of my aides, like Antonia Lu, the person who just brought us this tray."

"It can all be done quite easily," Cuslow said. "I'll take care of it as soon as I'm back at my Headquarters—or I can even call there now, if it's urgent."

"No urgency just yet. I'll try to give you advance warning, but the warning might be merely a call, to get them over here as safely and quickly as possible. I suppose your headquarters aren't too far from this hotel?"

"About eight minutes. I've an HQ force there all the time. We'll have no trouble making room for the added number it will take to bring these people when you call."

"Good," Bleys said. "How exactly would an escort like that be armed, and what would it consist of—in the way of officers and men?"

They discussed the nature and size of the escort, and from there went on to talk of Cuslow's soldiers in general; their organization, proportion of officers to men, and more general information about Cuslow's Headquarters' organization, about which Bleys' curiosity wanted to be satisfied.

Still, it was only another ten to fifteen minutes before they reached an end to their talk and Cuslow took his leave. Bleys saw him to the main lounge of his suite, where three other middle-aged officers were sitting, waiting for him. They said good-bye to each other cordially, and Bleys went back to the lounge where he had been talking to Toni, Henry and Dahno.

He had expected to find the room empty and to call the rest from wherever they had gone off on their own activities.

But when he stepped into the lounge, he found Dahno and Henry still there, evidently not having left but stayed put to listen to his conversation with Cuslow; and Toni joined them almost on Bleys' heels.

"By the way, and before you get back to what you were talking about, Bleys," she said as soon as they were all seated. "Both the CEOs and the Guilds called while you were talking to the Marshal. I imagine they were told he was here as soon as he showed up, and that was what triggered their calls. They both wanted you to come to their buildings for dinner and conversation. I explained to them that, now you were First Elder, you couldn't go to them even if you wanted to. For reasons of protocol, it would be necessary they come to you. Both of them told me then that they'd have to talk over doing that among themselves and get back to me. That was the total conversation, in both cases."

"I expect," said Bleys, "we'll hear from them in the next two days, then; maybe even early tomorrow. They're going to end by agreeing to come here. They don't have any choice. They'll both want to establish relations with me as soon as possible, now I'm back. Did you tell them they'd be meeting each other when they came to see me?"

"Not specifically," Toni said. "On the other hand, I rather emphasized the protocol element in any such meeting. They'd have to be remarkably dense if it didn't occur to them that protocol would also insist that, since they were two separate organizations, each tied into governmental control of this world, the demands of interstellar statesmanship would require you to meet with them equally—and very probably at the same time. If I'd said that in so many words, they might have had to find that situation a sticking point interfering with their being able to come to talk to you. But if they don't know it officially, then they can take part in such a meeting with easy consciences."

"Good," said Bleys. "As a matter of fact, I'm glad they called and you told us just now because meeting them was what I was going to talk about next. Henry, since the Friendly soldiers are going to be continuing their guard of this hotel and my suite, I'd like to pull the Soldiers of God in as much as possible. Have them ready. Off duty, but in the hotel and reachable at a moment's notice. It's best if there's to be any confrontation, particularly one involving any kind of force, that it be the Friendly soldiers and the local people who are involved, rather than our people and the locals."

"Yes, Bleys," Henry said. "I was thinking that myself. In fact, I've already told the Soldiers to stay put in their rooms for the moment, and I'll be letting them know whether they'll have the freedom of the rest of the hotel before today's out."

"I should have known you'd be ahead of me, Uncle," said Bleys. "At any rate—back to what I've got planned for meeting them. I want to bring together not only the Guild's top people and the CEOs' top people, but also the leaders of the People of the Shoe. If the Guild doesn't want to agree officially to going to a meeting at which the CEOs are present and vice versa, you can imagine how they'd both have trouble with the idea of sitting down with the People of the Shoe. On the other hand, just as the Guild and CEOs will put up with each other if they can claim that they didn't know it was going to happen and it was sprung on them by me—so they'll also put up with the People of the Shoe if they simply find them here. They've got too much to lose by getting up and walking out, any of them. That includes the People of the Shoe, by the way."

"What do you think you'll gain from the People of the Shoe?" Dahno asked. "Would you spell it out for us?"

"The People of the Shoe as an organization are simply one more organization on a world full of them," said Bleys. "But they're the closest thing to representatives of the general mass of New Earth people—the job-holders, as Anjo calls them. The job-holders are actually the main body of opinion on the planet; and it's what they want and need that will determine which way the planet's history builds. Of the three organizations—CEOs, Guilds and Shoe-people—only the Shoe-people really have the ear of the general populace."

"Yes," Dahno said, nodding. "I think you're right. So, speaking of the general populace, let's see what I can find about public opinion here for you, out on the street tonight and early tomorrow morning."

"If you don't mind, Dahno," said Bleys, "I'd like all three of you to stick as close as the Soldiers are going to be doing. In fact, even closer. Any one of you would make a rather valuable hostage for any of those three organizations, you know."

"Bleys," said Dahno, "I wouldn't say this in front of anybody else but Toni and Henry, but you know you have this bad habit of relying on—what can I call it? Momentum. To borrow a term from physics, you're a mass in motion as far as public opinion goes; and I've always felt you were a little bit too ready to take a chance on that momentum carrying you over a gap in your planning—the way a mag-lev vehicle might jump over a crumbled-away gap in a mountain trafficway, if it was traveling fast enough. You may *need* what I can find out for you out in the city."

"Maybe you're right, Dahno," Bleys said. "But against that, there's the fact that I might need your opinion—or Toni's or Henry's—on the spur of the moment, anytime in the next few days. Keep in mind that this meeting I'm talking about is the climax of all I've been working toward, since we left Association on this tour. I'm not so afraid of anything happening to you if you're taken hostage, though things like that can always turn dangerous. I'm afraid of being left without the counsel of any of you, at a time when I could need it, in the next few days. In fact, I'd like you to stay—all three of you—

even closer than the Soldiers. Your suites all connect with each other and mine without needing to step out into the hotel corridor. I'd like you not to leave your suite or any of our combined suites if you don't mind; at least until I feel it's safe for you to do so. Would you do this much for me?"

"I'll think about it," Dahno said. He was clearly not happy.

Chapter 43

Neither the CEO Club nor the Guilds called back that afternoon; but in the evening, as Bleys and Toni were in his private lounge, talking about the arrangements for the meeting the following day, the doorbell rang unexpectedly.

"Just a second—" said Toni.

She got up and answered it.

And admitted Anjo, controlling a cart with food and drink on it, into the lounge. The door closed behind him.

"There's a forged order from your room, for this," he said, abandoning it. "It's just part of the arrangement to get me in here. I thought you'd rather talk to me than someone else from the People of the Shoe."

"You're right," Bleys said. "Sit down. I want Dahno and Henry here with us for this."

He lifted his control pad to his lips and called them. Henry answered immediately and said he would be right over. Curiously, Dahno's phone did not answer, but took a message. Bleys left word for him to call and come immediately.

Sitting therefore with only Toni and Henry in Bleys' private lounge, both they and Anjo surrounded by the security blue bubble made by the Newtonian device that Dahno had acquired, Bleys turned to Anjo.

"It looks like we'll just have to go with three of us and you." he said. "But, come to think of it, don't you have some questions for me, first?"

"I do," Anjo said. "Your message said you wanted to see our leaders, in company with some other New Earth people. I took that to mean the top men and women in the CEOs and the Guilds. Was I right?"

"Yes," Bleys said.

"Then the first thing I need to know is how many of our leaders you want, and which ones in particular. You can't mean those who lead every separate group among us. There's several hundred different organizations in the People of the Shoe—they were separate organizations, originally. We formed what might be called a coalition only about eight years ago. It's gradually become a more unified, single outfit; but the leaders of the groups that make it up still have a strong voice in what's done by the whole organization, and considerable influence. You understand?"

He looked hard at Bleys.

"So," Anjo went on, "it'll make for hard feelings to leave out any of them; but it'll have to be done. Also, it'll be dangerous for the few I can bring. There's nothing the Guilds and the CEOs would like better than to snap up any one of us and squeeze us for whatever information we can give them about the Shoe."

"No, I don't want more than three or four," said Bleys. "Including you, of course."

"I can promise you me," Anjo said grimly; "I'm official head of the whole organization, after all—if only because I was the only candidate for the post that the others could agree on. But since I've been in, of course, those who want to displace me, or those who disagree with me—and there's a number of those, either because it's their duty to think of their own first, or they never did want me in office. They've got together and built their influence so that they're now perfectly capable of voting—the leaders, that is—not to come to your meeting at all. Or they might agree to send only four representatives, but with a list of demands against the CEOs and the Guilds that would make a shambles of the meeting."

"They'll be cutting their own throats if they do," said Bleys; and was jarred by the unexpected harshness of his own voice. "I'd suspected that sort of problem with your people, but not on the scale you mention—"

He was interrupted by the small chime from Anjo's wrist control pad, announcing a call for him. It kept chiming until Anjo touched the stud and the sound was cut off suddenly.

"Forgive me," he said, "but I've got only a few minutes to talk to you here. I had to borrow the number and job of one of the regular waiters. He's hiding. But that was another room-service delivery, and one of us has to take it. So—in brief: I can produce three other leaders for you; but I don't know what to do about their list of demands. In a situation like this, I'll just be one of the four. Technically the other three will be in a position to override any opposition I make to forcing the demands on the meeting. I'll try to squash that, of course. Maybe you can think of a way around that."

"Tell them," said Bleys, "if they insist on that, no one from the Shoe will be allowed at the meeting."

"You'd do that?" Anjo said.

"I would." said Bleys.

Anjo was silent for a second.

"The only other thing I can think of," he said, standing up from his float and stepping back toward the door, speaking as he went, "would be to suggest to the other leaders tonight that we elect you in my place as head of the organization of the Shoe. If it was you holding my office, none of them would oppose you in anything you wanted at the meeting. I can promise you, in the end they'll all follow you. But that's all I can promise. Think about it between now and tomorrow. I'll have four representatives, all right, myself included, at your Other Headquarters early tomorrow; and we'll just sit tight there until you call us, even if it's several days. But think about what those other leaders might want."

"I will," said Bleys, "and I really think there's a solution. Don't suggest anything to the other leaders yourself. My experience is there's always a solution with a lower price tag, if you think for a while. I'll do that. You just pick and bring who you can—but come yourself, in any case—"

His own wristpad chimed.

"Just a minute—don't leave just yet," he said to Anjo. Touching the stud that would put his conversation on *hush*, he lifted the wristpad to his lips and heard Dahno's voice by bone conduction in his inner ear.

"Bleys?" it said. Bleys touched a stud on his wristpad to carry his voice to the phone through bone conduction.

"I'm here, Dahno," he said silently, sub-vocally. "Anjo's with us. What I talked about earlier is true. This is a moment in which I could have used you with me. I'm glad you called. Where are you?"

"Oh, just a few minutes from you. In fact, I'm on my way to you right now," said Dahno, "Have Anjo wait."

"He can't, unfortunately," Bleys said. "So you went out after all. I thought you'd told me you'd stay in."

"I said I'd think about it," said Dahno. "But in any case you ought to know that my business for a long time has been one where lies are useful tools. I was right: I needed to go out and sample public opinion here. I've got something of importance for you. But it'll have to wait until I'm there. Get Anjo to wait, one way or another."

"I'll try," Bleys said.

He lifted his head from the wristpad and looked over at Anjo standing almost poised by the not-yet-opened door to the hallway.

"Anjo," he said, "Dahno is due here in just minutes. Are you sure you can't—"

"No," Anjo said. "The last thing you need is for me to be picked up and questioned here in this hotel. That'd be practically as good as telling both the Guild and the CEO everything you want done and what I'm up against in helping you, because they'd get the information out of me. I've got to go, and I'm going. I'm sorry—good-bye."

He turned, the door opened behind him. He went through it and it closed again.

"He's gone, Dahno," said Bleys, releasing the bone-conduction stud and speaking aloud. "Come as quickly as you can. Toni, Henry and I'll wait here for you. We're in the first lounge."

"So," said Henry, "he went out in spite of what you told him."

"I knew he would," Toni said.

"I was afraid of it myself," Bleys said. "But we all are what we are; and each one of us makes our own rules when it comes down to a final decision. Dahno is Dahno. He said he was only minutes away. We should see him shortly."

"Then we wait," said Henry.

They waited.

"—So you see," Bleys said, as soon as Dahno had arrived and Bleys had briefed him on what Anjo had told them, "Anjo knows as well as I do that my present appointment as First Elder would rule out my doing any such thing as taking office as leader of an organization on New Earth; a world where I'm not only not a citizen, but we're engaged in renting it half a hundred thousand soldiery. As a matter of fact, my not being a citizen alone would be a bar to accepting such a local office under New Earth law, let alone the laws of our Friendly Worlds."

"I don't see why he even suggested it," said Henry.

"To you, Toni, Dahno and me," said Bleys, "it's unthinkable. But of course he thinks differently. He himself is an outlaw; effectively in arms against his own government. He could be feeling that if he can put himself in that position, I ought to be willing to do so, too. What he doesn't take into account is, even if I wanted to—ignoring my rank as First Elder and turning against my own government—all my plans and, consequently, the only real chance I have of resolving this situation the way I want it, would be gone. I told him I thought I could think of something—or we could think of something. In line with that, Dahno, what did you find out, outside the hotel?"

"Just what I went to find out. The attitude of the New Earther man and woman in the streets and elsewhere. You might be a little surprised. Since our troops started arriving, a lot of people have been expecting the People of the Shoe to take a hand in the situation, somehow—though most I talked to wouldn't stick their necks out enough to name anyone in the Shoe, or the organization itself. They're all sympathetic with the Shoe, but I don't think the majority of the public will follow that organization as a whole, any more than they'd follow the CEOs or the Guild as a single choice for control of their world. They'd probably split up, following the groups that made up the Shoe—the ones Anjo told you about. The only single leader they'd follow, Brother, is you!"

"That's impossible," said Bleys, "although Anjo just suggested exactly that. But while I can safely let myself be named First Elder of Harmony and Association, since it's understood that I'm a citizen of a Friendly world—letting myself also pick up an official position on any other World, would make it seem I'm favoring some Worlds over others—and lose me the general all-New-Worlds' following I've still got to gain. If I'm going to forge all the Worlds into a single, unified, society—unified in purpose, if nothing else—they've all got to trust me. Otherwise, I can't lead, even if I lead from the shadows, the way I want to, with the help of local Others—ones not in obvious situations of power, but known by the people who've been running these Worlds up till now. That means I want the People of the Shoe recognized legally, but the Guilds and CEOs also have to stay in position; and at least appear as if they have as much power and control as they did earlier."

"I wish the Guilds and the CEOs had called back before now," Toni said. "Then at least we'd have some idea about whether the meeting was set, and when."

Bleys nodded. He turned to Toni.

"I think you'd better give them both a call. I know it's late, but in this case I don't think we have to worry about office hours. Tell them I regret not being able to accept their invitations in their original form, but you already explained the constraints upon me. Add that, actually, there are even more constraints than that. Because of my obligations as First Elder, my schedule, as I originally laid it out, has just been severely curtailed. The result is that I'm only able to see them tomorrow at a meeting in the early afternoon, here at my suite."

"What if I can't get through at this hour to anyone important enough to give that message to—at either CEOs or Guilds?" Toni asked.

"You'll get through," said Bleys. "I'd bet my future on it. Give the exact same message to each one; don't make any specific mention of any but the organization you're calling. As you said earlier, I think under the circumstances the CEOs won't be too surprised to see the Guilds here and vice versa. Since Anjo will have his people ready to come tomorrow, I want to bring them in as soon as possible before their leaders who weren't picked to come have time to get together and cook up trouble for Anjo in the Shoe organization."

"All right." Toni got up. "If you don't mind I want to go back to my own desk with the record of exactly what they said to me the time before. Then I'll bring in transcripts of all of them for you." She went out.

"Here are all the old transcripts, plus the new," she said, a few minutes later, coming back to the private lounge; where, in the interval, Dahno had been filling Bleys and Henry in on the specifically significant things he had heard from the people he had talked to outside the hotel, and why he had drawn the conclusions he had. He broke off as Toni came back in and accepted the transcript she handed him, as Bleys and Henry were accepting theirs.

They all looked at them. Bleys needed only a quick glance at each page. Dahno was almost as fast, but Henry read his, line by line, gravely, but without any noticeable change of expression. Meanwhile, Toni sat down. They waited for Henry to finish.

"I'd say they're eager, all right," Bleys said, flicking the end of the papers on the small table-float in front of him where his copy lay, as Henry laid his down. "Wouldn't you say so, Dahno?"

"I would, indeed," said Dahno.

"Any suggestions?" Bleys asked. Dahno and Toni both shook their heads.

"A few questions," said Henry. "Bleys, are you ready to meet them, yourself? Are you sure what you want to say to them; or how you want to deal with them? Also, should I have a few Soldiers standing by in adjoining rooms, just in case?"

"I can't imagine why any of our Soldiers of God would be needed," said Bleys, "and I assume it was they you were talking about, rather than the Friendly troops?"

Henry nodded.

"—And the last thing I want is any of the Friendly military involved in the meeting," Bleys said. "No great danger in their knowing after the fact, but what's known beyond a controlled area by even one person spreads quickly to just about everybody else—in this case, the public that Dahno went out to check on. On second thought though, it never hurts to play safe. Yes, Henry, bring in a few of your Soldiers; but make sure that they don't see the people coming in, or the people see them. Particularly, I don't think the People of the Shoe would appreciate their visit being known—at least, until they've left and are safely away someplace else."

He paused and looked around at the three other faces.

"Any other comments, suggestions, anything?"

"Oh, another small piece of information," Toni said. "You wanted the meeting set early in the afternoon. I set it for two o'clock, just after an early lunch hour, so that we won't be bothered with setting up any eating or drinking, except for the sort of nibble-and-sip refreshments, like those I set out for you and Marshal Damar."

"Good," Bleys said. "If you haven't already, you might call the Others' headquarters, under security, and give Ana Wasserlied warning about the Shoe people and the Friendly soldier escort; also, put off any meeting by me with her until after this other meeting tomorrow."

He glanced at the chronometer on his wristpad.

"Come to think of it, have there been any other important calls for me? Ana, maybe, or someone unusual and important? "

"Ana did call. I said you'd call her back as soon as you could," Toni said. "Were you expecting anyone in particular?"

"Not in particular," Bleys said. "Someone from offplanet, perhaps. But clearly you didn't get anything like that. It's just as well. I don't want to be disturbed between now and the meeting—the only exceptions being you three. I want to be able to push aside everything else and leave my mind free to work with what could happen then and how I ought to handle it."

He looked at Dahno.

"We're at the climax. This meeting's the break point I've been aiming for, ever since I started this lecture tour of mine. I've got to manage it right. In fact, I think I'll go lie down now, and if I sleep, I'll get up and eat something later on."

He paused.

"Anything else any of you want to bring up?"

"No," they each told him.

"In that case, I think I'll get to bed to be in shape for tomorrow. I feel like some sleep, right now."

And he did. As the other three got up and left him, he was feeling the touch of an unnatural weary emptiness within him. It could be one of the side effects Kaj had warned him could linger for years.

He became conscious that the muscles of his jaw were clenched. He made them relax; but the determination in his mind remained.

No side effect—no anything—would come between him and what he had set out to do.

Chapter 44

Morning: of the day of the meeting with the leaders of the CEOs, the Guilds and the People of the Shoe.

Bleys had been awake since dawn, but had not yet left his bedroom. He had taken no phone messages nor made any calls. He had written innumerable notes to himself and destroyed them. He had paced and thought, as on the morning back on Association, when Henry had come to offer himself as a protector. Only that had been lacking; though he had not realized he lacked it. He had been impatient, like the gyrfalcon, until now. But at last, oddly, coming on top of his poisoning—as if it was something he had found, rather than won—it seemed to him that finally the full strength he had sought, the power to hold his listeners transfixed, no matter whether they wished to hear or not, had finally come on him. That ability of the Ancient Mariner in Coleridge's poem—what were those lines again?

> *He holds him with his glittering eye—*
> *The Wedding Guest stood still . . .*

It was this that Bleys had reached for with what he had worked for and done; and he would need it this day, at this meeting with all those who must be brought under control, here on New Earth. He was pacing again, back and forth in a bedroom filled with high-noon sunlight through a transparent window wall, promising joy and a magnificent day to all those outside.

Bleys was blind to it. He was barely aware of his own tall body, in its striding back and forth between the two facing blank walls of the room. His mind was still examining and re-examining the possibilities of the meeting, dealing with one possible scenario after another, for what might develop, as fast as he could imagine them.

The possibilities were not endless; the number and characters of the participants in the meeting limited them. But he would be guessing at their emotional reactions, and those were what counted. He would be juggling three factions, and four individuals, within each faction.

Either he won here and now, or he lost everything he had gained so far. He must trigger each group emotionally to announce their strength before its proper moment. Then, without losing control of the situation himself, he must push everything to a final showdown . . .

His wrist control pad chimed.

"Time to go," its small feminine voice announced to the room at large. He had set it to answer from his wrist, rather than in the larger voice from walls and ceiling, so that it would rouse him as gently as possible from wherever his thoughts had led him.

"All right!" he said, to shut the small voice up, since it was beginning to repeat its announcement. Still, in spite of what he had just said, his emotional momentum carried him through several more strides and across the room completely, before he slowed to a stop.

He was completely dressed and ready, except for his cloak. It was heat-sensitive, just like the cloaks he wore for his public talks. It would have cooled, rather than overheated him. But he had not wanted to finish dressing before he had to go.

Now, however, he threw it around his shoulders and turned toward one of the blank walls of the room.

"Mirror!" he said.

Instantly the blank daylight sky-blue of the wall became a reflective surface, showing him to himself, full length, with the cape on and ready to face those coming.

Bleys' breathing checked. For a moment he merely stared, motionless, at his reflection, unmoving.

"Henry"—he began out loud, unthinkingly, but his mind finished the sentence silently—"*should see me now.*"

The change he had first thought he saw in himself after recovering from the poisoning seemed now to have gone a step further, under the impetus of this final make-or-break moment.

The rectangular face he saw in the mirror above the cape and below its dark brown hair, was still physically unchanged. But psychically it was as if it had moved a step deeper in the direction he had seen reflected before in that earlier mirror image.

It gave the single impression of all of its natural elements working together now to create one unmistakable image, of physical features lit by the purpose within him. His eyes under their dark brown brows appeared darker, focusing with unnatural concentration on what they gazed at.

His high cheekbones, his level mouth, his high forehead, now all together had the appearance of channeling a knowledge and understanding almost too weighty to be born by any single human. Altogether, what he looked at could be one of those many faces of the Satan in whose hands Henry believed Bleys was held. Not, perhaps, the most usual visage of that Darkness; but of a sad, powerful Satan.

It was a face that shook even him, so that, for a moment, he almost

turned from it—and yet, at the same time, it was the image he had been
working toward, all these years.

"—You're still here," said Toni's voice, suddenly behind him. With
an effort, Bleys forced his expression swiftly to an urbane expressionlessness. He turned to her, even as her voice was still going on . . .

" . . . You'll have to come now. The CEOs and the Guild people are
already here; and I've got the People of the Shoe out of sight in a side
lounge. You'll want to see them first, of course?"

Bleys had almost whirled upon her at the first syllable he had heard,
as if her voice had been the voice of an enemy. But instead he had remembered to turn casually. Still, he had been braced inside against seeing
in her the shock he himself had just felt. Instead, she only stared back at
him for a second. A slight frown line appeared between her eyebrows.

"Are you all right?" she asked.

He almost grinned at her, with the fierce joy that had suddenly awakened within him, hearing the other members of the meeting were here.

"Never better!"

"Well, if you're sure," she said, still watching him closely. "You know
Kaj warned you to avoid stress. And this particular meeting's an important
one, isn't it?"

"It couldn't be more important," said Bleys, "but I don't see how
there could be any stress in it." He knew he was lying as he said it; and
worried for a second whether Toni knew him well enough now, to see
through him to that. But she said nothing. "I don't think I'm in any danger."

"If you're sure," she said, her eyes still on him. "This is the high
point of everything you've done so far, isn't it? This is the moment when
everything comes to a head for you as far as New Earth is concerned?"

"That's right, and if it does, I should take a long stride toward what
I want from Cassida and Newton, too, since New Earth's necessary to
them. They expect a tussle, but it's not going to go the way they think.
It'll be like a four-handed card game, with the CEOs and the Shoe people,
at least, each thinking they've brought along a high card that will take
everything. Possibly even the Guild thinks so—though the Guild is riding
on the CEOs' coattails right now. All I need to do, though, is work them
into playing their cards ahead of the proper moment they should play
them. Then, having played them, they'll have lost most of their advantage
and I'll be the one to come out on top."

"Stress," Toni said flatly.

"Not really. Just a matter of my waiting for the moment to act. You
said the Guilds and the CEOs were here, too?"

"Yes," Toni said. "They're already in the meeting room—and probably wondering about the extra chairs at the table."

"Yes," Bleys said. "We shouldn't waste time, then. You're right. I'll
go now. But, yes, take me to the People of the Shoe first—did the Guilds

and the CEOs hold themselves each down to four representatives?" he added as they went through various rooms and down a short corridor.

"Yes. Both groups brought four representatives. Three of the CEOs you met at their dinner when we were on New Earth last. They've one person, though, wearing a head-blur; like those two Others who were spies in the Guilds and CEOs—you remember—they came to talk to you with Ana here in the hotel."

Bleys smiled.

"Yes," he said. "Have you got a recording of the CEOs coming in? I'd like to have a look at that blur-headed individual."

"The usual security recording, I suppose," Toni said. "Henry's been insisting we always make them now."

She punched at studs on her wristpad. The corridor wall behind them lit up with a life-sized three-dimensional image of four individuals coming into the suite through its main lounge door. There were Harley Nickolaus, Jay Aman and Orville Learner. The fourth, in a black business suit cut in the current New Earth fashion, was a shorter individual with the head-blur Toni had mentioned. Bleys watched it closely.

The recording followed them across the main lounge and through a further, side door to the meeting room.

"She—he—could be anyone," said Toni. "By the way, the shoulders of that jacket are padded pretty heavily."

The figures went into the meeting room. The image winked out and the wall was a wall again.

"I noticed," said Bleys.

"The CEOs didn't introduce their incognito person," Toni said as she went on again, "but I'd guess it's somebody new. Otherwise there'd be no point in hiding the identity—"

She broke off, turning through a doorway, whose door had just slid open before her. She and Bleys stepped into a small, fireplaceless lounge, where Anjo and three other people—two women and one man—sat waiting.

They got to their feet as Bleys came in. The other man was a little taller than Anjo; but with a face that seemed to show something of the same implacable heritage, though it was not tanned as Anjo's was. The two women were not much more than in their twenties, if that; remarkably healthy looking, sturdy young women, both of them, but standing differently and a little apart. One was a light blonde, with her hair cut fairly short and almost ice-blue eyes, holding herself very erect. The other, shorter, with comparatively light brown hair but with startlingly warm brown eyes.

The blonde wore a burgundy skirt, and tailored dusty-rose jacket, with a pale blue sweater underneath; the brown-eyed one a full emerald-green skirt and loose yellow tunic, sashed at her waist. Both pairs of eyes examined Bleys, but gave nothing away; and without knowing just what gave him the message, Bleys had the feeling that they were antagonistic, not only to each other, but to Anjo and his particular group within the Shoe. But any internal differences of their organization should not be something he would have to deal with at this meeting.

"I'm glad to meet you," Bleys told them. "What I want you to do is come just behind me into the room where the meeting's to be held. Four members from the Guilds and four from the CEOs are already there. When I go in, I'll announce that representatives from the Shoe are joining us; and the minute you hear me say that—the door will stay partly open behind me so you can hear—you come in directly, before they have a chance to speak. Sit down immediately in any empty floats you see. Pay no attention to whatever they start to say, then. I'll answer them. Am I clear enough about what I'd like?"

"I think so," said Anjo. He looked at the others. They nodded; and the blonde said "Yes!" rather crisply.

"Then come with me," said Bleys.

He turned, walked out, and followed Toni back down the hall, through one empty lounge and to an inner door of another. At this still-unopened door, Toni stopped and stood aside, motioning those behind Bleys to also stop, out of sight when the door was opened. She nodded at Bleys. The door opened and he walked through.

Seven faces on the bodies seated around a long conference table, turned to look at him. The eighth—the one with the blur—did not give any clue as to whether it had turned, let alone whether its owner was looking.

"I'm happy to see you here," said Bleys, quietly but quickly before anyone on either side of the table could start speaking. He stepped to the empty float-chair at the closest end of the long table, but did not sit down in it immediately.

"And I'd like you to welcome the other members of this particular meeting, four representatives from the People of the Shoe—I'm sure you know the organization."

He sat down.

The visible faces had jerked about to stare as Anjo and the three with him came through the doorway and went down to the empty chairs at the far end of the table from Bleys, Anjo sitting in the one that had him completely facing Bleys.

Now there was a moment's additional silence. Then the explosion Bleys was expecting came, from the individual he had expected it to erupt from first. Harley Nickolaus, who had seemed the most dominant among the CEOs' board members when they had met with Bleys before—the *Oldwolves Band-father*, Bleys found himself thinking, as he looked at Harley.

Harley had taken the lead at that dinner meeting at the CEO Club on his previous visit. Although Jay Aman, Harley's nephew and now again sitting at his right side, had struck Bleys as probably the best mind among the CEOs' leaders. But Jay would never be the first to speak in a situation like this. He was the kind to hold back and consider the situation first.

The same thing would be true of Orville Learner, who also had been at that earlier meeting and was now seated at Harley's left side. The person with a blur above his shoulders, beyond Learner, was a question mark; but at first glance Bleys had been sure that the face was hidden because it was someone intended to be unexpected among the CEOs; as if Harley and the rest had come with a shrouded weapon, to be revealed only when the time came for its use.

"You brought us here!" Harley almost stuttered, and his face darkened with congested blood in a way that would have concerned Kaj Menowsky, if he had been present. "Here—to sit with those?"

He jabbed a thick forefinger at the far end of the table, where the People of the Shoe sat. "It's not bad enough you spring these Guild people on us! Now you stroll in here with these work-people! I'll tell you what it is, First Teacher—First Elder—you give us no choice but to leave!"

He stopped speaking. Bleys said nothing, merely looked mildly at him. After the silence had stretched out embarrassingly with nothing said, Harley exploded again.

"Well?" he said. "What've you got to say?"

"Leave," Bleys said.

There was another silence that stretched out. Jay Aman started to whisper in his uncle's ear, but Harley brushed him off.

"Leave?" he shouted at Bleys. "What do you mean by that?"

"What I say," Bleys said. He lifted his wristpad to his lips, "Toni, Harley Nickolaus is leaving. A CEO member as important as he is deserves an escort of at least four of our people. Would you send in four, accordingly? Thanks."

"All right!" Harley shouted, jerking to his feet.

He kicked his chairfloat away from behind him and stepped back from the table. Jay and Orville Learner also slowly started to rise. But the figure with the blur for its head did not move; and, on seeing this, Jay sat down again and reached out to catch Orville's elbow. Orville looked, saw Jay and the headless figure still seated, and sank back in his own chairfloat.

The door opened and four of Henry's Soldiers of God came in. They came down the room and stood around Harley Nickolaus; who turned and stamped past them and past Bleys at the end of the table, the Soldiers still following; and went out the door, all five together. One down—and out, Bleys thought.

As the door closed, Jay Aman spoke.

"If you'll forgive me for pointing it out, First Elder," he said in a voice as quiet as Bleys', "this leaves us with only three representatives for the CEOs at this table."

"So it does," said Bleys. "Perhaps you can tell us, if necessary, what Harley Nickolaus would say to matters as we discuss them here. Speaking of discussing matters, shall we get down to it?"

"Forgive me also, First Elder," said Edgar Hytry, one of the Guild-masters on the opposite side of the table and the one that Bleys had had most to do with on his previous visit. "I thought this was to be an informal, casual gathering. On behalf of those who aren't here from the Guilds, as well as I'm sure the Guildmasters with me, we're as upset as the people on the other side of the table seem to be about those you just brought in—those sitting at the end right now."

His words were firm enough, but his voice also was as controlled as Jay Aman's.

"I'm surprised you should be, Guildmaster," said Bleys. "What's that old saying—'you can't make a cake without flour'? If there's to be any discussion of this world's future, along with the other New Worlds—as I rather expect there might be—the CEOs may be the shortening, and you may be the sugar, but certainly the People of the Shoe represent the job-holders who're the flour—the largest and most important ingredient of the cake that's New Earth's population."

"Perhaps," said Hytry, "but like our friends across the table, again, I didn't realize we'd come here for any kind of discussion of our World's people, or for any reason that would call for representatives from various parts of it. Also, we Guildmasters have always thought of ourselves as representing the job-holder. After all, that's why the Guilds were formed, to protect and help the job-holder."

"So I've been told," Bleys said. "But haven't you ever asked yourself whether your Guilds might not have evolved from King Log into King Stork over the years?"

"They've certainly done no such thing!" said Hytry.

"Haven't they?" Bleys said.

His trained voice gave the words a cutting edge. Hytry's face paled as Harley Nickolaus' had darkened from a similar emotion. But whatever else the Guildmaster had been about to say, he held back, possibly from a distaste for being also unceremoniously excluded from the room. Clearly, Bleys thought, Hytry was showing little faith in his fellow Guildmasters' getting up and walking out with him, if he threatened to leave.

"In that case," Bleys went on, "I'm sorry for you and Harley Nick-olaus. With the future we have before us, the very bright future we have before us, the most clear-sighted of leaders will be needed; and I'd always counted you among them."

Hytry stared back, slightly pop-eyed and uncertain, but still keeping his silence. *Two down.*

For now, at least, Bleys had the attention of the effective leaders of the Guild and CEOs' contingent fixed on him. He must use the oppor-tunity while he had it.

"In fact," he said, turning his attention to all those around the table, "that's my hope for every one of you. Because leaders like that are going to be needed. It's not just my point of view. Speaking as a representative of another World, I can honestly say we're concerned, in our own interest, that our other New World neighbors do well in the years ahead; and that those who direct affairs on each World are not only clear-sighted but capable individuals, sensitive and responsive to the people on their planet as a whole. Not to just one class, segment or organization on it."

Bleys paused, but none of those sitting there seemed to feel like answering.

"I take it you feel the way I do—as leaders on any World have to feel," he went on calmly. "So I'd like to talk to you, particularly, about this bright future I mention so much and so often to so many people."

Bleys looked for signs of impatience. For the moment, however, all the visible faces before him seemed only waiting and listening.

"Clearly," he said, "the time has come that the Exotics talked about—when, as separate Worlds, we could start to decay. Happily, the historic pattern that builds forward with every moment of human history and every action by every individual alive at that moment, is moving us all in exactly the right direction to cope with that."

There was a new interest now on the faces—and some puzzlement. Bleys continued.

"In the case of New Earth, it seems to me, the connection's already partly made for a more structured three-world social unit, with New Earth as trainer of engineers for new technology—technology taken to the point of practical production by Cassida, and originating before that as discoveries or ideas on Newton."

"I repeat," said Hytry, now in a firmer voice, "this is not at all what we came here to talk about."

"But *we* did!" said Anjo, suddenly and strongly from the far end of the table. "It's your working to fit our World in with Cassida and Newton that's made you try to push the job-holder farther and farther down toward being a slave!"

"I deny that!" Hytry snapped.

"Why bother?" Jay Aman said, calmly. "The job-holders are always complaining. This is just one of their standard lines, tailored to fit the present circumstance."

"Of course," said Anjo, turning on Jay, "you of the CEOs and the Guilds have been hand in glove in this whole process. You deliberately used this antagonism you pretended to have, like two millstones to grind the job-holders to dust between them."

"Rhetoric!" said Jay.

"Rhetoric to a certain extent, maybe," Bleys said before Anjo could answer, "but it seems to me there's also a certain amount of truth there. In fact, it seems to me there's a certain amount of truth and falsity in the positions of all three of your groups."

He looked down at the end of the table to meet Anjo's eyes himself.

"All three of you," Bleys repeated slowly.

Anjo's face did not express whatever reaction he might have been feeling. It was simply intent and ready as he matched gazes with Bleys.

Bleys' opinion of him went up a notch. *Three down*—no, the third cooperative, for the moment at least.

"I have to say I've more sympathy for the job-holders at the moment," Bleys went on. "They've certainly been the ones to suffer visibly, as far as their individual struggle to survive goes. You CEOs and Guildmasters have, on the other hand, had certain special benefits from your efforts. Where you've suffered, without knowing it, is in justification for the existence of your organizations, and the raising of the question of whether your own existence in the world of the future will be justified."

"You know, First Elder," said Jay, toying with the stylus beside a pad of paper on the table in front of him, "this is all rather abstract and theoretical. In our real world of New Earth—"

"In your New World of New Earth," Bleys interrupted him sharply, over-riding him both with tone and volume that made Jay's voice seem thin by contrast, "selfish concerns with personal advantage—and again this includes the People of the Shoe as well as the CEO's and the Guilds— have ended up pushing this planet to the point of open revolution!"

He had let a little anger surface in his voice; and he knew his face was showing it. Jay, who had opened his mouth, closed it again.

"If you'll look at the patterns cyclically repeated in the historic record," Bleys went on, in a calmer voice, "what's most likely now is an outbreak by the job-holders; their taking control of this world, and that control becoming more and more tyrannical—to the point where former CEOs and Guildmasters end up being brought to trial for past crimes against the New Earth people. You face a modern replay of what went on during the revolution in France on Old Earth, back at the end of the eighteenth century. To put it in more simple terms, the job-holders have suffered a low-level, long-term series of adverse effects from the last hundred years of New Earth history; while the Guilds and the CEOs have essentially saved up theirs for a shorter but much more intense moment of backlash from their actions."

"This is nonsense," Jay murmured to the stylus and the paper in front of him.

"Nonsense?" said Bleys. "Look at the people at the far end of the table there, Jay Aman. Take a long, open-eyed look at them. Then tell me you can't imagine the people sitting there would never decide your neck should be put under the blade of a guillotine—assuming an archaic machine like that might be revived for use on present-day New Earth, a few years from now."

Jay lifted his eyes from the paper, looked at Bleys and smiled; then deliberately turned his face to look at those at the end of the table. He gazed for a long moment—in fact, for more than a long moment—and, subtly, his features changed, lost their confidence; and his features became merely blank, so that his eyes remained locked with the unchanging attention on him from the end of the table, as if he was unable to look elsewhere. *Four down.*

"And you, Anjo, and the others looking at Jay Aman, right now," Bleys said, "can you promise everyone here that, if not you, others in the organization of the Shoe might not be ready to commit such judicial mass murder?"

The other Shoe people, beside Anjo, stared at Bleys.

"What you mean . . . " began the blonde, and fell silent. *Three more.* Seven all told.

"What he means," said Anjo, still watching Bleys, "is, we shouldn't only think about that, but ahead to the point where our own People of the Shoe would condemn us—us four, here now—and put *our* necks in the noose. But why're you so sure all this is going to happen, Bleys Ahrens? There have to be reasonable solutions to our situation. We don't *have* to have bloody revolution."

"For one thing—" Jay Aman broke in—"there are other solutions that don't involve revolution, but are equally bloody—"

He broke off deliberately, with a smile, in mid-sentence.

The heads of all those in the room had turned to Jay, to Orville Learner and the blur-headed individual sitting with them; for it was the CEOs who had officially begun the importation of the fifty thousand soldiers from the Friendlies, over half of which were already here. Jay had made the point that he or Harley had come here to make; but, Bleys was sure, ahead of the moment either one of the two had planned. The moment of climax near the meeting's end would have been their natural choice.

All down now—with the possible exception of blur-head, who had undoubtedly been expecting it. But the attention was all on Jay at this moment. That would need to be changed.

Bleys waited, giving them a moment to look. Then he spoke, before Jay could go on.

"—However, Jay Aman, I think it'd be a waste of time for us to consider any such solution, since there's one alternative that wouldn't be bad for anyone and would take the momentum of the present historic evolution, making sure it goes onward and upward to a better life for everyone on New Earth."

Their heads turned back to him; but slowly, most of their attention still on Jay.

"I wouldn't be here talking to you all now, if this alternative wasn't possible," said Bleys; "but it has to be part of a general all-New-Worlds effort. No one World, and no alliance of several worlds only, can make it work. It will need all, working together. The pattern of history has moved to a point where the predicted disintegration and decay will either pull down all of us—or none. What I see, in fact, is an ideal solution, but it calls for two hard decisions from every individual on all the New Worlds."

He stopped, giving them the chance to interrupt; but none of them did, including Jay, who was waiting calmly, with a small, satisfied smile on his face.

"One," Bleys said, "is ending for all time the attempts to dominate us by Old Earth, which has never really given up its dream of keeping the New Worlds as colonies.

"The second, by individuals and societies, is to face the fact that they have to remake themselves. They have to commit themselves to developing abilities they've forgotten they had; or face being discarded from the race. The people on some worlds—like the Dorsai and the two Exotic Worlds, unfortunately—I'm afraid are beyond saving. We'll probably have to leave them to their own natural end. But the rest of us—all of us—can live, flourish and grow forever if we go at it right. Properly handled, our future can disregard those three worlds."

All eyes—even Jay's—were on Bleys now. The names "Dorsai" and "Exotics"—those two legendary and still-potent powers among the New Worlds—had triggered off what was in effect a historic reflex. Even now, when nearly a century had passed, the wealth and acumen of the Exotics, the military powers of the Dorsai, could still possibly rise, like giants from their sleep, to spoil the best-made plans of any people on one or even all of the other New Worlds.

At last, Bleys held each of them at the table, like the Ancient Mariner . . .

> . . . with his glittering eye—
> The Wedding Guest stood still,
> And listens like a three years' child:
> The Mariner hath his will . . .

Chapter 45

Suddenly the atmosphere in the room was different. What Bleys had just said had painted some inherited, but still vivid, pictures in the minds of those at the table.

The two Exotic planets and the Dorsai no longer occupied the thoughts of people on other New Worlds the way they once had, when those three worlds were the ones to consider in any interstellar situation for the other human-occupied planets. But the images were still there. Images of the Exotics with their almost wizardly business skills and wealth in interstellar currency. Images of the legendary Dorsai, from a world of which it was said that the Grey Captains—as the leading mercenary commanders there were called—could, if they chose to band together rather than hiring themselves out separately, have raised a trained military force that all of the other inhabited Worlds together would not have been able to stand against.

Those around the table might utter public regrets over anything that damaged the society of any other New World. But behind the old fears was a deep desire to see both the Exotics and the Dorsai brought down to a position below all the rest of them.

Bleys had led both Jay and Anjo to expose their high cards; evidently, Hytry had none. Now was the time to wind things up.

"So," Bleys said, speaking into their silence, "we've got two jobs before us. One is the re-organization of the individual; the other is the re-organization of all the New Worlds into a single social unit."

He paused to give anyone there a chance to respond; but they were still held and silent, absorbing what he was saying.

"Achieving the second of these things, the re-organization of the Worlds, will lead us whether we like it or not, to a final confrontation with Old Earth; and necessarily putting an end for all time to her attempts to influence us, particularly through the Final Encyclopedia. To win that battle—and we have to win or be forgotten by history—we've got to begin a process of re-arming now. So that when we do confront her, it will be with enough power to back up what we say. Bear in mind: Earth's population still outnumbers that of all our New Worlds combined, if we subtract the Exotics and Dorsai from our social group—which, as I say, unfortunately we'll have to—"

For the first time there was a break in the motionlessness of his audience. The figure with the head-blur had moved slightly the arm he or she had been resting on the table next to the pad and stylus there. Bleys went forward rapidly without pausing.

"Happily, in this, my Other organizations can help. The people in them have been trained—and many more are going to have to be trained, to work with them—as a cooperative management system to tie their organizations on all the New Worlds together. It may sound too ambitious; to suggest tying our Worlds as a whole together the same way. But, in fact, I think there are parallels."

He took time out to let his last words sink in.

"As I said earlier, the historic pattern's been moving in the direction of a single New Worlds Society, anyway. There's the example of a three-world combination in this world with Cassida and Newton. The only drawback to it at the moment is that the plans have mostly been made by Newton—which hopes to control all the other New Worlds itself. What I work for is a community of Worlds in which no one World dominates all others. But what Newton's been doing for over half a century won't be wasted, since the alignment's already there. It'll require a shift of attitude in some people, though—don't you agree with me, Pieter DeNiles?"

The person with the blur where a head should be suddenly lost that blur; and the face of the man Bleys had met on Cassida emerged. The head and neck belonging to the face now betrayed how, indeed, the upper part of the jacket had been padded to hide the thin, stooped shoulders of age.

Bleys had noticed on Cassida how his face had been quick to smile, and how deep the smile wrinkles were around the corners of DeNiles' eyes under the graying eyebrows. Those eyes were now literally twinkling with amusement.

"I wondered how long it would take you to make the connection," he said.

The spell binding those around the table was broken. Bleys was no longer the center of the attention. They were all staring at DeNiles.

"It was the only reasonable conclusion," Bleys said. "I expected you here for this meeting. You made one mistake when we met on Cassida. It wasn't necessary to rub your frailty into me by having one of your attendants make an angry remark about the way I'd tired you out when we walked from your building to those trees. That was overdoing it. The attendants might have showed their resentment in many ways; but having one of them put the lesson in words to someone like me was bound to make me question it."

"I *am* old," Pieter said, "and that walk to the trees was rather hard on me, particularly keeping up with those long legs of yours—even if you did slow down."

"I'm sure it was," Bleys said. "But the impression you wanted me to have was that you were too old and frail to do anything like take a working trip to another New World. Only that could have been the reason for so much emphasis on your weakness; but I didn't actually begin to lose my last sense of doubt until I came in from that balcony on Newton, the evening Council meeting, after hearing and seeing a figure with a blurred head sitting there—" he turned to the others around the table—"forgive me, I should introduce the person you now see. Pieter DeNiles, Cassidan born, but apparently an invaluable voice in the Laboratories Review Council on Newton—if an anonymous one. Normally he attends Council meetings there under the name of 'the Gentleman.' "

"I don't think—" Jay Aman began; but Pieter cut him short.

"Don't make yourself seem any more foolish than you already have," Pieter said. "The First Elder already knows all about our connection with you CEOs. He could hardly miss it. It wouldn't take a Bleys Ahrens to figure out that, while the CEOs might be well off, raising the international currency to make an immediate payment on a contract for fifty thousand Friendly troops would be something that might be beyond CEOs' means."

"I'll have you know we have—"

Jay's voice was cut short again by DeNiles.

"As I said, don't make yourself look any more foolish," Pieter said. "Undoubtedly you can pay such a bill—eventually; but there's a tremendous difference between having that kind of credit on record and being able to draw down on it at short notice, to pay what you had to agree to pay to the Friendlies' government on that kind of contract. You needed us. Not that it makes much difference because you'd have had us helping you, anyway. First Elder, I think while you'll have some trouble convincing some of these New Earth people to go your way, Newton's populace is nowhere near that vulnerable. The social connections Newton has been setting up now for a matter of generations are firmly in place."

"Convincing isn't the word!" Jay almost shouted. His expression had changed, and his voice had begun to reach a pitch rather like that heard from his uncle before. "Speaking for the CEOs, we aren't bound to anyone, including Newton, even if we are somewhat in debt to them; and we don't intend to be bound to your plan either, Bleys Ahrens. Apparently—" he looked at Bleys and then DeNiles with white anger—"the two of you think you're the only ones who can make plans and carry them out successfully over a period of time. My uncle's not the fool that many people take him for; and even before his time, the CEOs were thinking ahead. It was inevitable that sooner or later the CEOs had to completely own New Earth—"

"I dispute that!" Hytry cried. "Our Guilds—"

"Your Guilds were never anything but unions for a bunch of sheep that don't know their own minds!" Jay snapped. "Except for your Guildhouses and your titles, you're no different from the People of the Shoe. It's the CEOs who own the corporations. It's the CEOs who control the planetary government. And it's the CEOs who are going to bring not only Newton and Cassida, but all the other worlds into line!"

Jay paused and calmed with surprising rapidity. He looked around the table slowly.

"All we ever needed," he said quietly, "was our own army. And now—we've got that."

They were all watching him. He let them sit for a moment and absorb his last words. Then he almost smiled.

"In fact," he said, "our planning has always run far ahead of that of two other people you've just been listening to at this table. That's something that ought to be of particular interest to you Guilders and you Shoes. You'd better face the fact that you may have been betting on the wrong horse. As an example of CEOs thinking ahead, I'll tell you now I arranged for the Commander of the Friendly troops on our World to come here shortly after this meeting was to start; and say he'd wait until it was over, so he could speak to me. I'll call him in now."

He lifted his wrist control pad to his lips.

"This is Jay Aman," he said, and his voice came back at them from the intercom structure in the walls and ceiling, "Marshal, would you come in now?"

He lowered his arm again to the table without waiting for an answer, reached to an inside pocket of his jacket and came out with a folded handkerchief, with which he wiped his lips. Behind him one of the doors to the room slid open, and Marshal Cuslow Damar stepped through it. He took a couple of paces into the room to stand behind Jay's chair.

"You sent for me, Mr. Chairman?" he asked the back of Jay's head. He looked exactly the same as he had when Bleys had seen him the day before. His uniform, his way of standing, even the expression on his competent face and an evident willingness to listen to anything, was the same.

Jay swung half-about in his chair so that he could look momentarily at the Marshal.

"We don't use that title in public, Damar," he said. "You'll have to learn that."

"My apologies, Jay Aman." said Cuslow, his tone of voice also unchanged.

"Granted—this time," Jay said. He swung back to face those at the table. "What I brought you here to do, Damar, is to stand there and tell these people if what I say agrees with what you know—that is, if I ask you whether it does."

"A pleasure, Jay Aman."

"For those of you who don't know him—that, of course, excludes the First Elder—the man behind me now is Marshal Cuslow Damar, commander of the troops we've just bought from the Friendlies. Actually, he was born right here on New Earth; but his father moved the whole family to one of the Friendlies—Harmony, I believe—when the Marshal was only eight years old. I don't remember just what age the Marshal is now, but it's a fair number of years ago since he was taken to Harmony. I mention this just to show how we of the CEOs plan ahead."

No one offered to question or dispute the information. Jay went on.

"Damar, is that correct?"

"Yes, Jay Aman."

"His father had a mission," Jay went on, dabbing his lips again with the handkerchief, "a mission for us. It was to live on Harmony and raise his family there. The Marshal was the third son, I believe, and they all went into the military; but the oldest two ran into accidents and died. The Marshal here, however, survived. He rose through the officer ranks to high command. When we talked to the Friendly government about buying these troops, we asked them to send, if possible, a commanding officer who had knowledge or experience with New Earth. Naturally, they sent us Damar. Correct, Damar?"

"Exactly correct, Jay Aman."

"Yes," said Jay. "You know, Damar, we consider anyone who was born on New Earth a citizen of it forever, so you know that you're actually a citizen of New Earth?"

"I've always known that, Jay Aman."

"As a matter of fact, I believe most of your family is back here now. Aren't they, Damar?"

"That's right, Jay Aman."

"In fact, I believe even his father is among them," Jay went on, but this time to the people around the table. "We have them under guard— protective guard, of course. Your father just returned recently, didn't he, Damar?"

"He got a message my sister was very sick," said Cuslow, "so he decided to come back. Happily, it turned out when he got here she wasn't as ill as he'd assumed from the message. In fact, I think he's got passage booked back to Harmony in a couple of weeks."

"All in good time, Damar." Jay was still looking at those around the table. "It's a great expense, even for a successful merchant like your father, to be taking spacecraft interworld like this. Let's see if we can't persuade him to stay and enjoy his native world a while longer. We intend to take care of him, you know; along with all the rest of your family, in spite of all the years he spent on Harmony. In fact, in spite of his becoming, necessarily we hope, among the most religious of those religious-minded Friendlies. And he did become just that, didn't he, Damar?"

"My father became a True Faith-Holder," said Damar. "This was acknowledged by all who knew him on Harmony. I've always told people there how proud I was of him and how I hoped someday to be worthy of achieving such faith myself."

"I'm sure you did, Damar," Jay said to the table. "However, at the moment I've got a duty for you. We've got two off-planet visitors here in this room. One of them, of course, is Bleys Ahrens, First Elder of the Friendlies, and the other's a visitor from Newton—just look for the oldest person here—a *'Gentleman'* named Pieter DeNiles. Our government has just decided these two are now persona non grata on New Earth; and accordingly you'll make arrangements now—I assume you brought some other military people with you?"

"I've some aides and a few enlisted men with me, who could come if I called them, Jay Aman."

"Yes, well, then, possibly you ought to do that now. I don't think Pieter DeNiles will give you any trouble; but the First Elder has rather made a fetish of physical exercise and might do something foolish. We wouldn't want him to get hurt—it might create an interstellar incident. So call your men in and escort the two off-planet now, by the first vessel headed interstellar. They can make their own arrangements from wherever it takes them."

"Just a moment," Bleys said. He reached inside his jacket and brought out a bound sheaf of paper which was the copy of the contract the Marshal had given him earlier. "I think you'd better have another look at your contract before you do anything drastic, Mr. Chairman."

He skidded the bound sheets down the tabletop to Jay, who knocked them aside.

"I don't need to look at it! I already know what's in it."

Jay produced his handkerchief and dabbed at his lips again, then went on more calmly.

"I think you're the one who might be surprised by that contract, Bleys Ahrens. We went over it very carefully, with the best of our legal experts. It contains all the points we demanded from the Friendly government. All of them. Damar, you have your orders."

"Indeed, Jay Aman," said Damar, "there's only the matter of consulting with my superior about a diplomatic matter like this."

Jay's face, which had by now recovered its usual color, went white again. His mouth twisted, and he spun about in his seat.

"What do you mean?" he said. "I'm your superior! I own you and your people! Do you understand that? I own you, all your military *and* your family. Particularly your family. Hasn't that penetrated your skull?"

"Indeed it has," Damar said. But now he was speaking over Jay's head to Bleys. "First Elder, do I have your permission to execute this order?"

"I think not in this case, Marshal," Bleys said. "I think Jay Aman— or the Chairman—whichever address he prefers—might be a little confused."

He looked from Damar to Jay.

"Jay Aman—or Mr. Chairman—" he said, "you really should look at that contract again. This time, you might keep in mind that it's modeled on a Dorsai contract; and the Dorsai have had a couple of hundred years of practice in making out military contracts. I'm saying nothing against your legal advisors, of course. But I think you'll find in there that the one who commands the Friendly troops on Harmony, if it comes down to a matter of making a decision for the use of any of them, is the superior Friendly official on the world at that time. I happen to be the one on New Earth at this moment."

Jay stared at him, unmoving and wordless, the handkerchief now crumpled but still held in one of his fists.

His lips moved slightly, but no sound came out. He swung about to face Cuslow Damar again.

"Did you hear me?" he said. "Do I have to remind you of your duty again—and your family? Particularly your father?"

"I love my family deeply," Cuslow said; and now there was emotion in his voice. "Above all, I love my father and would do anything to keep him and the others safe. But I have always striven to walk in his footsteps; and he, himself, would say that my duty to God comes first. And that duty requires me to obey the command of my superior, who is the First Elder, at the moment. Neither to God nor my superiors will I fail in my duty."

"Mr. Chairman—" Bleys said softly—and Jay spun back to face him across the table. "Did you really think the Friendly Worlds would lease you our children if their Commander was not a true man of the faith? I think you'd better look in that contract. Page seven, the section marked 'COMMAND AND DISPOSAL OF TROOPS UNDER CONTRACT.' "

Staring at him, Jay reached out blindly, closed his fingers on the sheet of paper he had knocked aside and pulled it to him. He turned pages.

"I think the eighth line down," said Bleys, "is where you'll find the words—beyond a colon, there—'... *the troops under contract shall be under the command of the senior officer present and his superiors, including the authorities on Harmony and Association who are committed to the supplying of the troops earlier enumerated.'* "

Jay Aman's eyes ran down the page and stopped. He looked up at Bleys again.

"I see it," he said; "What about it?"

"Jay Aman," Cuslow said behind Jay's head, "the First Elder is my superior officer."

If Jay's face had paled before, it became almost completely drained of blood now. He stared at Bleys.

"You see," said Bleys, "the Dorsai, as I said, have been honing contracts like these for a couple of centuries, now. Early in their time of supplying mercenaries on contract to other worlds, they were often cheated by contractees who tried to take control of the Dorsai troops with a commander of their own; on the argument that the only Dorsai left alive to command the troops was of inferior rank to their general commander, or some such excuse."

He paused, watching Jay's face; but Jay only continued to stare.

"To get around this," Bleys went on, "it became a Dorsai practice to name some extra senior commanders who did not go out with the immediate shipment of troops; but remained on the Dorsai, available to go wherever someone was trying to do something like this and take over command. Pending their arrival, the troops would operate only under the standing orders which you'll find enumerated at the very end of the contract. You can look those up, too, if you like; but briefly what they say is that even if they're down to one enlisted man, he—by definition—is acting commander of the existing forces under contract, until a more senior officer arrives."

While Jay still sat unmoving, the door behind him opened again. Two majors, a lieutenant and four enlisted men in the uniform of the Friendly expeditionary force came through and stood behind Cuslow Damar. The sound stirred Jay finally and made him turn. He stared at them, then turned back to Bleys.

"This is all non—" he began, then stopped.

"Marshal," said Bleys, standing up, "I think I've done as much as I usefully can here. Neither Pieter DeNiles nor I will need to be escorted off-planet; though I imagine we'll each be leaving soon, in any case. You might alert an Honor Guard on stand-by basis for me."

He looked around the table.

"One more thing," he said. "Marshal, from this point on, you'll take advice—advice only—when necessary, from Ana Wasserlied, the Head of the Others organization on this world; whom I now appoint my deputy; and if you need direct contact with any of the influential groups represented here, speak to Anjo for the People of the Shoe, Edgar Hytry for the Guildmasters, Jay Aman for the CEOs—and in case the matter of Newton or Cassida should come up at all, with Pieter DeNiles, if he's still here—or, if he's not, the chief diplomatic representatives of Newton or

Cassida. Now, good afternoon to you all. Marshal, you and those with you might as well come with me."

He walked away from the end of the table toward the waiting officers.

"I think I'll go with you," Pieter said, pushing back his float-chair and standing up. "Wait for me, please."

He caught up with them just as the officers were standing back to let Bleys go first. Just before he passed through the door, however, Jay called after him.

"Wait!" he shouted. "Speak to me? After this, you want them to speak to *me?* Why?"

"Because you're the most capable of the CEOs," Bleys answered, without looking back.

He went out. Pieter DeNiles, Cuslow Damar and the other soldiers followed; and the closing door shut out sight of all those in the room behind them.

Bleys and those with him had stepped into an adjoining lounge, empty of people, the yellow walls of which picked up the now-full mid-afternoon sunlight. Bleys turned away from that sunlight to go through a further door in the wall beyond, and they followed him into the hall down which he had come originally to join the meeting.

"If you'd slow down a bit . . . " said DeNiles.

Bleys checked his stride and waited for the older man. The officers, including Cuslow, had politely kept pace behind the two of them. When they were once more all together, Bleys went on more slowly; and a little way down the hall they turned in through another door into the general lounge of the suite's main entrance.

"I've got to sit down," said Pieter.

"Certainly," said Bleys, guiltily conscious that, without his thinking, from habit his legs had lengthened their stride again. He reached out to grasp a chair-float and pull it to Pieter, who dropped into it with a small sigh of relief.

Bleys found another float for himself.

"Marshal," he said, sitting down, facing Pieter, "Pieter DeNiles will probably be going back to his hotel. After that he'll want freedom from interference by New Earthmen until he leaves."

He glanced at Pieter, who nodded.

"Perhaps you might get together three or four officers and some men to stay in touch with him and make sure he has an easy time of it and gets off all right."

"I'll arrange that right away, First Elder," said Cuslow, and went over to a thin, tall and very straight-backed, young officer, who was standing talking to Toni.

"Thank you," said Pieter. "How did you know it was me in there?"

"You didn't make it easy for me," Bleys said. "By the way, congratulations on your performance as Jack, the anonymous double member—both for our Others and for the CEO Club. It couldn't have been easy to not only move, but talk, like someone with a half-century's-less life experience than you."

"I was an actor—a professional actor—for a while, years ago," Pieter said mildly. "But you haven't answered my question."

"I didn't connect you with Jack until I walked with you on Cassida. Even then, it was hard to believe it. But the leg movements had the same signature," said Bleys. "In the case of Jack, you remember, I'd sent you all away just so I could see you and Jill walk out of the room. If you were a professional actor, you must have been told that the hardest thing about oneself to disguise is the manner of walking. You walked naturally, in a way that suited your age, when I was with you on Cassida, as you did here. But the movements were alike enough to give you away."

"You didn't see me walk on Newton," said Pieter.

"No, but you were clearly the dominating factor in that Council Room, and entirely too intelligent to let the Council follow that foolish plan of Half-Thunder's unless you knew a great deal about me. Enough to think I stood a good chance of surviving such an attack; and if you had been that interested in me for some time, I suspected you were looking for someone like me—just as I was looking for someone like you. Combine that with what I said there and the earlier effort made to make me think you couldn't travel interworld; and I could be pretty sure you'd be at any meeting like this where you knew I'd be. All you had to do was come here and wait."

"I came when the first of your Friendly Soldiers arrived," Pieter said. "But you say you were looking for someone like me? Why?"

"I assumed there had to be someone tying all three worlds together. After the amok attack on me, I was pretty sure it was you. If it was, I could almost predict how you would react in the meeting we've just left. You did."

"I believe I did," said Pieter, and sighed. "I'm definitely getting old."

"I don't agree," said Bleys. "Multiple contact is always dangerous to secrecy, and you'd have wanted to see me in action. Also, it must have been incredibly hard for you to move like a young person when you were walking away from me on New Earth."

"It was," Pieter said. "It required taking some rather uncomfortable medication before I met you, so I could override the limitations of my body as it presently is, for even a few moments. Once the door was closed behind us, I pretended to turn my ankle; and Jill—whoever he or she was—helped me back to my own transportation. But maybe you knew about that, too?"

"I didn't," Bleys answered. "By the way, are you Cassidan? Or are you really a Newtonian?"

"Oh, I'm Cassidan," Pieter said. He had his breath back, evidently; for he spoke with relative ease in spite of looking rather small and frail as he sat in the chairfloat. "But the best minds are on Newton and that drew me there—though I'm not a scientist or researcher myself."

"If that Council of theirs on Newton is a sample of their best minds," said Bleys, "you must have been disappointed."

"No," said Pieter, "and yes. No, I wasn't disappointed. And yes, you're right. The Council has never been made up of people from the top class of Newton's minds—you can't pry the top people away from their work. But from just below the top class—and even just below that—those with a hunger for political power end up on the Council. So, yes to that last part of your question. The Council would have been disappointing to me, too, if they'd represented the best Newton had to offer. But for the actual best on Newton, I've been willing to work all my life—though most of them hardly know I exist. The best may be few, but they're valuable; and they need whatever's necessary to get their work done." He paused to smile at Bleys.

"Now you tell me. I was listening to your general aims, just now in there, with a great deal of interest. What are your larger intentions toward Newton and Cassida?"

"You were probably the only one there who was," said Bleys. "Everyone else was concerned only with what might affect them, personally and directly."

"Probably natural of them," Pieter said. "But I've lived long enough to know that if someone sneezes on Old Earth, eventually someone on Newton catches a cold. But, you haven't answered me. What, specifically, are your intentions toward Newton?"

"The same as my intentions toward New Earth or any other of these Worlds," Bleys answered. "I don't intend to interfere with the local social machinery—or, rather, I'll interfere as little as possible. Whoever's governing can go on governing, if they've the capability for it. But I want to see all the New Worlds combine and head in the right direction. As I may have said, either in the meeting just now or to you on Cassida, I'm a philosopher. All I want is to spread the point of view of my philosophy as widely as possible and have it accepted by as many people as will do that."

"That's a reasonable view, of course," Pieter said.

Cuslow Damar had returned. Standing beside Bleys, he leaned down to attract Bleys' attention.

"First Elder," he said, "I—"

Chapter 46

Bleys woke to dimness. It was as it had been each time before—a sudden transition, as if no time at all had passed—except for the fact that now he had not wakened to find himself talking uncontrollably. Gloom enclosed him again like a thick fog; in which he could see no figures, not even the comforting one of Toni that he had become used to finding there.

"No!" he exploded, out loud. "Don't tell me I just dreamed about getting well—"

The figure of Toni did resolve out of the dimness, then. He saw her mistily, but close beside him; and her voice came strongly and comfortingly.

"No," she said. "It was just a blackout."

"Just a blackout?" Bleys could not put his finger on how he felt. It was disagreeable, but there was no focus to it. It was not pain, but a sort of unpleasant universal feeling all through him. A general unclearness and stupidness clogged his thinking; and suddenly a sensation very close to panic pounced and fastened its claws on him. "Did I collapse? Did Pieter DeNiles, or any of the soldiers see me collapse, or act strangely—anything like that?"

"No," said Toni's voice, "Cuslow and his officers left; then one officer and some enlisted men left with DeNiles. You seemed just as usual, then. You said you were a little tired and you were going to take a nap. You lay down, and later, when we went to find you, we couldn't wake you. We got Kaj, and he said it was to be expected. He had warned you that episodes like this would occur from time to time. You remember—I asked you if you were all right and reminded you what Kaj said before you went into the meeting. They're supposed to be less and less frequent, though, as time goes on."

"I can't afford"—Bleys broke off—"but you're sure no one noticed anything?"

"I'm sure," Toni said.

"Good. That's all that matters, then."

Toni said nothing—pointedly.

But Bleys felt a tremendous relief. The dimness became more dim around him. Then brightened, then dimmed again.

"Can you hear me?" It was the voice of Kaj Menowsky. Some time seemed to have passed. Bleys was vaguely aware that although he could really see nothing but the dimness and their two blurred figures, his surroundings had changed. His voice rang in his ears as if it echoed off walls more close to him than the ones that had surrounded him when he had been speaking previously.

"Yes," said Bleys. "Where am I now?"

"That's good," Kaj said. "You're more conscious of what's about you than at any time before. You're on board ship, on your way back to Harmony. Now tell me. How much stress did you have before and at this meeting?"

Bleys' mind pondered the question. He seemed to think for a long time, but either Kaj was very patient or it was not as long as he thought.

"I suppose," he said at last, "you'd say it was all stressful, from the time the meeting was set. But I didn't feel stressed—at any time. I simply felt as if I was operating at top power."

He hesitated, thinking of his talk with Pieter DeNiles.

"Some unexpected developments came up after I left the meeting— but they were very welcome developments."

"But there was prolonged stress?"

"Yes," said Bleys. "How can you have any kind of situation like that without stress?"

"Tell me about the situation," said Kaj. But now he was evidently talking to Toni because Bleys could no longer see him and his voice seemed aimed in a different direction. He was aware of Toni answering, without his actually being able to make out the words she was using; and he drifted off again.

Then he woke to the fact that Kaj was with him once more.

"Can you hear and understand me all right?" asked Kaj.

"Certainly," said Bleys; and in fact, it seemed to him that the dimness was better lit than it had been before—or perhaps his eyes were focusing better. The figures of both Kaj and Toni were less fuzzy and imprecise.

"I should tell you," Kaj said, "you've got to choose between what you call top speed and this kind of reaction, but I'd be wasting my breath, wouldn't I?"

"Yes," said Bleys.

"I thought so. These blackouts," said Kaj, "will be coming from time to time, as I told you. Don't try to fight them. I suspect you're instinctively trying to fight this one. Don't. Just relax and ride along with it. The less you bring them on—and the more you're able to accept them, the better chance you'll have that they'll become shorter, easier and trouble you less and less."

"But how long—" Bleys started, and then could not think how to phrase the ending of his sentence the way he wanted.

"How long will they bother you?" Kaj said. "That depends on you. What you do and what kind of person you are. I can't tell you that. It all depends on how much real damage you sustained, how good you are at repairing yourself—mentally, emotionally and physically—and probably on a certain amount of individual genetic strength, which we don't know yet how to measure. You'd be wise to just accept these episodes for the indefinite future—a matter of some years, perhaps, before they cease completely. In fact, what will probably happen is that you'll realize one day you haven't had a blackout, or any other such problem, for a matter of some years. Then you'll have to think back to when it actually ended. Because the exact moment of its ending will be invisible, in the end."

"I see," said Bleys. But secretly, inside himself, the determination had already formed that he would find a way of mending himself, some way of self-repair more effective than Kaj expected. He had handled everything else he had come up against in life. He would handle this.

Whether or not this decision was a factor, from then on he did recover with a rapidity that was at least gratifying—if not startling—to those around him. From the moment of his conversation with Kaj, it seemed his recovery from this particular blackout accelerated.

His vision sharpened; and, little by little, at Kaj's instructions, Toni allowed more and more light into the room. Bleys discovered directly why it was good sense to keep it dim, when inadvertently the control command she sent the window wall of his bedroom was overstated, and more light came in than she had intended. It was almost as if the illumination was a solid fist striking him in both eyeballs. He grunted, as one grunts from a powerful and painful unexpected blow. But already Toni had the light back down where it should be, and as quickly as he had felt the impact of sudden brightness, his reaction to it had vanished.

In any case, within twenty-four hours, the room was darkened only slightly; and by that time, he was not merely up to sitting on the edge of his bed, or in the nearby chairfloat, but had reached the point where he was on his feet and pacing—perhaps a little unsteadily, but pacing—back and forth.

"Why can't I leave this room and do some real walking?" he asked Kaj, at this point.

"You probably could," Kaj said. "But I'd rather play safe. Stay here for another twenty-four hours, do anything you want inside the room, but stay close to your bed in case you get to feeling dizzy, or uncomfortable in any way. If you do, I want you to lie down, relax and forget about everything. Just push everything else aside."

"I can do that while I'm walking," Bleys said.

"Nonetheless." Kaj was firm.

So Bleys stayed in the room another twenty-four hours. But he began to have visitors; and while Toni, who had been with him all the time, was still there for most of it, she was now joined by other people. Though in the case of Henry, who was the first of those to get in to see him—she left the room on her own initiative to give him privacy in which to talk to Bleys.

"How are you, Bleys?" Henry sat down by Bleys' bed. He brought the words out as if he was requiring a report from some subordinate, but Bleys was not misled. Long before he was fully grown, he had come to know the inside Henry as well as he knew the outside Henry. Henry was most likely to appear his sternest when he was most deeply stirred by his own personal emotions.

"I'm just fine, Uncle," said Bleys. He knew Henry liked to be called "Uncle" by both him and Dahno, but would not admit this, even to himself—so that he was embarrassed if either one of them did it under any but casual—or special—private and emotional conditions. The particular minute changes in his expression were unreadable now, even by Bleys; but Bleys was satisfied that this was one of the times when Henry accepted and enjoyed being so addressed.

"I'm glad to hear that, Bleys."

"It was just some aftereffects that will crop up from time to time, Kaj says. Looks a little spectacular, but actually I hardly noticed it from the inside."

This was a literal truth because of his blackout; but it was also very much a twisting of the truth as far as his reaction to it, once he was awake enough to realize what had happened to him. Secretly, Bleys regarded anything like the episode that was now passing away from him, as he would have a deadly enemy. Anything like such a disability was to be killed, squashed—destroyed as soon as possible. But it was better not to tell Henry that.

"Good," Henry said briefly.

"But how are you, Uncle?" Bleys asked. "You were wounded, back on Newton, and we haven't really had time to talk."

"Perfectly healed." Henry's tone ended any discussion on that matter.

That was the last mention of what had happened to either of them. He and Henry talked about the surviving Soldiers, the trip back to Harmony, which Bleys could not remember, and the hotel Bleys was now in, which was the same one he had been in on previous occasions, but on a different floor than he had ever been on before. But shortly, Henry took his leave, ordering Bleys to rest and refusing to stay longer and possibly tire him out any more. Actually, Bleys was fretting at being bed-bound and would have enjoyed the company.

Then came Dahno.

Toni had stepped out of the room when Henry had come to talk. But she stayed when Dahno entered; and Bleys noticed that behind Dahno, Henry also slipped back in, and sat down in a float by Toni against the farther wall, forming an unobtrusive, two-member audience.

"How are you?" asked Dahno, dropping his large body onto the chair-float beside the bed on which Bleys was lying—and jacking the seat up to give his legs room to stretch out.

"I'm fine!" Bleys said. "The one we ought to all worry about is Kaj Menowsky. Perhaps we should have him taken off for a general physical and mental examination, with emphasis on an attitude of runaway concern and overprotectiveness. I'm lying here now only as a favor to him. Perhaps I ought to say, a favor to his medician's qualifications."

"Nothing wrong with resting," said Dahno. "It never hurts to play safe."

"A stitch in time saves nine. Prevention is better than cure—that takes care of that subject, and I apologize to Kaj in absentia if I seemed to doubt his wisdom. We can find other things to talk about, can't we?"

Dahno grinned.

"All right," he said. "You're a fox, Brother. Here you had me thinking that you'd folded up, with two-thirds of what you'd set out to do not done; and it turned out you'd done it after all. I was all set to ask you what I should do about Cassida and Newton until you were in shape to start doing things yourself, and now I find you'd taken care of it, after all."

Bleys smiled back at him. "You worked out what happened, then," he said.

"It was pretty plain, once I looked into it closely," Dahno said. "Tell me something. Did you have your eye on Pieter DeNiles from the beginning? Or did he just fall into your hands by lucky chance?"

"Both," said Bleys, thinking back to his climb along the side of the building on Newton to the balcony outside the meeting place of the Newtonian Council. "No, that's not right. We'd have found the possibilities in him, sooner or later. But it was the best thing that could happen that he was here and made one of the CEOs group at the meeting—by the way, you might start a deliberate search on the other worlds for other people who have the same happy combination of intelligence, influence and ability to control matters; but I don't think you'll find many. If we do find some, though, we want to try and use them in our command structure for the single-community of New Worlds. Move them in high up in the ranking with the Others we've been training."

"I've already started to look," Dahno said. "But you're right—we aren't going to find many that good, let alone already in place. I've got to get to know DeNiles better. Now, there's a politician!"

"A statesman," Bleys said.

Dahno brushed this aside with a large hand.

"Statesmanship's only good politics on a grander stage," he said. "But a DeNiles is something to put in a vault and treasure. He could give lessons to Richelieu—the power behind the throne of Louis the Thirteenth—that's the King of France, in ancient times on Old Earth."

"I know about him—Armand-Jean du Plessis, I think you mean," Bleys said. "As you say, DeNiles could be even more capable."

"Well, there you have it. And we've got the advantage of that ability, in having DeNiles himself. Evidently he's willing to lead Cassida and Newton into the net for us without their even realizing it's happening. Beautifully done, Brother. Maybe you'll tell me now how you managed to do it."

"I talked about what I wanted. DeNiles' aims coincide with mine—for the moment, at least—that's all. But how'd you find out he was going to work with us?"

"He called me just before we took you off New Earth this time, when he couldn't get through to you," Dahno said. "He effectively let me know we'd be together—not in so many words, of course. But what did you say, exactly, that captured him?"

"I wouldn't call it capture—with someone like him," Bleys said. "He's still his own man, as he's always been—"

"Just a minute—" Toni interrupted. Bleys looked up to see her and Henry coming toward the bed, with their chairfloats scooting obediently along behind them, like a couple of trained pets. They sat down beside Dahno.

"This sounds like something Henry and I should have a part of," Toni said. "I didn't know you'd recruited DeNiles in any way; and I don't see how you did it in the little time from when the meeting started until he left. Certainly in the meeting—and we three were all listening in on that—there was nothing to indicate it."

"No, it was after the meeting. And I wouldn't call it recruited, either," Bleys said mildly. "What happened, in effect, was that we just had time to make a deal before the blackout hit me. That's one reason I was worried that he or one of the others might have noticed something different about me. If he knew I had a weakness, he's still someone who could exploit it with a vengeance. He's far and away the most capable person I've encountered so far—except for one."

"Hal Mayne," grunted Dahno, "of course."

"Yes," said Bleys. He remembered the bearded figure in the cell on Harmony. "Hal Mayne."

"That boy's an obsession with you," said Dahno. "I've got to meet him, too, someday and find out why you rate him so highly."

"He's not a boy anymore," Bleys said, "and as far as his being the best I've met so far—that's excluding family, of course; I don't worry about you."

He smiled at Dahno.

"I think I could handle him," Dahno said, thoughtfully. "DeNiles, I mean. It would depend, of course, whether the situation we met on was his home ground or mine. And then he's got an edge over me as far as life experience goes. That's two handicaps I'd be carrying, just to start out with. But I think I could do it. I agree with you, though, Bleys; I'd hate to guarantee anything like that."

"I've seen some cracks in him," said Bleys, "and that would work for us, as a weakness in me would for him. You yourself know, Dahno, any crack can be exploited."

"Just a minute," Toni said. "Let's get back on track. You were telling us you made a deal with him, just before you blacked out. I was in the room with you. I didn't hear anything like the two of you coming to an agreement."

"It was all over in the space of a few minutes, if not seconds," said Bley. "He actually made the first offer."

"How?" Toni demanded.

"I didn't mean to keep it a secret from all of you," Bleys said. "It's just that I've been concentrating on getting well and wanting to think through the possibilities. No, he did make the first move. He must already have decided during the meeting that he'd rather not fight me if he didn't have to. He made his offer by telling me what he'd worked for all his life."

"We heard him, listening in on the meeting," said Henry. His eyes had lost whatever gentleness they had held when he had come in to talk to Bleys. "He'd worked for Newton's dominating all of us on all of the other worlds."

"No," said Bleys. "He's worked only for a very small group of people, on Newton alone. He doesn't care about Newton's plans for conquest. He doesn't care who runs Newton. All he cares about is that the best minds among the scientists there are protected and have everything they need. As long as he can make that supply secure, he considers his life worthwhile."

"Interesting," said Dahno.

"Isn't it?" Bleys said. His voice was growing hoarse. He reached out and drank from a water beaker on his bedside table.

"He's dedicated himself to serving them—which, in fact, means he's serving all humanity in the long run," Bleys went on more clearly. "I think, Dahno, he's seen and understood the forward-working of the fabric of history. He just hasn't concentrated on it the way I have. Essentially, he simply wanted me to guarantee that his special scientists would be able to go on working for the race as a whole. I told him that as far as I was concerned, I didn't care who ran the worlds, either; that my goal was a philosophical one. He said that was reasonable—which essentially meant he'd work along with me—then I blacked out."

"The main thing is, he's agreed to work for us," Dahno said.

"With us, not for us," said Bleys.

"Oh, I understand the difference, Bleys, believe me." Dahno said. "I'm glad Toni made you come up with the details though, now; though I'd have dug them out of you, eventually. I think perhaps I ought to try and see DeNiles before he leaves New Earth, from what you say. If you'll forgive me, I'll get a letter spaceshipped off to him now. Start setting up a connection."

He got up from his float-chair.

"Yes," said Bleys. "Good idea."

He rose abruptly, throwing his legs out of the bed, and got to his feet. The same excited, almost-violent surge of expectation was on him that had been in him on Association, just before the lecture tour had started and when he had been waiting to hear how Toni's talk with her father about coming with him on the trip had been settled.

"I don't care what Kaj Menowsky says," he told them. "There's too much to be done, and no real difference between now and twelve or fourteen hours from now. I'm through with that sickbed!"

Chapter 47

The ways by which they had finally come together hardly mattered. Its stages had been so imperceptible and the ultimate conclusion so inevitable, that Bleys, at least, had to put out unusual effort to recall the exact steps of it.

But the exact steps really did not matter. For one thing, the inevitability of their joining had become certain from the moment Bleys became aware that he was compulsively pouring out all his innermost secrets to Toni, as she sat by him during the first stages of his reaction to the genetic antagonist with which Newton had infected him; and that certainty had been fixed in place for all time, later, when succeeding days passed and Toni made no reference at all to what she had heard.

They had drifted together, accordingly, as two bodies in space might approach each other under the pull of their mutual gravity, but without accelerating as they came closer; so that the moment of their joining was not one of violent impact, but as gentle a meeting as that of two free-floating water lilies on the deep but certain current beneath the waters of a slow stream. So that the first time they were in bed together, it was as if they were merely continuing what had gone on over a long period before; and even what was new, was at the same time familiar, expected, comfortable and happy.

For Bleys it was a happiness such as he had never had before in his life, and never imagined having. They lay there in the dim bedroom, relaxed in the comfort of the afterwards, companionably close, side by side and looking up at the tiny lights of the starscape filling the ceiling.

" . . . And how about Hal Mayne, then?" Toni said after a long silence. "What about him?"

"I've been planning on going down to Ahruma tomorrow and seeing him again," Bleys said. "I can't leave him in that cell. I meant to call Barbage and say I was coming two days ago; but all this replanning that we've been doing since Pieter DeNiles became available's kept me here. On the one hand, having Pieter frees up the efforts of our Other organizations on the rest of the Worlds. On the other, it pushes us ahead of schedule—we'll have full use of New Earth, Cassida and Newton much sooner, because of him—even if a lot of the actual connections and controls still have to be put in place."

"You expected as much or more, if you could recruit Hal Mayne," Toni said.

"Yes. I still do," Bleys agreed. "But I've never dared count on him. I'll try again tomorrow, though. If he shows any sign at all of being willing to work with me, I'll open up to him completely—or as completely as I can to anyone . . . "

He turned his head slightly for a moment to look at her profile in the darkness; then brought his eyes back to concentrate on the star points in the ceiling.

"Anyone except you. But then, I don't know, even if I tried, if I could tell someone else as much about myself as I told you."

"No," Toni said quietly. "I don't think you could."

"That's why I was so sure I'd lost you, then," Bleys said. "That's why I'd never dared open up to you at all, before. I was sure you'd be repelled, hearing what I had to do. It's still hard to believe you weren't."

"Of course," she said, still in the same soft voice. "There were things you said that shocked me, but there were other things that counteracted them. One was how wonderful humanity could be, if only it would recognize its possibilities and try to realize them. Always, you said, it had failed in that. Its individual members had ended by going after baubles and toys, each in their own lifetime; and the real effort has to be given to have its effect beyond many lifetimes."

"There's no other way."

"I know there isn't, Bleys-of-mine"—he felt her fingertips gently stroking across his chest—"I know it now. But don't you see, with that end in view, nothing else matters—except that you matter to me."

"That's a ridiculous name for me!" Bleys smiled in the darkness.

"But it's true," she said, "and it's mine for you."

"I know," he said. He reached for her hand without looking, and their fingers intertwined. "As far as I can belong to anyone, I belong to you. But I'm not free to belong completely—to anyone. I'm an artifact of the Historic Pattern. I've always belonged to it and will to the end of my life. It decides what I do. I can't break loose from it any more than I can make myself subject to any other person, group or thing—nor should any person, unless that person wants to. It's one of the ends I work for."

"I knew that a long time ago," Toni said. "Do you remember, back before we left Ecumeny and Association for New Earth at the start of all this, how I told you I had to speak to my father before agreeing to go off-world with you? It was one thing to work for you while you were there on Ecumeny; but it was something else to commit myself to being one of those who helped you anywhere, with anything you decided to do in the future."

"I remember," Bleys said. "I more or less paced the floor, waiting for you to get back and tell me *what* your decision was. I know how strongly Henry feels about certain things, and I was sure your father would feel strongly about some things himself."

"It isn't quite the same," Toni said. "We're a traditionalist family; but the observance of the things we hold important has naturally evolved since my grandfather's great-grandfather left Old Earth. Still, there was the responsibility to our family name—the Ryuoji name—that had to be considered. Following you, I could be risking it; and I had to know whether my father trusted me to do what was right, always."

"But he approved," Bleys said.

" 'Approved' isn't quite the right word," said Toni. "I told him what I believed your aims to be; and that I wanted to be with you and help you reach them."

"And what did he say, exactly?" Bleys asked.

"Inochi o oshimuna—na koso oshime!" Toni answered.

"The language of your father's ancestors is one of the Old Earth tongues I don't know," said Bleys. "What does it mean?"

"It doesn't translate literally in Basic, very well," Toni said. "You have to understand our heritage to understand the meaning of it. Perhaps it could be rendered as *'Put your life at risk, as necessary, but never your name.'* He was trusting me, you see? You do know the French language of Old Earth. Have you ever run across the saying in that tongue, *'Fais ce que dois—adviegne que peut, c'est commande au chevalier.'* "

"Yes," said Bleys, "Conan Doyle quotes it, I think, in his historical novel, *The White Company*—in Basic it would be something like *'Do what you ought, no matter what comes—this is the commandment of the knight.'* "

"Yes," said Toni, "that and my father's words don't both say the same thing, but both have something in common. I've wanted to tell you what he said for a long time. But it's only now that we can talk about such things."

"Yes," said Bleys, "because now you know everything, and you're still with me."

"I know up to the point in time where you stopped talking," Toni said. "Since then, knowing you, I know your plans will have gone on developing, the way they're always changing and developing. Are you still planning not to try bringing either the Dorsai or the Exotics into your community of New Worlds?"

"Yes," Bleys said, "That's something that won't change. Part of the reason is that I can't influence either the Dorsai or Exotic people the way I can those on other Worlds. Another part is the fact that if Dorsai and Exotics come to join us finally—as I hope they will, even if it's several centuries from now—they'll have come only because they themselves decided to. I could no more move them than I could move a True Faith-Holder, or a Fanatic, on Association or Harmony. What the Exotics live for and the Dorsai live for is beyond argument."

"So"—Toni turned on her side in order to watch him as he lay, still staring at the starscape above—"what are you going to do next? Are you still planning to see next about gaining controlling influence on Sainte Marie?"

"I'm not sure," Bleys said.

"It's such a small world, largely Roman Catholic, mostly rural, with not much technology," she said. "If time's of the essence, as you kept saying when you were sick, wouldn't you be better off turning next to building control on either Ceta or Freiland?"

"Yes," Bleys said. "Possibly. Time is of the essence. It has to be. It'll take three to five years to build a position from which we can talk to Old Earth on even terms—and that's with the cooperation of *all* the other New Worlds except the Exotics and Dorsai."

"Then, why not Ceta or Freiland?"

"Partly to avoid a lot of bloodshed. In the case of Ceta, it's still broken up into a number of small, independent countries. They'd need to be taken over one by one, and they're quick to fight among themselves if any change is made in the balance of power among them. It would really be best to leave Ceta to be the last, so that they'd come into my family of New Worlds simply because they couldn't afford to be left outside. As for Freiland—I was hoping to avoid it for the moment, if I could. I want to give Newton, Cassida and New Earth time to settle into the idea that they may be the only three that are closely tied together, and feel comfortable with me pulling strings on them from behind the curtain."

"Coby," said Toni, "could be almost more useful than Sainte Marie, even if it is smaller."

"But it's relatively unimportant in the larger balance of power—that among all the other New Worlds. My recruiting people there wouldn't look so alarming to those on the Worlds I haven't gone after yet," he said. "Also . . ."

"Yes," Toni said, when he did not go on, "also what?"

"It's a little ridiculous."

"You can't be ridiculous with me." Toni gave his fingers a slight squeeze.

"Well, then," he said. "You know about Donal Graeme, who ended up Secretary for Defense of all our New Worlds, a century ago?"

"Of course," she said. "As I know about Julius Caesar, Genghis Khan and Napoleon—probably more about Donal Graeme than those others, because he's more recent in history."

"You know he had twin uncles, Ian and Kensie Graeme?"

"Yes."

"As I say, this will sound ridiculous, particularly from me. But, you remember that both Kensie and Ian were on Sainte Marie, and it was there that Kensie was assassinated?"

"I know the story. Yes," Toni said.

"I read about it myself, when I was very young. So young, I was sneaking adult books because I'd outgrown the child books they'd given me. Another Dorsai, one of the Morgans who lived close to the Graemes at Foralie, wrote about it in his own casual autobiography. He was there, on Sainte Marie, in the Dorsai force hired by the Exotics to oppose some who were hired by revolutionaries on that world. An opposing force hired from our own Friendly Worlds. You remember that Ian and Kensie were twins; and how, suddenly, unexpectedly, Kensie was assassinated by the revolutionaries themselves, at a time when theoretically the opposing forces were at truce?"

"Oh, yes."

"Well, that's it," Bleys said, his face still looking upward at the starscape, "as I say, I read it when I was very young; and something about Kensie's death and what it meant to Ian touched me very deeply. Touched me for Ian, I mean. Ian, you see, was something like I've always been—isolated, at a distance from everyone but his twin brother. And then Kensie was killed, and Ian had to keep the mercenaries of his soldier force from going like avenging angels through the town where it happened, because everybody loved Kensie."

Toni squeezed his hand again, but without saying anything.

"It seemed to me then—I was still with my mother, but I was old enough then to know she didn't love me, she'd never loved me," said Bleys. "—It seemed to me that I could feel what Ian must have felt losing Kensie. And that I could understand it only because I was like him. He was a dark man, you know. He stood apart from everyone; and he never said anything about Kensie's death, or gave anyone a clue to his feelings. But I felt them."

His voice hesitated, and once more Toni squeezed his hand reassuringly.

"Ridiculous, as I said," Bleys went on. "but aside from everything else, that's always been with me. I think—it's just a feeling—but I feel that Ian will rest a little more quietly in his grave, once I've made sure that Sainte Marie will be one of the worlds where, in the long run, there'll be no more assassinations—and no more assassins."

Bleys was silent, and she let him be silent. But into that silence there came after a few moments, the chime of the phone on her wrist control pad. By mutual, almost telepathic understanding between the two of them, all speakers from the surrounding rooms, had been shut off. Bleys' phone was shut off, and only Toni's emergency channel remained alive. She had left word that Bleys was not to be disturbed under any circumstances, and she only in the greatest of emergencies. She reached to pick up the control pad from the small table-float on her side of the bed and lifted it to her lips.

"Yes?" she said.

She lay still for a moment, listening.

"Under no conditions," Toni said clearly.

She listened a moment or two more, then sat up against the patterned shadow of the quilted headboard on their bed.

"How urgent?" she said.

Bleys pulled himself up into a sitting position beside her. She continued listening a long moment more.

"Wait," Toni said to her wrist phone and turned to Bleys.

"It's Barbage," she said. "He says he has to talk to you. He's been trying to get through to you ever since he found out you were back here on Harmony. I'd left orders you weren't to be disturbed by anyone, but evidently whoever just went on phone duty let him ring through. Do you want to talk?"

"Yes," Bleys said. He reached for his own wristpad by his side of the bed and slipped it on. His fingers found the correct studs automatically in the dimness.

"What's this all about?" he said into his phone.

"Great Teacher—Hal Mayne hath escaped from his cell ten days since!" came the sharp voice of Barbage. "I was gone that day to the new Core Tap site, where there had been a successful sabotage that will hold up work a matter of months. While I was absent, the guards at the cells, without orders from me, tried to take Hal Mayne to a hospital. But their ambulance became stuck in the crowds filling the trafficways in excitement over the sabotage; and because the leading saboteur—Rukh Tamani—was to speak to them. Mayne escaped from the ambulance while she spoke. The guards will be dealt with, of course—I do not call thee about that. But a street informer told within two hours of Mayne's escape that he had seen someone like unto Mayne being admitted to the Exotic Embassy. If Mayne is in that Embassy, no Militia can go after him. We need thy voice in high places to get permission to go look for him there."

Bleys sat for a moment, looking neither at his wristpad nor at the starscape above, but just into the darkness.

"Great Teacher?" came Barbage's voice. "Am I still connected to thee?"

"I'm here," said Bleys. "If the Embassy has taken him in, there's nothing I can do."

"The Eldest could give special orders for us to go in," said Barbage. "It is certain he is still there. We had Militia surrounding the Embassy within minutes; and the informer stayed, watching until the Militia came. He tells us no one had left but a tall, stout Exotic who is known as an accredited staff member. We need only thy word to help us go and get him."

"No," said Bleys in the same dead level voice in which he had answered to begin with. "The Exotics are still a power between the stars. I can't suggest to anyone in our government that we create an incident with them at this time. Consider Hal Mayne gone."

"But, Great Teacher—"

"No," said Bleys, "he is gone. Call off your Militia."

He broke the connection, stripped off his wristpad and lay back down again. After a moment, Toni took off hers also and lay back down beside him. Bleys was lying still, staring at the starscape again, as if he were lost in it, and had forgotten not only the conversation, Barbage and Hal Mayne, but her as well.

Toni touched him very lightly with her fingertips on the skin of his upper right arm.

"Bleys?" she said very softly. "You would only have to say a word in McKae's ear—"

"No," said Bleys, without moving. "He's gone off-world by now. That tall Embassy staff member would have been him. The Exotics could do that easily. There's no use. It's settled now. He's not to be reached by me."

Bleys said nothing more, and Toni waited; and when he said nothing more, she spoke again.

"Can you tell me?" she asked finally. "Why is he so valuable to you? What is there he can do for you that you can't do without him? You've won New Earth, Cassida and Newton—everything you went for, without him. But you act as if you'd just lost your best friend. What was it you needed him for, that much?"

Bleys did not move. His gaze was wholly on the starscape, and nothing else.

"A friend," he said.